CAIRO
Unzipped

CAIRO
Unzipped

by

MONA FUAD

www.hispubg.com
A division of HISpecialists, llc

Inquiries should be addressed to

HIS PUBLISHING GROUP
P.O. Box 12516, Dallas, TX, 75225
info@hispublishinggroup.com

Published by HIS Publishing Group

Library of Congress Control Number: 2012924068

ISBN: 978-0-578-11039-4

Printed and bound in the United States of America

10 9 8 7 6 5 4 3 2 1

First Edition

"In studying history, it must be borne in mind that a knowledge is necessary of the state of manners, customs, wealth, arts, and science at the different periods treated of. The text of civil history requires a context of this knowledge in the mind of the reader."

— Sir Arthur Helps on History

Mona Fuad

ABOUT THE AUTHOR

MONA FUAD WAS BORN IN ALEXANDRIA, Egypt and was educated in Catholic schools in Cairo. At sixteen, she won a bathing beauty contest and the Miss Egypt pageant. Soon after, she won a *Jennifer Jones* lookalike contest and was offered a movie part portraying Jones in the Egyptian version of *Duel in the Sun* with Gregory Peck and Joseph Cotton. She played a role in *The Ten Commandments* and in the television series *I Spy*. Mona appeared in many Egyptian films becoming a star.

Mona loved show business and desired to travel the world. She once told her movie producer, "I would like, one day, to see Paris." To which he replied, "My dear, you are in Paris!" Egypt, at the time, was the Paris of the Middle East and a wonderful place for a young actress to make her mark on the world. Egypt was good to her, for the most part, until she fled along with all Europeans, when the government evacuated Egypt soon after the exile of King Farouk.

Reluctantly, leaving her beloved Cairo behind, she lived in Turkey, Spain, Bangkok, and France before moving to America. In 1971, she pioneered the first artificial fingernail business, Mona Nails, in Dallas, Texas. She opened over 75 franchises exclusively dedicated to acrylic nails and began manufacturing the product. She altered the landscape of the nail business, which exists today in cities all over the world. Many in the industry still credit Mona for providing them with the *American Dream*. Her innovative talent and personal dedication to the nail industry created hundreds of thousands of jobs. The acrylic nail industry has grown into a 35-billion dollar industry worldwide.

EVIL EYE

Middle Eastern people wore the *evil eye* pendant to ward off the *bad eye* curse, which usually came in the form of a malevolent expression of ill will. Popular belief conveyed that some people had the capacity to gaze at a person or animal in such a way as to cause bad things to happen. The gaze might appear to be an innocent look or a compliment, such as "Your baby has beautiful eyes" or "I see that you are doing well in your investments." People in Egypt felt the *evil eye* was something to beware of, something to avoid.

The *evil eye* is mentioned in the Bible in Proverbs 23:6, 28:22, and Mark 7:22 (KJV) and is synonymous with envy, jealousy, and covetousness. The *bad eye* curse started in early Greece and spread to all the countries throughout the Middle East and Asia. Turkey, Egypt, Lebanon, and most Muslim countries have the strongest fears associated with the effects caused by the *bad eye*.

People thought there were a number of things they could do to ward off the *bad eye* curse. The practice of Muslim women wearing the headscarf is said to be an attempt to ward off compliments on her beauty and, thereby, avoid bad luck. Babies are thought to be protected from these compliments by bundling them in layers of clothing so they can barely be seen.

Most, however, preferred the *evil eye* pendant, which originated from the belief in the God of Horus (depicted as a person with the head of a falcon). The *Eye of Horus* represented the right eye of the falcon and was believed to hold the power necessary to prevent evil phenomenon from happening to the wearer.

The *evil eye* design was later enhanced by the Egyptians who crafted the *Hamsa*. This pendant was an eye mounted in a metal hand, preferably gold or silver, and held palm out toward the potential threat. They might wear it on a bracelet or necklace or as a part of a simple pin. In the case of babies, which they believe most vulnerable, parents hung the eye on the baby carriage. The wearer would say the word *Hamsa* three times and, thus, be protected from envy, jealousy, or any other ill that had been directed at the wearer. The *evil eye* in some countries is called a *Blue*.

INTRODUCTION

The story you are about to read is true. Out of respect for individual anonymity, Layla's name along with several others, has been changed. However, the integrity of the facts is preserved, and the fictional elements woven into the story only lend to enhance the plot. Please refer to the appendix where you will find a map of ancient Egypt and information about Amenemhat III, the Egyptian labyrinth, and the pyramid at Hawara.

PROLOGUE

DURING THE 1930s, because of the turmoil in Europe, Egypt became a melting pot of people from the various European countries from Greece to Russia that were being put to the fire by the Nazis. Egypt was under English mandate and became a place of great opportunity for European families.

How could Egypt be best described? It was one of the most beautiful and interesting places in the world. People could eat breakfast at the Mena House restaurant in front of the Pyramids and the Sphinx and then ride horses in the desert afterwards. Or they could visit the best European shops

Tea on the porch of the Mena House

where silks from France, clothes from Italy, beer from Germany, and woolens from England were sold.

Every nationality had a specialty in Egypt. The Italians were butchers, the French were shopkeepers, the Armenians made leather goods including shoes and handbags, the Jewish ran the banks and large department stores and were the managers of most large businesses. The Jewish also built the movie studios and rented them to film producers. The Jewish community thrived, mainly because they spoke excellent Arabic and could communicate with the workers.

The royalty and the rich attended European schools so that they might learn foreign languages. Most, including the future King of Morocco, attended the same French and Italian schools. They are the same schools that two Russian Princesses who escaped persecution in their own country had attended.

Pierre Mendes France, President of France, married a Jewish girl from Cairo. Her father was the owner of Cicurel, the largest department store in Egypt, but like many non-Egyptians, he would be forced to flee in 1957 with only his baggage and five dollars in his pocket.

Even the middle class families of Egypt had many luxuries. It was not unusual for a family to have two maids on a daily basis and another who came once a week to maintain the property and shine the brass. One of the favorite outings the locals loved was to picnic in the desert. Families loaded up tents, chairs, and cooking equipment along with their horses and servants in preparation for staying a week or more. The desert was the quietest place on earth; only the wind could be heard. It was a wonderful place for people to gather their thoughts uninterrupted.

Groppi, Soliman Pasha Square

Also available was a variety of entertainment: singers from Greece, dancers from Russia, and movies from America. Egypt drew all of the most popular American and European personalities, such as Maurice Chevalier, Yves Montand, Charles Aznavour, Charleton Heston, C. B. De'Mille, Rita Hayworth, the Russian Ballet, and many more. The famed Opera House featured the most popular contemporary stars of opera and ballet. Many came to Egypt for the weather or other pleasures, and they loved to bask in the mineral springs located in Helwan, just south of Cairo.

Crystal chandeliers and elegant furnishings adorned many of the bars and nightclubs. At the English and French Clubs, members could swim and play tennis, bridge, and other card games. Health and social clubs and coffee shops, like Groppi that had porcelain dolls as decoration with Persian carpets on the floor. There was horseracing, golf, pigeon shooting and duck hunting. You name it; Egypt had it, and all in luxury.

➤➤➤

Young King Farouk

At the time, Egypt's leader was King Farouk, who was a mere sixteen years old when he ascended the throne. His official title was His Majesty Farouk I, by the grace of God, King of Egypt and Sudan, Sovereign of Nubia, of Kordofan, and of Darfur. His Majesty had life and death power over the whole population of Egypt. He was Turkish and Armenian by birth and considered himself more Europe-

King Farouk's Autos

an than Egyptian. His Father had sent him to be educated at the Royal Military Academy in Woolwich, England, which was a British Army military academy for the training of commissioned officers of the Royal Artillery and Royal Engineers. However, he never matriculated. Regardless, he spoke five languages fluently.

He was a charmer and led a lavish lifestyle, which was unpopular at the time, especially by the elected government officials, although they swore allegiance to his throne. Farouk had four palaces and his annual salary was 125,000 British Pounds plus

Al-Mahroussa, the royal yacht, weighed 4,561 tons, had a 164-man crew, and quarters for 24 passengers

an additional 125,000 British Pounds allowance for palace upkeep and odd expenses (2012 - $700 thousand). His personal fortune inherited from his father in 1936 was estimated to be around $50 million dollars (2012 - $250 million) and was derived primarily from taxes from cotton, manufacturing, and other sources.

In Egypt, if you were interested in purchasing a car, the dealer would say, "You may purchase any color but red." Red was reserved for the King. No one was allowed to drive a red car except King Farouk. He had a number of models at each Palace, and his estate maintained four Rolls Royce autos for special occasions.

King Farouk was a world-renowned coin collector. He amassed over 8,000 coins of great value, and his coin catalog filled over 300 pages. One of his gold coins, a rare 1933 American Double Eagle, sold at a London auction for more than seven million dollars. The Double Eagle coin was considered the most valuable coin in existence at the time.

The handsome, young King fit the times of Egypt, just as Gandhi fit the times of India. He was a Muslim who thought like a European. He had no interest in the local culture unless it benefitted him. When Farouk left Egypt on his yacht, *Al-Mahroussa*, he declared, "Egypt, *merde**. In ten years there will be only five kings left in the

---

*   crap (French)

4

Layla

world: the King of England and the four kings in a deck of cards."
In his disdain for the people of Egypt, he said, "If I give money
to the people today, they will eat today, they will eat tomorrow,
but they will be starving again the following day."

There were some 500,000 Europeans living in Cairo, and most
spoke at least five languages. It was estimated that in the 1940s,
there were some 85,000 Greeks, 75,000 Jews, 50,000 French,
and perhaps 300,000 other nationalities in the capital city.
Conversations were colorful. It was normal to hear people mixing
together the best words of each language; a word of Russian here,
a word of French there, some descriptive Arabic words, and a little
Yiddish for humor. Many families continue with this type of dialog
today.

The Europeans who were adopted into Egypt adored their
new King. Farouk was a person who understood them, he was
a person who helped them, and he was THE person who gave them
status in their new world. Farouk became their friend and showed
it by creating many opportunities. It was common for Europeans
who were properly educated to be appointed as the president of a
bank or head of a company. Many received the best jobs simply
because they knew how to read and write. They also owned shops
and factories and frequented the best hotels and restaurants.

Previously, Europeans had not been welcome in these establishments. Hotels and restaurants had frowned upon anyone not considered a member of Egypt's elite, landowners, Pashas, or religious figures. There were a few cultural and religious problems, but for the most part, the Europeans were left alone. These circumstances, of course, created jealousy and resentment among the local Arabic population.

➤➤➤

Many soldiers and sailors during the late 30s and early 40s filled the streets of Cairo. It seemed every man wore a uniform and was looking for a woman. Prostitution increased to huge proportions during this period. Many times it was the parents who got the girls started. The girls solicited business from the balconies of their homes, similar to Amsterdam's Red Light District, but rather than standing in windows, the girls sat on balconies wearing silk kimonos with no underwear. The kimonos conveniently slipped open with every movement. In broken English, they shouted to the soldiers, "How about Zig Zig, right now, five pounds?" Zig Zig was an Egyptian term meaning *a good time*. The parents profited tremendously from their efforts. *Etait Le Bon Temp Pour Tous, une rejoussance formidable*.

Layla was a radiant individual standing five-seven, which was tall for an Egyptian woman. She had long hair, blue eyes and was physically gorgeous. Men were intimidated by her looks, which had them mumbling and forgetting what they wanted to say.

Her manner was graceful and calm, her voice low and pleasant to listen to. Her sincere smile was quick to appear and quick to go away when it was no longer appropriate. She had the type of face a person could look into and learn from. If Layla could be described in one word, it would be honest.

Layla had no knowledge of her birthday. No birth certificate had ever been issued, and her mother didn't think it important

---

* A good time for all, a formidable rejoicing. (French)

to tell her. Instead her mother, Helena, answered her curious questions about her birth with, "What do you care? You're eating, aren't you?" Layla estimated her birth to have occurred sometime in 1926 or 1927, which would make her about eight years old when she was forced to work in 1935. She didn't have a religious background, never attended church, but claimed Christianity as her religion.

Mona

Mona Fuad was born in 1933. Her parents were very well respected in Cairo. Mr. Fuad was president of a large tobacco company, and her mother was well esteemed among the social elite. Mr. Fuad spoke Italian, Arabic, and several other languages. Mona's grandfather had arrived years earlier with one possession, a sewing machine. He soon built a reputation as one of the most respected tailors in all of Egypt. Being of European descent, the family had always been considered reputable.

Mona had shiny black hair, turquoise colored eyes, and an hourglass figure. When she looked at you, her piercing eyes, made you feel like she was looking straight into your soul. It caused you to doubt yourself and wonder if what was coming out of your mouth was what you intended to say or if it was even the truth. She had a way about her, if she didn't like what she heard, she could easily cut you into pieces with her words. That is if you were lucky.

Her beauty was extreme, which seemed so opposite from her character. She was a real tomboy, great at every sport and ready to fight any boy twice her size. By the time she was twelve, she had been expelled from every European boarding school in Egypt. Word got out about this mischievous child and no other schools would admit her.

Mona was sixteen years old when she first met Layla. Mrs. Fuad owned a small hotel in Helwan near the mineral springs. She catered mainly to the wealthy and the English military officers during World War II.

Layla and a friend named Lucy rented rooms in the hotel. Mona's mother forbade her daughter to talk to either of them, saying, "If you talk to those girls, people will think you are one of them."

Mona was just too curious about a girl who was so beautiful. She often sneaked in and talked to Layla when her mother was away. Layla was always very open, truthful, and sweet to Mona. She even offered her advice on boyfriends. Layla would go on to live a life of adventure and intrigue. Mona believed she was somehow a better person knowing Layla and having shared in some of those adventures.

Mona still remembers the day Layla confided, "I have heard it said we are all born into sin. I wasn't introduced to it until I was eight years old when my Uncle Max raped me."

CHAPTER ONE

THE YEAR IS 1956, AS THE SHIP SLIPPED SILENTLY THROUGH
THE MEDITERRANEAN FOG HEADED FOR ROME...

LAYLA STOOD GAZING at the disappearing coastline as the
ship ambled slowly out to sea. Her knuckles whitened as she
clenched the handrail and closed her eyes, allowing visions of 1952
to spiral through her mind. It was the year of Cairo's bloodiest revolution, and her homeland was in turmoil. The choking plumes
of billowing smoke, the raspy yells of shopkeepers as looters
grunted under the weight of new treasures, baton cracks followed
by shrill cries in the streets. Even her beloved Shepheard's Hotel
was in ruins, smoldering in protest to the frequent Molotov cocktails it could no longer absorb. It was clear to her now-these images
officially marked the end of her life in Egypt.

Somewhere in the Suez Canal Zone lay the bodies of 50
Egyptian Auxiliary policemen, unaware of the chaos their deaths
would herald. Joining them in their ignorance were the British
troops who opened fire upon them during an uprising. Within
hours, riots had swept across the country, setting ablaze anything
remotely connected to Britain or Europe. Police went to the private
homes of known Europeans and demanded entry. To refuse meant

a beating, jail, or even death. One by one, cafes, hotels, cinemas, restaurants, nightclubs, and even the famous Cairo Opera House fell victim to the onslaught of anti-European fervor. The mobs looted numerous shops, including the famous restaurant, Groppi, where rioters stacked dozens of ornate decorative porcelain dolls in the street and burned them. In all, 750 establishments were extinguished in a cloud of smoke and fury.

Because of the large contingent of European guests, the Shepheard was one of the first to go. Mobs cheered as priceless Egyptian antiquities were dragged out of the hotel and quickly met with hacksaws and machetes. Sadly, the same was true of some of the guests. After dousing the Shepheard with gasoline and setting it ablaze, the "British Club" was given a similar fate. Layla's grip tightened as she recalled the cries of the jumpers leaping from second story balconies only to be beaten to death by the angry mob below.

She opened her eyes slowly. Four years had passed since the revolution began, and Layla was fortunate enough to have been evacuated by the US Navy along with most of the Americans and foreign nationals. She looked at the ship, admiring the craft that had just saved her from her tumultuous homeland and now inched closer to Italy with every crashing wave. Her mind then drifted to the mission she and Mona had received from Chuck. Italy would serve as a good launching pad for their objectives. A hand suddenly touched her shoulder and startled her out of her trance. She spun around, quickly identified the intruder, and let out a restrained sigh. "Oh, Spence, you scared me very much. You must know better than to sneak up on a lady this way."

"Layla, you look ravishing, but you seem worried about leaving Egypt. Are you okay?"

Spence had been handy when Layla was boarding. Like everyone, in such a hurry to flee, she didn't know the protocol. He had extended a hand and asked to carry her bag. He was an officer in the

Marine Corps and had secured passage in Alexandria for the evacuation. Upon meeting Spence, she had immediately been attracted to him. Standing tall at six-two, with piercing blue eyes, a barrel chest, and strong hands, he had a magnetic affect. His features were dark, accented by a firm jaw line and bulging biceps.

As was her custom, she knew how to take advantage of the amorous effects she had on men, especially a man in uniform. Soon after boarding they absconded to his berth like a couple of schoolchildren fleeing the scene of a crime. There, as usual, she caved in to his affectionate caresses.

Now, standing on the open deck, thoughts ripped through her mind like the ship's hull tearing through the white caps tipping the waves. "Spence, I am so overwhelmed with emotion I don't know whether to be happy or sad."

"Talk to me. What's going on?" he whispered into her ear.

As Spence held her tightly from behind, she could feel the warmth of his body and the rhythm of his breathing. She so wanted to open the window of her mind, but it was sealed tight as if protecting her from the storms of life, "This is the first time I feel free to live life on my terms."

"What do you mean?" Spence asked, his eyes closed, his senses intoxicated by the scent emanating from her skin.

Placing a finger over his lips, she said, "Just hold me."

❯❯❯

She heard the banging of dishes in the kitchen. Layla entered slowly and noticed her Aunt Ahti working alongside her mother. Her aunt and uncle slept over on poker nights, which were regular occurrences at Layla's family's house.

Her Uncle Max was a heavyset man with broad shoulders. Not too tall, but he was built solid like a rock. She was a sound sleeper, but remembered a startling feeling between her legs and sensed an acrid smell, the smell of alcohol on his breath. There had been a sharp pain, a tearing if you will and then it was over. The next morning she awoke finding blood on her legs and sheets.

"Mother, Uncle Max did something to me last night; there is blood everywhere," Layla said trembling.

"Child, come here. You are so full of wild stories. What in the world am I going to do with you?" Let me take a look, "See here. You have a cut on your leg, and you have been bleeding. Quit making things up." With an open hand, she slapped Layla hard across the bottom and said, "Get to the sink and make yourself useful. Dry those dishes."

Her Aunt Ahti approached and inspected the cut. "Don't you ever repeat that lie. It could ruin Max and our children if it made its way to the street. Truth told, you walk in your sleep. Maybe you got up in the middle of the night and hit something causing the cut on your leg." Ahti stared down at her with cold piercing eyes.

"But, why is their pain down there, you know, in between my legs?" Layla countered as she turned and darted back to her room. Passing through the living room, she was startled when her Uncle Max stepped in front of her. She winced at the sight of him. He grabbed her shoulders and dug his fingers into her skin. Layla struggled to get free. "Stop hurting me," she cried.

"You ungrateful *gâtér*. You should be grateful that Aunt Ahti and I look out for you. God knows your mother is worthless. Hell, we don't even know how old you are. There is no birth certificate. Shit, girl, even your mother doesn't know how old you are. As far as the authorities are concerned, you don't exist. You best remember that the next time you make such a wild accusation. We'll kick you out into the street and then what will you do? Who would take care of you then? Yani?"

Yani was her mother's boyfriend. He was the reason her father, Hushiel, had left. Her father was an attractive man with sandy

---

* brat (French)

12

blonde hair, a color which was very unusual for a Jewish European. Disgusted by his wife's continued infidelity, he moved out and rented a room from an old friend named Hannah. Hannah was a classy lady and a successful seamstress. Layla never knew whether they ended up being lovers, but she did know that Hannah was always sweet to her. With no daughter of her own, Hannah sometimes took Layla to the store and bought her shoes and other necessities. With her leftover material, she would make her a dress or coat. Layla was very grateful and enjoyed visiting Hannah.

Layla always wondered what her Father saw in her mother. Helena was average height, somewhat fat with brown stringy hair. She was not at all good looking. In time, Layla came to realize her mother and Yani were deserving of one another. Yani was of Greek origin, slight in build, wiry, and dark. He had one of those pencil thin mustaches and jet black hair combed straight back, covering a slightly bald spot. He had calculating eyes that reflected his deceitful and lying nature, and he had no job unless gambling qualified as employment. He just leeched off her mother.

One night when Yani came for dinner, he asked as he took another swig from the bottle of ouzo he and Layla's mother were sharing, "Helena, how old is that girl of yours?"

"She is only eight, but she is a feisty one, always making up stories and such. I don't know what I am going to do with her. I think it is time she started earning her keep around here. Tomorrow I am taking her to that seamstress, you know, the one that is always after me to work for her," Helena said, getting up from the couch and heading to the kitchen.

"She has the body of a girl much older. You're going to have to fight the men off with a baton. They will be crawling all over this place." He grabbed her arm. "Where do you think you are going? Come back here and lie with me."

"Yani, you're just horny as usual. Give me time to finish cleaning up. Sit back, relax, and think about what I'm going to do to you. I won't be long."

Yani had his own agenda. He waited for Helena to exit the room, then got up, and ascended the small flight of stairs leading to Layla's bedroom. As usual, Layla didn't hear a thing, for she was fast asleep. She was a very sound sleeper. Her brothers used to tease, "A bomb could go off, and Layla would not stir."

"Layla, are you awake? I want to show you something, Layla, Layla?" Yani thought to himself, "Good, she is out like a light and won't feel a thing.' He unzipped his trousers, pulled back the sheets, and carefully pulled up her nightgown exposing her naked body. Being the *perver** he was, he parted her legs and violated her.

"Yani, where are you? Come see what I have in store for you."

Startled, he pulled back and lifted his trousers. Looking down, Layla just lay there with eyes closed, no idea her innocence had been violated again.

Slowly closing the door to her room he yelled, "Be right there."

Similar to the experience with her Uncle Max, there had been a sort of awareness on Layla's part, like in a dream where she couldn't tell if she were asleep or awake. She remembered hearing a faint whisper, but could not make out the words. Upon waking, she felt that sick aching between her legs. Scared and not knowing what to think, she ran to her mother.

Instead of consoling her daughter, Helena clamped her hand around Layla's arm and peered viciously down at her. "You have a great imagination, always accusing people that they are touching you, when it is not true. Don't you dare tell anyone about this, you little liar."

---

*   pervert (French)

She brought her other hand down hard on Layla's bottom all the while tightening her grip. Layla tried to free herself but to no avail. Helena continued hitting her until exhausted. She let go and said, "*Imshi* *". The pain was excruciating, not just on her bottom, but deep down inside was also the emotional pain. The reaction of her Mother scarred her for life.

Now with Uncle Max looming over her she felt about half a meter tall. It would be the last time Layla would say anything. She didn't care to be yelled at or punished. She was not a complainer. She didn't understand; she was just a young girl, sad and lost, with a mother who was usually swimming in a bottle of ouzo and a father who was ignorantly absent.

It wasn't the last time her uncle or Yani visited her room. After awhile, Layla learned to accept the abuse as a normal part of life. The mornings after, she rinsed and washed their filth from her body.

---

* Get out. (Arabic)

CHAPTER TWO

THE BOAT HIT A LARGE WAVE almost knocking the two them off their feet. "I'm cold, Spence," Layla exclaimed.

Spence could feel her shivering body in his arms. He wrapped his coat around her shoulders. "Here this will help keep you warm."

The deep foghorn from the ship sounded and the crew could be heard rousing the passengers, "Time for everyone to move inside." The ship was now outside the bay heading toward the deep, with Egypt growing fainter in the distance. The crew anxiously secured the deck in preparation for their long voyage.

Layla shook her head, totally ignoring the warning sound. Her hair was blowing in the ocean breeze, and her thoughts, as if one with the ship, drifted out to sea. Layla had a sister and four brothers, all about three years apart. It was fortunate Yani hadn't touched her sister; of course, Layla was better looking and more developed. At eight years old, she didn't know what was real or imagined, but she determined at a young age that if she let men fondle her, she could have anything she wanted or needed.

Spence whispered, "Layla, what do you say we go back to our berth and warm up?"

Smiling, she turned and nestled her chin on his chest. "Sounds wonderful."

The other passengers were descending the stairs toward the berths. They were cozy rooms consisting of nothing more than a bunk bed with a small space in front about eighteen inches wide. Not bad if all you had on your mind was sleep, but somewhat noisy for what Spence had planned. Along the way Layla caught sight of Mona on the deck. Mona had been on the opposite side of the boat watching as her beloved country vanished into the horizon.

She called out, "Mona, come. I want you to meet someone."

"Hey girl, what are you up to? Something intriguing would be my guess," Mona said as the curves of her mouth eased into a smile.

"Spence, I want you to meet a friend of mine. Mona, this is Spence, he is an officer in the Marine Corps traveling to Rome on leave. He was nice enough to help me with my bags when we boarded."

"*Enchantér*," Mona extended a hand.

Peering into her eyes in a rather flirtatious manner, Spence took her hand, brought it up to his lips, and said, "The pleasure is all mine."

Layla continued, "Mona's husband, Chuck, is in the Air Force and works for the American Embassy. He arranged our passage on the ship."

"Spence, you had better be careful with Layla," Mona teased. "She can be addictive." Mona and Layla both let out a laugh. Mona knew Layla all too well. They continued toward the berths.

Chuck, Layla, and Mona had been upset by the fact that King Farouk had double crossed them. Chuck had secured their passage out of the country, with their destination being Rome. Chuck's plan was to meet them, which would allow the three of them ample opportunity to gather information and exact their revenge on Farouk. They weren't about to sit back and let him take them after everything they had been through. They were determined Farouk had to pay for his deception and the murder of their friend.

They approached Spence's door, which he opened while stepping aside to let Layla enter. "Spence, it was nice to meet you," Mona said realizing for the first time Layla was staying with him.

"Dinner is around 6:00. Should we stop by on our way?" Spence asked in a suggestive manner.

Mona and Charlton Heston

Mona with Cecil B. Demille

Mona

Mona agreed and walked to her berth.

"What do you think, Spence?" Layla said.

"Think about what?"

"Don't try to fool me I saw you looking her up and down. She is gorgeous, and you know it. What you don't know is she is a famous

Egyptian actress. She had roles in many films. Did you ever see *The Ten Commandments* with Charlton Heston?"

"You have to be joking. She was in that movie? It's considered a classic back home."

"Yes, and let me tell you, Heston was quite enamored with her. If he had his way, it would have been he and Mona instead of Chuck and Mona. Cecil B. DeMille was so impressed by her performance that he decided she would be perfect for a movie he was directing. She got a call from Charles Liftschits, an Egyptian producer whose father had built movie studios close to the Pyramids, asking her to come to his office. Mr. Liftschits told her DeMille was looking for a girl like Mona for a movie they were making called *El Cid*, starring Heston. He told her the part was hers if the studio consented, but her producer, Bahari, wouldn't release her from her contract. Liftschits went on to sign his second choice; a scarcely known beauty from Italy named Sophia Loren. It was Sophia's first film in America."

"You've got to be kidding, Sophia Loren?"

"Mona was so mad. As soon as she received word, she went to Bahari's office. His secretary made the mistake of blocking the entrance and without missing a step Mona punched her, broke her nose, and walked past her to confront Bahari.

"I would have given anything to see his face. Mona tells me it was a look of sheer terror. She proceeded to give him a firm piece of her mind, in French I think, I don't remember now. Anyway, she tore up the contract and threw it in his face. Disgusted, she turned and walked away never to return. Turns out, Bahari was madly in love with her and was afraid he would lose her. He had been telling everyone they were dating."

"Wow, she must be a feisty one."

"Oh, you have no idea. If you look close, you can see the mystery in those green eyes. Mona is as smart as they come. She has been my role model, but until recently, I haven't followed her lead."

"What do you mean?"

"Mona is straight. As I've told you, not so with me. Mona's mother made sure she was protected over the years. Being a good looking woman in Cairo can be both a blessing and a curse. She moves with such rhythm and her features have always had a mesmerizing effect on men. Let me tell you she drives the men wild without even trying.

"Then along came this young Air force officer named Chuck. He was quite the looker in his own right. He is a tough sort, but in a loving way. He has this cute way he smiles accompanied by a slight chuckle. You can't help but like Chuck. He flew on a B-17 during the war. I think he was the guy in that little ball on the belly of the plane firing those big guns. He said he shot down a bunch of German planes. Anyway, you can imagine how tough you would have to be to fly in one of those death traps."

"Yea, I have several friends who flew B-17s. Where is Chuck now, I'd like to meet him?"

"Chuck, being the heroic type, stayed in Alexandria to ensure that all Americans found safe passage out of the country. His plan is to meet us in Rome as soon as he is able. If you are still with me, you'll get the chance to meet him then."

➤➤➤

Mona's husband, Chuck, was considered "essential personnel" at the American Embassy. He had remained behind to ensure the successful evacuation of all Americans and foreign nationals. On October 29, 1956, he notified his staff they would be evacuating all dependents from Egypt because of an impending attack by Israeli forces in the Sinai Peninsula.

Cairo International Airport was closed to all traffic, thus precluding any evacuation by air. Radio Cairo reported that the airport was, at present, being bombed by French and Israeli aircraft. Of course, the report was later revealed as propaganda.

Chuck checked his watch and responded to the Colonel's inquiry, "Its 10 o'clock, and I am making final preparations for the Embassy staff and their dependents. We've assembled most of the people employed by American companies and foreign nationals friendly to the United States. My staff logged all the names so we can trace them throughout the evacuation process. Seems French aircraft are on a bombing raid, so we won't be able to reach the planes at Cairo Airport. We are switching to our alternate plan and loading them into staff cars and private vehicles and heading to Alexandria. We should make it to the Cecil before nightfall. The plan is to rendezvous with the sixth fleet vessels and load them on to the ships."

"You're doing a great job, Chuck," the Colonel praised. "Keep up the good work. Let me know the moment you arrive at the hotel. If you need anything, you know how to reach me."

"Yes, Sir"

Colonel Hal Roberts had been placed in charge to see that all evacuees secured safe passage out of the country. He had a posh room at the Hotel Cecil, which seconded as his command post. The hotel was a glamorous structure that opened in 1929 and served as a prime venue for grand balls and other social activities in Alexandria. It was the best hotel in town.

Chuck descended the steps of the Embassy where people were frantically loading luggage into the vehicles. Raising his voice in competition with the surrounding noise, he yelled out, "Everyone, hold up for just a minute. Listen up. Look we need you to stay calm. Planes are bombing the airport so we have to change our plans. We are heading to Alexandria to meet up with the sixth Fleet. There is a chance we will experience some opposition along the way, so if anyone approaches, ignore them. No one is to exit their vehicle under any circumstance. I'll be in the lead car. Where is Jonathan?"

Jonathan raised his arm and waved. "Folks, this is Jonathan. He is my lead associate here at the Embassy. He and his team will be bringing up the rear of our convoy. Does anyone have any questions?" Chuck waited for a response, "If you need anything at all, see either Jonathan or myself."

Hotel Cecil

Stunned by the day's events, everyone nodded agreement. Chuck turned and quickly walked back inside to attend to some final business before leaving the Embassy. Chuck's calm demeanor and command of the situation had a peaceful effect on the evacuees. He made it seem routine, just another day in Cairo.

"Jonathan, is everyone about loaded? We need to pull out as soon as possible. The French and Israelis are running bombing raids on the airport, Cairo West; and threats from the Arab population are escalating."

"You bet, sir. Most of the baggage has been loaded, and we've already started putting people in the vehicles."

During WWII, Jonathan served in the Army, 101st Airborne, so he was right at home in the midst of the chaos. Shortly after the war, he had opted for an Embassy position, and Cairo was offered. He had been a good steward to Chuck and could be counted on in a bind. Within the hour, approximately three hundred people were loaded and on the road. The bombing was now visible from a distance and appeared to be from French aircraft.

"Jonathan, come in, do you hear me?"

"Yes sir, loud and clear," Jonathan said bringing up the rear.

"Look we need to be on the alert. No matter what, keep moving and stay up with us. The locals are unpredictable."

"You bet, Sir. We've got your back."

The trip for the most part was uneventful. Alexandria was approximately 200 km and under normal circumstances would take slightly over three hours to navigate. However, convoying civilians in private vehicles was definitely not a normal excursion. Chuck and Jonathan agreed that improvisation would have to be an intricate part of the plan. With a long stretch of desert separating the two cities, there was no way to foresee what maintenance issues might arise. Thus, they loaded what spare parts they could find: batteries, belts, tires, and of course, extra fuel. With all the breakdowns, rest stops, and false alarms, the trip took eight hours to complete.

The roar of the plane's engines could be heard as it screamed past the convoy. Suddenly there was an explosion that shook the ground. Shrapnel splattered the side of several vehicles, but the damage was minimal.

Chuck called on the walkie-talkie, "Jonathan, is anyone hurt? Give me an update."

"It appears everyone is okay and still moving. We took some damage to the six-by, but the old boy is holding up well." Jonathan was proud of his rugged BTR-152 armored personnel carrier. It had become his hobby upon purchasing it in Cairo. The vehicle was Russian made and the BTR stood for Bronetransporter. The Russians had provided many of them to third world countries after the war. Chuck enjoyed ribbing him about spending his off time working on the vehicle not to mention his time sourcing parts. But, Jonathan was proud of her on this day. It was serving the convoy well by pulling a trailer loaded with excess luggage, spare parts, and gasoline.

"Good, we have to keep moving."

"I'm with you. Let's get the hell out of here."

Members of the convoy were scared to death with planes buzzing overhead. The lead vehicle moved at a good pace, hindered only by the occasional vehicle abandoned along the way. The Embassy flags Jonathan had placed on the front of their vehicles made them appear official. People seemed curious but kept their distance. The convoy finally arrived in Alexandria, pulling up to the Hotel Cecil around 6:30 that evening.

Military personnel were waiting on them and had the surrounding area locked down tight. Several had been ordered to escort them inside upon their arrival. As instructed, Chuck radioed the Colonel as soon as they entered the city. "Good to hear your voice, Chuck. How was your trip?"

Chuck laughed and said, "It wasn't easy escorting a few hundred screaming children. Of course, the kids were a handful too. All in all it was fairly uneventful. We took a hit between here and Tanta, but no real damage. Planes were screaming overhead most of the day, which kept everyone on edge. Believe me, they are ready to board the ship and say goodbye to Egypt. How are things here in Alexandria?"

The Colonel, picking up on Chuck's joke, said, "Ha, yeah, the adults know to be scared, but children just see it as a big adventure. We could learn a thing or two from them." Switching to a more serious tone he continued, "Everything here is calm for the most part. We are in a blackout situation, so let your people know. Chuck, they also need to understand, even though things appear calm, we consider this a night *under fire*. There have been reports of people looting stores, and a few are setting fires. The locals are managing, but you know as well as I how quickly things could heat up. Let's keep them inside the hotel until we get word when to board. I would suggest having them ready at 0500 tomorrow. My men will escort you to the harbor. I'll send over the latest Intel report."

"Yes, sir. I will brief my people and make sure everyone is ready to go," Chuck said before signing off.

"Jonathan, tomorrow morning we need to make sure everyone is up and ready to pull out by 5 o'clock. Colonel Roberts and his men will escort us to the port where everyone will be cleared through Egyptian customs before boarding the ships."

Jonathan remarked with pride, "I've already notified the desk to make sure all rooms are alerted at 4 o'clock. This should give everyone plenty of time before we pull out."

"I received an intelligence report stating the Alexandria Harbor could be the next target. It confirms that Cairo Airport is now being bombed by unidentified aircraft and that the invasion of Sinai is underway. Israeli forces are occupying Egyptian territory at 'Jeep speed.' The 80,000-man Egyptian Army, equipped with Russian tanks and artillery, have been seen fleeing on foot, many leaving the engines running in their vehicles."

"We should be safe here, don't you think?" Jonathan asked.

"Hell, I don't know. This place is red hot, and there is no telling what's going to happen. Look, once we get these people loaded we need to contact the Ambassador and determine who else needs refuge. I want us out of here as soon as possible."

The next day, the bombing of Alexandria's outer harbor began, thus making it a clear *evacuation under fire* for the evacuees being loaded onto the ships. The US Fleet Commander, Charles Brown, entered the Ambassador's office agitated. "Ambassador Hare, I just got word from the Egyptian Naval Staff indicating that the Alexandria outer harbor, our route to open water, has been mined by British aircraft. We believe this report to be false, intended to keep the inner harbor from being a target of the British bombs. However, on the outside chance that it might be true, we are not going to risk several hundred lives, mostly women and children. We need them to sweep the harbor."

"What do you propose, Commander?"

"Contact President Nasser and express your concerns about the mines and demand he take action to ensure the safety of our vessels."

"I'll get right on it and let you know what I find out," said Ambassador Hare, turning to his secretary. "Joan, get President Nasser's office on the phone. Tell them it is a matter of national security."

Joan was the Ambassador's secretary and had volunteered to stay by his side until the military decided it was time to move out. "Sir, I have Nasser on the line."

"Put him through. President, this is Ambassador Hare. We have a major issue, and I need your assistance.

"What can I do for you, Ambassador?'

"We have it on solid intelligence that your people have moored mines in the Alexandria outer harbor to thwart movement of our vessels. We need you to move minesweepers into place and pave the way for our exodus."

"Ambassador Hare, I have no knowledge of any mines. I believe the information you have received is false. You might want to contact the British Ambassador, Humphrey Trevelyan. My intelligence officers tell me his people are the culprits. Besides, I would be pleased to assist your Navy, but I am afraid we haven't any minesweepers.

"Sir, I don't need to tell you that Eisenhower is ready to give the order for a US invasion."

"He must do as he deems fit, but I repeat, I don't have knowledge of any issues to block your exit or equipment in place to assist you."

"Good day. I will be in touch," the Ambassador's voice trailed off as he lowered the phone and placed it back in the cradle.

As expected, British Ambassador Trevelyan denied the claim as well. However, not long after he spoke with Trevelyan, Joan handed him the following message:

Egyptian Government has information that the entrance to Alexandria Harbor has been mined by British aircraft.

*American transport ships may leave Alexandria Harbor during
daylight under their own responsibility. It is required to know
the number, type, and position of said mines to decide if sweep-
ing can be carried out. You may refer back to British authority
through your Naval authority. Recommend using Bougas Pass
to seaward. Wishing you and your passengers Bon Voyage and a
safe return home.*

"Joan, get me Commander Brown on the phone."

"Yes sir," Joan responded, already dialing the number at headquarters.

"He is on the line, Sir."

"Commander, the Egyptians are stirring up trouble, trying
to turn us sour on the British. I spoke to Nasser, and he is denying any knowledge of mines being moored in the harbor. However,
I just received correspondence to the contrary and a request for the
British to provide the location and number of the mines. I think
it best for you to respond at this conjecture, considering time is of
the essence. We need to send Nasser a clear communiqué demanding those sweepers be set in place post haste. He needs to know
the President is growing weary of his lies and propaganda."

"I'll take care of it at once. That bastard had better move his ass,
or we'll be moving it for him. Thank you for your call."

The following message was sent by Commander Brown to the
Egyptian Foreign Office,

*Charged, as I am, with the safety of more than a thousand women
and children, I consider this refusal to sweep G, P, Channel
a most unfriendly personal gesture toward me. Your cooperation,
in fact, has been outstanding, but such refusal to adequately
insure our safety on departure tends to lessen mutual cordial
relations obtained up to now. Therefore, I urgently request that
immediate and positive action be taken to insure our safety.*

Ali Sabri, the Egyptian Minister in charge of the harbor responded with his own message:

Egypt denies putting mines in the harbor. I believe Egypt has a minesweeper, and if there is one, please use it. The minesweeper will be allowed to precede the American vessels.

The Commander fired back:

Our Assistant US Naval Attaché has reported that Egypt has nine minesweepers, five Russian and four others. We will expect your immediate attention to this detail.

The final message on this subject came from the Egyptian Naval Commander Admiral Suleiman Ezzat. The message stated,

I cannot sweep mines due to unknown number, type, and position of mines. I further guarantee that the Egyptian Navy did not mine the harbor; however, as a final gesture of good will we will place a minesweeper at the head of your convoy and precede you through the channel. Request your estimated time of departure.

The evacuees departed Alexandria at 4 o'clock on November 3. The ships were full, which left twelve Suez Canal pilots stranded. The pilots had been hired soon after President Nasser nationalized the canal. The US Navy Destroyer *Sumner* was commissioned to Port Said to pick up the Pilots. Unfortunately, word came through that the attack by the British forces on the canal was imminent, and permission to enter Port Said Harbor had been denied. The *Sumner* was instructed to change course and rejoin the Sixth Fleet.

Chuck got a call from the US Naval Attaché asking him to assist in the pilots evacuation, to which he responded, "No problem, I'll make other arrangements. We will get them to safety. I'll put in a call to the Fleet Commander. I understand they have been ferrying troops in and out of the Canal Zone. It might be possible to get a helicopter in for a quick pick up operation. We'll hang tight back at the Cecil until I receive word."

Cradling the phone he said to Jonathan, "See if you can arrange a secure line to the Fleet Commander Brown. He's an old golf buddy of mine. They have been transporting people from the various ships which are stuck in the canal."

Jonathan arranged the call and before long had Brown on a secure channel. "Commander Brown, this is Chuck Gaskin."

"Chuck, how's the golf game?"

"My sand shots have improved since I've been stationed here."

"Ha. I bet. What can I do for you?"

"I have fourteen men in need of evacuation. Is Dan Harding still aboard?"

"I believe he is. Do you want me to have him make the pickup?"

"Yes sir, at Port Said."

"Let me see what I can do. By the way, I want a rematch at Royal St. George's. I believe you still have some of my money in your pocket, old buddy."

With his signature laugh Chuck answered, "I don't hit the ball as far as I used to, but I'm sure we can arrange a game."

"I'll be looking forward to it. Good luck with the evacuation."

Not long after hanging up, Chuck, communicating via two-way radio, received a call. "Chuck this is Captain Jaap of the USS Corral Sea. We understand you need transport out of the Canal Zone.

"Yes sir, that is correct."

"Good. Appears I have one of your old B-17 buddies on board, Dan Harding. We have been communicating with Commander Brown and will be dispatching him in a Sikorsky H-19."

Dan and Chuck had flown over 30 missions together during the war. The mission that bonded them for life happened in May of 1945. Chuck spent the majority of his missions in the ball turret, located on the underbelly of the plane. The turret was armed with 50-caliber machine guns that rotated in every direction except up; they shot from the horizon down. The ball turret protected the aircraft from fighters below or on the same level as the bomber.

One day, Chuck's crew had been short a navigator, and Chuck was the only other crew member with navigational experience. They pulled Ronnie, a gunner from another crew, to man the ball turret. As they were returning from a bomb raid over Germany, they ran into heavy flak, anti-aircraft shells, and took a hit that knocked out their hydraulic and electrical systems. The turret controls were so badly damaged they couldn't open the hatch. It was locked in the *guns up* position, leaving the hatch down and impossible to open. Dan was forced to make a decision about whether to ditch in the channel or crash land, wheels up, at the base in England. If they ditched in the channel, the ball gunner would be killed on impact or drown in the turret; if they crash-landed, he would die on impact because the turret would be sheared off the aircraft when it hit the ground.

By the time they reached the base in England, they were flying on fumes. Having exhausted all options, the brass ordered them to make a crash landing. In his mind, Chuck could still hear Ronnie screaming and agonized knowing he was supposed to be in the turret that day. Memories like that don't ever leave a man; instead, they bond men together in a way only someone with combat experience can understand.

"Thank you, sir. Why don't you call me back on the secure channel once Dan is in route and have a definite ETA?" Chuck said.

"I understand you have twelve men to be extracted. Is that correct?"

"No sir, the figure is fourteen, including myself and one other Embassy employee."

"We only allowed for twelve to be extracted. Any more will put the chopper over capacity. Ambassador Hare informed me that

Jonathan and you were staying behind at the Embassy. Has there been a change in plans?"

"Not if that's what the Ambassador told you. We'll direct them and make sure they rendezvous on time." Chuck signed off.

Chuck put a call through to Joan at the Embassy. "Joan, this is Chuck Gaskin. Is the Ambassador in?"

"Yes, let me get him on the line."

"Chuck, Hare here, we have been attempting to reach you."

"Sir, we have everything under control and are preparing to evacuate the remaining people. Captain Jaap just informed me that you want Jonathan and me to remain in Alexandria. Is that correct?"

"Yes, I'm afraid so. I won't know for how long until I receive word, but with a skeleton crew we should be able to handle anything they throw at us. Sorry, Chuck. I know this must be disappointing news."

"No problem. It comes with the territory."

"Thanks Chuck, let me know if you need anything, I owe you one."

Jonathan had entered the room and was listening. Chuck turned and said, "There has been a change in plans. The Ambassador wants us to stay."

"Yea, I overheard. Oh well, just another day in paradise."

"One of my old Air Force buddies responded to our SOS and is in route to Port Said to make the pickup."

The helicopter set down as planned. The roar of the blades grew louder as the men neared the craft. They came to a stop and piled out of the vehicles. Dan slid open the glass on the side of the fuselage and yelled, "Where is Chuck?

One of the pilots yelled, "He had to stay behind. We're it."

"Get your boney asses in gear and get loaded. I'm revving up for takeoff in five whether you're on this old bird or not," Dan said surveying the area.

Tahrir Square

"Oh shit, you boys better hurry. Looks like we have company."

Off in the distance were two army trucks with machine guns mounted on top heading their way. Another few minutes and they would be in range, and they could all kiss their asses' goodbye.

The men hurriedly pulled down the side entry door and started boarding as the helicopter started to jerk skyward. Dan wasn't taking any chances. When the last two jumped aboard, the thrust of the 600 hp Pratt & Whitney engine took them airborne. They heard a faint sound of machine gun fire; however, the Egyptians were either terrible shots or the chopper had loomed out of range. The men were lying on their backs breathing heavily, glad to be fleeing the hellhole Egypt had become.

➤ ➤ ➤

Meanwhile, Chuck, Jonathan, and a few other Embassy personnel who stayed behind, watched the destruction of the harbor as they listened to Cairo radio reporting the British were bombing the canal. Of course, the Egyptian Army, not the British, was responsible. They were blowing up vessels, cranes, and pile-driving dredges and had damaged the walls of the canal locks, all the while blaming it on the British.

Nasser was filling the airways with propaganda and could not be trusted. He was in rare form. The Egyptian Army had been hiding all of their *Russian* made equipment, including tanks, armored cars, and jeeps, in garages below residences in a suburb of Cairo called Zamalek. After the evacuation, Nasser had all the equipment brought out and organized a parade through the streets of Cairo, claiming it to be a *Victory Parade*. Although he had lost the Suez Canal and the Sinai, his entire army had been routed from the desert, and Egypt had been saved from complete occupation by President Eisenhower's ultimatum to Israel.

The main square in Cairo, *Midan Suliman Pasha*, was renamed *Tahrir Square*, meaning *Victory Square*. Nasser even went so far as to order the tearing down of the marvelous bronze statue of Suleiman Pasha, a famous hero in Egypt, and the statue of Ferdinand De Lesseps, the Frenchman who developed the Suez Canal. Nasser still held a grudge with the French for adopting a secret agreement with the British to take over the Canal.

CHAPTER THREE

BACK ON THE SHIP HEADING FOR ROME...

SPENCE COULDN'T REMEMBER the last time he had met anyone who could make him feel more alive. Besides Layla's beauty, he was taken by this air of innocence about her, an innocence that didn't coincide with her flirtatious ways.

Layla broke his chain of thought. "Chuck knew just how to handle Mona. The night they met, I had been asked to assist at the American Embassy. It was the fourth of July, and Mona was one of the hostesses at a fundraiser for orphaned children.

"Throughout the evening, Mona walked through the crowded room with a tray containing tickets. Anyone purchasing a ticket would be granted one dance with her. Mona could be heard saying, 'Hey fellows, you know how much you want to support our cause. Dig deep into those expensive pockets and exchange your money for a dance with me.'

"Of course, no one turned her down. The men searched for their wallets as their wives punched them in the sides. It was such fun to see Mona work the room. She was quite the charmer.

"What she didn't know, Chuck had been watching her most of the night. He was enamored by her beauty and the intelligent way she handled the guests. Soon it was his turn to make a donation. He stood, speaking with a few of the officers, when Mona approached, tray in hand, and made her request. Chuck smiled and laughed that signature chuckle of his and asked how much for the whole tray. He didn't know it at the time, but Mona had melted at the sight of him. Before she could answer, Chuck threw twenty pounds on the tray and said, "I guess the dances are mine. Spence smiled and said, "I like Chuck already."

Layla kissed him gently on the cheek before continuing, "Chuck has always been infatuated with Mona and the surrounding culture. Chuck loves to be in the middle of the action, and living with Mona is a new adventure each day. He has often said, 'Mona has never known a dull day.' He loves to tell the story about arriving home one afternoon to find pieces of cotton in the yard. Mona failed to tell him she was having their cotton mattresses fluffed. She had hired a special worker to open up the mattress. He was using a tool like a bow and arrow to shoot the cotton into the air to fluff. He then gathered up the pieces and resewed the mattress. For Chuck, the fluffing of a mattress was very uncommon, considering he had been raised on a farm and was content to sleep on hay if necessary. He loves Mona for her exotic nature."

Admiring Layla's excitement, Spence asked, "Is there going to be a problem with Chuck getting out of the country?"

"No. Chuck will be fine. I'm sure he has a solid exit plan. That's what I like most about Chuck; he just gets things done. In fact, I've always had a crush on him. But boy, if Mona thought for a minute I was making advances with Chuck, friends or no friends, she would just as soon cut my throat. You don't mess with Mona, her man, or her friends. She is loyal to a fault," Layla said, leaning against his side as she purred and ran her hand up his leg.

Spence could feel the heat of his body increase as his blood rose quickly to his head. All he could say was, "Um, be careful, or I might explode."

Layla just smiled and said, "Don't you dare. I have much more in store for you."

The two disappeared under the covers not to surface for several hours. She had kept the company of many men; therefore, it was not unusual for her to be present in body and absent in mind. Her thoughts rocked with the movement of the boat as she drifted back in time.

$$\text{\textbackslash\textbackslash\textbackslash}$$

The thought of her uncle and her mother's boyfriend made her sick to her stomach. They continued the abuse against her will. One morning, she awoke well before daylight crying. She put on her clothes, left the house, and took off running. The dust flew from her heels, and the wind in her face felt good. Her young mind was confused.

Her mother just didn't seem to care. Layla was in constant pain, and all she knew was something was not right. There was no one to talk to. She longed to be loved, to be held, to be caressed. It's how she felt when her father had put his arms around her. In his arms, there was such comfort and peace; she loved that feeling. Little did she know the longing for love and affection would create negative roots deep in the recess of her heart. Those counterfeit roots over time would fuel her desire to keep the company of men.

She felt her life was doomed so she ran as fast as she could, running away from what, she did not know. She just wanted to get away. Anywhere was better than home. Up ahead, she heard the sounds of drums and saw people dancing. Curious, she drew closer to the house and peeked through an opening in the fence.

Zaars were a common occurrence in Cairo at the time. Many people were superstitious, believing evil spirits had inhabited their home, workplaces, and families. They felt the poverty they were living was a curse from evil forces. Due to poor sanitary conditions, one child died out of every four born. However, when an Egyptian was asked for an explanation, all he or she could say was, the *bad eye* brought on the fever. They held Zaar ceremonies to rid themselves of the *bad eye*.

The event took place in the back yard of a home, starting late at night and continued well in to the early morning hours. The leader started by piling chairs on one another until a height of about six feet was reached. Then a sheet was draped over the chairs and a tarbush placed on top. The tarbush or *fez* (Egyptian hat), which looked like an upside down pail, was worn by most Egyptian men. The structure represented the devil.

Those present who thought themselves possessed danced around the devil structure to the sound of beating drums. The one hosting the party led the dancing, and everyone else followed. When he was exhausted, the host would fall to the ground. Then the others would bring out a live sheep, and while two men held the sheep over the host, they cut its throat letting the blood cover the host's body. The guests, who had their own private curses to cure, scrambled for the blood to touch their bodies. Outside, in the street, a large group always gathered after the ceremony when the host would throw pieces of the sheep into the street. The poor scavengers would scurry and fight for a share.

Layla watched as people ran around the sheeted structure, making wild gyrations. She slipped in through the opening that was just large enough for her tiny frame. No sooner had she cleared the opening, than she was confronted by a blood soaked image staring at her as if to say, "You have no business here." She froze like stone. Her eyes widened with fear, and a feeling of warm liquid ran down her leg. She had peed in her pants. The scene was unlike anything she had ever seen. She wondered if these events were always happening in the early morning hours of Cairo. It was the first time she had been awake, much less outside, that early.

Someone screamed, breaking her trance, so she turned and scurried back through the opening and ran as fast as she could. In a confused state, she felt like demons were chasing her. Thoughts flooded her mind like water in the streets after a desert rain.

She didn't stop running till reaching the backdoor of her mother's house. Slamming the door behind her, she went to her room where she collapsed on the bed and sobbed deeply.

➤➤➤

It was the aftermath of WWII, and strange things were happening all over Cairo. Most didn't understand the times; they just accepted what life had become. There was a major divide between the rich and the poor, which was the case in most societies. It was more obvious in places like Egypt where people gathered in the streets begging for food.

Layla confided to her brother, Akins, about the strange event she had witnessed. He told her that she had been cursed with the *bad eye*. Layla had no way of knowing what it meant to be cursed.

"Layla, the bloody figure was the devil, and he placed a curse on you. I know an old lady over in Helwan. People say she knows how to break such a curse. I'll take you there tomorrow."

Layla had trouble falling asleep worrying about the day's events and believing she had been cursed by the devil. Nightmares plagued her throughout the night. She was haunted by visions of blood soaked people chasing her through the streets. Several times she awoke drenched in sweat. The morning sun shone through her open window, and a cool breeze swirled around the damp sheets waking her. She could still feel the effects of the fear that had gripped her so tightly through the night.

"Layla, you awake?" Akins whispered peeking around the door.

"Yes, but, Akins, I didn't sleep much. I had bad dreams all night. People were chasing me. Take me to see that old lady. I pray she knows what to do."

"Get your clothes on, and we will slip out the back door. Hurry before anyone else wakes up."

Layla felt a sense of comfort. She and her brother didn't speak much. He was not healthy, and her mother was always babying him.

She couldn't keep from thinking maybe her whole family had been cursed by the *bad eye*. That would explain his poor health and the poverty they lived in.

Her thought was disturbed by her brother's voice. "Come, we must hurry."

They walked to the outskirts of Cairo and entered Helwan where just a few homes lined the streets. The homes were in disrepair, but there was a certain mystique about them, leaving observers to think that at one time or another they must have been distinguished. Helwan was located in the southern part of Cairo. The Khedivial Astronomical Observatory was located in the area, built around 1903 to watch Halley's Comet. During the early part of the 20th century, the town was the site of RAF Helwan, a major British airbase that was later used by the Egyptian Air Force.

However, the most curious structure, and one weighing on Layla's mind, was the psychiatric clinic. As they passed by, she felt an eerie feeling at the sight. It was located on top of a hill in a large home. Constructed in 1940, it would later come to be known as the Behman Hospital, the first and largest private psychiatric hospital in Egypt.

"Akins, that's where the crazy folks live; it gives me the creeps. Are you sure this lady isn't some escaped lunatic?"

"You do have a vivid imagination. I will give you that. Look there's the home I told you about." He pointed to a faded, blue frame house with pinkish trim worn by the effects of the sun. Many roof tiles were missing and could be seen taking up residence around the perimeter. An ornate iron fence surrounded the property, but the paint was peeling like skin scorched by the sun.

"Layla, knock on the door. Let's see if anyone is home."

Layla looked up at Akins and said, "Why don't you knock?"

He just shrugged his shoulders. Her little hand was shaking so hard, but she managed to ball it into a fist and rap at the door.

"Harder, knock harder. No one could hear that."

As she lifted her feeble hand for another rap, the door swung open. Layla almost fell forward, but caught herself. Startled, her brother jumped a foot off the porch.

"What do you want?" asked the old lady in the doorway.

She had to be at least 100 years old, Layla guessed. Her skin was wrinkled like leather worn from years laboring in the sun. Deep lines formed around her mouth and chin. Her eyes, like her hair, were black as night. Neither Layla nor her brother could speak; their mouths hung open, and they stared into those dark and seasoned eyes.

"Well, I don't have all day. Tell me what you want, or I'm slamming this door."

"Madam," started her brother, the quiver of his lips evident, "my sister ran into a yard where they were holding one of those Zaar meetings to ward off the *bad eye*. She came face to face with a blood soaked devil, and he placed a curse on her."

Layla looked into the lady's eyes and was held spellbound by her piercing stare. The woman then stepped to the side and motioned them into the house. The interior was strong with the scent of incense. Tapestries lined the walls between windows which allowed sunlight to flood the room. Hanging from the center rafter was a chandelier, its dangling crystals shooting rainbows of color on to the ceiling. Layla was stunned by the sheer beauty of the room.

Pointing to an odd piece of furniture, the old lady said, "Sit down and tell me what happened. You must tell me every detail. Do not leave anything out. Do you understand?"

Akins and Layla took a seat on the récamier, which had two raised ends, nothing on the long sides, and was upholstered in a red velvet material. Akins kept his eyes glued to the plank floor worn by the years. He would confide later that he was scared to death the lady was a witch and might place a spell on them.

Layla related the abuse she had endured from her Uncle Max and Yani and the Zaar she had witnessed. After finishing her story, silence loomed like the smoke swirling up from the incense resting in a small vial on the table beside her.

"Did you leave anything out?" the old woman asked.

"I don't think so."

The old lady leaned back in her chair, brought her boney hand up to her chin, and rubbed the palm of her hand across her mouth. Without blinking, she peered deeply into Layla's eyes as if searching for something deep within her soul. Several minutes passed.

Layla was startled when the lady stood and said, "Wait here." Then she disappeared through a curtain separating the front room from the rest of the house.

Akins was about to crawl out of his skin. "She is strange, Layla. I don't know if I did right by bringing you here. I might have made things worse. Maybe she did escape from that insane asylum."

Layla looked over at him and said, "My life couldn't be much worse. Uncle Max and Yani taking turns with me and mother drunk most days. I will take my chances. Besides, there is something about her I like. I don't understand it, but I feel a certain peace in her presence."

When the lady reemerged, she had a fine chain dangling from her closed fist. Walking over to Layla, she again locked eyes with the young girl and peered intently as if confronting something lingering within.

Breaking the silence, she said, "I am going to give you this blue *evil eye* necklace. You must wear it around your neck and never remove it, do you hear?"

"Yes ma'am," Layla said, realizing for the first time she didn't even know the woman's name.

"You have been cursed by the *bad eye,* and this *evil eye* pendant is the one thing that can protect your soul." Then she repeated, "Never remove it!"

Frozen in a trancelike state, Layla felt a strange presence, "I won't ever take it off."

"Take it and leave. You are never to return here. Do you understand me?"

Placing the pendent over her head, Layla felt a sense of comfort, believing it would provide protection for her and those close
to her. Layla left the house walking with a noticeable strut and her
head held high.

❭ ❭ ❭

Layla attended an Italian school and graduated the second grade.
She continued for a while in the third grade before her mother
put her to work at a seamstresses shop doing hems and such.
She worked there for a couple of years.

The seamstress' name was Madame Oni. She was a tiny thing
about five feet, two inches tall and thin as a rail. Layla used to wonder if she just didn't have enough to eat. Later, she discovered
Madame Oni was such a hard worker that she didn't take much
time out to eat.

Madame Oni liked Layla, and when she thought Layla was ready,
allowed her to deliver clothes to customers. Layla enjoyed
the street and looked forward to the deliveries.

"Layla, listen to my instructions. I want you to deliver this
blouse and skirt over to Pasha Nahib's residence. He is a very
demanding man, but his wife has him wrapped around her little
finger. Everything must be perfect, do you hear?"

"Yes Ma'am, I will be sure not to make a mistake."

"While you are there, she has some items of clothing to pick
up that need altering. Bring them back and tell her we shall return
them in a week or so. Be sure to collect the two pounds for the
alteration."

"Yes Ma'am," Layla said, picking up the package off the counter
and heading toward the door.

"Layla, one more thing..."

Pausing and turning Layla asked, "Yes, Madame Oni, what
is it?"

"Be careful. She has a vulture for a husband. He likes young girls. If you have any problem with him, run back here, and I will take care of him."

As Layla cleared the shop door, she heard Madame Oni mumbling, "*Perver.*" Madame Oni knew Layla had a hard life at home, and caring deeply for her, she felt a responsibility to protect her whenever she could. The Nahib residence was located in Heliopolis, a wealthy part of town. Baron Empain, a prominent European entrepreneur, arrived in Egypt in January 1904 and a year later established the Cairo Electric Railways and Heliopolis Oases Company. The company bought a large stretch of desert northeast of Cairo at a low price from the government, and in 1907, the Baron built the new town of Heliopolis. The city was designed to be a city of luxury, with broad avenues and all the modern conveniences, including running water, drains, and electricity. In time, the city included the Heliopolis Palace Hotel, a golf course, a racetrack, and a park. The area was populated by aristocratic Egyptians as well as some European nationals.

Layla scaled the front steps of the house to find tall front doors made from rough-hewn wood hung on brass hinges. She pulled back on the large brass ring and let go. The force of the blow could be heard throughout the residence.

After a few minutes the door creaked open, and a rather obese man filled the doorway, "Yes, may I help you?'

"I have a delivery for Mrs. Nahib from Madame Oni," Layla replied.

"Please come in. We have been expecting you." Pasha Nahib wasn't a bad looking sort, but his belly hung over his belt and his shirt was unbuttoned revealing an apish amount of hair on his chest.

Layla couldn't get the word "perver" out of her mind. She entered the house and was taken aback by the sheer opulence of the décor. Two large Roman statuettes of naked ladies stood guard over the entry to the house, and a circular stairway spiraled up past a thick beam attached to the wall on either side. The beam supported a chandelier hanging from what appeared to be a fabric encased chain. Artwork lined the walls on all sides.

Baron Empain

Pasha Nahib turned and pointed down a long hall. "Please put the package in the kitchen."

Layla obeyed and walked forward, still taking in the sites along the way. She instantly felt a bump on her behind and realized it was Pasha giving her a light tap as she passed by. Again the thought "perver" echoed through her head.

"Haha, my, that is a tight little bottom, young lady." Smiling, she turned, gave Pasha a flirtatious wink, and skipped off toward the kitchen. Of course, her gesture excited the old man, and he quickened his pace in hopes of closing the gap between them. She entered the kitchen and set the package on a tile lined counter.

Baron Empain's residence

"Hello, my dear. You must be Layla." The voice startled her. It belonged to Mrs. Nahib, who was sitting in the parlor off the kitchen in an armchair, her legs resting on an ottoman with a book opened in her lap.

"*Oui*, Madame. I'm Layla, and I have your skirt and blouse. I believe you have items I am to return to Madame Oni for alteration?"

Out of the corner of her eye, Layla could see the Pasha bent over, elbows resting on the large island counter in the middle of the kitchen. She could feel his stare.

"Layla, sweetheart, see that bag in the corner?"

"*Oui*, Madame."

"It contains the items you speak of. Did Madame Oni say when I might expect them?"

"She can have them back to you in a week, if that meets with your approval."

"That would be wonderful." Then ordering her husband, she said, "Dear, don't just stand there pay the girl!"

"Layla what was the amount?" he asked taking out his wallet.

"Two pounds sir," Layla replied with a wink.

Pasha took out an additional one pound and smiling like a schoolboy said, "Come, I will escort you to the door."

Layla thanked the lady of the house and turned brushing past the Pasha on her way out of the kitchen. He felt his blood pressure mount as he turned and watched her cheeks swivel under the sheer, long skirt she was wearing.

She came to a stop at the door and stepped to one side while saying, "Please do me the favor of opening the door."

Still gaping, he said, "Oh yes, where are my manners?" Putting his hand on the knob, he brought his other arm around her and pulled her close. She lifted the package creating a barrier between them and smiled. Returning her smile, he allowed his hand to slide down the curvature of her spine and rest atop her buttock.

"Sir, don't you have something you want to give me?"

He said giggling, "Indeed I do."

"I believe Madame Oni informed your wife the alterations came to a total of two pounds."

He cleared his throat and said, "Oh...uh...yes, here you go, and Layla there is an extra one for you." With a raised brow, he asked, "Will you be making the delivery next week as well?"

"I guess you will just have to wait and see, won't you?" Slipping from his grasp, she shot through the now open door. Whistling, she proceeded down the steps to the street. Excited at the exchange between them, the Pasha stood in the doorway, watching her departure.

Upon arriving at home, she gave the extra money to her mother to help with the rent. From that day on, she determined to earn as much money as she could so her brothers and sister would never go hungry.

It was around this time that Layla's mother, Helena, set up an exchange service of sorts. She would send Layla to her male friends telling them she needed money for food or clothes. Of course, the men fondled her and sent her home with the money.

One day, Layla was told to visit the butcher. Of course, her mother knew the butcher was going to fondle her daughter. She had made the arrangement in exchange for liver and steak. Later that night, Helena was taking care of Akins. He had a severe case of asthma, which he contracted at the age of two. He was also anemic, thus, very susceptible to colds and other diseases. The doctor informed Helena the boy needed to eat liver or steak cooked lightly. She would wait until the other children went to bed around seven o'clock or so and then go to the kitchen to prepare his meal.

Layla was aroused by the enticing aroma and drawn into its clutches luring her to the kitchen. Finding her mother laboring over the stove, she asked, "What are you cooking so late?"

"I'm cooking liver for your brother. The doctor ordered it."

Layla watched in silence and then headed back to bed. At that moment, she understood why her mother had been sending her to the butcher. She held the thought close, "If I let the butcher fondle me, my brother will get well." She returned to the butcher time and again thinking her brother's asthma would improve. Even at a young age, she understood the family needed her.

What might appear strange by normal standards was a way of life in Cairo. People found a way to survive. Layla was learning how to use her beauty to get anything she wanted. Many girls at the time fortunate enough to sport good looks and a shapely body learned to do the same. Layla was different from most in that she always had this keen sense of commitment and understanding that family came first. She was very responsible, even in the employment of the seamstress.

Madame Oni began receiving more and more calls. Many of the husbands met on a regular basis at Café Riche. It seemed they were sharing their experiences. Word was that Layla was a feisty girl and had a fun way of flirting when making her deliveries. Anonymity at the Café was honored. Knowing each other's secrets made them vulnerable. Layla, in the meantime, kept silent in order to protect the customers and Madame Oni. Business picked up as word about Layla circulated among the men.

Layla had no way of knowing these events in her young life were leading her toward a life of prostitution. All she knew was flirting had become an easy way to earn a few piasters or even an extra pound. Her motivating factor had always been the support of the family. Soon, however, she would meet a streetwise young girl named Lucy who would show her how she could ask for more, a lot more. Men were more than willing to oblige, which led to her formal introduction to a life of prostitution, her profession for years to come.

↘↘↘

Layla was about ten years old when she met Lucy. Lucy was two or three years older but wise beyond her years and street smart. She was taller than most of the boys, had jet-black hair with brown eyes, and like Layla, well developed for her age. Lucy had a unique look about her, not beautiful, but attractive. She wasn't nearly as good looking as Layla, but she could hustle. Becoming best friends with her, Layla learned about the street from Lucy over the years.

Layla and Lucy played together and dreamed of a day when they would live in a palace and marry a prince. Their adventures became a wonderful way to escape the mundane and oftentimes troubling events of their lives. Layla came to love the street because of her friendship with Lucy.

Lucy had a cynical side, a result of the deep distrust she had for men. Like Layla, the men were always taking advantage of her.

Café Riche

At an early age, she learned how to manipulate them to get what she wanted. Along with this knowledge, she developed a thick skin. It was not wise to get on her wrong side, or you might wake up to find a part of your body missing.

For instance, some of the boys from down the street came to play. The leader was a kid named Oubastet. Lucy didn't much care for him, but he had a crush on her. Everyone knew it, but she wouldn't as much look at him. This particular day, he was through being embarrassed by her in front of his friends. He sneaked up and grabbed her from behind and in front of her friends pulled up her skirt and attempted to run his hand down her panties. Lucy squirmed, just enough to break his hold and kicked him between the legs. He gasped in pain as Layla and Lucy ran off. Oubastet, beet red, couldn't move, much less chase them. All his friends doubled over in laughter.

The next day, Layla saw Oubastet sobbing. She overheard him mumbling something about his cat being nailed to a fence. She ran to Lucy's house, eager to tell her the news. Lucy just looked up with a smirk, raised her eyebrow, and said, "Oubastet had it coming for what he tried to do to me. I bet he thinks twice about annoying me again."

Layla didn't dare say anything. Like her other secrets, she kept this one to herself. Still she wondered how Lucy could be so cruel as to kill a cat, such an innocent animal. Truth be told, she admired the defiant air about Lucy. People learned not to joke with Lucy, and being her friend, they didn't joke with Layla.

Lucy had an inner strength and was afraid of nothing. Layla found herself drawing upon that strength in difficult situations. She was rough in her own right and could take just about anything thrown her way; however, she always maintained a certain sweet demeanor, which Lucy lacked. Their completeness of one another was the main reason they became and remained so close, unwittingly they played a role in molding each other's character.

Not having anybody else to talk about the incidents with her uncle and Yani, Layla decided to confide in Lucy. Lucy focused all her attention on Layla and listened, not once interrupting her. Tears flowed from Layla's eyes and down her rosy red cheeks. Lucy wrapped her arms around Layla and held her tightly.

"Your arms around me feel just like it does when Pappa holds me."

"Look, I know this doctor. His name is Kamuzir, and he can check you and let us know if everything is okay." Then as her eyes lit up, she asked, "Layla, are you a virgin?"

Being so young, Layla had no idea what Lucy was asking. With a tilt of her head, she questioned in return, "Lucy, what is a virgin?"

"Oh, Layla, you are not that stupid, are you? Virgins are pure, meaning they have never been penetrated by a man. You really don't know, do you? I mean, did your uncle or mother's boyfriend ever put their penis inside you?"

Starting to cry, Layla murmured a faint, "I think so."

With a grin Lucy said, "I know. Maybe I will let them play with me, and then I will cut off their penises and hang them on the fence next to Oubastet's cat."

They both grew weak from laughter.

"Don't worry. The doctor is a very smart man. He will be able to tell if you are a virgin. Come, let's run to see the doctor."

So off they went, like a couple of wild, street Arabs racing along the sidewalks of Cairo. It was a warm day and the sun was shining. There was a peculiar lightness about the air. Layla ran as if she were floating above the ground with a sense of adventure at her feet. It was a feeling she had never experienced before. There was renewed hope birthed in her that day. She was drinking from Lucy's well of character, and the taste was sweet.

❯ ❯ ❯

Lucy and Layla slowed as they drew closer to the center of town, holding tight to the storefronts and avoiding passersby. Lucy grabbed Layla's arm as she yelled, "It's Café Riche. Slow down, I want to peek inside. Do you know what is in there?"

Layla had no idea and responded by shaking her head from side to side.

"This is where all the Beys, Pashas, and other important men about town gather. They smoke from the hookah and talk business." She led Layla over to a side window of the café, and the two of them bent over, their little buttocks sticking out, as they peered through the window.

Several men were sitting around puffing at hoses attached to a brass pot sitting in their midst. Neither Lucy nor Layla knew the substance they were smoking was hashish, from which the men gained a euphoric feeling accompanied by much laughter. Upon closer inspection, there seemed to be one man who was the center of attention. Layla found herself drawn to him like iron to a magnet. He was rather large, but dark and handsome with a pencil thin mustache and wearing small round sunglasses. She felt a fluttering in her heart by his presence and apparent importance.

The girls were startled when two big hands grabbed each of them by the shoulder, and the burly man said, "What are you two little spies up to?"

Fear gripped them as they were led inside the café. The men fell silent as they turned to see the two innocent looking girls. Layla didn't know she was about to meet the King of Egypt, King Farouk, for the very first time.

With a slight laugh, their captor said, "I caught these girls peering in through the front window. What do you think we ought to do with them?"

The man whom Layla had been admiring followed with his own laugh. Removing his glasses he said, "Bring them to me I must interrogate these spies. We must find out how much they heard about our dealings."

The other men laughed and followed his lead by shaking their heads and whispering, "You two are in big trouble."

Mesmerized, Layla found herself staring into the depths of the man's eyes. They were intriguing, almost sphinx-like.

He looked at her with a look of concern and asked in a baritone voice, "What is your name, girl?"

"Please, sir, don't hurt us. We didn't hear anything."

"Silence. I asked your name," he said holding a flat hand up toward her face,

"Layla, sir," she was so afraid she thought she might pee in her underwear. Then out of the corner of her eye she could see Lucy. Lucy had that cynical look about her, and Layla was thinking, "Lucy, you can't cut off his penis in here."

The man continued with a stern voice, "Let us all get a good look at you two. My, what striking women we are producing here in Egypt. Look, gentlemen, a blonde with blue eyes. My sweet, those blonde curls, blue eyes, and nice round rear end are going to serve you well in life."

All the men roared as the King made suggestive glances up and down Layla's body.

She didn't know what to say, so she asked, "Would you like to touch me, monsieur?"

The men laughed even louder. King Farouk taken back by her advance, turned red, smiled, and said, "*Imshi*", and if I ever catch you spying here again, I will have your heads. Do you hear me?"

"Yes sir." They said in unison as they turned and ran past the bodyguard to the front door, not stopping until they were both out of breath a few blocks away.

"Layla," Lucy yelled, "Do you know who that was?"

"No, but he was so strong and handsome," she replied with innocence.

"That was the King of Egypt, King Farouk," Lucy blurted out with excitement. "Did you see the look on his face when the other men started laughing?"

"No, I just thought he was like all the other men and wanted to touch me. I don't know why I said it; it just kind of fell out of my mouth."

At the time, she couldn't remember ever laughing so hard. It was a memory she would not soon forget. When they settled down long enough to get their bearing on where they were in relation to the doctor's, Lucy excitedly said, "We are here. We are at Doctor Kamuzir's house."

➤➤➤

Lucy and Layla walked up the short flight of stairs and rang the bell. The doctor lived in the Zamalek district of Cairo. The area consisted of quiet streets lined with 19th-century apartments and villas. Filled with many fine restaurants, bars, and open-air cafés, the area was also a favorite area for many Europeans who settled in Cairo.

---

*   Off with the two of you. (Arabic)

The doctor's home was a large two story villa. The front door was ornate iron, and two large clay flowerpots sat on either side overflowing with Narcissus plants, named for their narcotic properties. The door opened, and Abdou, the doctor's *boab* (porter), a rather sophisticated looking sort in a *galibia* (garment), made inquiry as to their purpose.

"We are here to see Doctor Kamuzir," Lucy said in an authoritative tone.

"Do you have an appointment, young lady?"

"We don't need an appointment. You just tell the doctor that Lucy is here to see him."

"Wait here, and I will tell him you are here."

Lucy looked at Layla and said with a slight giggle, "You just wait. The doctor will see us. After all, he is my uncle!"

Layla had been amazed at how Lucy stood up to the man and with such verve, but now she was shocked at what she had just heard. She had no idea that Lucy's mother had a brother, much less that she had a doctor in the family. She thought they were poor.

The door opened and a handsome man stood smiling down at them. "Lucy, my dear, how are you? What can I do for you?"

"Doctor, my friend does not feel well, and we had nowhere else to go. Will you take a look at her?"

"Yes, my sweet little niece, anything for you."

The doctor was Lucy's mother's half brother. Her grandmother had been married to a wealthy European at the time of WWI and had one child by him. When the father was killed fighting in France, her grandmother had been devastated. Their son, Doctor Kamuzir, had been well educated and attended medical school. Late in life, Lucy's grandmother fell in love, remarried, and had another child, Lucy's mother. The doctor always took care of his half-sister, but he wasn't very fond of her lifestyle. She became a prostitute when their mother died.

Knowing how difficult life was living with his half sister, the doctor had a special love for Lucy. He also admired her street smarts.

She didn't let anything or anybody keep her from what she intended to accomplish.

"Come in, girls. Let us step into my study," the doctor said, sliding the doors open.

Layla entered the home and stood mesmerized by the interior. The room appeared enormous to a now wideeyed Layla. It had a high ceiling and walls lined with books. A ladder with hooks at the top rested on a polished brass rod that was attached to the wall at various intervals. The bottom of the ladder had rollers, which allowed it to be maneuvered around the room. There was a large desk in the center of the room with a settee in front of it and two antique chairs on either side. The settee was adorned in dark burgundy leather, the color of which could be likened to a rich merlot wine.

Doctor Kamuzir asked them to sit down and instructed Abdou to brew some tea.

Then a sense of helplessness came over Layla. She looked over at a beautiful, ornate, grandfather clock predominately displayed in the room. She could not keep her thoughts from wandering back to her uncle Max and the many times he had lifted her up to see the very same type clock in his house. She was told he was teaching her to tell time, but each time Uncle Max always lifted her high, held her there for a long time and then slowly slid her down his body, stopping when she was about waist high for a few moments in order for him to feel her presence on his genitals.

The doctor interrupted, "Ladies, I am a busy man, so please tell me how I can be of service."

Layla had never been called a lady, so at once the doctor was elevated to a godly status in her eyes. Lucy in her bold tone said, "*Son oncle viens dans sa chamber ce met sur elle pendant qu'elle dort.* *"

With a sad look he asked, "What is your name?"

---

* My friend's uncle comes into her room while she sleeps and lays on top of her (French)

She said in a shy tone, "Layla."

"Layla, it would be an honor for me to assist you. Lucy, I am going to escort Layla to my examination room. Why don't you wait here? We won't be long."

"Sure, but make sure she is okay and find out if she is still a virgin."

Abdou entered the study balancing a tray with three cups and a small teapot. "Abdou, be so kind as to pour our guest some tea. I bet she might enjoy some of those fresh baked scones the cook prepared this morning."

Abdou set the tray down and picked up the teapot. "Yes sir."

"*Yalla**, follow me."

As they exited the study, the doctor led Layla down a long hall to an open door. The scents of the home filled her nostrils. She smelled the cedar lining the walls in his study and a light hint of mint emanating from the tea Abdou had brewed. Pictures dotted the wall along the way. Many appeared to be important men and their wives. However, one person common in all was the woman standing next to the doctor. Layla assumed her to be his wife.

Entering the room, the doctor said, "Layla, this is my examination room. I want you to sit up here and tell me what happened in your own words. I want to hear the story from you."

Layla felt so respected that someone asked with interest about what had happened to her. Tears welled up in her eyes as she related the abuse from her uncle and Yani and the reaction of her mother and aunt.

Then she said, "Tell me, where did the blood come from?"

Shaking his head, the doctor looked at her. "Layla, we are going to find the answer. I need you to take off your clothes. You can put them on that chair. Here is a gown for you to put on, and when you are finished sit back up on the table. I am going to leave the room while you undress. Remember, there is no reason to fear. This procedure is normal for all of my patients. Soon you will hear

---

*   Come (Arabic)

a knock at the door. If you have finished putting on the gown, please respond. I will come back in and examine you, and we'll talk some more."

The exam room was different from the other parts of the house. The walls were white and smelled of a hint of ammonia. Cabinets lined the walls and were filled with small vials. Layla assumed they held medicine. The table had wooden legs and a leather surface, which was lined with a thin piece of white paper. There were also two weird looking contraptions at the end of the table. She did as told, stripped off her clothing, and slipped on the gown. When finished, she sat back up on the table and waited for the knock. She wasn't scared at all.

Not too many minutes passed before there was a slight rap at the door.

"Layla, are you ready?"

"Yes, Sir."

The doctor came back in the room and walked over to where she was sitting. Speaking in a soft tone he said, "Okay, Layla, let me explain what I am going to do. I am a women's doctor, and my patients come see me once a month for a checkup. This means I check their privates, the area between their legs." Pointing to the weird contraptions at the end of the table, he said, "I would like you to sit back and lift your knees up and slip your feet into these stirrups. What I am about to do may feel uncomfortable, but at any time if you feel pain, please tell me, and I will stop. Don't be afraid. I'm here to help, not hurt you. Do you understand?"

"I guess so," Layla said enraptured by the attention the doctor was showing.

"This tool is called a speculum and will help me open you up a so I can check your cervix. I will also be taking some samples with this brush."

Layla did as she was told and realized it was cold sitting on the paper with her bare behind. The doctor had a small instrument in his hand and brought it between her legs.

In a whispered tone, he said, "Oh, okay... I see...um, it is as I suspected."

Before she knew what he was doing, he stepped back and said, "Well, that wasn't so bad now, was it? Okay you can sit up. I'm going to retrieve Lucy from the study and give you a moment to dress." He left the room.

A few minutes later, there was a knock on the door. "Come in," Layla called.

With a smile from ear to ear across her face, in pranced Lucy, followed by the doctor. The doctor began. "The hymen is a thin membrane of tissue that surrounds the vaginal opening. Layla, it has been torn, but for the most part there is no damage. I have sad news; you are no longer a virgin. It is not my custom to interfere in my client's personal life, but because you are so young I will make an exception. Would you like me to speak to your mother about the results of my test?"

Layla sat up and responded, "No sir, please do not tell anyone. If my mother learns that I came here today, she will beat me."

"Layla, it is not right what they have been doing. Someone needs to know. These men should be exposed and punished."

"If my uncle gets in trouble, it would just kill my aunt. Her children would be shamed. Please promise me you will not tell anyone about this."

"It is against my better judgment, but I promise. But you must make me a promise in return. You will come to see me the first week of every month, and Layla..."

Layla looked into his eyes and said, "Yes, Sir."

"Remember, if you ever need help, I am here."

Later he would confess to her that he feared for her safety, knowing the authorities would ignore any report of abuse. As such, the report would have placed her in greater danger.

After Layla dressed, Lucy grabbed her by the arm and said, "Doctor, we have to go. Thanks for seeing us, and I will make sure she keeps her promise."

"Be careful you two."

Exiting to the street, Lucy said with excitement, "Oh, Layla do you know what this means?"

Of course, Layla had no clue and indicated as such with a slight shrug of her shoulders. She was still trying to figure out why being a virgin mattered.

Lucy continued, "Oh this is such a great day. Don't you see, Layla? Now that you are no longer a virgin, there is plenty of money to be made. I know a man named Albert. He owns a dance club and would be happy to let us work for him. We can make much more than we do now."

"What do we have to do?"

"We let the men lay with us and do what your uncle and mother's boyfriend have been doing. They will pay as much as ten pounds to lay with us, sometimes more."

She did not quite understand what her future and new adventures meant. Layla felt like a whole new world was about to open up to her.

` ` `

The next day, Layla, still excited about the previous day's events, hurried to Lucy's house but found it empty. Fear gripped her. "What in the world had happened?" It made no sense to her. At first, she thought she had gone to the wrong house. She reoriented herself but realized it was Lucy's house. It was like Lucy and her family had vanished in thin air.

She wouldn't learn until later that when Lucy returned home the previous day, men were placing all her family's belongings on to a big truck. Her mother had instructed her to pack her clothes in a large suitcase she had set out. Her mother's boyfriend had taken a job in another town, and they were to leave that night. Similar to Layla, Lucy rarely saw her real father; incensed at his wife's infidelity, he too had taken his leave. Lucy had fought with her mother, which of late had become a common occurrence.

"I don't want to go, and you can't make me. I will run away, and you will never see me again, ever."

"Lucy, quit being so theatrical. Besides, it's a wonderful town on the coast. Look at it like one of your wild adventures. It is a good opportunity, and we need the money. Don't you mess this up, or I will make your life a living hell. Do you hear me?"

"It's not fair."

"Just get your things together and put them in the case. We are leaving tonight." Her mother spun on her heels and slammed the door on the way out.

Something broke in Lucy's spirit, and tears flooded her face, causing her nose to run. Frozen, she sat cross-legged in the middle of her room. She couldn't remember the last time she had cried, but it felt good. She felt a peace come over her and knew what she needed to do. Lucy had a plan and moving was not part of the plan. She packed everything she could into the large suitcase and climbed out the window.

Layla was alone at home when she heard the knock at the door. Pulling back the lace curtain to see who it was, she saw Lucy. Barely able to contain her excitement, Layla unlatched the door, flung it open, and threw her arms around her. The force of her embrace caused them both to stumble and fall to the ground where they remained, laughing and glad to be together again.

Once inside, Lucy shared her plan. "Layla, after our visit to the doctor, I arrived home, and mother told me we were moving. We fought then, and I packed a suitcase and slipped out the window. I wasn't about to leave town, not after the news we learned from the doctor.

"I went to see that man named Albert, the one who owns the dance club. I asked him for a job and mentioned you. He hired me and said that you were welcome as well. So, what do you say?"

"Lucy, I have something I need to tell you. On my deliveries for Madame Oni and when I go on errands for Mother, I have been letting the men fondle me. None of them have been demanding sex, but I have been making extra money on every delivery."

"Layla, you are smarter than I gave you credit for. I knew you had it in you. Albert said many soldiers are coming to Cairo and are lonely for affection. They have lots of money, and we can make ten to twenty pounds several times a day. All we have to do is spread our legs and let them have their way."

Layla chimed in, "Well, if I can make a lot of money, so be it. After all, it couldn't be any worse than what Uncle Max or Yani are doing to me."

Lucy straightened and said, "No, in fact, the soldiers will treat you with more respect than your old fat uncle and that sleaze your mother calls a boyfriend."

The girls started dancing at the club, which was somewhat innocent. They put on shows and flirted with the customers encouraging them to drink up. However, Albert was quick to put the word out, and the first week, Layla, only twelve years old, entertained a few soldiers in the back room.

Her first customer was the most difficult. At first, she was hesitant to let him penetrate her. However, Albert had spoken to the man and let him know it was her first time as a prostitute. He was gentle, moved slowly, and didn't attempt to force himself into her. It was the first time she had felt pleasure at the touch of a man.

Several days past, and Layla's mother received a call from Madame Oni, "May I speak to Layla?"

"Madame Oni, she is not home at the moment. May I ask why you are calling?"

"She hasn't been to work in over a week, so I was concerned something had happened to her."

Her Mother being clever responded, "Oh, she has been spending time with her father. I will speak with her and get back to you. Sorry you had to call."

"No problem. She is a special girl and has been doing an excellent job. I'd hate to lose her."

Layla arrived home late that night and was surprised to find her mother waiting up. Nervous, she held out ten pounds and said, "Look, Mom, I've had good luck at work. This should come in handy."

"Layla, where have you been?"

"Nowhere in particular, why?"

"How is your job at Madame Oni's?"

Layla could tell by her Mother's tone that she knew more than she was letting on.

"Why do you ask? Is Madame Oni mad at me?"

"I should say so, considering you haven't been to work in over a week. You want to tell me where you have been every day?"

"I took a job at the dance hall with Lucy. It is much more rewarding than running errands for Madame Oni."

"Have you been letting men make love to you?"

"What does that mean?"

Helena slapped her across the face and said, "It means *baiser**. You know what it means, so don't play innocent avec *moi***. *Est ce que tu deveins une grue?* *** "

"Maybe and why not, Yani and Uncle Max have been doing it to me for a long time!"

Helena brought her hand up again ready to slap her, but stopped just short of Layla's cheek. "Interesting, how do you like it?"

"I can make a lot of money." Then she turned and ran from the house, as she had many times before.

Layla had concluded the streets were a normal way of life. They were to become her market place.

---

*   fornicate (French)

**   with me (French)

***   Are you becoming a whore? (French)

Helena paid a visit to Albert the next day, and they came to an understanding. Helena would set a room up at the house and make all the preparations. Albert would send the men, and they would split the proceeds. That's when Helena, her Mother, became Layla's pimp. She was trapped, and not even Lucy was able to help her.

Soon, Helena set up shop on the balcony of their home, which became a pseudo sex factory. She would have Layla sit with a silk kimono making sure she flirted with the passersby. Another ploy would be to have Layla approach the soldiers on the street and ask if they would like a zig zig. If they responded in the affirmative, she was to negotiate a price and lead them to the room Helena had prepared. Helena always set out two glasses of wine and stood at the door to collect the money. She even had the audacity to ask, "What about my *bakshich**?"

Being pulled from school after the second grade, Layla had never learned to read or write. Her mother was too busy with her own life, which was spent with her gigolo, Yani. Over time, Layla became self-taught in a variety of ways. For example, at first she didn't know English. When she went out with the English soldiers, she had trouble communicating. One of the girls she met at the time spoke English, so Layla related in French to her what she wanted to say and the girl translated in English. The men thought she was funny and enjoyed her accent. She had quite the sense of humor.

Layla would approach a soldier smiling and say, in French, "*Mon cher petit chou*," which sounded good, but translated into English was, "How are you, my dear my little cabbage?" Regardless the men loved when she spoke to them that way. Sometimes she would just say, "*Bonjour mon ami? Voulez-vous dormir avec moi?* **" Once they understood, the answer was always yes.

She also spoke to them in Italian, for the language was so much more romantic than Greek or Arabic. Men enjoyed it when

---

*   tip (Arabic)

**   Hello, how are you? Do you want to sleep with me? (French)

she would say in Italian, *"Como esta, vera casa mia?* At first they didn't understand what she was saying so they would just smile. Then she would translate the words into English: "How are you, do you want to come to my house?" They stared in awe, not believing she was a prostitute, and then fell all over each other to be the first to respond. She had fun with them, making their time together more exciting than it was with the other girls.

When she met the same men again, she had them tell her things, so she could go back to her girlfriend for the translation. She also began reading books in English and over time came to speak the language fluently.

Layla wondered about her life. Maybe things would be different if she would have been born in another place and time. Layla's primary relationship with her mother was one of anger and impatience, and deep down she felt her mother must hate her. Helena was always using her as an object, an object to please herself. She never had time for her, except when there was money to be made. Layla was just a body to her.

Layla couldn't stand being controlled by her mother; however, she was more concerned about supporting her family than about her own well being. She was dedicated to her sister and brothers who depended on her. In time, the thing that would save Layla from her mother's evil clutches was her mother's own fear. Helena was paranoid that Layla would leave and go to work for another madam.

Helena and Yani were rolling in the dough, but their monetary gain would be short lived.

➤ ➤ ➤

It was July 1941. Layla, now fourteen, was walking the street when she ran into Hannah, her father's landlord. "Layla, you poor thing. Are you still working these dreadful streets?"

"Hannah, how else am I going to support my family? Mother won't work, and my brothers are trying to finish their education so they can get proper jobs. Any money Father gives us, she spends on Yani, that worthless boyfriend of hers." Hannah listened as she looked at her in a curious way. "Stop looking at me like that, I'm okay, I'll be fine. You know me; I can take care of myself."

"Can you, Layla? Let me see something," She said lifting the hair covering Layla's neck. "How long have you had these spots on your neck?"

"The spots, oh those they are nothing. They showed up a couple of weeks ago. It's just a rash or something; I'm planning to see Doctor Kamuzir tomorrow."

"I have seen spots like these before. You need to see the doctor right away."

"What do you mean? I'll be okay, I need to work. I don't want another beating from mother."

"Layla, listen to me. You might have a disease. If my suspicion is correct, you are putting your customers at risk. It is very contagious. You come with me, and I'll figure something out about your Mother. I'm more concerned about your health at this moment."

Doctor Kamuzir was more than happy to see Layla and asked his nurse to put them in one of his exam rooms. "Ladies, my 10 o'clock appointment just showed up so give me a few minutes, and I will be in to see you."

"Yes, Doctor. Thank you."

Soon there was a knock at the door. "Yes, come in."

"Hello Layla! To what do I owe the pleasure of this visit?"

"I have a rash on my neck, and Hannah thought it best if we came over and had you take a look."

"Let me see," he said pushing her hair to one side.

"Ummm, I am going to get a sample from the area and also have my nurse draw some blood so I can run some tests.

Turning, he said to his nurse, "I want you to draw about 15ml of blood." Then he took Layla's hand in his. "I don't want you to be alarmed, but the rash is similar to those I have seen caused by a specific venereal disease. It is called syphilis. However, until I get back the results from your blood test, I won't know for sure. Regardless of what we find, I'm certain it is treatable."

The nurse drew blood and placed a small amount into three glass vials. The doctor concluded their time together by saying, "Layla, I won't have your results for a couple of days. We will give you a call when the tests come back. Will you be staying with Hannah?"

"Yes, and Layla I won't take no for an answer," Hannah said in an authoritative tone.

"Good, I will give you a call as soon as I have conclusive information." He rose and gave Layla a soft kiss on the cheek. Then looking her in the eyes, he said, "I'll take care of you. Don't worry."

Hannah had no idea what else was going through Layla's mind. The rest of the day was a blur. Hannah took her home and insisted she stay with her until the tests came back. Layla couldn't sleep thinking something terrible had happened. She clasped the *evil eye* pendant and called out, "Lord, help me, please don't let me die. My brother will not be able to get his medicine. My family will starve."

Layla went into Hannah's room. "Will you hold me? I'm scared."

Hannah responded by holding out her arms. "Of course, dear. Come here and lay down beside me," Layla trembled in Hannah's arms, and the tears began to flow. Her sobbing came in droves interrupted by an occasional gasp for air. However, the warmth of Hannah's touch soon calmed her, and she fell asleep. The next couple of days she slept most of the time, not realizing how exhausted she had become.

Hannah peered in to see if Layla was awake, "The doctor called and would like us to come in as soon as possible."

"Good. I will be glad when this ordeal has passed, and I can get on with my life. I feel so confused."

They arrived at Doctor Kamuzir's that afternoon, and his nurse led them to the examination room. Soon the doctor poked his head in. "How's my girl holding up?"

"Doctor, it's been a nightmare the last couple of days not knowing what to expect. Tell me you have good news."

"I have good news and some not so good news, but nothing life threatening."

Layla and Hannah just looked at each other as if reading one another's mind. "What does that mean?" they each thought.

"Now, now let me explain. The not so good news is you have been infected by syphilis. The sores on your neck are called chancres. The reason you haven't experienced much pain from them is that they form during the primary stage or the first 20 or so days from exposure."

"What is syphilis, Doctor?" Layla asked.

"It is a highly contagious venereal disease. Your blood test confirmed my suspicion showing traces of treponema pallidum in your blood."

"How did I get it?'

"The obvious answer is through intercourse, but you can also catch it through direct contact with a carrier. I am going to give you a shot today, and I want you to return once a month until we know for sure you are free from the disease."

What's the good news, Doctor?" Hannah asked, tilting her head in a curious manner.

"Layla, what are we going to do with you?"

"Tell me, am I going to die?"

"No, no nothing like that, but you are pregnant," he said wondering who the father was.

Silence filled the room for what seemed an eternity. Layla had been sitting on the exam table, and, as she descended, her legs became weak, and she started to collapse. The doctor caught her under the arms and guided her to a seat.

"What am I going to do? I don't know anything about babies. What's going to happen to me? Is the disease going to harm the baby?"

"Slow down now. Calm down. Everything is going to be all right. The best I can tell, you are about two months pregnant, so I'm not sure how the disease will affect your pregnancy. We may have caught it early enough, and in most cases the treatment prevents complications.

"What am I going to do?"

"The way I see it, you have two options. You can abort the child, or you can have the child. I know several couples who can't have children and would love to provide for a baby. Please understand, I have known many women who opted for an abortion, and all of them have regretted the decision. It is the root of much pain in their lives. Human life is precious, even when it is unexpected.

The thought weighing on her mind, Layla asked, "What about you, Doctor? Are you okay?"

Hannah just looked at the two of them with a blank stare. She had no idea why Layla would be asking this question. Layla had been a regular client of the doctor since that first meeting with Lucy, but six months earlier, their relationship had changed.

One day Layla had been feeling lonely, and it occurred to her she had missed her appointment that month. She had called to make sure Kamuzir was in the office; his assistant confirmed he was.

It was a beautiful spring day, and the flowers were in full bloom. The doctor's assistant greeted her. "Layla, Doctor Kamuzir asked if you wouldn't mind waiting in his study until he finishes with a client."

"I don't mind at all," she said entering the study like she had on many occasions. Looking around, she reflected on the first time she and Lucy had visited. She remembered all the pictures, especially the one with the doctor and a woman she had assumed to be his wife. Kamuzir's wife had been a well-respected woman around Cairo when she was diagnosed with a rare form of cancer. The doctor researched the disease and contacted peers around the world in hopes of finding a cure. He never left her side, but always felt he had let her down. She died a horrible death. Abdou told Layla the story and now several years later, Doctor Kamuzir was still alone.

Her thoughts were interrupted by the doctor's greeting, "Hello, Layla."

Layla was wearing a yellow sundress held together by only two straps loose around her breasts. She hadn't noticed, but her nipples were erect expressing the passion she was feeling. Kamuzir wasn't prepared for the sudden rush of heat that shot through his body. His pulse quickened as he gazed at her sensual appearance. He had always acted professionally, but he had become more and more excited at the thought of her visits. She had developed into a beautiful woman since that first day he had investigated her virginity.

As he stood staring at her, Layla picked up on the electricity in the room and moved toward him bringing her hands up to his face. "Hello, Doctor, I have missed you," she said rising on her toes, spreading her lips, and letting their wetness rest on his cheek. She could feel his passion as he pressed up against her.

Overcome by her innocence and beauty, he had been unable to resist. Pulling her close and holding her tightly to him, he said, "Layla, I am burning at the thought of you beneath that dress."

Nose to nose, they gazed into one another's eyes. Both were breathing heavy as he kissed her, their tongues intertwining. He was mesmerized by the softness of her lips and the sensation in his groin. He cupped her bottom in both hands giving it a little squeeze. She lowered her hands from his face down to his chest and began unbuttoning his shirt.

His chest hair felt good against the top of her breasts which were peeking out from her dress as he held her tightly. Layla rotated and scooted him back until he felt the edge of his desk bite into his back. Turning, he lifted her up on top of the desk and stepped back admiring her beauty. Unlatching his belt and letting his pants fall to his ankles, he reached into a box on his desk and took out a condom. Layla took it from him, placed it on him, then grabbed him with both hands, and led him between her legs.

The doctor trembled as he penetrated her and rocked to the rhythm of her hips rising to meet his every thrust. He collapsed on top of her with an amazing feeling of ecstasy. It would not be the last time her sweetness would engulf him. Over time, he became addicted to the feelings she invoked.

"Layla, you make me feel like a man ready to take on the world. You, my dear, are special. I hesitate to say more for fear your pretty head will grow too large. Now I guess I better return to my doctor role, don't you think?"

"Um…only if you promise to let me make this a regular payment for your services."

The doctor raised his hand, rubbed his chin with his thumb and first finger, and said, "I don't know, Layla. I must respect the doctor-patient relationship. It is of the utmost importance."

Running her hand across his privates, Layla smiled. "But, Doctor, isn't that what you just did?" They embraced in a hearty laugh.

"On second thought, why not? Come as often as you like."

"And you as well, my doctor," Layla said with a full portion of mischief in her voice.

Layla was having sex with the doctor, and Hannah sensed the connection between them. The doctor asked if he could speak to Layla alone.

Showing a slight smile, Hannah nodded her head and said, "Layla, I will be at the front door."

"Layla, I have been careful to use protection when we have been together. I am fine. It is you I am the most worried about. You must attempt to contact anyone you have slept with in the past month. I know this might be impossible, but do the best you can.

"When I was over at the University it was brought to my attention that the authorities are concerned by of the number of reports. They fear an outbreak has occurred. Please be careful and make sure you return monthly for the shots."

She was relieved the doctor had exercised wisdom and that he wasn't upset with her. As she started to cry, he put his arm over her shoulder and pulled her close.

"Doctor, you know Albert, the owner of the club where I work?"

"Yes, his wife is one of my patients."

"He has not been so wise. He called me to his office one day and told me he was burning with passion. His wife was pregnant, and he asked if I would satisfy his desires until the baby was born. I was more than happy to oblige, and we have been meeting once a week. What if he is infected and gave it to her?"

"You must tell him to bring his wife as soon as possible, and I will examine them both. Being her doctor, it will be easy for me to make something up. I can give her the shots and tell her they are vitamins which will ease her pregnancy and improve the infant's health."

Layla was horrified and for the first time felt shame. She had to get word to Albert right away and cringed at the thought of telling him and not knowing how he would react. Hannah was waiting by the front door when Layla emerged from the study. As they stepped out on the curb, both pensively watched the cars slowly navigating the street before them.

Turning to Hannah, Layla said, "My eyes feel like windows, and I'm looking out at an unreal world. Everything is moving, but I don't feel like I'm a part of it. It's as if I'm in a stupor fully awake, but numb to everything around me. Hannah, thank you for helping me. I am forever in your debt."

"Layla, I'm here anytime you need me."

"Look, I need some time to sort all this out. Do you mind if I don't go back with you?"

"I guess not, but promise me you will come to me if you need anything at all."

"I promise," Layla said reaching over and kissing her friend on the cheek.

As Hannah hugged her and turned to walk away, Layla noticed Hannah's tears. Layla tilted her head and looked up. The clouds were like white sails moving across the backdrop of the blue sky. She hailed a taxi and headed for Albert's.

Entering, she found him sitting at the bar and in a hurried tone began telling him about all that had happened. When she told him about the nurse drawing blood, he stopped what he was doing, rose from his chair, and moved toward her, "Layla, slow down what are you talking about? What is wrong with your blood?"

With tears forming in her eyes, she said, "Please don't be angry with me; forgive me. I had no idea. I am afraid for you and your wife. The doctor says he must see the two of you right away. Your wife and baby are in danger."

"Layla, I just left her a while ago; she is fine. What are you ranting about?"

"Albert, I have syphilis."

Albert stammered backward falling into his chair which shot out from underneath him, causing him to fall to the floor. He landed flat on his butt.

Albert managed to get up, but he was in a state of shock. After a brief silence, he asked, "What am I going to do? I can't tell Julia I might have given her a disease. Wait, maybe she doesn't have it. I mean, we haven't had sex in over a month."

"The doctor wants you to schedule an appointment as soon as possible so he can check the two of you. He said he can just tell her she needs vitamin shots that will help her pregnancy. She doesn't have to know. I am so sorry, Albert. I had no idea until Hannah noticed the spots on my neck."

Albert lifted her hair and said, "I was meaning to ask you about those. Are you going to be all right?"

"Yes, he said we caught it in the early stages and is confident that with shots I will be fine. Albert, it can be a deadly disease, I am more concerned for your wife and baby. Please promise to get her to the doctor as fast as you can."

The doctor checked Albert, and they discussed the plan for his wife. Kamuzir administered the shots telling her they were vitamins necessary for the health of the baby and to offset the anemia she had been experiencing.

Layla questioned how she would live with herself if the baby and/or mother died. Layla cried out to God while clutching the amulet around her neck. 'Lord, you just have to let them live. If you have to take a life, take mine. It's not worth much anyway.'

The doctor's sources had been right; there was an epidemic going around Cairo. The police were scouring the streets where the prostitutes hung out. They were loading up any women they could find and taking them to the station for testing.

Layla was nearly home when the police pulled up and told her to get in. She was taken to the police station with several other girls. Having no one else to turn to, she called Albert for help in hopes she could still count on him. Albert agreed and contacted his good friend, the head of police, who allowed him to come pick her up before the testing. She would have been in big trouble had they found out she was a carrier.

❯❯❯

Over the next few days, Layla took refuge in the back room of Albert's club. The small bed she and Albert had shared suited her just fine while she hid from the authorities. Layla started feeling ill in the mornings. Scared, she went back to the doctor. He took her into the exam room, and they went through the normal routine. He let her know everything was okay; she was just experiencing morning sickness. Knowing she needed the support of family, he suggested she should go to her mother's house.

Finding out she was pregnant came as a complete shock. It was the farthest thing from her mind. Again, life began to unravel. Desperate and needing to confide in someone, she decided to take the doctor's advice and go to her mother.

Entering the front door, she could see Helena at the back of the house in the kitchen. She took a deep breath and walked toward her. It had been several weeks since they had spoken. Her mother heard the door close and spun around on her heels. She was both excited and mad at the sight of Layla walking toward her. As Layla neared her, Helena could see the tears on her daughter's cheeks.

"Where have you been?"

"Mother, I am pregnant.

They stood staring at one another until Helena broke the silence, "You can't take care of a baby. You must have an abortion."

Layla was surprised by her mother's words. There was no sense of love or caring in her voice. It should have come as no surprise, but she had secretly hoped her mother would wrap her arms around her and tell her everything would be okay. The more her mother insisted on an abortion, the worse Layla felt. She ran from the house, like she had done on so many occasions before.

She just couldn't bring herself to consider an abortion. She had a good nature about her that was always in conflict with the life she was leading. Working the streets from age twelve had been difficult at first, but in time she accepted it as a normal way of life. The thought of becoming pregnant never occurred to her. She turned to Lucy once again for love and an honest opinion.

Lucy opened the door, surprised to see her. "Layla, where have you been? I have been looking all over for you. Get in here," she said looking to the right and left as if expecting someone. "The police are on a rampage. Syphilis has broken out in Cairo, and they are scared to death. They are pulling girls off the street and any-one found infected will be quarantined at the hospital. They won't be allowed back on the street."

Layla collapsed on the couch lining the wall inside Lucy's front room. "Lucy, you have no idea what I have been through. I've been hiding out in the back room over at Albert's."

After relating the events leading up to her arrival, she said in a whisper, "Lucy, it's not just Albert's wife I'm worried about. I am pregnant."

Lucy took it all in and said, "For a minute, I thought you said you were pregnant."

"That's exactly what I said."

Lucy looked at her, her mouth agape. "Oh my God, girl. I don't know if I should laugh or cry. What are you going to do?"

"Mother is insisting I have an abortion, but I feel if God allowed a baby to be placed in me, then I am going to have the baby. There is no way I can kill a baby. How could I be so selfish? So I've made up my mind!"

"I am behind you one hundred percent. You'll see it will be the best thing that has ever happened to you. Do you have any idea who the father might be?"

"I have thought about it, but you know how many men I have been with. How could I be sure? Besides, what does it matter? The man would probably side with my mother and insist I have an abortion."

Sitting down next to her, Lucy consoled, "So true, so I'll take care of you."

"Lucy, you are an angel. I can always count on you."

"We can count on each other. You would do the same for me. Hell, who knows when that might be?"

Lucy rented several rooms in the hotel that Mrs. Fuad owned and out of necessity had been acting as a Madame for several of the girls. Layla had been doing much soul searching, even visiting a church. It was then she decided to move in with Lucy.

At Lucy's, Layla was able to isolate herself from everyone. Her closest customers had no idea what had happened. Many contacted her mother, inquiring of her whereabouts. Pretending to know, her Mother promised she would contact them when Layla returned. Of course, it cost them a sizeable sum. Her mother always found a way to prosper at Layla's expense.

Some say the loss of innocence occurs when the reality of life hits in a way we cannot deny. It is at that moment a person has a choice of living in the present, or reverting to some safe place in time found in the inner sanctum of the mind. Others might deem it as a coming of age. In Layla's case, it was the unfortunate evolution from a damaged childhood to a fragile existence leading to adulthood. Her life up to this point had been a continuing experience that had widened her awareness of evil and the resulting pain in the world around her.

Layla awoke sweating. The clock on the nightstand read 10 pm. Doubling over she gasped at the pain ripping at her insides. She screamed as the pain intensified. She called out, but no one else was at home at the time. Exhausted, she lay back on her bed, her head flooded with thoughts." The streets are not good. I must make a change. I can't go on living like this. I would rather die than continue the ways of my past. What will I do?' Another sharp pain shot through her tummy, and then it happened...she lost her baby.

The room swirled, and her head began to spin. She was alone with the pain and her thoughts of shame. After a long period of time, she regained some semblance of sanity and realized she needed to seek help. Knowing Darius was usually curbside in his taxi, she made her way to the front door, and upon opening it, experienced the first sign of relief. There was Darius, seated in his taxi. She cried out in hopes he would hear and come to her aid.

Unlike most cab drivers in Cairo, Darius was Italian and a tenderhearted young man. In a rare moment, he had landed a job while studying at the local university. Because he was different from most cab drivers, Layla and the other girls requested his services. He would drive them anywhere they wanted, even if they didn't have money. Of course, upon their return they always gave him a generous tip. Layla and Darius became good friends, but no sex was involved. He always played the gentlemen, which provided her a level of peace and security.

A shrill voice broke the silence. He noticed movement out of the corner of his eye. Startled, he swung his head around and saw Layla standing in the doorway. Through the open window he yelled, "Layla, are you okay?

"Darius, please take me to the doctor," she said barely able to stand.

"Wait right there," he said this while scooting across the bench seat of the cab. Hitting the curb with both feet, he bolted up the few steps to where she stood and scooped her up in his arms. He noticed she was pale as a ghost as he placed her in the front seat. Slamming the passenger door, he moved around to the driver's side, climbed in, and started the engine. The tires screeched as he threw the car into gear and hit the gas pedal.

Doctor Kamuzir was sound asleep when the pounding awoke him. Darius was encouraged when lights came on in the entranceway. He yelled, "Hurry, she's almost dead."

Doctor Kamuzir started to open the door and was pushed back as Darius barreled through, almost out of breath. "Doctor, it's Layla. She lost her baby." The doctor directed him to the examination room.

Layla felt the doctor washing her with a hot towel. The warmth was soothing, and the pain subsided. Her face was pale, and her cheeks were moist with tears.

The doctor reached down and put his arms around her as she buried her face in his chest. "There, there, everything will be all right."

Layla lay back on the table and drifted off to sleep. Darius had been standing by in a state of shock before moving to a chair and collapsing. Mentally exhausted, he too was soon fast asleep.

Overwhelmed with emotion, Kamuzir sat down, thinking how hard life had been on her. He knew the ache in his heart was the love he felt for her. After a while, he nudged Darius, "Wake up. Help me get her to the bedroom. She is sound asleep and needs to rest. She won't be returning home tonight."

The two of them lifted her and walked her to the bedroom down the hall. Doctor Kamuzir pulled back the comforter, exposing satin sheets lining a thick mattress set in a magnificent canopy frame. The tall bedposts, attached with cross bars draped with a tapestry on three sides, rose to the ceiling. The other furniture in the room was a side table with an antique lamp, a dresser directly in front of the bed with a round vanity mirror, and a wicker chair next to the door. The walls were painted a comforting pale green, which set off the subtle glow from a small crystal covered light attached to the ceiling above the bed.

Layla opened one eye as they laid her on the bed. Once she was stabilized, the doctor spoke. "Layla, I am going to keep you here overnight just to make sure you don't have any complications. Please rest assured everything will be okay."

He lifted the satin sheets up around her neck. Silence filled the room. Now all that could be heard was her breathing and an occasional moan. The two of them stood motionless and admired her beauty. Even now, there was a glow emanating from her which had a dizzying effect on them.

Breaking the silence, Darius whispered, "Doctor, is she going to be all right?"

"She'll be fine."

It was late the next morning when the Doctor cracked the door and looked inside. Calling her name, he noticed she was awake. She was comfortably nestled among the satin sheets. "Good morning. How do you feel?" the doctor asked in a hushed tone.

"I'm sore, but otherwise okay."

The doctor sat down beside her, and she rose up to meet his outstretched arms. They embraced for several minutes, the doctor's shoulders moving from side to side in a comforting motion.

CHAPTER FOUR

ONE DAY, LAYLA AWOKE WITH A SENSE OF CALMNESS. It was as if she had emerged from a cloud through no effort of her own, and her vision was unimpeded. The day would prove to be the beginning of a deliverance of sorts, as she heard an inner voice echoing in the quiet recesses of her mind, 'Your life is not measured by your actions, but by your heart.'

Later that day she received news: Albert and Julia were the proud new parents of a baby boy. Julia had given birth to a healthy four kilo baby, and both mother and baby were doing fine. Layla felt like celebrating, but instead just looked skyward and said, "Thank you, Lord."

Over the next few weeks, she began questioning her life as a street prostitute; things just weren't the same. It was around this time she met Thomas. He was impressive in appearance, towering over her with broad shoulders and a slender waist. His family owned a soap factory and was very wealthy.

Layla fell crazy in love with him. At first, Thomas showed off his newfound beauty by taking her to the finest restaurants and nightclubs around Cairo. Layla was enamored, seduced by his style and the way he lavished her with gifts and tailored clothing.

She shared her desire with Lucy. "I'm thinking of quitting the business. The street is taking too big a toll on me."

"What will you do? How will you live?" Lucy said surprised.

"You know Thomas, the one who is always calling and wanting me to go out? Well, he has caught me or so it seems. I can't stop thinking about him. Lucy, I believe it is love."

Lucy said with a mischievous grin, "Girl, you must follow your heart. What I wouldn't give to find some wealthy man to take care of me."

Layla moved from Lucy's place into an apartment with plenty of room and a large picture window looking down on the street below. A French professor owned two sections of the building, Thomas rented one section, and a lady who owned a perfume lab rented the other.

Seldom did Thomas spend the night; instead, he offered excuses about being expected at his parents' house or about an important meeting in another town. Within a couple of months of her moving into the apartment, they arrived home from a night out, and he accused her of looking at other men.

"I saw you look at that scum."

"Thomas, I love you. Who are you referring to?"

"Don't you dare play stupid with me, Layla, or I'll knock that smile off your face."

"But, I haven't looked at..." Her words trailed off as she felt the smack across her face. Thomas delivered a blow with the back of his hand that knocked her off her feet. As she fell back on the bed, he continued, "Stop your lying tongue. I don't want to hear it. You are always flirting every time we go out."

Crying Layla grabbed his arm in an attempt to comfort him. "My eyes are for you. It is not my fault if men look at me, but I never look back. Why do you take me with you then?"

Again, she felt the sting of his hand. She entertained feelings of guilt, thinking maybe she had been flirting. That's when the anger began to rise up in her, but at the time, she didn't know how to deal with it.

Layla met Mary, who worked for the owner of the perfume lab, and the two of them became good friends. She confided in Mary about Thomas and about how she felt. Mary had been watching in painful silence. She hated the way Thomas had been treating Layla. One day she waited to make sure Thomas was gone and approached Layla. "I am going to tell you something, but if Thomas finds out, he might kill the both of us."

"Mary, what in the world do you know that would put you at risk with Thomas?"

"He has been seeing another woman."

Layla said, "You mean he is cheating on me?"

"I'm afraid so. I have a girlfriend who works at the Kit Kat Club who tells me he goes there all the time with one girl."

Layla felt like someone had dumped ice on top of her head. She stood frozen. Here he was leading her to believe he was traveling for his soap business. Always the loyal one, the thought never crossed her mind he could be cheating on her.

"Mary, you must help me, otherwise I won't be able to sleep. I must get back my pride from out of the gutter."

"What do you propose?"

"I need to find somebody better than him, richer than him, and single. He needs to be a strong man that will not be afraid of Thomas. When he sees that I am on to his game and not willing to sit back and take his abuse, he will have a change of heart. However, at that point I will be the one telling him to leave. He will be begging me to take him back, but where am I going to find such a man?"

To Layla's surprise, Mary smiled and said, "I've got the man for you."

Stunned by her sudden response, Layla asked, "Who?"

"Shakir, the owner of the shoe factory across the street, is always asking about you. He has seen you on a number of occasions through the large window in your apartment. He is always begging me to introduce him. He goes on and on about how pretty you are. Thinking I was offering protection, I told him you were married. All I have to do is call him and tell him you are available. He'll come running."

"Oh, please do."

There was a knock at the door. Layla opened it and was quite surprised. The man standing in front of her was handsome and well dressed in a silk suit with an ascot around his neck. "Are you Layla?"

"Yes, please come in."

He nodded and stepped through the doorway. "I am Shakir. Mary suggested I come over and make your acquaintance. I trust she has told you I have been asking for an introduction."

With a flirtatious giggle, Layla answered, "She did mention there was a handsome man who has been making inquiries."

"I know how Thomas has been treating you, and I want you to know I don't think much of his arrogance. You deserve to be respected."

"That is the sweetest thing anyone has said to me in a long time."

"How about a night on the town, anywhere your heart desires?"

"You know I would like that, and I have just the place, the Kit Kat Club."

"Good, it's a date. How does 7 o'clock sound?"

Layla reached up, kissed his cheek, and said, "I'll be ready and waiting."

Layla could have sworn she heard him whistling as he turned and walked away. Then again she thought, "maybe it was the wind."

Mary loaned her the money, and Layla visited the hairdresser. She then selected her sexiest dress and adorned herself with some of the jewelry Thomas had given her. She was going to make sure every head turned when she entered the club.

Shakir arrived at seven and appeared nervous when the door opened. He had failed to ask if Thomas would be a problem when he arrived. Fortunately, he was out of town on business.

The two of them went to the Kit Kat club, and several of Thomas' friends were there. She danced with Shakir in an overtly amorous way making sure all in attendance noticed. Thomas never showed, much to Layla's disappointment. She had hoped he would see her in full dress with another man. Knowing Thomas had another woman, his friends didn't suspect much. They assumed Layla had finally caught on and moved on with her life.

She was frustrated when Thomas came home and didn't inquire about the other man. She was repulsed by his touch, thinking to herself, "How could I have ever fallen in love with this guy? He is disgusting."

Layla and Shakir continued to go out until it became obvious to everyone Layla was dating behind Thomas' back. However, no one dared say a word; all of his friends were fearful Thomas would kill someone if he found out.

Layla went over to the lab. "Mary I've had it. I can't take his hands on me anymore. I packed a bag and set it close to the door. When Thomas comes home tonight, I am going to give him a piece of my mind. I need you to keep an ear out, and if you hear me scream, call the police."

After taking a deep breath Mary said, "What time do you expect him?"

"You know Thomas, there is no telling. I just need you to be on the lookout and be ready."

"Don't worry. I'll be ready."

When Thomas showed up, Layla was standing by the packed bag just inside the door. In his usual tough tone he said, "Where the hell do you think you are going?"

Layla unleashed on him. "I know all about your little whore! I have friends who have seen you out with her on the nights you tell me you are at your parents or away on business. You are nothing but a liar."

"Layla, whoever is feeding you that garbage is the one lying. I don't have eyes for anyone but you," he said reaching out for her.

Layla took a step back, "Really, you have never been to the Kit Kat Club with another woman?"

"Tell me who told you these lies."

"It doesn't matter, Thomas. It's over between you and me. I have a lover, and for the past few weeks we have been going out for all your friends to see. I am surprised they don't care enough to tell you."

"I don't believe you. How did you find someone stupid enough to be seen with you knowing I would come after him and might kill him?"

"Wouldn't you like to know? Why don't you ask your friends?"

"You are making all this up."

Layla looked him right in the eyes and said, "I'm packed, and I'm leaving"

He said, "Oh no, you don't. You don't walk out on me."

Stepping closer, she said, "Just try to stop me and see what happens to you."

Layla thought for sure he was going to haul off and slug her, but he was intimidated by the confidence she portrayed. He had never witnessed her inner strength before. She picked up her bag, walked passed him, and left the apartment. Thomas didn't go after her because he was in a state of shock. It was the first time a woman had ever spoken to him with such authority.

Layla boarded a train for Alexandria with plans to meet her new lover. He treated her with the utmost respect, but upon her arrival, she made it clear she was not ready for another traditional boyfriend. "Shakir, let's be friends. I am not ready to have another affair."

"Whatever you desire, Layla. I just want to spend time with you."

She returned to a life of prostitution, once again accepting it as her fate in life. Of course, she and Shakir had sex, and he spoiled her to no end. He became one of her best customers. He loved to take her camping and even taught her how to shoot a rifle. As with most of her regular customers, they became good friends.

Thomas, on the other hand, was miserable. He had seen something in her on the day that had ignited a passion in his groin. He visited her mother daily to inquire about her whereabouts. Of course, her mother had no idea where she was, and Layla wasn't about to tell her.

Several months passed, and Layla entertained a series of other men in hopes of changing her lifestyle. The first was Simone whose father owned a big department store. He was very handsome, and Layla was instantly taken with him. Unlike Thomas, he was nice and gentle with her. He let her go to the store and pick out anything she wanted; suits, pocketbooks, shoes, or stockings. He had a box at the racetrack where he liked to show her off. All the women would stare in envy, wondering who the enchanting woman was with Simone. Unfortunately, his father found out about their relationship and sent him to Switzerland.

That was the end of Simone.

At the racetrack, she was introduced to a trainer named Claude. He had been a jockey, but a growth spurt cut his career short. Standing five feet, nine inches tall he was too large for the horses, so he became a trainer. He was a rugged sort who excited something deep within her, and soon she fell in love.

After a while, times were tough economically, and Claude was having trouble finding training jobs. Knowing Layla had amassed a large collection of jewelry, he convinced her to hock it to support the two of them. In her mind, money was secondary to the love she had for him.

It was about this time that a Saudi Arabian Prince who owned several racehorses noticed Layla. He heard rumors of her background and desired to make her acquaintance. One day, he approached Claude with a business proposition. "Claude, I would be honored if you would enter my employ. I have seven horses in need of a good trainer."

"It's possible I could fit your stable into my schedule," Claude said attempting to disguise his excitement.

The Prince said, "I tell you what, arrange a date for me with the young lady living with you, and my horses are yours."

Heliopolis Racetrack

Caught off guard, Claude didn't know how to respond.

"What is your answer?" the Prince pressed, knowing Claude was broke and needed the income.

"Let me think about it," Claude said in an uneasy tone.

Claude went to Layla and shared what he believed to be good news, "Layla, I have a business proposition that has come to my attention. There is a wealthy Prince who would like the pleasure of your company. In return, he will give me a job training seven of his horses."

Layla looked at him in disbelief. She stepped back a full foot and asked, "A business proposition, is it?"

"Yes, strictly business. If I am able to train his horses, we will not be wanting for anything. It is a proposition that is too good for us to pass up."

With a stern look, Layla responded, "Let me ask, Claude, how will you feel when I return from his boudoir knowing I have slept with him?"

"Layla, I won't treat you any different, I promise. It's just business," he said in his most convincing manner.

Layla went to visit Lucy and shared the day's events. As usual, Lucy provided the sound advice Layla had been accustomed to. Without hesitation she said, "He is nothing more than scum. If he loved you, he would not be willing, under any circumstances to share you with another man. Get rid of him. You don't need him pimping for you. If you let this happen once, it will be easier the next time."

Layla said in a whisper, "I have been a one man woman, always loyal. I was willing to give him everything, and what do I get in return? You are right, Lucy. I am sure not going to let another man profit at my expense. Claude is a worm and not worthy of my company."

There was a dilemma lingering deep within her heart. Operating below the threshold of consciousness was the division between her mother and father. She had this longing to be loved and to spend the rest of her life with one man. However, every time she let herself get close, the men seemed to have one thing in mind, a lust for her beauty.

That was the end of Claude.

Layla returned to Lucy at the hotel, but continued visiting the racetrack. Clutching the *blue eye* gracing her delicate neckline, she thought, "I vow never to work the streets again."

CHAPTER FIVE

LUCY WAS SINGING AS SHE HUNG HER LINGERIE over the rod in the bathroom. Layla peeked in. "Lucy, I have a proposition for you."

Lucy turned toward her, "Come on in. What's on your mind?"

"There is a better way to make a living than working these God awful streets. I have learned from my time at the racetrack that all the foreign dignitaries, military officers, and other men of prestige stay at the Shepheard's Hotel. Why don't we go have a drink and check it out?"

"Sounds good to me; I could use a drink."

Layla always dressed smart, but on this day she intended to be at her best. Picking up her lipstick she outlined her sealed lips making sure the gloss spread evenly. Next was the eyeliner and, as if stroking a canvas, she highlighted her eyes with just a hint of black.

Lucy had instructed her well. She could hear her words echoing, 'Layla, when applying makeup less is more; let your beauty speak for itself.'

The powder puff, soft against her cheeks, left a hint of pink. Dipping it again, she dabbed the top of each breast protruding from her lacy bra. Sitting back, she inspected her handiwork and had to admit God had blessed her with good looks. She picked up the ivory handled hairbrush and stroked her hair. Responding to the bristles, the blonde curls bounced into place. Her hair had a silky feel and glistened from the sun streaming in through the open window.

Rising, she picked up the dainty pink underwear and placed one foot in and then the other. She pulled it up and around the curvature of her hips to just below her belly button. She had chosen the silk chiffon dress, simple but elegant. With a wiggle, she brought the dress up across her bare legs past her waist to its final resting place below her shoulder blades. The silk with its slightly wrinkled appearance accentuated every curve. The men would eagerly wonder what lay beneath.

Reaching around and straining a bit, she pulled up the zipper. The blue, *evil eye* pendant, which had become a permanent fixture, now graced her neckline and rested between the waves of her breasts. Smiling, she spun around while looking in the mirror.

Last, she donned silk pumps with short heels. Standing five foot seven, she didn't want to tower over the men. The shoes were meant to accent her long, sleek legs, allowing them to work their magic.

She stepped into the hallway as Lucy was closing the door to her flat. Turning, Lucy stopped and stared. "Layla, you look great. "

"As you do, my dear. Shall we be going?"

"Indeed," Lucy said, bumping her with her hip.

The cab idling at the curb awaited their arrival. Darius was aroused watching the two of them descend the steps. Breaking his stare, he simultaneously opened both doors on the passengers' side. He was relieved the girls were entertaining a new venue. He had always felt, but didn't think it his place to say, 'Ladies don't walk the streets; they frequent the respectful venues around Cairo.'

After all, many of Cairo's elite were nothing more than kept women legitimately servicing their husbands. Women were not well respected in Cairo, and it was common knowledge that most men cheated on their wives.

Shepheard's Hotel and it's front entrance

"Darius, be a dear and drive us to the Shepheard's Hotel, and Darius dear..."

"Yes Madame?"

"Do make it snappy. We have important business to attend to," Layla said in her most elegant voice.

They all shared a loud laugh as he pushed in the clutch, slipped the car into gear, and pulled away from the curb.

✦✦✦

The Shepheard's Hotel was one of several hotels built in the 1840s to accommodate Egypt's increase in tourism. Located on Ibrahim Pasha Street, its original name was Hotel des Anglais and was British owned. Samuel Shepheard, an Englishman from Northamptonshire, England, purchased the hotel in 1841 with a Mr. Hill, who at one time was the head coachman for Pasha Muhammad Ali. Samuel bought out Hill in 1845 and later renamed the hotel after his namesake. Needing more room, Shepheard took over an old palace next door.

Through the years, the hotel would be named among the world's most famous retreats.

Shepheard's Hotel was considered as much a focal point in Cairo as the pyramids. With all the modern charms of Egypt, the hotel was set against a background of extreme antiquity. The Egyptian government had long allowed many of the ancient antiquities to be stored at the Shepheard. Samuel Shepheard had used them to adorn the entryway, lobby, halls, and rooms. Some of the artifacts were well over 2,000 years old. There were statuettes of the Pharaohs, incredible rugs, and art of alluring beauty.

Thousands of years of mysteries were stored in the decorations that adorned the hotel, and just as the surrounding landscape, many of those mysteries had yet to be revealed. In the presence of the artifacts and the grandeur of the hotel, guests got the feeling of being part of an ancient civilization with a direct line from the Pharaohs, yet part of the modern world. Kings, Princes, and other famous people from all over the world loved staying at the Shepheard's Hotel because it was like staying in a museum.

Woven into the tapestry of Egypt's exotic history, the hotel was Napoleon's headquarters in 1849, and the British military used it as their headquarters after the turn of the century. It maintained a glamorous and rare mystique for over one hundred and fifty years and was considered one of the finest Cairo had to offer. Out on the terrace, socialites wearing their most appealing Edwardian attire lounged in the wicker chairs, and waiters ambled about in their baggy clothing and fezzes.

Because the hotel hosted a diverse clientele over the years, the London News once wrote, *"Perhaps in no hotel in the world do you find such an assembly of people of the rank and fashion from all countries as are found daily sitting down to the table d'hôte in the grand salon."* An international social Mecca, the hotel was world renowned for its exterior grandeur and opulent interior.

Popular with British and American tourists, the Shepheard's Hotel became known as a special symbol of Britain's colonial rule. It drew an eclectic mix of statesmen, soldiers, archaeologists, antiquity dealers, movie stars, and artists, all with time

Hotel lounge and stairway

and money to spend. When discussing the social life in Egypt, an Egyptian lady could be heard saying, *"In Egypt, it's a shame to work."* Of course, her British or American counterpart would respond, *"In our country, it's a shame if you don't."* Egypt was a mysterious place to be in the 1940s and early 1950s.

Layla and Lucy stepped from the cab and ascended the steps adorned by iron railings and enormous palms on either side. The doorman was eager to open the door as they made their way inside the Hotel.

"Lucy, let's go to the Napoleon bar and see if we can find some unsuspecting gentlemen to enter into some stimulating conversation."

Lucy giggled and said, "I'll follow your lead."

All heads turned as they entered and located seats at the bar. Theodore, the bartender, beamed at the sight of them. "Layla, you are more beautiful than ever, and Lucy, my dear, the pyramids can't compare with your radiance."

Theodore knew them when they all worked together at Albert's. His adoration made their entrance seem normal. Layla and Lucy laughed in relief that a trusted friend was behind the bar.

"Theodore, you are still the charmer. How have you been? It has been way too long, my friend," Layla said.

"Ladies, how about a drink on the house?"

"What do you recommend, sir?"

"I'm glad you asked. I've been playing around with a drink made famous during the war at Harry's bar in Paris. It is known as a *sidecar*. Named thus because a captain was ushered to the bar each evening in the sidecar of a motorcycle. He desired something to take the chill off, and the bartender felt brandy would be just the ticket. However, brandy was not served as a pre-dinner cocktail, so the bartender took the liberty of adding some orange flavored Cointreau and fresh lemon juice. You two can be my Guinea pigs and let me know what you think."

Lucy smiled, "We would be delighted." She then turned to Layla and said, "Lady Luck must be with us tonight."

"Indeed, she is."

"Theodore, do you speak much to Albert these days?" Layla asked.

"Occasionally. You knew his wife had another baby?"

"No, I didn't, but that is wonderful news."

"It was a girl this time."

"Give my regards if you speak with him." Layla was still haunted at times by the memory of her infection, so to hear he was happy and doing well was a relief.

"Will do. Umm, ladies, I believe you have some admiring gentleman looking this way."

Lucy and Layla had become so engrossed with Theodore they hadn't noticed the two soldiers in dress uniform. Theodore set two fresh drinks in front of them, looked to his right, and said, "Guess who?"

Lucy nudged Layla with her elbow. "They are quite handsome, don't you think?"

"Indeed they are."

Careful, not to act interested, Lucy and Layla nodded in their direction and returned to their small talk.

It wasn't long before one of the soldiers approached and asked in a heavy British accent, "Mind if we join you for a drink?"

Layla smiled and said in French, "Oui certainement, mon cheri." The two soldiers had no idea what she had said. They just looked at each other and accepted the girls' smiles as an invitation. Translated, Layla had said, "Yes, certainly, my darling."

Layla thought he was going to faint with passion right there at the bar. His big blue eyes sparkled as he melted into the chair beside her.

The other chap nestled up next to Lucy, and the four of them conversed for a good half hour before Layla whispered into her soldier's ear, "Est-ce que vous rester ici a l'hotel." Looking at her with a blank stare he said, "Excuse me, bartender, do you speak French?"

Theodore laughed and said, "She asked if you are staying here at the Shepheard?"

Excited, the soldier nodded in the affirmative. Layla then rested her hand on his thigh and whispered, "Would you like to finish that drink in your room, Cheri?"

Tongue tied, the soldier looked over at his friend, winked, and then motioned to Theodore to prepare their check.

The four of them vacated the bar and headed for the hotel elevator. Upon entering, they made their way up to the soldiers' room not to be seen again for another hour.

Leaving behind two very satisfied customers, Layla and Lucy entered the elevator. Adjusting her dress, Layla said, "Lucy, can you believe how easy that was?"

Excited, Lucy answered, "It was absolutely marvelous. They were such gentlemen."

The door opened to an elderly couple who had been waiting. Layla said, "*Bonjour vous faite un beau couple* (Hello, you two make a handsome couple)." The woman beamed as her husband squeezed her hand, "Merci."

Layla and Lucy returned to Theodore who was still behind the bar. Smiling from ear to ear, he set drinks in front of them. Layla held up her glass and said, "Lucy let's toast to our new venue."

Lucy clicked the rim of Layla's glass and said, "It has been long overdue, but welcome all the same."

They laughed and enjoyed the rest of the evening deciding they had doled out enough affection for the night. The Shepheard's Hotel would prove to be a wonderful haven for the ladies for a long time. Layla referred to the hotel as her *home office*.

Theodore introduced her to most of the staff with whom she became good friends. Not looking the part of a prostitute, she always acted with class and carried herself in a professional manner, thus, management was content to look the other direction. Layla's personality soon endeared her to all who frequented there. Management determined she was good for business and provided her a special table in the bar.

This table was where the military officers, foreign dignitaries, and other rich men would come to inquire about spending time with her. She would invite them to sit and have a drink. If she liked them, she would share her price. Once negotiations were complete, she would set a time to meet in the customer's room.

❯❯❯

Layla missed the racetrack, so she asked Lucy to accompany her one Saturday. Dressed in their finest attire and donning hats, off they went. Darius, their appointed chauffer, continued to take great delight sharing in their adventures. It was a wonderful sunny day, and as usual, the track was packed with locals, foreign tourist, diplomats, and many of the social elite.

When dating Claude, Layla had made friends with several of the employees, so gaining access to the paddock and other areas was no problem. She and Lucy went down to the paddock area to survey the horses, but more importantly the owners. After a while, they returned to the main club area where they secured a table.

"Layla, have you ever met Henrietta?" Lucy asked.

Layla said, "Maybe, but I don't believe so. Point her out."

"Oh, trust me, you would remember if you had. That is her over there holding court in front of the men."

"Who is she, a famous movie star or something?"

Lucy let out a hearty laugh and said, "Quite the contrary. She is one of the most, if not the most, famous madams in all of Egypt."

"You don't say. So who are her clients?"

"King Farouk is one of her biggest. Of course, she caters to the Beys, Pashas, most of the foreign diplomats, and many rich tourists."

"Wow, she has a weird look about her."

"That's because she is somewhat blind."

"What do you mean somewhat blind? Isn't that like being a little bit pregnant?" They both laughed at the thought.

"No, I mean she is blind, but rumor has it that if you hand her a bill she can hold it close and discern the amount. No one dares cheat her."

Layla sat for the next few minutes, admiring the way Henrietta handled the various men who approached and made what appeared to be casual conversation.

Lucy rose from her seat. "Wait here, I am going to say hello and see if she would like to have some company."

Before Layla could respond, Lucy was prancing off in Henrietta's direction. Layla continued to soak in the beauty of the day and reminisce about her time with Claude. She had loved him and still remembered the pain and disgust she felt the day Claude wanted to set her up with the Prince.

Lucy tugged at her arm. "Henrietta would like to make your acquaintance."

Layla looked over where Henrietta was sitting and noticed she was looking back. She tilted her head as if to say hello. It would appear to the casual onlooker they knew one another.

"What did you say?"

"I told her you would enjoy meeting her, and we would be over soon to join her."

"Lucy, what do I want to meet some blind madam for? We don't appear to be having any trouble locating suitors at the Shepheard, now do we?"

"I just thought it would be fun. She is a character and does know everyone who is anyone. What do you say we go over and have a drink and see where it goes from there?"

"Okay, maybe for a while, but keep in mind we came here to meet men, not women." Together Lucy and Layla walked over to the blind madam.

"Henrietta, I would like you to meet a dear friend of mine, Layla. Layla, this is Henrietta."

"Sit down, girls, and join me. I was just getting ready to place a bet on the second race."

Layla was awestruck that she was betting on the horses. She wondered how Henrietta, being blind, would know which horses to bet on.

"Layla is it?"

"Yes ma'am, that's correct."

Holding out a racing form Henrietta said, "Be a dear and read me the information on the second race."

Layla looked over at Lucy and said, "Well, I guess I could do that."

With excitement in her voice. Henrietta said, "Great, which one should we go with?"

"Oh, I don't know much about the ponies, Henrietta, but the number six horse has a good rear end on him."

They all laughed, and Henrietta said, "The sixth horse it is. Lucy, would you be so kind to put two pounds to win on number six?"

"Sure. Henrietta," Lucy said as she took the money from her hand and took off toward the betting windows.

"*Maintenant que nous sommes seule nous pouvons etre moins formel. Quelle est votre profession, Layla?*[*]"

"If you are familiar with Lucy's, you can guess mine."

"Ha, seems we share the same line of employment. However, at my age I prefer lining up the engagements more than fulfilling the engagements, if you know what I mean."

"Yes, I do."

"You see that group of men over to my right?"

Layla was amazed wondering, how in the world could she know who was sitting off to her right.

"You are wondering how I know who is sitting off to my right considering my condition."

"To be honest, yes, I was."

"My hearing, dear, it is better than most. When you lose one of your senses, you gain increased awareness with the other senses. They have been wondering who the good looking blonde is I am sitting with. Come close and let me look at you."

Holding out her hand, Henrietta stroked her cheek and then ran her hand across her hair down to her shoulders. Slipping back in her chair she continued, "Well now, I see why they are so enamored with you. You must be one of the rarest beauties in all of Egypt. Let me ask you, dear, what have you been making working out of the Shepheard?"

"How did you know I was working out of the Shepheard?"

"Dear, it is my business to know my competition," Henrietta said with a sly laugh.

Layla tilted her head not knowing what to think about her newest acquaintance.

---

[*]   Now that we are alone we can get down to business. What is your profession, Layla? (French)

"Besides, Lucy told me before the two of you came and joined me."

Now they were both laughing and not paying attention to the men lingering around, straining to hear their conversation.

"I command twenty pounds on average."

"What if I could pay you fifty? Would that interest you?"

Layla sat up in her seat, "You can do that?"

"Oh, you have no idea the money we can make, and Layla dear, from now on, please call me Henrietta. What do you say we look at the third race and focus on more pressing matters?"

Layla picked up the racing form and began reading the lineup of horses and their jockeys for the third. She felt a stirring deep inside, and a warm feeling poured over her from head to toe. It was the warmth she had been longing for.

Lucy reappeared and tossed the ticket on the table. "Layla, Henrietta, I just bumped into an old friend, so if the two of you don't mind I would like to join him."

Layla said, "Go ahead. I think Henrietta and I have some business to discuss. Have fun!"

Henrietta smiled in Layla's direction and said, "Yes, indeed we do."

The bell sounded, indicating that the gate had opened, and the second race was under way.

"Oh my, here we go. Layla, keep an eye on number six, dear."

Layla turned toward the track excited by the day's events. Sure enough the sixth horse won by two lengths, and they both yelped with joy.

"My dear, I do believe the number six has proven to be an omen of good things to come."

"Henrietta, I do hope so."

The rest of the day sped by for Layla and ended with Henrietta sharing her phone number. "Dear, call this number in a couple of hours, and I will have good news for you."

Henrietta took a liking to Layla, offering free room and board and sixty percent of everything they made. Henrietta had other girls, but she didn't care too much for any of them. She didn't trust them. Some of the girls had attempted to cheat her by asking customers to come to their house so they could avoid paying Henrietta her forty percent. To their surprise, Henrietta's clients would call to let her know about the girls' deceit, and she didn't take the news lightly. The girls soon regretted their decision. Henrietta had several brutes at her beck and call that would pay the girl a visit, and she would never be heard from again. Layla didn't think too much about these girls because she was always honest with Henrietta.

Layla felt the same responsibility to take care of Henrietta that she felt with her brothers and sister. She considered her more of a mother than Helena. Layla moved out of Lucy's and took up residence at Henrietta's. From that day on, Henrietta became Layla's madam. Saturdays and Sundays were spent at the track where they shared a special table.

Many times Henrietta sent Layla ahead early in the morning to survey the horses and visit with the jockeys. There were all types of horses with different pedigrees. She wrote everything down, reviewed it with Henrietta, and then placed the bets. While Layla was away placing the bets, men approached Henrietta and inquired about her. Picking and choosing by hearing only their voices, Henrietta booked Layla's entire week. Business flourished.

CHAPTER SIX

BACK ON THE SHIP HEADING FOR ROME...

UPON RETURNING TO THEIR BERTH, things heated up between Layla and Spence. The bunk bed squeaked in a rhythmic fashion, tapping the wall in step with their passion. The sounds of their lovemaking were evident to those walking along the narrow passageway outside their door.

Exhausted from their exchange and breathing heavily, Spence rolled over onto his back and stared up at the ceiling. Layla rolled over too, feeling safe ensconced next to his naked body. Suddenly she was overcome by a sense of nostalgia. "Spence, would you like to hear the story of how I met the King?"

"King Farouk?" Spence questioned.

"Of course. He's the sole King in Egypt, isn't he?"

"Why do I get this uneasy feeling that there is a lot more to you than meets the eye?"

Stroking the hair on his chest, Layla smiled and said, "Oh you don't know the half of it."

He shot her a quick glance, shook his head, and looked back at the ceiling.

King Farouk judging the Bathing Beauty contest

Rasel-Tim Palace

"Every year there was a *Bathing Beauty* contest held at the Helmea Palace. All the girls wanted to enter because of the sensational prizes: Christian Dior shoes, beach hats, modern bathing suits, and Chanel purses. King Farouk sponsored the event and paid for all the prizes. Of course, his motive for hosting the event was to survey the local girls.

"Mona and I, along with several friends, entered and paraded through the theatre in skimpy bathing suits. As you might have expected, Mona won the contest, and I came in second. The King's right hand man was a guy named Pulli."

Spence rolled over and rested on one elbow, "I heard he was always propositioning prostitutes for the King. Wasn't he like his pimp or something?"

A cold shiver inched up Layla's spine, but she didn't let it bother her. She was used to hearing comments that had a disturbing effect. The thought crossed her mind that maybe she shouldn't share her life of prostitution. She wouldn't put it past Nasser to have some of his cronies in disguise out to gather information from people fleeing the country.

She proceeded with her story, but with a cautionary tone. "Antonio Pulli was not necessarily his pimp, but his procurer. He made sure whatever the King wanted was at his disposal. Pulli was 16 and Farouk 8 when they first became friends. Pulli's father, Francesco Pulli, was the court electrician at the Rasel-Tim Palace during King Fuad's reign.

"Since Farouk and Pulli got along so well, and Farouk wasn't allowed to have ordinary friends Farouk's father, King Fuad I, thought it would be good to keep Pulli around. It wasn't long before the two became inseparable. They have been friends ever since."

Spence just shook his head and said, "So the King has been isolated most of his life."

"Not just that, but his mother, Nazli Sabri, was into the occult. She was known to sit with her soothsayer with a boiling cauldron in their midst. It was common knowledge she held frequent séances and kept pornographic images around her apartment. All of this had a terrible, degrading effect on Farouk.

Farouk's mother
Nazli Sabri

"Nazli married Ahmed Hassanein in secret. He had been Farouk's tutor. He was a good-looking sort, born of Scottish decent; therefore, he had much lighter skin than most Egyptians. He was nicknamed 'Lawrence of Arabia of Egypt' and later became a Chief in Farouk's Royal Cabinet.

"The night of the beauty pageant, Mona paraded up and down the runway and paused in front of King Farouk and shot him a flirtatious look.

"The King nodded as she quickly strolled away. Donning her robe, she noticed Pulli rising from his seat. It was common knowledge Farouk had a penchant for beautiful girls and would send Pulli to do his bidding. Most girls were happy to oblige, and few dared to deny him. Occasionally, he would offer expensive gifts, such as real estate, to entice his prey."

"You have to be kidding. No wonder the country is so broke. The despot has been raping the Egyptian people," Spence said sitting up and crossing his legs Indian style.

"Not just that, many of the Pashas and other Egyptian men escorting women steered clear, fearing he might take a liking to their wives or girlfriends. He was known for his wrath when refused the company of a woman he coveted."

Spence frowned. "He would be missing something if he tried to take my woman."

Layla let out a good laugh and continued. "When Pulli got up from the table, it scared Mona. She asked me to do her a favor and act her double. I put on her robe and placed a scarf over my head as Mona slipped out the rear door. Sure enough, Pulli rounded the corner and approached yelling, 'You there, come to me. What's your name?'

"When I told him my real name, he said, 'Wait, you are not the winner.' Then his beady little head started rotating on his neck looking left and right in an attempt to find Mona. Frustrated, he began to question where she was, but acting innocent, I said, 'Sir, I have no idea who you are referring to.' He fired back, 'You know who I'm talking about, the winner!' He then shot past me saying, 'Get out of my way.' I felt proud protecting Mona's honor.

"Afterward, some of us decided to meet up later at a local hot spot, L'Auberge Des Pyramid. Returning home, I slipped into a cute yellow dress with big black polka dots before heading out for a night on the town."

Layla leaned up, crossed her legs, and sat across from Spence. "My friends and I were dancing, having a good time when there was a commotion at the door. King Farouk entered with Pulli and five or six other men. It was common at the time for nightclubs to reserve a table for him. It made no difference when he showed up: the nightclub staff was expected to be ready. He would frequent several clubs, but only stay thirty minutes or so, just enough time for his men to scan the club for female prospects."

"Unbelievable. He was nothing more than a predator," Spence said feeling the hair on his neck standing up.

"I guess you could say that. We continued to have a good time, but little did I know the King had been obsessed with counting the dots on my dress. Soon, Pulli approached and asked me to join the King for a drink. That's when Pulli realized I was the girl backstage at the pageant. He said, 'Oh merde, it's you again. I guess this is your lucky night. The King requests your presence at his table, and he won't take no for an answer. That is, if you know what's good for you."

King Farouk and Pulli

"Of course, I can be a smart ass, so I retorted, 'I would love to meet him. What does he prefer to be called? Heine, Kingie, Farouky? What should I call him?'"

Spence and Layla laughed. Spence thought to himself, "I like this gal."

In her best Pulli imitation, she said, "'You had better watch yourself, young lady, or the King will have your head. In fact, it would be better if you didn't say anything.' Thus, off I went like a school girl going to meet the most popular boy in school."

Spence took a deep breath, "I'll be damned. So that's how you got to meet the King of Egypt."

"Spence, it was actually my second time to meet the King."

"What do you mean? I thought you asked if I wanted to hear how you first met the King."

With a sly smile she said, "No, I asked if you wanted to hear the story how I met the King. I didn't say it was the first time."

Spence just shook his head trying to hang onto every word.

"I met him at the Café Riche when I was nine years old."

Spence said, "I have heard it rumored that Café Riche is where all the rich socialize and discuss politics."

"Yes, that's right. Lucy, a good friend of mine, and I were peeking through the window at the Riche. Farouk was inside with several other men. One of his bodyguards saw us and forced us inside. There we were, standing before the King. I became quite enamored by his looks and the mystery behind his piercing green eyes."

"Did he recognize you at the club? Is that why he picked you out?"

"No. When I asked if he remembered me, he studied me up and down to see if there was something he had missed. After a momentary silence, he just shook his head and said, 'I think I would have remembered meeting someone as stunning as you.' Flattered I went on to tell him about the incident at Café Riche. He erupted with laughter, and everyone in the club turned to look. He had a booming laugh that always drew attention. He couldn't believe the little blonde haired girl had blossomed and was now sitting at his table."

"That's an amazing story."

"That night he invited me to Alexandria where the *Al-Mahroussa*, his stately yacht, was moored. I spent four remarkable days basking in the sun."

Spence didn't know what to think of Layla. He was about to question her about her fling with Farouk when there was a loud knock at the door. It startled them, and Spence reached for a towel hanging off the end of their bunk.

Layla lay back down in silence and pondered, "Maybe this really is the end of it all. Maybe I will never see Egypt again, never see the city, the richness, the clubs, the bazaar, and oh the desert." Sadness engulfed her, and her mind drifted off into the past...

Sitting with Farouk among the dunes with the backdrop of the pyramids, Layla felt like the rest of the world didn't exist. Everything she needed was provided, and she felt safe from the rest of the world. Nobody but the King could touch her, and nobody could disturb her. The isolation of the desert provided her a feeling of comfort, as if protecting her from the abusive nature of so many.

Some of her favorite dates with the King were when they went camping in the desert a few miles from Cairo. There wasn't any place on Earth like it. There was complete silence, complete darkness, and when the wind blew it was like the sound of music. Layla loved those times. She didn't think about the bad things she had experienced; to her the past was all good, for she had met the best and the worst of people.

Squirming in her seat, Layla said, "*Cheri*, that tickles."

Farouk had a foot fetish, and Layla remembered thinking to herself the first time he sucked on her toes that this is one fetish she could get used to. Now here was the evening breeze cooling the air, and the King was playfully kissing her feet. She thought, "Life doesn't get much better than this."

The year was 1951, and they were attending the annual duck hunt being held near Lake Moeris, originally named Lake Qaroun, northwest of the Faiyum Oasis located 80 kilometers southwest of Cairo.

The lake derived its name from the biblical account found in Numbers 16. Korah and his followers had rebelled against Moses and Aaron. Moses spoke out against them to God, *'But if the LORD creates a new thing, and the earth opens its mouth and swallows them up with all that belongs to them, and they go down alive into the pit, then you will understand that these men have rejected the LORD. Now it came to pass, as he finished speaking all these words, that the ground split apart under them, and the earth opened its mouth and swallowed them up, with their households and all the men with Korah, with all their goods.'* In Egypt the story was told that Korah could touch any object and turn it to gold. Many still believed the gold lay hidden beneath the lake.

Hieroglyphics depicting geese

The area was one of the birds' favorite breeding and nesting grounds. The European flyway for ducks, and geese provided thousands of waterfowl each fall. The birds flew in from Europe proper, as well as from southern Russia, to winter on the nesting grounds in Egypt from the Delta of Egypt to Aswan Lake.

The hunt in Egypt was a unique affair, and the wealthiest men of Egypt, visiting members of Royal Families such as Saudi Princes, and, of course, the King were among those in attendance. American and European dignitaries were invited on a routine basis. It was the most long-standing venture of this type known to mankind. There were countless references and drawings of ducks and geese contained in the hieroglyphics discovered in the tombs of ancient pharaohs. The ancients considered the birds essential to life in Egypt. They provided a source of food, fertilized the fields, and entered the food chain of other creatures populating the area. Ducks and geese, or *bat and wiz* in Arabic, were indeed very important visitors to the wetlands of Egypt.

The event was world class and took the combined effort of many transporting truckloads of equipment that included tents, flooring, and cooking units, not to mention gun bearers, musical groups, and, of course, the guns and ammo actually needed to hunt the birds. Farouk brought at least ten stewards and several bodyguards. His field kitchen, designed to feed up to a thousand men, was used to prepare all of the meals. He invited the best chefs in Europe, and they prepared an exquisite spread of Egyptian, Moroccan, and European food. Only the very best foods, champagnes, and sweets were served.

The men left camp early in the morning to hunt and returned in the evening while the stewards prepared everything for the night's festivities. There was, however, one ironclad rule for the hunt: no wives. The only females allowed were mistresses or belly dancers, and just a few mistresses made the cut.

Layla had been invited by Doctor Kamuzir, as usual, acting as a front for King Farouk. Layla would spend the first day with the doctor. Then she would entertain some of his friends before finally entertaining the King. She had been an instant hit among the men.

King Farouk duck hunting

One of Kamuzir's closest friends was General Rahman, head of National Security. The moment the General laid eyes on Layla, he wouldn't let the doctor alone. "Kamuzir, you have to hook me up with that woman."

"I don't know, General. Farouk might have both our heads if I set you up with Layla." The doctor loved rattling Rahman's cage, so he felt it better to leave him hanging.

"The hell with Farouk. He doesn't give a shit about anything or anybody but himself. He could care less if I spent some time with one of his mistresses."

"I'll give it some thought and let you know this afternoon."

"Look, Doctor, I've got to have her. I can't keep my eyes off of her. I think I might go crazy if you don't set something up."

"Right, General. You are really hurting for women. Like I said, I'll let you know this afternoon."

The doctor spoke to Layla and suggested she entertain the General. He knew out of all the men at the hunt, the General was the most generous with his money. The General's infatuation with Layla soon became common knowledge, and his staff laughed about it behind his back.

Many of the men, including the King, brought horses. Layla and the King took a ride at sunset, which Layla loved as she breathed in the beauty all around. Now here they were sitting outside the tent listening to music, Farouk licking her big toe in a blissful trance.

"Layla why don't you come spend a few days on the *Al-Mahroussa*, and we can continue what we've started."

"Yes I'd love...to. Umm, that feels so good."

He looked up, proud of himself. "Good. My Nubian chauffeur, Mohammed Hassan, will drive you to Alexandria at week's end. Let him know what you need, and he will make sure it is waiting when you arrive.

❯ ❯ ❯

It was late afternoon, and the yacht was decorated as usual. At the rear of the ship was a large open deck with two large "L" shaped couches lined with thick cushions and throw pillows. Between them was an ornate table with a glass top. The staff was instructed to line the cushions with mink fur every morning.

Layla loved soaking up the sun while lounging on the mink. Normally she lay naked, nestled among the fur lined cushions. Of course, Farouk enjoyed the view, enamored by her sleek tan body set off by the mink backdrop. He liked sitting at her side, running his fingers up and down her legs while kissing her feet. At present, she was clad in a sheer wrap that accentuated her every curve and invited the curiosity of the staff.

"My dear girl, soon we will have an important guest arriving. He is bringing me a package of great value. The news of his arrival has me in a wonderful mood. I have also prepared a surprise for you, but you can't say one word to Pulli. Instead, I want you to lay here by my side and wait to see what I have in store," Farouk said this with a slight grin and a mischievous look in his eye.

He had stirred her curiosity. "Cheri, what are you up to now?" She glanced around scouring her surrounding in hopes of gleaning a clue that might reveal his surprise. It was a known fact that the King liked pulling practical jokes. She had a sneaky suspicion that he was on the verge of orchestrating another; however, nothing seemed out of the ordinary.

Farouk stood to inspect the boat nearing the ship and waved his hand; he nodded approval to the crew. Soon a seedy looking character climbed aboard. Aswani walked with a limp as if one leg were shorter than the other. He had a scraggly beard growing from a boney chin and a nasty scar on the side of his face just below his right eye. He was carrying a leather case held tightly to his chest.

"Aswani, you look like a dehydrated camel. Age has not been kind to you, my friend. Come take a seat and have a drink. Tell me, how are things at the dig site?" Farouk turned to Ahmed Ali and ordered him to bring a round of drinks. Ahmed Ali, clad in his usual red and gold uniform, was Farouk's personal dining steward and always assumed a position directly behind the King.

"Incredible, seems we are unearthing fresh relics daily unlike any found in a long time."

"I see you brought the prize?"

"Yes, your Highness. Would you like to discuss my find?"

"No, we will look at it later. I am expecting Pulli any minute, and I would like him to be present with us. Speaking of Pulli, I want to confirm what you shared with me. Are you sure he made the decision to become a Muslim?"

"Yes, your Majesty. I heard it myself, and others were present as well. We were having drinks on the courtyard of the Auberge de Pyramid, and Pulli was ranting how you had been twisting his arm. He mumbled something about getting back to his religious roots, that you were encouraging him to accept the fact he was a Muslim. He went on and on, finally saying, "Well, the King doesn't know it yet, but I became a Muslim. I am just waiting for the proper opportunity to tell him. I know he will gloat at the news. After all, he has been after me for years to make the decision to become Muslim." Aswani sat back with a big grin, and his eyes narrowed in an eerie snake-like manner as he spotted Pulli walking up from the stern of the boat.

Pulli called out, "Aswani, you made it; we meet again. I see you found King Farouk and made Layla's acquaintance."

Pulli wasn't fond of Aswani, but he had set up the details of today's meeting and arranged Aswani's transport to the *Al-Mahroussa*. "I hear told you have something of value to share with us," Pulli said not intending to waste time.

Farouk interrupted, "Hold on, Pulli. Our guest just arrived. In fact, Aswani and I were just talking about you. Don't you have something you would like to share with us?"

"I don't believe so. What possibly could I be hiding?" Pulli stated in a defensive manner.

"I didn't say you were hiding anything," the King said looking at Aswani and Layla, "Did I say Pulli was hiding anything?"

They both shook their heads to the contrary.

With an offensive tone Pulli asked, "Aswani, what lies have you been telling?"

"Sit down and have a drink," Farouk said in a commanding tone.

Pulli knew what Farouk was asking; he just didn't feel the timing was right. He grabbed a glass, positioned himself across from Aswani, and gave him a look that could kill.

"Let us toast to Cairo's beauty and the fortunate discovery Aswani has brought to our attention," Farouk bellowed with a big grin.

Pulli hesitated and reluctantly brought the glass to his lips. If one looked closely, he might swear Pulli had steam flowing from his ears.

"Pulli, drink up so we can have another. This is a day to celebrate," the King urged.

For no other reason than obedience, Pulli downed his drink. Suddenly there was a loud thud as Pulli dropped face down on the table. Layla gasped in shock. Laughing, the King placed his hand on Layla's arm and said, "Don't worry, he is not dead. I just slipped him a mickie to sedate him. We are going to circumcise him."

Wide-eyed, she yelped, "You are going to do what?"

"We are going to circumcise him because he became a Muslim. There is no such thing as a Muslim without the circumcision, so we are going to circumcise him."

Layla placed her hand over her mouth, "Oh my God. Boy, will he be hurting."

All the King could muster as he began his dirty work was, "Yes, that he will." The staff came over, lifted Pulli's limp body, and moved him to an open spot on the deck where they had prepared a soft bed of blankets and covered them with some sort of plastic. Farouk instructed them to strip off his clothes. With knife in hand, Farouk performed the deed and motioned for them to bandage the wound.

Layla couldn't help thinking, "Poor Pulli, such a pitiful sight, laying there passed out with nothing on but a bandage around his privates." She turned to Aswani and said, "You just never know what the King will do. That is the most gruesome event I have ever witnessed, one I hope never to see again in this lifetime."

Aswani laughed at the sight, proud that he had been the one to break the news to the king. The three of them continued with their drinks and afterward enjoyed a scrumptious meal under the stars. To set the tone, Farouk had one of his personal violinists serenade them with a Mozart concerto.

Layla couldn't remember a day when she had experienced so many emotions. She had laughed at Farouk's antics and had cried on behalf of Pulli, as if she felt his pain. All in all it was an interesting and fun day for her. Poor Pulli was out cold and had no idea of the indecency performed on him.

Soon after the completion of their meal, Farouk stood and stated, "I'm calling it a night. After all, the staff will be waking us early in the morning. Aswani, you'll stay the night. You don't want to miss the excitement when Pulli wakes up. Come, Layla, read me a bedtime story."

She knew full well what the King had in mind. He was about to let the fun and games of a different sort begin. Off the two went, leaving a pathetic looking Pulli and a satisfied Aswani behind.

⟍⟍⟍

The staff, true to Farouk's command, had stirred them at daybreak to make sure they were on deck to witness Pulli's awakening. Aswani, now awake, had fallen asleep the night before while lounging on the deck. Layla walked out admiring the beauty of the morning. The sun, just beginning to peek over the horizon, shot a wondrous array of colors across the water. The coolness of the ocean breeze swept across her legs left bare from the opening of her robe.

Farouk arrived on the scene holding a glass of ice water. He ambled his way over to the spot where Pulli lay snoring and then glancing back at the others and with a mischievous smile tossed the water into Pulli's face. Pulli opened his eyes while shaking his head and propped himself up on his elbows. "What the hell, who..., what..., is going on?" he asked, surprised to see everyone standing over him.

That's when the pain hit him. He looked down and screamed in terror at the sight of the bloody bandage wrapped around his privates. "What happened to me? Your Majesty, you are behind this you oversized..., what have you done to me?" Pulli said pausing between words so not to say something he might later regret. Even in pain, he was smart enough to know his place with Farouk.

Farouk not able to contain himself said smiling from ear to ear, "Pulli, now you are a true Muslim."

Aswani enjoyed seeing such opposite reactions: the delight in Farouk's eyes and the terror in Pulli's. Layla stood spellbound thinking how unbelievable it was for the King to pull off such a trick. He was quite the joker. After everyone had settled down, the King asked Layla to excuse him and invited Aswani to join him and Pulli in the ship's conference room.

"Aswani, what do you have for us?"

"Not much, just the one document which has eluded you all these years. Had you found this earlier, you would be basking in antiquities."

"Can you show it to us?"

Pulling the tube from a leather case, Aswani said, "Yes, but we don't dare unseal the document for fear excess exposure to the atmosphere will accelerate deterioration. I took pictures so we could study the document without putting it at risk."

"Aswani, I appreciate your forethought. Now, let's have a look."

Aswani pulled out a number of photos. Farouk was surprised at the clarity of them. The papyrus was aged but in good condition.

"How fragile is the original?"

"It's hard to say. It appears to be well preserved, wrapped in an animal case, and then wrapped in gauze like fabric. We found it among several other documents, all of which had been treated with extreme care. However, once exposed to light and air, decomposition would accelerate. No one can predict how soon, but it would be prudent to preserve it in a controlled climate under glass as soon as possible."

"I'm proud of your efforts. What was that figure we agreed upon?"

"You know good and well the figure, ten thousand pounds."

"Ah, but we don't know if this document is real. Until I can get confirmation, I'm not going to pay you ten thousand pounds. I will have confirmation within the month, and we can conclude our business at that time."

"Farouk, I'm not leaving this document without my money," Aswani said nervously pulling at the hair on his scraggly beard.

"Must I remind you, until we have confirmation, you have nothing more than a stolen antiquity. What do you propose, Aswani?"

"Your Highness, I have been loyal all these years, and now I have finally found something which could very well contain evidence confirming this myth of yours. I feel I should receive an advance."

"I'll tell you what I am willing to do, one thousand now and the remainder upon confirmation."

"Six thousand and not a penny less," Aswani countered.

"Fine, I'll give you two thousand today and the balance when I receive word from my source."

"Five thousand and the balance sent to my Swiss account upon confirmation."

Farouk remained silent in an attempt to see Aswani squirm. The silence was deafening to Aswani who was well aware of Farouk's lack of integrity when it came to money.

Fidgeting Aswani said, "Your Highness, do we have a deal?"

"Aswani, you are a smart man and drive a hard bargain. I don't know." Farouk paused for effect. "Of course, we have a deal.

"Aswani, come with me. I'll get your money and see that you are properly escorted to shore," Pulli said.

Unknown to Farouk, Pulli didn't intend for Aswani to reach the shore. He didn't think it prudent to have a loose end like Aswani who could come back later and use his knowledge of the document to blackmail them.

≻≻≻

Diplomatic relations between the Soviet Union and Egypt had been established by mid 1943. Moscow established an Embassy in Cairo. In 1948 Cairo signed an economic agreement with Russia which would send Egyptian cotton to the Soviet Union in exchange for grain and other resources. Many Soviets were sent to Egypt at this time to assist in the construction of plants and factories.

In late 1951, Farouk was still a young ruler at twenty-eight years old, but he had been in power for thirteen years. Sergey Alexeyevich Lebedev had been forty-eight when he was sent by the Soviets to Egypt. Sergey was an expert in complex systems. At the time, he was in charge of the Kiev Electro Technical Institute. Most of his work concentrated on electrical systems. Farouk had studied some of Sergey's principles while attending the Academy. Over the years, he had kept up with Sergey's work in the Soviet Union.

Eager to meet him, Farouk invited Sergey to dine at Abdin Palace. There Farouk learned Sergey was working on a super computer. In 1948, the West had started designing electronic computers. All the scientific magazines were awash with articles, but the technology remained a secret. Sergey was fascinated with the work being done, and in late 1948, the Soviets made a decision for him to focus his full attention on the development of a super computer. His first computer was about to be formally introduced.

Once the document had been discovered, Farouk had an epiphany of sorts. Sergey's computer might very well be able to unravel the fractal code the document was based on. The bond that was formed that night in the palace might very well prove to be more profitable than Farouk could have ever imagined. The King put in a call to the Egyptian consulate and requested a secure connection. The next day Farouk received a call saying he was being patched through.

The phone rang in the lab and the Russian answered, "Алло... Слушаю Вас? * "

Farouk responded, "*Попросите пожалуйста...* ** "

The voice on the other end interrupted, "You speak excellent Russian, your Highness."

Farouk almost dropped the phone, "Um, whom do I have the pleasure of speaking with?"

"This is your comrade Sergey."

With a sigh of relief, Farouk said, "Sergey, how in the hell did you know it was me?"

---

*   Hello, who is speaking? (Russian)

**   May I speak to... (Russian)

"Your Russian is good, but not that good," Sergey said, enjoying a good laugh at the King's expense. "How are things in that God forsaken land of yours?"

"Much better than in Russia. At least I'm not freezing my ass off in snow up to my waist." It turned out to be one of the coldest winters in Russia's recent history. Moscow had received record-breaking snow the previous month.

"Your Highness, rumors are running rampant. I hear things are heating up. How are you holding up?"

Farouk said, "I feel like the rear end of a camel that's been out in the desert too long, but still bright as the night stars."

They shared a laugh before Sergey said, "Surely, old friend, you haven't called all this way to just chat about the weather."

In a serious tone, Farouk said, "Before we proceed, you must agree to keep our conversation quiet. The information I am about to share with you concerns sensitive material, and all knowledge of its existence and contents must be held in the utmost secrecy for purposes of Egyptian National Security. Do you understand?"

"Of course, your Highness. Living in my country, one of the keys to staying alive is learning to keep secrets."

Farouk presented him with the proposition. "Sergey, what if I were to tell you that I found a document revealing a secret passageway in one of our pyramids that might lead to an ancient treasure trove of antiquities?"

"I wouldn't be too surprised. There are many myths surrounding the ancient pyramids in your country."

"What if said document contained fractal codes which needed to be deciphered. Do you think your computer could be of use?"

Sergey had not expected to hear such a question. He pondered for a moment and said, "It would depend on a number of random criteria."

Farouk said, "Such as?"

"How sound the document is. I mean is the material strong enough to be handled, are the codes complete and legible, and various things of this nature."

"With all of those in the affirmative, could your computer decipher the document?"

"Well, of course, computers are nothing more than number based systems. Analyzing a mathematical document would be an elementary task."

"I am prepared to make a sizeable deposit in a Swiss bank account bearing your name," Farouk then went silent, letting the full effect of what he had said sink in. Farouk knew times were difficult in Moscow. Sergey had confided in the King when they first met how provisions were limited and many families, including his own, were struggling. Working on special projects had afforded him a better lifestyle than most, but lately times had become worse.

Farouk continued, "I am willing to pay you twenty thousand pounds, half now and half upon completion. What do you say? Want to give it a try?"

Sergey just about fainted. Things were so bad in Russia, that he and his family could barely put food on the table. He didn't want to sound too excited, so he allowed the silence between them to linger.

Farouk broke the silence. "What is your answer?"

Sergey was still thinking. "Excuse me, and please do not confuse my silence as a lack of interest on my part. I was wondering how you plan to get the document to me."

"You met Pulli when you were here did you not?"

"Yes, but if memory serves me correctly, he is not very fond of my company."

Farouk laughed and said, "Yes you are correct. That night at dinner you were speaking so far over his head he couldn't see the words. He can be somewhat insecure, but he is still the one person in Cairo I can trust. He will be on what appears to be a routine vacation. So not to bring unnecessary attention, our Ambassador in Moscow will meet him upon arrival and deliver him to his hotel.

I have an operative in Russia that I trust with my life. Once Pulli is settled in at his hotel, my operative will contact him. I have already made the necessary arrangements. I am just waiting to hear the answer I am longing from you."

"This will be risky, but I do believe it is possible. I am not sure how long it will take, but I can get word back to your representative at the appointed time."

"I knew you would come through. Oh, one more thing."

"Yes?"

"No one at the Embassy has knowledge of the package's contents. When you are finished, you will be communicating to my operative. Just send a message saying the project is complete."

"What is your plan once Pulli has arrived?"

I believe you receive periodic deliveries from Rusal, an aluminum company."

"That is correct."

"My operative knows someone who drives for them, and he is now employed by me. He will sneak Pulli into your facility with the artifact. Once the van is past your guards, it should be easy for Pulli to meet you and deliver the document. If all goes as planned, the driver will exit the same way, and no one will suspect a thing."

Sergey broke in and said, "Your Highness, if I might offer a suggestion? To divert attention, it might be better if I am at the gate when the van arrives. We don't want to take any chances. If I am there, I can have the guards wave the van through."

"Sounds like a smart idea. Pulli will be catching a plane tomorrow morning and barring no unforeseen incidents should make it to your facility three days from today."

"Your Highness, how will I return the results?"

"My operative will be in touch. I thought it would be best for the two of you to decide on a meeting place where he can pick up the document along with your findings. I need to ask you to work as fast as possible on this. As you stated earlier, things are unstable here."

"Yes, I will do all I can." Sergey hung up the phone thinking, "Well, dying in front of a firing squad is better than starving to death."

\>\>\>

"Pulli, you will travel to Russia and deliver the document. You must tell Sergey to make haste in the deciphering process. He will have knowledge of the documents contents, but he is not to know the true nature of our business.

Pulli appeared startled. "Your Majesty, this is like nothing I've done before, entering a foreign country with one of our national treasures, stolen no less. If I am caught, the Russians will have my head and send my body back to Egypt in a very small bag."

Farouk laughed. "Pulli, it's either the Russians or Nasser. Which do you prefer? Take your pick. Of course, it must be your ass alone if you are caught. I will deny all knowledge of the document's existence. Furthermore, if you decide to doublecross me, I will hunt you down and it will not be a circumcision I will be performing. Pulli, can I count on you?"

Pulli hesitated weighing his options as a momentary silence filled the room.

"Can I count on you?" Farouk repeated growing frustrated.

Pulli straightened up and responded, "Haven't you always been able to count on me?"

Farouk rolled the edges of his mustache between his thumb and first finger in a circular motion and said with a grin, "I suppose so."

"Yes, yes, you can count on me, but I'm telling you if that Russian bastard gives me any trouble, I am going to stick that computer up his *tochus* (Yiddish for rear).You remember how he acted when you were drooling over him, trying to get his people to build the generators? He wore his arrogance like a bad wig."

Like morning fog rising from the Nile, laughter lifted the heaviness looming in the room. For the first time in months, Farouk and Pulli felt like there might be a way to remain in Egypt and thwart Nasser's plan.

Smiling at the thought, Farouk said, "Considering his computer is the largest of its kind in the world, that would be a sight to see. Good luck with that one. He is a smart son of a bitch. There is no denying he has his nose so high we could use him as a khamseen detector."

"Agreed. Now where is this so called super computer located?"

"It's housed in a secret facility some 50 miles outside of Moscow. Gaining access will be near impossible, but I have crafted a plan."

Pulli raised an eyebrow and asked, "So how do you propose I penetrate a secure Russian facility?"

"Don't worry. My reach extends well into Russia, and I already have people working on the details. You'll pretend to be on vacation. I've lined up a Russian escort who will lead you on a tour of the famous sites in Moscow. Upon your arrival at St. Basil's Cathedral, we will make a switch and a double will take your place. It is a large structure with many tourists so, it's a perfect spot. He will continue in your place until you return from the facility.

"At the meeting place, you will be pushed into the back of a delivery vehicle where you can hide for the trip out to the facility. I've contacted Sergey, and he will be waiting. Upon your arrival at the facility, he will meet the van at the front gate, letting the guards know to allow it access. Once inside, you will pass him the document and exit the same way back to Moscow."

"Yeah, I'm sure it will be that simple," Pulli said, rolling his eyes and throwing his arms in the air.

"Just listen. Returning to Moscow, you will be reunited with the escort, reassume your identity, and finish your vacation. I figure with your condition down below, you won't be tempted to do anything stupid and let some cute Russian girl pump you for information."

Pulli shifted his weight in the chair. "I don't know, your Majesty. It seems farfetched, if you want my opinion."

"I don't recall asking for it, but I do want your ass on the next plane to Russia. Hell, Pulli, you know how bad things are getting. I don't know how much time we have. The French, British, and Israelites are all unhappy, Nasser is breathing down my neck, the Assembly is siding with him, and the people are restless. Not to mention the Americans, who are just waiting for me to make a mistake.

"If we find this entrance, and it contains the antiquities you and I have been searching for all these years, there is not a person in this country who won't consider us heroes. Nasser and his band of thugs won't stand a chance of kicking me off the throne. My son's position will be established, and my family's lineage will be secure."

Farouk was overjoyed. It was the first time he had any legitimate proof the mine existed. He was nine years old when he first heard the story. People in the palace used to laugh at him because he believed what they deemed a fairytale made up to entertain children and guests. Now, he was like that nine-year-old boy, barely able to contain his excitement and close to finding out if all the stories he had spent a lifetime pursuing were true.

Farouk put his hand on Pulli's shoulder. "Oh one more thing, no ouzo on this trip. We don't need you spilling your guts. I am depending on you. I know you will not let me down."

Pulli exited the room, shaking his head wondering what he had gotten himself into. Farouk sat gazing out at the courtyard taken by the beauty all around him. At that moment, a flood of emotions hit him. He thought, "I guess it's not until one is on the verge of losing everything that he realizes how blessed he has been. Here I am in one of the most intriguing places in the world. Oh how I will miss it."

He was rattled out of his daydream when the steward approached. "Your Highness, lunch is ready. Would you prefer to dine on the terrace today?"

Ignoring his steward, Farouk said under his breath, "But, then maybe I won't have to leave. Maybe just maybe I will have the last laugh. Ha, ha, Nasser, I am about to stick one up yours."

"Sir, I didn't quite understand."

"Oh, excuse me. Yes, set up on the terrace. I am expecting Shri Panikker, the foreign ambassador from Nepal and some other foreign dignitaries. Please show them to the terrace when they arrive."

"Yes sir," the steward responded, slowly backing away.

Many countries in the region were uncertain what the future held for Egypt; thus, ambassadors were setting appointments with Farouk in an attempt to assess the volatility of the situation.

﹀﹀﹀

The next day Pulli boarded a flight out of the country with plans to travel through several cities before flying into Moscow. As the plane landed, he sat looking out the small port window thinking, "If we are caught, the authorities will hang us in the Square. You don't steal the antiquities in Egypt and expect a slap on the wrist. Fellow Egyptians will castrate us, and the international archaeological community will call for our heads. What a spectacle that would be. On the other hand, Farouk has always been a lucky bastard. He might just pull this off, and if he does, I'll be right there with him to bask in the glory. I guess it's worth the suspense to find out. Hell, when Nasser takes over, I'm done anyway; I might as well go out with a bang.

When the plane came to a rest at the gate, Pulli unlatched his lap belt and, still clutching the leather case, rose from his seat. When the side door of the plane opened, he felt a rush of cold air and then a tug at the case. Looking back, he came face to face with a well dressed man. In an instant, he was reminded of a conversation with Farouk, who had shared Sergey's warning, "You can always recognize KGB men by looking at their shoes. They will be shined, made of the best leather, and fit properly. They will look different than the normal Russians in general; better clothed, better groomed, well proportioned, and always arrogant.'

The man fit the description, so Pulli assumed he was KGB. Clutching the case tighter, he said confidently, "Diplomatic," in his best French.

The man narrowed his eyes and said, "*Извините сэр, я не хотел Вас толкнуть.**" He then let go of the case.

Saint Basil's Cathedral

Breathing a sigh of relief, Pulli made haste toward the exit and descended the steps. Once on the tarmac he looked around and observed how barren and deserted the landscape seemed. Upon entering the terminal, there was little excitement, no crowds, only the shuffling of feet as he walked through the terminal carrying his baggage. Still shaken by the incident on the airplane, he entered the line leading to a check barrier where police were thoroughly examining each person.

The policeman asked, "*Ваш паспорт, пожалуйста. Ваше имя? Где проживаете? ***"

Pulli flashed his Diplomatic Passport, and the man waived him through the barrier. Clearing the first hurdle went so smoothly, it gave him a sense he might accomplish the mission in spite of his earlier feelings of dismay. Exiting the terminal, he spotted the driver from the Egyptian Embassy standing next to a limousine. Recognizing Pulli as he approached, Alexander opened the door and offered to take his luggage. Pulli climbed into the back seat as the driver placed his bags in the trunk. Alexander settled in behind the wheel, and soon the limo was pulling away from the terminal.

Pulli sighed, then let out a laugh, and said aloud, "This should be an adventure."

---

*   Excuse me sir, I didn't mean to bump you. (Russian)

**   Your passport, please. What is your name? Where do you live? (Russian)

Alexander turned and said, "Excuse me, Sir. Do you need something?"

"No, no I'm fine. Everything is fine."

"Sir, I have been instructed to drop you at the Metropol Hotel. Do you want me to take you to the Embassy prior to our arrival at the hotel?"

The Hotel Metropol, nicknamed The Tower of Babel of the 20th century, opened in 1901. At the end of the 19th century, Savva Mamontov brought together the top artists and architects of the time to build a structure indicative of the modernist era known as the Silver Age of Russian art. There were 362 rooms, two restaurants, nine banquet rooms and the only hotel with hot water, refrigerators, elevators, and telephones. In 1917, during the Bolshevist reign, the hotel served as the residence to the Russian Executive Committee and was known as the Second House of Soviets. In 1930, the government allowed the hotel once again to join the ranks of world-class hotels. In order to impress the international community, the government booked all celebrities and foreign dignitaries into the hotel. During the Second World War, the hotel was set up as a press center for Western correspondents.

The hotel would prove to be a good home base for Pulli while in Moscow because it was located opposite the Bolshoi Theater, close to Red Square and the Kremlin.

"I don't believe so Alexander. I am tired from my journey and think it best if I just rest."

"Should you need anything during your stay, I am at your service."

"I plan to visit the Embassy in the morning and attend to some business. Why don't you plan to pick me up around nine?"

"Yes sir, will do."

"Afterwards, a good friend has informed me that my itinerary has all been arranged. We are going to visit every tourist attraction in Moscow. I am sure by the end of the week, I will be exhausted."

Farouk had sent along a special correspondence and instructed Pulli to hand deliver it at the Embassy. It was intended to make his trip appear official. However, so not to arouse suspicion, he informed the Embassy that Pulli would be spending a few extra days taking in the sights. The next day Pulli made a token visit to the Embassy and then returned to his hotel where he was to meet an operative named Greta.

Sitting on the patio of the hotel restaurant, Pulli was enamored by the beauty of the young lady looking his way. Nodding, he acknowledged her stare, and to his pleasant surprise, she nodded in return and headed toward his table. She had long brown hair pulled back in a tasteful ponytail tied with a red ribbon and accentuated by a long scarf draped around her neckline. The scarf just covered her rather large plump breasts, which had the men in her path straining, curious to get a peek. She was wearing a woolen skirt cut just above the knees revealing long sculptured legs, and her bottom twitched from side to side with each stride. Pulli caught himself staring, so he looked the other way and picked up his glass. Arriving at his side the gorgeous woman said, "Pulli, your picture does not do you justice; you are much better looking in person. My name is Greta. May I join you?"

Pulli turned, fumbled his glass, but caught it before it hit the floor. He couldn't help thinking he might have a heart attack right there in the restaurant. Excited by her appearance, his penis began to throb in pain from the recent circumcision. "Damn," he said out loud.

"Excuse me, is that anyway to greet a young lady?"

"Oh, no, I was just reacting to my embarrassment at almost dropping my glass. Please forgive me. Please have a seat. May I offer you something to drink?"

"No thanks."

Leaning forward he asked, "How did you come by my picture?"

"Dominique, who works for your King Farouk, asked if I would like to act as a tour guide for a distinguished Egyptian diplomat, and I agreed."

"Ah good, just what I wanted to hear. One can never be too sure if they are in the correct company especially in this country. So what is our plan?"

"Dominique will meet us at St. Basile Cathedral in twenty minutes. He's prepared a mask from a synthetic material which I must say is scary."

"Scary? Why is that?"

"Well, the resemblance to you is uncanny, I had no idea someone could prepare a mask to look so real."

"Oh, so if I'm correct in my interpretation, you are saying I look scary?"

Laughing, she said, "You know what I meant. But, on second thought..."

Changing the subject, Pulli asked, "The Cathedral is in Red Square, is it not?"

"Yes, just about three or four blocks away. In fact, we should be heading in that direction."

Pulli summoned the waiter who was prompt in bringing the check. They both arose and started for the door. Of course, all eyes were on his companion.

Pulli was walking tall with one of the most radiant women in Moscow on his arm. "Tell me, Greta, how are things here in Moscow?"

"Not good, food is scarce. Of course, you won't notice staying at the hotel and walking the streets here, but in the outlying areas, people are hurting. Life in Russia is difficult," she said and pointed in the direction of the Cathedral. "There is the van."

Pulli noticed a couple of vans in that direction. "Where?"

"There, the white one with Rusal Aluminum painted on the side. We will need to walk around to the other side. Don't be alarmed, but as we pass, you will be pushed inside and Dominique will step out to take your place. He and I will continue walking, and the van will pull away as if nothing happened."

Before Pulli knew what was happening, a man came from behind a column, hit him, and knocked him sideways into the open cargo door of the van. As Dominique emerged, the two of them shared a brief glance. Pulli was amazed at the man looking at him. It was like looking in a mirror and seeing his reflection. The door slammed shut, Dominique took Greta by the arm, and the two of them headed toward the entrance to the Cathedral.

The van jumped to life as the driver pulled away from the curb and headed away from Red Square. The facility was well on the outskirts of town. The trip would take them about one and half hours to complete. Nervous, Pulli hid himself under a tarp in the cargo area of the van and waited.

Not knowing what to expect, the driver neared the guard gate. He had been told Sergey would be waiting, but approaching, the driver saw no sign of him. He slowed in hopes of delaying his entrance to the facility and thought, "Come on, Sergey. If they catch me, the Siberian front during the war would seem like a vacation compared to what they will do to me.'

No sooner had the driver finished the thought than Sergey emerged next to the guard shack. He waived a hand, motioning them to proceed as the arm blocking the entry lifted. Sergey leaned in through the open window and asked, "Can I catch a ride?" He then came around and jumped into the passenger seat. The driver nodded to the guard as he passed and pulled into the facility.

Once inside, Sergey said, "Pulli, my boy, are you back there?"

Pulli responded in a muffled voice, "Yes, and I'm freezing. Man, if I knew it was going to be this cold, I would have worn some long underwear."

Sergey laughed and said, "We'll be at my lab in a couple of minutes, and you can warm up before returning to Moscow."

Inside the lab, Pulli shuffled his feet in an attempt to get warm as Sergey handed him a glass containing a clear liquid. "Here, drink this. It's Russian vodka, known for taking the edge off."

Replaying what Farouk had said and ignoring his counsel, Pulli grabbed the glass and said, "Don't mind if I do."

He downed it, and the warmth of the liquid moved down his throat to his stomach. The feeling was divine as he thought, "It's too damn cold in this place not to enjoy a shot of vodka." He held out his glass and said, "Sergey, pour me another."

Sergey was more than willing to comply. Clinking Pulli's glass, Sergey offered a toast. "Let us drink to Egypt and her ancient artifacts."

Pulli said, "Yes, let's do." He closed his eyes and let the nectar linger in his mouth this time before allowing it to trickle down his throat.

"Pulli, we had better take a look at that case you brought and conclude our time together. The driver will be back from his rounds, and you will need to make your exit."

Pulli pulled opened the leather case revealing several photographs and the document sealed in the original covering. "It should go without saying, the document is fragile considering it is more than two thousand years old."

There was a knock at the door to the lab. Pulli pulled the gun from his leg holster and moved to the side, looking questioningly at Sergey.

Sergey looked back at him and said, "Settle down. It's probably the driver."

Opening the door, Sergey greeted one of his colleagues inquiring about his lunch plans. Pulli, afraid he might enter the room, stood ready to subdue him. The thought came to him, "if he finds out I'm here, there will be hell to pay. I might not make it out of Russia and the document could be lost."

Sergey, however, was quick on his feet saying, "Gorskey, I don't have time. In fact, the Kremlin has me working night and day on the computer. Excuse me, but I must pass."

The door closed, and Pulli breathed a sigh of relief. Then another knock and Pulli jumped back, assuming Gorskey had returned. This time it was the driver asking if they had concluded their business.

Still jittery, Pulli holstered his weapon and said, "Sergey, you know what to do. Once you conclude your findings, contact Dominique, and he will make plans to meet you in Moscow. We'll coordinate with him about the results and return of the document. We will be expecting periodic updates. You can use the secure line at our Embassy to call King Farouk. I can't emphasize enough that time is of the essence. Do you need to escort us to the gate?"

"No, that would draw unwanted attention. They don't usually stop anyone on the way out of the facility."

The driver gestured the coast was clear, and he and Pulli moved fast, making their way back to the van. Pulli hid back under the tarp and literally held his breath until the driver informed him they had cleared the gate. Pulli pushed aside the tarp and grasped the handle of the gun removing it from the holster strapped to his left leg. He pulled the silencer from his coat pocket and slowly screwed it on to the barrel. He wanted to be ready in case any unexpected visitors stopped them.

As they entered Red Square, Pulli looked out the front window to get his bearings. As soon as the van came to a stop the door slid open. Pulli was crouched down, pointing the gun as Dominique stepped in and pulled the mask from his head, "Damn Pulli. Get the gun out of my face!"

Pulli lowered the weapon.

"Were you planning to use that thing?" Dominique stated anxiously.

"If it hadn't been you entering the van, I wouldn't have hesitated."

"It's a good thing I was wearing the mask. By the way, Greta was pleasant company and just so you know I took care of her needs to save you the embarrassment."

"What?"

"His Highness told me about your delicate condition, and I thought it best as your double to do you a favor."

"Thanks, but I am healed and feeling fine. Now that she has had a rookie, I can show her what a real man is like." Pulli thought, "I'm going to kill that fat bastard if Rahman and Nasser don't beat me to it."

They shared a laugh as Pulli unscrewed the silencer and returned it to his pocket.

"You had better go. We don't want to draw attention. Greta is just inside the entrance. Be careful and have a good vacation, my friend." They shook hands as Pulli exited the van.

＼＼＼

Pulli had a wonderful time while in Moscow. Unfortunately, he wasn't as healed as he led Dominique to believe, so he and Greta got along better than they might have otherwise. She had been excited to show him all the sites and was well versed in the history of Moscow.

Meanwhile, Sergey unsealed the document and carefully scanned it, allowing the results to be entered into the tape drive of the computer. The document wasn't holding up well under the scan and would more than likely be destroyed. However, upon completion, he was encouraged by the computers response and felt confident he would be able to decipher the fractal code.

Farouk received word Pulli had landed and made it back safely without raising suspicion. Every day was nerve racking. He had made several appointments in an attempt to stabilize relations, but things were not going as planned. It seemed every move he made was the wrong move. Pulli's return gave him renewed hope.

"Your Majesty, there you are. I respectfully have a complaint. Dominique informed me you had fun at my expense disclosing my decision to become a Muslim."

Farouk laughed. "I couldn't help myself. I figured it might take the pressure off and give you an out with the lady."

"Well, it was rather embarrassing, but all worked as planned. Sergey has the document, here I am, and no one is the wiser."

"Yes, he's already made contact to let me know he was able to download the contents to his computer. However, it appears the original was too fragile and is ruined."

"To hell with the original. No one around here cares about antiquities. If his computer can decipher the code, that's all we need," Pulli said.

"Nothing seems to matter anymore. While you've been gone, things have heated up. I don't think we are going to be welcome in Egypt much longer." Frustrated, Farouk yelled, "These scum have screwed me to the hilt. We are so close to the discovery of a lifetime, and it seems all might have been in vain. There is no way we can get close to the pyramid, much less penetrate the interior."

As the political tension mounted, the men loyal to Nasser and Rahman were pressing in on Farouk. People were protesting in the streets, and Farouk's every move was being monitored. The Moslem Brotherhood was demanding his head; thus, his ability to carry out the extraction was now in jeopardy. Knowing Farouk's penchant for women to satisfy his lustful desires, the leaders allowed Pulli to move about freely.

"Your Majesty, you're forgetting something."

"What in Allah's name are you rambling about? This isn't the time to be playing guessing games. What in the hell do you mean? What am I forgetting?"

"The duck hunt is always held at Faiyum Oasis, and Layla is one of the few woman allowed to stay overnight in the tents. Why not figure a way for her to gain access to the pyramid. No one in their right mind would suspect her of attempting to steal an artifact."

"Pulli, my man, you surprise even me. What a grand idea. If I recall, last year the doctor set her up with several of his closest friends. In fact, General Rahman was among them, and rumor has it, he still has an eye for her. He is in charge of security around the pyramids and the other ancient structures.

"She could entice him to let her have access for an adventure of sorts. I don't think he would suspect her of foul play. Pulli, you have rejuvenated my soul. I do believe we may have a go at the ancient myth after all. Get her on the phone and tell her she is needed at once. We need to move quickly. There is no time to be wasted. But, wait."

"Wait hell. I thought you just said..."

Farouk cut him off, "You're forgetting one small detail, the entrance to the Pyramid at Hawara is about 7 or 8 meters under water. How on earth do we expect Layla to carry out the plan much less find the entrance when it is hidden under water?" Farouk said crossing his arms over his chest, his eyes narrowing.

Pulli straightened in his chair and with eyebrows raised shot the King a sly smile.

"What are you smirking about now?"

"You remember the event a few months back at the US Embassy?"

Farouk said, "Yes, how could I forget? I met that foreign dignitary from Turkey, and we had a nice romp." They both laughed.

"Sir, you are quite the playboy, but had it not been for me, you never would have met her."

"What do you mean? She couldn't take her eyes off of me."

"She didn't even know you existed until I approached and informed her she was in the company of royalty."

"She did have a tight ass, didn't she?" Farouk said, his thoughts drifting further off course.

"Your Majesty, focus man. Is fornication all you think about?"

"What, oh I'm sorry. I just had a moment remembering that blissful night when Egypt and Turkey embraced and became intimate. Okay, where were we?"

"The night at the Embassy."

"What about it?"

"Do you remember speaking to Joseph Locke, the new Marine Guard stationed at the Embassy?"

"Pulli, this must be a record. Twice in the same day, you have wooed me with your intelligence. Of course, I remember the brute. Even with my girth, he made me feel small given his size. Did you know he was a Navy frogman during WWII?"

"Hell yes, I know, why do you think I brought it to your attention in the first place?" Pulli said frowning and shaking his head.

"One can never be sure with you," Farouk shot back, in rare form as he poked Pulli in the belly with a pointed finger.

Farouk always maintained good relations with the American Embassy. A few weeks earlier, he had received an invitation to attend a cocktail reception where several foreign dignitaries were being hosted. While there, he had entered into a conversation with one of the Embassy employees. Farouk was fascinated to learn the man had been an underwater demolition expert during the war. Now, sitting here with Pulli he had renewed vigor, thinking the game was still afoot. "Um, do you think he might be interested?"

"One never knows until he asks, now does he?" Pulli said with a sly grin.

Deep in thought, Farouk looked past Pulli while stroking his bearded chin with his thumb and first finger. Silence lingered in the room as Pulli sat back and watched Farouk. He knew a plan was brewing by the look on Farouk's face.

King Farouk's Chef

"I've got it. The coral reefs off the coast will be our bait. Get in touch with him and let him know we are going snorkeling and would like him to join us. I will speak to Layla ahead of time about the plan and then suggest she entice our frogman to teach her how to scuba dive. If he is like most men, he won't be able to say no. If all goes well, I will pull him aside and propose an adventure. I'll need to be careful how I present the information, in case he decides it would be in his best interest to share the news with Nasser and his people."

"I'll set it up," Pulli said nodding agreement.

Little did Farouk know, but Layla had already been introduced to Joseph, and he had instantly fallen for her. In time, Farouk would discern their affection for one another and considered it a form of security. Farouk felt love weakened a man. The guard wouldn't dare cross him knowing that doing so could bring harm to the one he loved.

Rising from his chair, Farouk slapped Pulli on the back, almost knocking him to the floor, "Pulli, my boy, my appetite has returned. Would you care to join me for lunch?"

"You bet I would. Any chance of getting an aperitif to prepare our pallets?"

"Pulli, I do believe all the years you have spent in my company are finally having a positive impact."

They both laughed and the earlier tension released its grip. Farouk summoned Ahmed Ali, who was standing silently behind him, "Ahmed, ask Beta Ali to select a nice sherry for us prior to lunch being served."

Beta Ali was Farouk's head chef and had spent the better part of the day preparing the King's luncheon spread complete with lobster and muttonchops.

Beta oversaw all meals prepared at the royal palaces and traveled with the King. Beta's father was the first Egyptian chef in the palace working for Farouk's father, King Fuad. Prior to Fuad, Egyptian royalty had always preferred European chefs.

"Pulli, once Joseph meets Layla, and she sets the hook, we should have no problem reeling him in," Farouk said before sipping his sherry.

↘↘↘

Joseph was new to the Embassy. During the war, his underwater demolition unit had been assigned to search for mines before the boats came in to Omaha beach on D-day. When they first shook hands, Chuck, Mona's husband, extended his right hand and rested his left on Joseph's shoulder. That's when he noticed Joseph's solid build. He had a commanding presence about him and was quite a good looking guy.

He and Chuck had hit it off from the beginning. They enjoyed many of the same activities, especially a good round of golf. When Chuck introduced Joseph to Mona, she immediately thought of Layla. Mona had a sense the two of them were destined for each other. If she had her way, Joseph and Layla would fall in love, and Layla would put aside her life of prostitution. Because Divine Providence at times took too long, Mona decided she would expedite the process and introduce them.

"Layla, we want to introduce you to a guy. His name is Joseph Locke, and he just started working at the Cairo Embassy. He and Chuck have become good friends, and we agree you might like each other."

"I know what you are up to," Layla said with a giggle, "but I trust your judgment. Go ahead and set it up."

"Okay" ' Mona grinned back with her devilish smile. "Saturday is the monthly get together over at the TWA club. I'll see if he can join us. We'll introduce the two of you over drinks, which will give you a chance to talk and become acquainted. Plan on us coming by around six to pick you up"

Layla was ready when Chuck and Mona pulled up. As she descended the steps, Mona said, "Chuck, look at her. No one would ever know she is one the most sought after call girls in Egypt."

Chuck nodded while admiring her. The rear door of the vehicle opened, and a beaming Layla poked her head through and said, "*Bonjour mon cher Chaueffer*. Shall we continue to the Embassy for fun and games?"

"Layla, you look beautiful. I love your dress," Mona said.

"Thanks! I bought it especially for tonight. You look beautiful as well! Maybe we'll all get lucky tonight."

They shared a needed laugh as Chuck gunned the engine, sending them on the way to the Embassy.

Mona turned and rested her elbow on the back of the front seat. "Layla, you are going to enjoy Joseph's company. After all, I know how much you like a military man. You might not want to come on too strong at first. Give him a little time to warm up to you."

With a devious gleam in her eye Layla responded, "You know, I'm also shy, so we should get along just fine." All three roared as Chuck slowed as he approached the entrance.

Chuck held the door for the ladies, and upon entering, they could hear Fats Domino in the background singing *Sixty Minute Man*. People were milling around making small talk.

Every month the Embassy hosted a party for employees to take the edge off, especially of late, given the tension around Cairo. The club was a great place for community. The ladies had a regular bridge game, and the men opted for an occasional game of poker. There was a refugee from Palestine, an international bridge champion, who started giving lessons. With not much else to do during the day, all the women had signed up. Mona and Layla among them had enjoyed learning the game. Of course, to make the game more interesting, they played for small amounts of money. The two became partners and playing for money had forced them to learn faster. It wasn't long before they perfected their strategy and usually returned on the winning side.

Chuck saw Jonathan, his lead associate at the Embassy, talking with Joseph and some of the TWA employees, so he asked, "What would you ladies like to drink?"

Layla spoke first, "Ask the bartender if he knows how to make a sidecar. That's what I order from the bartender at the Napoleon. They are divine."

"Sure thing. Mona, how about you?"

"Sidecar sounds good to me, one of the same."

"I'll grab Joseph and the drinks and be right back," said Chuck.

Soon Chuck returned with a small tray of drinks and the handsome Marine Guard. "Joseph, I would like you to meet our friend Layla. Layla, this is Joseph. He is a new addition to our staff here at the Embassy."

Holding out her hand, Layla said, "It's a pleasure to meet you."

"I believe the pleasure is all mine. Nice to meet you."

"Layla, here's your drink."

Layla didn't hear a word Chuck said as she and Joseph locked eyes. For a moment, they were in a trance as if they were alone in the room.

"Ah," Chuck said.

Layla looked over and said, "Excuse me, Chuck. Did you say something?"

Chuck laughed and said, "Yes, a bomb just exploded, and the building is on fire!"

They all laughed as Chuck passed out the drinks. He then motioned for them to sit at a nearby table. As expected, they all got along well and soon were entrenched in conversation. Chuck bragged about some of the bombing raids he had been on, and Joseph entertained them by telling stories about his dives. On occasion, Mona and Layla got a word in, but for the most part,

Layla was content staring at Joseph, thinking how much she liked him, already envisioning them together.

Mona interrupted. "Joseph, allow me tell you a funny story."

Joseph shifted in his seat and gave Mona his undivided attention.

"I got a call from my good friend Clement; his family owns a jewelry shop here in Cairo. This Saudi Prince wanted to buy watches for his entire harem, so Clement begged me to come model the watches and offer advice about which ones to give as gifts to his women. He wanted me to convince the Prince to buy the most expensive lines, which were Rolex, Piaget, Audemars, Piguet, and more. I met the Prince, who kissed my hand and told me how enchanting I was. Of course, he took my advice and selected 80 Rolex watches. He then told me to pick one out for myself. Thinking of Clement, I selected a wonderful lady's Rolex adorned with lots of diamonds."

Looking over and touching Chuck's arm, she continued. "Chuck likes this part of the story. I sold it back to Clement as soon as the Prince left."

Smiling, Chuck nodded his head in agreement.

"The Prince's chauffeur came back to the shop half hour after they left and invited me to go to the Prince's desert palace near the Pyramids to have dinner with His Majesty."

Mona paused for effect, and Joseph said, "Did you go?"

"Please understand, it's not every day a lady is asked to dine with a prince," she said looking over at Chuck, raising her eyebrows, and smiling. "No, I politely declined. Chuck was due any minute to take me out that evening. We spent some of my day's earnings going to the best places in Cairo."

The girls giggled, and Layla said, "Oh, Mona, I would take Chuck over a prince any day."

Mona reached over and gave Chuck a big kiss. Of course, he just smiled and winked at Joseph.

Joseph rose from the table and held out his hand. "Layla, would you like to dance?"

Abdeen Palace (exterior) and parlor

Chuck and Mona watched as the two held each other and danced to a slow, romantic song, which Joseph had so carefully calculated. Mona's intuition had been correct; Joseph appeared to have fallen for Layla. Of course, most men did; she had a mesmerizing effect on them. Her natural beauty radiated, and on this night, the stars were aligned just right.

About that time, "Paper Doll" by the Mills Brothers began playing, and they began to comfortably melt into each other's arms, swaying to the music.

➤➤➤

Pulli contacted Layla to let her know the King requested her presence. He seemed more secretive than usual with her on the phone, "Layla, Hassan is on the way in the limousine. Be ready when he arrives." The phone went dead.

She was waiting at the curb when the limousine pulled up. She climbed in, and before long, they were pulling up in front of the palace. Strangely, Pulli was waiting outside by the entrance. "His Highness wants us to wait in the red parlor. He has important news to share with you."

Entering the parlor, they each took a seat and waited for Farouk to join them. It wasn't long before he entered and crossed the room with an excited gait. He bent down and kissed her on the cheek. "Layla, it's good to see you."

Abdeen Palace Entryway

"It's good to see you too, but why all the secrecy?"

Not being one for politics, Layla didn't understand what was happening in Egypt. Concerning matters of state, she was most ignorant. She believed her political ignorance was one of the reasons her customers preferred her company over other girls. Of course, they also were attracted by the fact she never discussed her associations outside of the boudoir; she always respected their anonymity.

Sitting across from her and leaning forward, he cupped his hands under his chin and rested his elbows on his knees, "The time has come that I must leave the country I love, and there is something I want you to do for me. But before I tell you what it is, let me let me share a story with you. Amenemhat III in the 15th year of his reign built a pyramid at Hawara."

"Isn't that where the annual duck hunt is held?" Layla asked.

"Precisely. Legend has it that while his people were excavating the site preparing to build, they uncovered the entrance to an ancient gold mine. It is common knowledge the pyramid at Hawara contains some of the most complex security features of any pyramid ever discovered in Egypt. Thus, it was thought Amenemhat hid many of his prized possessions somewhere deep within. Among them was a lost text similar to the Rhind Mathematical Papyrus."

Layla interrupted, "I've heard of that document. I think it's on display in a British museum."

Farouk shot a surprised look at Pulli and continued, "That's correct. It dates to the second intermediate period of Egypt and is one of the earliest depictions of Egyptian mathematics. Many believed

Mohammed Ali Pasha al-Mas'ud ibn Agha

there was another text that was never found, a text holding the secret to the mystical powers of the Great Pyramids. With this knowledge, along with one of the richest finds in Egypt's recent history, I would be able to convince the authorities to reject Nasser and his followers. I would again be in a position of power. This would preserve my son's rightful place on the throne."

"That's quite a story, but what does it have to do with me?" Layla asked.

"My great, great, grandfather, Muhammad Ali Pasha, spent a lifetime trying to find the entrance." Farouk rose, took a deep breath, and began pacing, "In his later years, he crafted stories of his own adventures to the children in the palace. No one took him seriously because he had become so ill and senile. This was how the legend was passed down and continues to this day. Pulli and I spent hours when we were young trying to find the document. Didn't we, Pulli?"

Pulli was bored, and his eyes had grown heavy. He was close to drifting off to sleep when Farouk slapped him across the back. "Pulli, pay attention."

Pulli nodded in agreement. "Yeah, we used to have some wild adventures, and searching for it almost got us killed."

"Pulli, you remember Aswani, our shady antiquities dealer from the Nile valley, don't you?" Farouk said laughing as he reflected on the event that took place aboard the *Al-Mahroussa*.

"Do I remember? It's because of him you damn near cut off my penis." Pulli wasn't in the mood for Farouk's antics. "Can we just get on with it, sir?"

"Layla, the leather case Aswani brought aboard the yacht that day contained a document, which might hold the answer to the mystery. Aswani was leading a team taking part in a major archeological project near the pyramid at Hawara. They unearthed an area and found several clay pots sealed, thus preserved. Inside they found ancient documents wrapped in gauze similar to the material used in mummifying bodies. Several of the documents held mathematical equations; others looked more like construction drawings.

"A few years ago, I commissioned Aswani to help me locate the entrance. One of the documents caught his attention. It had hieratic writing at the bottom, which he interpreted to mean, *golden entrance*. Aswani knew the ancients used drawings and other sketches to hide secrets. This particular document was far more complex than any he had ever encountered. Being in charge of the dig had its advantages, and he had been able to separate the document, seal it, and slide it into the leather case.

"The drawing is made up of fractal dimensions, which is a concept Egyptians have used for centuries in building labyrinths. Some believe they were used to conceal generational secrets, which were then hidden to be retrieved in the afterlife."

Layla was now sitting on the edge of her seat. "Haven't they discovered an ancient labyrinth near the pyramid at Hawara?"

"Yes, this is why I was eager to see the document. Pulli set up the meeting telling him I would meet his price."

"So he wasn't on the yacht to witness Pulli's circumcision?" Layla said casually, glancing at Pulli with an empathetic look.

"Do the two of you revel in reminding me of my pain? Too bad Aswani met such an untimely death. No one knows with certainty what happened to him; he just sort of disappeared," Pulli said winking at Farouk.

Knowing better than to ask, Layla ignored Pulli. .

"So why go in to all this detail with me? I don't have access to the kind of knowledge it would take to decipher the paper."

"Ah, but you have an important position to play, my dear, should you accept my offer. Have you been invited to participate at this year's annual duck hunt?"

"You know I have. Doctor Kamuzir invites me each year so you don't have to. I am looking forward to spending time with you in the desert."

"It appears I won't be making the hunt this year; however, General Rahman will be, and from what I understand has taken quite a liking to you."

"Yes, I suppose he has, but what does he have to do with any of this?'

"He is in charge of the security for all the surrounding pyramids and other ancient structures. We believe you could entice him to let you take a tour."

"Wait a minute, wasn't that the pyramid that flooded?"

"Yes, why?

"You want me to go underwater? How would I do that? How could I possibly...?"

Farouk cut her off. "I'll pay you two hundred and fifty thousand British pounds." He went silent to let the full effect of the amount permeate her conscious mind before adding, "Fifty to start and two hundred upon delivery."

"Did you say two hundred and fifty thousand?"

"Yes."

"There is a Marine Guard new to the American Embassy who was a Navy frogman during WWII. His name is Joseph Locke."

Layla gasped hearing Joseph's name, making it hard to breathe. With her heart pounding, she coughed in an attempt to disguise her shock.

"Are you okay?"

"Yes, I don't know what happened. I guess all this intrigue is somewhat overwhelming. Go on."

"I met him at the American Embassy and enjoyed some of his tales about the war. I even invited him to join me sometime on my yacht. It occurred to me he might make the perfect accomplice. With his skill and training along with the information from the document, it should be no problem finding the mine. Therefore, I intend to make him an offer, and if he is like most ambitious young men, he will be delighted to make some extra money."

"How are you going to make the offer?" Layla asked.

"Pulli is going to extend an invitation for him to join me next weekend for a diving excursion aboard the Al-Mahroussa. Of course, you will be aboard and after introductions, ask him to teach you how to scuba dive. Pulli and I are betting he won't turn you down. This will prepare you for the mission and allow you to entice him to accept my proposal."

"Are you sure they are still going forward with the hunt this year?" Layla said.

"My sources say they are. With me out of the way, Rahman and Nasser see it as a good venue to garner the necessary support and select certain people for positions of power.

"Believe me, Rahman's mind will be on much more important matters than guarding pyramids. What do you say, Layla, will you do it?"

Unsure how his plan would unfold, she thought to herself, "Two hundred fifty thousand pounds. I could change my life with that kind of money."

Layla's mouth curled into a smile as she said, "How can I turn you down, your Highness?"

❯ ❯ ❯

Returning to Henrietta's place, Layla put a call into Chuck. When he picked up, she began to speak without introduction. "Chuck, you are not going to believe what happened to me today."

Montazah Palace

Recognizing her voice, he said laughingly, "No, Layla, and I wouldn't dare guess."

"Farouk plans to invite Joseph to go diving aboard the *Al-Mahroussa* and wants me to flirt with him so he will help him find some ancient document."

Layla couldn't wait to let Chuck and Mona in on the plan. Knowing she could trust the two of them, she was both relieved and excited. She was sure the two of them could play a part if Joseph agreed to help. Chuck was resourceful, so she could use his help. Layla had always had a crush on him, but in her thinking what girl in her right mind wouldn't. Chuck was steady in everything he did and had that kind of solid father figure a woman always looks for in a man. She felt safe around him.

"Chuck, are you sitting down?"

"Layla, what are you saying?"

"Farouk will pay me two hundred and fifty thousand British pounds if I can retrieve some ancient piece of paper," she said pausing for effect.

After a long silence, Chuck said, "At today's conversion rate that would be umm, that would be, let's see approximately $700,000 US dollars. So what's he want you to do?"

"Farouk believes there is a hidden mine within the pyramid at Hawara. Something about his great, great, something or other passed on an ancient myth, and Farouk and Pulli have been searching their entire lives for the treasure. An archeologist found a coded document that reveals how to find the entrance and where the document is stored. He wants to use Joseph because the entrance is underwater. You know, it's curious, but do you remember the story about when Farouk's wife gave birth?"

"Uh, no I don't think so."

Layla continued, hardly waiting for an answer. "Farouk and Pulli discovered some ancient cannon from the Napoleonic era. Farouk was asleep on a remote beach when word reached him that Queen Farida had given birth. As he was arriving at the Montazah Palace in Alexandria, he heard the guns going off."

"You mean the gun salute indicating whether it was a boy or a girl?" Chuck asked.

"Yes, exactly."

Chuck's tone of voice changed. He was now fully attentive. "I do remember the story. There were forty-one guns so Farouk knew it was a girl. I believe they fire one hundred and one if it is a boy. So what's the connection with his offer?"

"When Farouk told me this tale and offered all that money, I thought about that story. It occurred to me that he has been obsessed all these years with ancient antiquities. You know the palaces are full of pieces from the Pharaonic period. Maybe just maybe, he has found something."

"So what are you going to do?"

"Chuck, I know Joseph was an underwater expert, but I don't know anything more about him. Don't get me wrong I like him, but if he and I were to locate some ancient mine, how would we get the document to Farouk and collect all that money? I need somebody I know. Someone I can trust with my life. Do you know anyone like that?"

Chuck started laughing and said, "Okay, hold on just a minute. This is a lot to take in over a short phone conversation. Let me get this straight. Farouk has some ancient myth he is chasing, and he wants you to coerce Joseph into helping you find some ancient document you don't know even exists, and he will pay you two hundred and fifty thousand pounds, is this correct?"

"Yes, that's about it. Will you and Mona help?"

"This may be one mission I need to defer to Mona on. Do you know what would happen if you were caught stealing an Egyptian antiquity?"

"But, Chuck, he is the King. Who would dare do anything to us?"

"Layla my girl, have you kept up with the news? Egypt is a hotbed, and everyone is out for a piece of his ass."

"Oh well, if you and Mona won't help, I guess I will just have to find someone else."

"Okay, I get it. Like I said, let me discuss it with Mona, and I'll let you know what she says."

"Thanks, Chuck. You're a dear," Layla said before hanging up.

The next day Chuck shared Layla's proposition with Mona, and she too become excited, "Chuck, I'm up for an adventure. We really wouldn't be stealing anything. It would be more like we were procuring a document on behalf of the King. If we are caught, we can show them the location of the mine. At worst, they would just kick us out of the country. Hell, eventually it looks like that's what it is coming to anyway. What do we have to lose, honey?"

"I guess you're right. What do we have to lose? Let's see, my job and possibly a military court martial. That's just what the United States would do. Then there is Rahman and Nasser. If they didn't kill us, they would just put our heads in a sling, throw us into some ancient dungeon, and throw away the key."

Chuck paused before finishing, "On the other hand, I have been somewhat bored sitting on my ass at the Embassy."

Mona looked at him, tilted her head, and smiled. "Now, that's the Chuck I married. I had a feeling you had already made up your mind."

Chuck shot her a sly grin and said, "I'll let Layla know."

Chuck thought he was going to have to pull Mona off the ceiling she was so high with excitement. Having lived in Cairo her whole life, she was bursting at the seams to leave the country. She had watched the bastards tear apart the Cairo she loved. Now it seemed the bygone era had come to an end, never to be realized again. The money would allow them to live just about anywhere they desired.

↘↘↘

Chuck called and spoke to Layla, "Hey, I wanted to call you first thing this morning. I spoke to Mona...." Chuck's secretary came into his office, interrupting the conversation.

Cupping his hand over the mouthpiece of the phone he asked, "What do you need?"

"Joseph just arrived. Should I send him in?"

"Yes, please do."

"Chuck, did I hear you say yes?"

"No, well not exactly that was my secretary. Look, I spoke to Mona, and we're up for an adventure."

"Chuck, that's the best news I've heard in a long time!" Layla exclaimed.

The volume of her voice caused Chuck to hold the phone out from his ear. "Layla, Joseph just arrived, and I would like to run the plan by him and see if he is up for it. What do you think?"

"Great, go for it. Would you like me to swing by and we can discuss it together?"

"You know, that would be great. How soon can you be here?"

"I'll get Darius to drive me, say thirty minutes."

"Okay, we'll see you then."

Joseph walked into his office. "Chuck, you wanted to see me?"

"Yes, come in and take a seat. I've got something I want to run by you." Chuck explained the situation to the best of his ability, and Joseph listened without saying a word. "What do you think?"

"You know, I've heard some farfetched stories in my time, but this one takes the cake. I've heard Farouk is off his rocker; now I know he is. Even if we could get into the pyramid after all these years, what makes him think some ancient document holds the secret to the mine's location?"

"He's willing to pay two hundred and fifty thousand pounds."

"When do we leave for the pyramid?" Joseph said his eyes widening.

Chuck laughed, "I thought that might get your attention. Layla's on her way, and we'll go deeper into the proposition when she arrives."

➤➤➤

It was a superb day, and Layla had risen early to go for a walk. She had a pot of tea at a quaint little place on the square. When she returned, the phone rang; it was Pulli. "Layla, Hassan and I are on the way to pick you up. We want to arrive in Alexandria promptly at 10 this morning. Make sure you are ready when we arrive."

"Pulli I enjoy the sound of your voice. Will we have some time together before we have to pull out?"

"Damn it, Layla. Cut it out and get your ass in gear. We can always find another deserving young lady to take your place."

"Sure you can, Pulli, and the King would have your ass."

"Layla, one of these days I am going to make up for all the lost time these past two years. I'm going to show you what it's like to be with a real man."

"Don't worry, I'll be ready." Layla had fun joking with Pulli given his tendency to take life so seriously.

The horn honked, and Layla grabbed her bag. Descending the stairs, she saw Abdul Metaal emerge from the passenger side and open the rear door. Abdul was Farouk's personal steward and handled many of his affairs.

She enjoyed riding in the King's limo and the respect it garnered. The trip to Alexandria didn't take long in the lap of luxury. The yacht was moored in the usual spot. It always took her breath away to see it in all its glory. She wondered yet again, "How did I get from a balcony offering Zig Zig to soldiers to the elite docks in Alexandria to mistress to the King? Life has been good."

"Ma'am," Abdul was holding the door and trying to get her attention.

"Oh, I'm sorry, I was lost in thought."

"The King asked if you would be so kind as to board and make yourself at home in his suite. He will join you in about an hour."

This was the normal routine, which she preferred. It afforded her time to prepare for his Highness' arrival. She would slip into her most alluring nightie, powder her nose, and place perfume in all the right places.

"Abdul, has the other guest arrived? Joseph's his name, I believe."

"Not to my knowledge, but he should be here soon. Shall I alert you when he arrives?"

"No, the King has plans for us to meet at lunch."

Joseph arrived not long after Layla and was escorted to his room in the forward part of the ship. There was a note waiting, inviting him to the aft deck at noon to dine with the King.

Farouk felt his pulse quicken, knowing what was waiting for him. Entering the room, he was not disappointed. He found Layla lying on the bed in a sheer red nightie clearly revealing the fullness of her natural blonde beauty. Crossing the room he said, "Layla, oh how I am going to miss you."

Unzipping his trousers, she replied, "Shhhh, don't talk about things that haven't yet happened. Instead, let us enjoy the moment." He and Layla spent the next hour entangled in passion.

〉〉〉

With his sexual appetite sated, the King was in a good mood. When Joseph walked up, Farouk was eating grapes from a crystal bowl. The spread of food before him was, indeed, fit for a King.

"Joseph, come sit down. It is great to see you again. I'm so glad you could join us. How is your room? Does it meet with your approval?"

"It's great. This is quite a ship, your Highness."

Farouk chuckled. "That it is. Would you like something to drink?"

"Water with lemon would be great, thank you."

"Abdul, please take care of our guest."

"Yes, sir," Abdul said already picking up the pitcher.

"Joseph, I have someone I want you to meet. In fact, here she comes now."

Joseph turned to see Layla walking toward them wearing a bikini, the latest fashionable bathing suit. It was a two-piece model which left little to the imagination. He had intended to act surprised when she arrived. However, he didn't need to act; his jaw dropped at the sight of her.

The King watched as Joseph seemed to be taking the bait. He was confident Joseph would be more than happy to take him up on his offer, especially if it meant spending time with Layla.

"My dear, come. I want you to meet Joseph Locke, a good friend of mine. Joseph, this is Layla. I hope you don't mind, but I invited her to join us for lunch."

Joseph stood and cleared his throat, "Uhhh, no. that's fine. It is a pleasure making your acquaintance."

"Your Majesty, you didn't tell me he was so handsome," Layla said, brushing passed Joseph and bending over to give the King a kiss. Of course, she held the position just long enough to give Joseph a full view of her posterior.

"Layla, you look good enough to...have lunch with," the King said laughing.

They each took a plate, settled back, and enjoyed a wonderful lunch as the crew prepared the ship to sail. The captain gave the order, and soon they were moving through the bay toward open water.

"Layla, Joseph was a frogman during the war."

"Your Highness dear, you are so funny. Joseph looks like anything but a frog." She looked over at Joseph and asked, ""What in the world is a frogman?"

"Well, ma'am, my unit spent most of the war under water, so it's just a nickname they gave us," Joseph said with pride.

Layla flashed her most alluring smile and said, "My, my, maybe there is a prince somewhere behind the frog."

They all laughed, and then the King asked a leading question, "Joseph, isn't it called scuba diving today?"

"Yes sir. Jacques Cousteau coined that term a few years ago. It is short for self-contained underwater breathing apparatus. He and Emile Gagnan developed an open-circuit unit where you inhale compressed oxygen from a tank. It allows you to stay under water for extended periods."

"Layla, I bet Joseph would show you how to scuba dive if you asked him."

Giggling she said, "Oh, would you, Joseph? I've always had a thing for frogs."

"I would love to, but I'm afraid I don't have the equipment."

No sooner had he finished his statement than two crewmembers emerged with tanks and all the necessary accessories.

Joseph said, "I should have known a ship like this would be well stocked with just about everything imaginable. You know, sir, teaching her to swim with the tanks might be overkill for a one-day excursion. Do you have snorkeling equipment? It would be better to break her in slowly."

When Joseph met Chuck and Layla at the Embassy and discussed the extraction, he had suggested they use oxygen rebreathers to penetrate the entrance to the pyramid. During the war, rebreathers were developed by Dr. Christian Lambertsen, a military expert. He designed them specifically to be used for underwater warfare. Less bulky than tanks, they gave the diver more maneuvering ability and proved most efficient for shallow water. Layla had assured them the crew kept snorkeling equipment on board.

Farouk instructed the crewmembers to return the tanks and bring up the snorkeling gear. He then picked up the phone from the cradle beside him and said, "Captain, we have two guests who would like to explore the coral reefs. Please let me know when we are in place. So, it is settled. You two can have a go at it. I would join you, but I think my scuba days have passed. You know, Joseph, Egypt is a special place. We have pyramids, oases, rivers, and such. The country is rich in history."

"Yes, I have heard. I hope to have time to explore many of your ruins. I have always been somewhat of a history buff. It's one of the reasons I requested the guard service at the Embassy."

The Captain could be heard over the intercom ordering, "Slow all engines and prepare to anchor. Your Majesty, we will be moored and ready in ten minutes."

"Joseph, you and Layla have fun. I will rejoin you in an hour or so and will be eager to hear about your adventure."

The King rose and winked at Layla. She returned the wink, knowing he intended her to seduce Joseph in hopes of drawing him into their operation.

"Oh, Cheri, come go with us. It won't be the same without you," Layla said to Farouk.

"No, no, you two have fun."

"Well, okay, if you insist."

Layla turned to Joseph and said, "Shall we?"

Joseph looked over at the equipment, "Sure, let me check everything, and then I will show you some things here on deck before we enter the water."

Not many things made Joseph nervous, but feeling the passion emanating from Layla had him shaken in a pleasant way. He helped her place the mask with the attached snorkel over her head.

"Layla, I want you to practice breathing through this tube."

"Okay, here goes."

"If water gets in your mask, you just lift your head out of the water and pull forward on the front of the mask. If your snorkel fills with water, just blow hard through the mouthpiece," Joseph said demonstrating with his own mask and snorkel. "We will practice swimming on top of the water at first. You will be amazed at the visibility. Do you understand everything so far?"

"Yes, I believe so. I think I'm getting the hang of it."

"I can guarantee you one thing."

"What is that, Joseph?"

"All the sea creatures will be wondering who the stunning fish is swimming around!"

She rested her hand on his forearm and kissed his cheek. "You are too kind."

Blushing, Joseph said, "When we enter the water and you get the hang of breathing through the tube, we're going to dive. When I give the signal, this is what I want you to do: bend at the waist and pull your knees and arms up to your chest. Then take a deep breath and push your legs straight up. This will thrust you downward and help you to go deeper. Since your lungs will be full of air, you'll need to release a small amount as you descend. We will swim around for a few seconds, and I will motion for us to go back up. At that point, put your arms straight up and pull down while letting your air out as you ascend. Got it?"

"I believe so, but please be patient with me."

Layla climbed down the stairs on the back of the yacht leading into the water. Joseph jumped in fins first and then swam up close to her. The Mediterranean was magnificent, sky blue in color, crystal clear, a delightful temperature, and known for the many species of coral and sea creatures.

Layla adjusted her equipment and they began swimming around. She adapted and in no time was ready to dive. Joseph motioned downward, and off they went. Joseph was surprised how easy it was for her to descend. He took her hand and put it on the top of his trunks. She caught on and held tightly as he took off swimming with Layla in tow. After about thirty seconds, he pointed up, and she released her grip, thrust her hands upward, and let out some air. Soon she was bobbing on top of the water.

Layla glowed with excitement. "Joseph, that was wonderful. Let's do it again, shall we?"

After several dives, they swam back toward the ship and climbed the stairs. Joseph couldn't help fixating on Layla's bottom as she climbed aboard the yacht. He pulled himself up on the deck and found himself aroused by the day's activities.

Farouk appeared comfortable sitting on the deck reading a book. "Ah, there you are. How was your dive?"

Like a young school girl on her first field trip Layla said, "You wouldn't believe how colorful the reefs are. I had no idea there were that many different colors. Fish swam right up to my mask. It was amazing."

"Your excitement makes me happy. Joseph, I am grateful to you for showing Layla such a good time. Come dry off and have a seat, rest awhile. I have something important I want to ask you."

Joseph set their equipment off to the side, took a towel from the steward's outstretched arm, and said, "Thanks."

"My pleasure, sir. Can I get you something to drink?"

"Yes, water with lemon."

Joseph dried off and sat across from Farouk. Layla, already dry, had wrapped the towel around her head turban style and was sipping wine from a long stem glass.

"Joseph, as I said earlier, our country is blessed with many antiquities. I have come in possession of a document confirming the location of an ancient mine hidden deep within one of our pyramids. It is a matter of national security, and I am afraid once Nasser takes control, it will be lost forever. What is most unfortunate is I don't have the access I once enjoyed."

"They are troubling times, but what business is it of mine, sir?"

"Most people don't realize that our pyramid at Hawara flooded, and the entrance is some eight or nine meters underwater. Seeing you maneuver today, the thought occurred to me that you might be able to swim down to the entrance and with this document locate the ancient mine. There is a story that has been passed down through the generations about a famous papyrus hidden deep inside. I am concerned robbers will find the precious artifact and attempt to profit by selling it to the highest bidder. The document needs to be secured and placed in a museum. I will pay you a handsome amount if you would be willing to serve Egypt in this capacity."

"Sounds like a fun adventure, but you make it sound too easy. Why do I get the impression there is more to this? What's the catch?"

"I understand your reluctance, but I assure you, there is no catch. It will be difficult locating the entrance and navigating the interior; thus, I need someone with your ability."

"Correct me if I'm wrong, but don't you Egyptians frown upon anyone attempting to steal your antiquities? Going in alone would probably not be in my best interest. I don't like playing the scapegoat."

"Granted, the pyramids are guarded twenty-four hours a day and not everyone can gain access, but we have someone who will accompany you on the journey."

"And who might that be?"

"Why, Layla of course. She has been invited to the annual duck hunt, which is always held a short distance from the pyramid. She believes she can secure permission for the two of you to explore the depths of the pyramid. You will pretend to be on an adventure; no one will suspect your true intention."

Joseph looked at Layla and questioned, "You knew this all along?"

Layla tilted her head, winked, and said, "Joseph, this is the first I have heard of the plan."

Joseph played his part by shaking his head and acting as if he were frustrated by her comment. "How much do you intend to pay me if I agree?'

Farouk thought to himself, "Everyone has their price."

"I will pay two hundred and fifty thousand British pounds; fifty to start and the balance when you deliver the document."

Maintaining his poker face, Joseph responded, "Um, interesting. You know, I saw a lot of action during the war, but things have been somewhat boring around the Embassy. It might be fun to entertain some excitement," Joseph paused before saying, "I'll do it. Consider me in."

Farouk beamed from ear to ear, suggesting everyone get some rest, shower, and reconvene on the deck at sunset.

❯ ❯ ❯

After the day's events, Farouk was pleased with himself. Layla stepped out of the shower as Farouk sat admiring her beauty, "Layla, I want you to spend some time alone with Joseph. We need to make sure he can be trusted. With my exile imminent, I can't afford to take a chance on someone doublecrossing me."

"How am I going to get alone with him without arousing suspicion?"

"I'm going to say I have some important business which has come up and suggest the two of you have dinner in my absence. I don't think he will be too disappointed."

Farouk and Layla were sitting on the deck as Joseph walked up. Looking out at the ocean, he said, "Man what a great view."

"Joseph, come sit down next to Layla. I just received word about some unexpected business requiring my attention and must leave you to enjoy this captivating sunset. Why don't I have my chef prepare something special?"

"That would be great. Who in his right mind would turn that down? That is, if it's alright with Layla," Joseph said turning toward her.

"I never turn down a free meal."

Laughing, Farouk stood and said, "Good," He then bent down, kissed her, and whispered, "I'll join you around 9 or so in my stateroom."

Walking away, he said something to Abdul, who turned post haste and disappeared down the stairs.

Layla was thinking, "Here I am, sitting on one of the most luxurious yachts in the world on one of the most exquisite evenings of the year."

"Joseph, life doesn't get much better, do you agree?"

Turning toward her and resting his arm on the back of the seat, he said, "I saw many things over the past few years that harden a man. I would agree at this moment and looking at you, life doesn't get much better." Layla leaned over and kissed him. Joseph felt his temperature rise and asked, "What do I owe that pleasure to?" he asked.

"That was just about the best thing a girl could hear."

Abdul walked up and interrupted, "Excuse me. May I interest you in an appetizer?"

Layla scooted back into her seat and brought her knees up to her chest. "Joseph, you must try these; they are wonderful," she said taking one from the tray.

Reaching out, Joseph took one and put it to his lips and with a strange look said, "Mind me asking what it is?"

Layla laughed at the site on Joseph's face. "It is called *Batarekh* or Egyptian caviar served on toast with melted butter."

Joseph choked when she said caviar; he had never been a big fan of anything fishy. They enjoyed a good laugh, and soon several of the stewards were rushing around preparing the table with various delicacies. They enjoyed a wonderful meal as the sun slid beneath the horizon.

Farouk made it back to the room right at nine and found Layla brushing her hair in front of the mirror. "Cheri, darling, come take a shower with me."

Farouk enjoyed making love in the shower which required Layla to be almost acrobatic given his size in relation to the shower stall. On this night in particular, she intended to satisfy his every desire.

Afterward, sitting on the bed and drying off, she said, "Your Highness, I want to ask your permission about something involving our little adventure."

Farouk feeling relaxed slipped on his robe and turned toward her, "Permission about what?"

"Joseph and I were discussing the details of our little adventure over dinner and agree it would be best to assemble a team."

His curiosity stirred, Farouk asked, "What do you have in mind?'

In a joking manner she said, "You know I am a crafty sort, and Joseph; well it goes without saying, he is well trained, but we agreed it will take more than the two of us to pull this off. He asked if I knew Chuck Gaskin at the Embassy. I told him Mona, Chuck's wife, was one of my best friends. He suggested Chuck might be a good person to bring in. Turns out, Chuck has access to diplomatic pouches and 24-hour access to certain military aircraft. He also said Chuck showed him some of the photographs he had taken of the pyramids and other historical sites. He thinks they might help."

"Sounds interesting," Farouk said, tying off his robe and sitting on the bed.

"Joseph believes we could use the diplomatic pouches to send information out of the country for safekeeping, or, in case you are deposed, communicate our status. Access to military aircraft would allow us to leave the country undetected in order to rendezvous and make the necessary exchange. What do you think?"

"Given the fact you are one of the few who could even get close to the pyramid at this most tumultuous time leaves me with few alternatives. Seems like a good plan and not bad for a simple girl of modest means," he said with a curious gleam in his eye.

To quell any suspicion, Layla leaned over, put her hands on his thighs, and said, "I would like to take the credit, but Joseph came up with the details. We just agreed it would be best for me to speak with you."

"Let me check this Chuck out with my sources. Give me a couple of days, and you will have my decision." He pulled her down on the bed while removing her towel.

>>>

Farouk decided to spend the remainder of the week at Montazah, his summer palace. It had been three days since he had entertained Joseph and Layla aboard the *Al-Mahroussa*. Layla was wandering the streets in Alexandria, visiting some of her favorite stores. Hassan was to pick her up at 3 o'clock.

As usual, he was on time, and the limousine was right where he said it would be, but she noticed Pulli leaning against the passenger door.

Walking up to the car, each arm full of bags, Layla winked, "Pulli, be a dear and open the door."

Pulli rolled his eyes. "The King requires your presence back at the palace. It is a matter of extreme importance."

"My, Pulli, you sound so authoritative today. You know that turns me on."

"Get off it, Layla, and get in the car."

Pulli was the one person who didn't dare make an advance. The king would have his head if he did. It was all right for others to entertain her company, but not Pulli. His not being able to have her had created tension between the two of them, and Layla rubbed it in at every opportunity.

Upon arrival at the palace, she was ushered inside and led to the King's bedroom. Farouk was standing in the doorway as she approached. "Did you have a successful shopping trip?" he asked.

She pulled out a sheer black nightie and held it up. "*Cheri*, you should see all the dazzling things I picked out just for you."

"Layla, you look more enticing today than ever. Come to me and let me feel your warmth. Ecstasy is always but a moment away when I am in your company."

Layla smiled and with her blue eyes full of playful allure said, "*Cheri*, you are making me blush."

Farouk lifted her dress up and over her head, revealing tender breasts outlined in a lace bra and dainty panties hugging the curvature of her hips. This was the moment he cherished most. Taking a step back, he paused to admire her body. He was known for his penchant toward pornography. It was common knowledge that he possessed one of the largest collections in the world. However, he once told Layla that none of it elicited the excitement he felt in her presence.

The sun streamed in from the west window while a gentle breeze cooled their naked bodies and electrified their surroundings. As Farouk lay back on the satin sheets, Layla rolled over on top and mounted him. Taking her time she guided him into her. He shivered upon entry, and his eyes rolled back in his head. They rocked for several minutes as she moved her hips up and down.

Farouk spoke as his body started to quiver. "Layla, it is indescribable how you make me feel. Your soft skin and sweet smell have a dizzying effect. OH, LAYLA... I am going to explode, harder now, harder, OH MY LAYLAAAA... AHHHH... UMMM..." and with a final sigh, he closed his eyes, and she collapsed into his arms, feeling the pounding of his chest with each heart beat. His breathing was heavy and his body wet with perspiration.

Thinking to herself, she laughed, "He might be a king, but he is in no way *king sized*." Having sex with Farouk had always been challenging because of his rather large and rounded belly and small penis; however, there was always something about Farouk that turned her on more so than any of her other clients.

Their lovemaking was filled with a passion she seldom experienced. He had a certain charm and was always gentle with her. In her youth, men had not always treated her with the dignity she experienced with Farouk. There had always been a longing on her part for a fatherlike touch from a man she admired. Farouk satisfied this longing, thus explaining what she was feeling on this day.

She knew this could very well be their last encounter. A breeze swirled through the room, and sadness engulfed her. Her feelings came as a surprise because she did not let emotions interfere with her profession.

She had learned this the hard way in her experience with Thomas and the others she had fallen in love with. As a result, she remained focused in the moment, careful not to fall prey to feelings that might interfere with her ability to be intimate with her clients.

After a long nap, the two of them rose. "I have some wonderful news to share with you, but let us attend to more important matters first, shall we?" Farouk summoned his steward, "Ahmed, bring me a bottle of the 1921 vintage from the cellar." Ahmed smiled and vanished from the room.

Farouk then donned his usual silk robe and positioned his ascot. Layla slipped into one of the many silk kimonos he purchased for her. They sat in front of the large floor-to-ceiling doors leading to the terrace overlooking the ocean and breathed in the cool air swirling through the room.

"Nasser is pressuring me more and more each day, and there seems to be no compromise or agreement to be reached. Soon I will be forced to flee the country. I am going to miss you more than you will ever know."

"Where will you go?" Layla said turning to face him, genuine concern in her eyes.

"I'm thinking Rome. I have friends there who will receive me. If I could stow you away on the *Al-Mahroussa*, I would do so."

Ali returned with two long stem crystal wine glasses, and a bottle resting in a champagne bucket with a white cloth draped across the neck.

"Layla, you have no idea the surprise I have for you. The champagne I am about to open is not just any champagne mind you; it is Dom Pérignon."

Interrupting, she said, "Oh, but King I have tasted it on many occasions."

"No, Layla, you have never tasted this particular vintage. Do you know when Dom Pérignon was first bottled?"

"You know I haven't the faintest idea."

"It was in 1921, but it wasn't put on sale until 1936. My Father acquired several boxes from Simon Brothers in the United Kingdom, and it has been stored in our cellar ever since."

He unwound the wire from the top of the bottle and removed the wrapper. He nudged the cork until it exploded across the room and ricocheted off the adjacent wall. Farouk laughed like a kid shooting a gun for the first time. He handed Ali the bottle, and he proceeded to pour a fair amount into each glass before requesting his leave.

Farouk lifted his glass while swirling the nectar and then lifted it in the air for inspection. "Layla, how am I ever going to be content again, to leave the country I so love? Is there anywhere in the world that compares? Sadness is my constant companion these days, but the news I have to share with you brings life to my old sore bones. I have inquired of your Mr. Gaskin, and it seems he is a very well respected at the Embassy and with our Egyptian authorities. I was unable to uncover any evidence to the contrary. Therefore, I give you my blessing to share our secret with him; however, I will require a meeting. Pulli will set it up so not to arouse suspicion. No one else must know of our plans. Are we in agreement?"

Layla lifted her glass to his and at the clink of the crystal stated, "I pledge on the blood of my ancestors, my loyalty and secrecy to our mission." Then she giggled.

"Good. I will set the meeting and at the appointed time will provide all the necessary information."

They sipped the sweet delicacy which Layla compared to a creamy truffle as it swirled around in her mouth and flowed down to her tummy. Along with their lovemaking, the wine contributed to the warmth she felt all over her body.

〉〉〉

Upon returning from Alexandria, Pulli made arrangements for Chuck and Joseph to visit Abdin Palace for a meeting with Farouk. Entering the elaborate foyer, they were greeted by Farouk himself. "Gentlemen, I have been expecting you. Please follow me. I think it best if we retire upstairs to the Red Salon where we can have an air of privacy from my well-meaning stewards."

Farouk led them up a grand stairway lined with an ornate handrail. The walls were adorned with portraits of women. Farouk acting as tour guide said, "The pictures you see depict women who were part of the royal dynasty of Mohammed Ali."

Chuck and Joseph looked like a couple of deer crossing a country road and frozen in the headlights of oncoming traffic. Neither of them had ever visited Abdin. They ascended the stairs, awed at the level of opulence all around. Abdin was considered the most magnificent royal palace in the world.

Reaching the top floor, Farouk continued, "You will recognize the furnishings in this area which are predominately Louis XV. Down that hallway are the private apartments for the Queen and me. Of course, the furniture in that area you will notice is French 18th century in the style of Louis XIV."

Chuck was curious, but knew better than to ask. He had heard the King had a special harem room where the Queen was kept in strict seclusion. There she entertained select groups of women throughout the year. He was also tempted to ask to visit the massive theatre

King Farouk in the Red Salon

where she was relegated to sit in a special screened in box.

Farouk stepped to the side and said, "We'll meet in here. Please, gentlemen, have a seat."

The Red Salon was one of four reception salons; the others were the White, Diplomatic, and the Suez Canal suites. On one wall hung a rather assuming image of Farouk's father, Fuad I, painted by Philip de László.

"Ah, come here, boy," Farouk said looking at the dog now entering the room.

"Gentlemen, may I offer the two of you a drink?"

Joseph squirmed, feeling uneasy in the presence of the dog. Farouk noticed his reluctance and said, "Don't worry. He is quite tame. He is a champion Alsatian Loretto, a breed of German shepherd."

Watching Joseph squirm, Chuck smiled and in his casual manner said, "I'll take a scotch straight up."

Joseph said, "Scotch suits me just fine."

Farouk smiled too. "I have just the thing. Abdul, bring us a bottle from the most recent shipment. Gentlemen, consider yourselves lucky. You are about to taste a rare delicacy. Bill Smith Grant, the owner of The Glenlivet & Glen Grand Distillery, just sent me a 12-bottle case. He expects to get about 3,000 bottles out of twelve casks distilled from product dated May 12, 1937, the date of George IV's coronation. Thus, he has aptly named it Coronation Glenlivet. No one outside the distillery has ever tasted it."

Farouk lifted his glass and said, "Enjoy."

Each of them closed their eyes and savored the ambrosial effect of the liquid. Their sighs could be heard throughout the halls of the palace.

Setting his glass down, Farouk said, "Continue to enjoy the scotch while I bring you up to speed on our plan. Several months ago, I came into possession of an ancient coded document, which I believed contained information how to locate the entrance to an ancient mine hidden within the pyramid at Hawara.

"Last year the Russian government sent several high-ranking officials to oversee construction of some of our projects. One of the officials was Sergey Alexeyevich Lebedev, a Russian scientist. During his stay, we developed a close friendship, and he shared the work he was doing on the construction of a supercomputer. Thinking he might be able to break the fractal code the document is based on, I sent the document to him."

Joseph asked, "Excuse my ignorance, sir, but what is a fractal code?"

"Fractals are a unique design the ancients used to build elaborate mazes and other structures. From a layman's perspective, it can be explained using a theory known as the *Koch snowflake*, which was first described by the Swedish mathematician, Helge Von Koch. He concluded that a snowflake is but a multiplication of one simple design confined in a small area. Please, hand me a piece of paper and pen from that desk," Farouk said pointing to a fascinating desk made from cedar, ebony, and brass.

Noticing their admiring eyes, Farouk said, "The writing desk is a Louis XIV bureau Mazarin with Boulle marquetry. It was owned by Cardinal Jules Mazarin who was Louis' regent in the mid 1600s."

Chuck handed Farouk the pen and paper and noticed Joseph rolling his eyes.

Farouk continued speaking while sketching a circle and small diagram, "If we placed a portion of a snowflake in the middle of this circle and examined it using a powerful microscope, we would find the whole snowflake is but a multipli-

King Farouk with his dog

cation of this simple design," Farouk said, pointing to his diagram. "Thus, a fractal is a mere multiplication of a design which can be reproduced infinitely without ever moving outside the circle.

"The ancient labyrinths were constructed using this basic principle. Of course, we know them as mazes today, a design multiplied within a set boundary. The goal, as you know, to conquering the maze is to start at the beginning and wander in hopes of discovering a section with a differing design, which when followed leads to the exit. It is a remarkable concept of mathematics."

Chuck interjected, "This is interesting in light of the recent discovery at the base of the pyramid at Hawara."

"What discovery is that, Chuck?" Joseph asked.

Farouk exclaimed, "The labyrinth! Herodotus, an ancient scribe, visited the structure and wrote about it. We always felt it existed, but until late had no evidence supporting his writing. The labyrinth is a horseshoe shaped group of buildings. The translation of Herodotus' description states, *'If one were to collect the walls and evidence of all other efforts of the Greeks, the sum would not amount to the labor and cost of this structure.'* The maze was said to surpass the greatness of the pyramids. It had twelve roofed courts with doors facing each other. Six faced north and six south, in two continuous lines, all within one outer wall. There were also double sets

Hawara Pyramid

of chambers, three thousand altogether, fifteen hundred above and the same number underground."

"Can you imagine how many men it must have taken to build it?" Chuck asked, looking at Joseph.

Farouk took a sip of scotch and continued, "My great, great grandfather, Pasha Muhammad Ali, was the Father of modern Egypt, hereditary Vizier of Egypt, and Governor of Nubia, Senna, Kordofan, and Darfur. He ruled from 1805 until 1848 when his senility left him too incapacitated to govern. He died a year later. However, he told a story which has been passed down from generation to generation.

"According to him, King Amenemhat III was a pharaoh of the Twelfth Dynasty of Egypt. He ruled from 1860 BC to 1814 BC and was regarded and is still considered the greatest monarch of the Middle Kingdom. He built the pyramid at Dalphar, which we know today as the *Black Pyramid*. The original planners miscalculated the load requirements and the foundation did not support the massive wall sections, thus a collapse and many were killed. Frustrated, the King instructed them to abandon construction and move to a secondary location at Hawara.

"While excavating the site in preparation for laying the foundation, several workers unearthed an ancient passageway. Word was sent to the King, whereby he told his serfs to cease work. It was decided that the King would hand pick a select team from his staff to enter and explore the inner depths of the passage. These men were sworn to secrecy.

"The King learned the passageway led to ancient underground mine. One of the rulers of an earlier dynasty had discovered a rich deposit of gold ore. It was believed the gold mined had funded lavish lifestyles of several rulers and financed campaigns of war, which led to the expansion of the kingdom.

"During that time, one of the famous historians spoke of several accidents that occurred during the construction of the pyramids. My grandfather perpetuated the rumor that Amenemhat had orchestrated some of these accidents in order to silence those with knowledge of the passageway. Grandfather presumed the secret had so consumed Amenemhat that he couldn't bring himself to share it with anyone.

"Amenemhat was an interesting man and full of mystery. The Pyramid he built at Hawara is a mysterious work of art. There are secret passages and trap doors built into the interior to ward off would-be robbers. It was rumored some of Amenemhat's enemies found out about the mystical parchments in his possession. Fearful of them being stolen, it is thought that he hid them inside the mine."

"That would explain why they weren't found in his tomb," Chuck said, setting his glass on the table beside his chair and leaning forward.

Farouk smiled. "One of these documents was discovered, the Rhind Mathematical papyrus, and is on display in a British museum. However, even scholars today believe it to be copied from a document originating during Amenemhat's time. The original being written by Ahmes, a scribe to Amenemhat III during his reign.

In the opening paragraph, Ahmes presents the papyrus as giving, 'accurate reckoning for inquiring into things, and the knowledge of all things, mysteries...all secrets.'

"I assume it would be my grandfather's contention that the main document is not the Rhind papyrus, but a document not yet discovered, containing information how to unlock the mystical power of the pyramids. Ever since hearing the story as a young boy, I have been searching in hopes of finding the location.

"Recently a coded document came into my possession, which not only confirms the existence of the ancient papyrus, but has instructions on how to find the mine's entrance. It is my desire to find the entrance and locate one of the richest finds in Egypt's recent history. Armed with this knowledge, I will be able to tap into that mystical power source and regain power, thereby establishing my son's rightful position to the throne."

At this last statement, Chuck and Joseph glanced at each other as if reading one another's mind. "Farouk is off his rocker."

Chuck spoke up first. "Umm, okay, that's an incredible story."

Chuck didn't have a problem believing an ancient text existed, but that's where he drew the line. Mystical power sources were way over his head, and he sure didn't believe in magic.

"So what are you proposing, sir?"

"You may be aware of the annual duck hunt to be held at El-Faiyum Oasis this year. Well, our mutual friend Layla has been invited. It is my hope she would seduce General Rahman, who is in charge of security for all Egyptian antiquities, and convince him to let her and Joseph do some exploring. For this, I am willing to provide a large sum of money."

Looking at Joseph, Farouk said, "I have already offered Layla and Joseph a sizeable sum. I assume you have shared the arrangement with Mr. Gaskin?"

Joseph nodded in agreement. "Yes sir. Indeed I have."

"Chuck, what do you say we skip the bull and get down to business. Are you in?"

Labyrinth

Chuck glanced over at Joseph, who sat stonefaced. An earlier thought crossed his mind, "If you are caught, it's not just your career, it's your ass."

Silence hung in the air like the incense emanating from the ancient Chinese censer in the corner. Chuck extended his right hand to Farouk and said, "I'm in."

Shaking Chuck's hand, Farouk summoned Abdul to his side and whispered, "Bring the case."

Abdul left the room and then reappeared carrying a black briefcase. Joseph looked over at Chuck and smiled. Farouk motioned

175

for Abdul to place it on the table in front of them, "Please, open the case."

Chuck popped the latches on either side and opened the lid, revealing several stacks of British currency and a manila envelope.

"Count it if you like, but you will find it contains fifty thousand pounds. The envelope contains the instructions you will need, the information from my Russian source."

Rising, Farouk said, "Abdul, will show you the way out? I have some pressing issues to attend to. I'm depending on you gentlemen. Good luck."

They shook hands, and Farouk exited the room.

＞＞＞

Chuck entered the Embassy the next morning and poured a cup of coffee. He noticed Joseph and asked, "How are you holding up since our meeting with Farouk yesterday?"

"I'm good. I have to admit I didn't sleep well last night. The whole story seems farfetched, but intriguing none the less. I've given it a lot of thought, and if what he says is true and the guy in Russia accurately deciphered the document, we might be able to pull it off. At the very least, we attempt entry to find it impossible. Either way, I don't see we have that much to lose. We still get to keep the fifty thousand already collected. What are your thoughts?"

"I've been up since four this morning poring over all my notes. Mind if I run through my plan?"

"No, by all means let's hear it."

"The hunt is being held along the Nile in the Faiyum Oasis, which is right at the base of the pyramid. The doctor usually sets Layla up with several of his friends. This year, I'm going to suggest she ask him to move General Rahman to the beginning of the list." Chuck looked up from his notes and noticed the frown on Joseph's face.

Chuck set the notes down, "Joseph, I need to know one thing."

With a hint of frustration, Joseph answered, "What is that?"

"Can you handle knowing Layla is going to be sleeping with these men? I need to know because if you can't, I'll call Farouk and tell him the deal is off. Mona and I want you to know that you and Layla mean more to us than the money. We are willing to walk away."

"To say it doesn't cause a wrenching pain in my gut would be a lie, but I have worked under some of the most stressful conditions, and I never let my emotions distract me from my goal."

Chuck knew behind Joseph's eyes was a seasoned professional, one tough son of a bitch, and they were going to need his expertise if they were going to pull this off. "Enough said, so listen up."

"Yes sir."

"The plan will be for her to seduce the General and secure approval for the two of you to swim down to the entrance and explore the pyramid. She will present you as a curious friend and pretend you have been intrigued by the fact the entrance is flooded and the challenge it presents. She will also ask for an escort from the pyramid back to Cairo. At the conclusion of the week, there is always a tremendous amount of movement with crews breaking down and dismantling the tents so an escort will also provide safe passage back to Cairo. I'm hoping asking for an escort will keep him from becoming suspicious."

"Have you thought about how I'm going to rendezvous with her to gain access?" Joseph said shifting in his seat and crossing his legs.

"You'll meet her at the security checkpoint. Once cleared, the two of you should have ample time to don your equipment and locate the entrance. If all goes as planned, you will exit the same way and return to Cairo where I will park a car on the outskirts of town."

Joseph cocked his head and ran a hand through his hair. "What do we know about the entrance? Since it's been under water, do we have any idea what to expect?"

Resting his elbows on the armrests of the chair, Chuck said, "Locating the entrance might pose a challenge. You will face some unknowns, which you will have to contend with. For that reason, we need to think through all possible scenarios."

Joseph interrupted, "My suggestion would be to construct a mockup to explore the contingencies. Would it be possible to find a warehouse or obscure building we could use?"

"That's a great idea. Let me check around. I am confident we can find a location. The tough part will be concealing our plan. We will need to be careful not to leave any evidence behind that could draw suspicion."

Joseph said, "Maybe King Farouk could provide a location."

With concern in his voice, Chuck said, "I don't know. For some reason, I don't have a good feeling about his involvement. We know he is unstable and somewhat desperate with all that has transpired. Security has been increased, and they are limiting access to the palace. His involvement would bring unwanted attention. If Rahman suspects something, he could have us tailed, which would more than complicate matters. It might make better sense to leave the King in the dark as much as possible."

"How long do you think Farouk has before they kick him out of the country?"

"It's anybody's guess. Hell, I'm wondering where he will go."

❯❯❯

Joseph took the rest of the afternoon and thought through all the scenarios he and Chuck had discussed. He also put together an equipment list. The next day Chuck's door was open as usual, and he was hard at work.

"Chuck, you got a minute?" Joseph knocked to let his presence be known.

"Joseph, come on in," Seeing the paper in his hand, Chuck rose from his chair and crossed the room, "What ya got?"

"Since you are our go-to guy, I'm going to need some special equipment," Joseph said unfolding the paper.

"I'm sure I can get whatever you need," Chuck said with a gleam in his eye.

"Okay first I need a Foca PF, which is a French camera and stands for *petit foca*. It is made by a French company, Optique & Precision de Levallois."

"That will be easy. I already have an account with them. We purchased some special equipment from them awhile back.

"Will they let you purchase direct? It might be better in the long run not to have any record of our purchases at the Embassy."

"Good point. I don't think they care as long as they get their money. I'll check into it. What else do you need?"

"Next, I need what is called a 'Tarzan,' which is a special housing designed for the camera. The casing comes with a foam rubber sleeve for the camera and an outer housing made of aluminum. It has two controls, the shutter release and the film advance, and is held in place with four nuts and sealed with a flat gasket. The housing is watertight, which keeps the camera waterproof. It can be acquired from a French company named Beuchat.

"The next item might be more difficult to acquire, I need the *DSEA* rebreathers I told you about. This stands for *Davis Submerged Escape Apparatus*. I think they can still be procured from the British company, Siebe Gorman. The units are limited to a depth of 6 to 9 meters, which will suit our purposes fine.

"These are compact, lightweight and have two canisters, one for carbon dioxide and the other for oxygen. They come with a rubber-breathing bag, which contains a canister filled with barium hydroxide that scrubs our exhaled carbon dioxide. The second canister, held in place by a pocket located on the lower end of the bag, holds about 56 liters of pressurized oxygen. This canister is equipped with a control valve, connected to the breathing bag.

"When you open the valve, oxygen is admitted into the bag, thus charging it to a pressure equal to the diver's surrounding water pressure. The canister with the carbon dioxide absorbent is connected to a mouthpiece with a flexible tube. The unit also comes with a nose clip since all breathing is through the mouth. We don't want Layla breathing in through her nose, or we will be in a heap of trouble.

"Oh, one more thing, make sure they provide the goggles included with the kits. I don't use one because when I did my training I discovered my eyes were especially suited for underwater operations. Luck of the draw, I guess, or someone upstairs knew ahead of time what I would be doing during the war. Layla, on the other hand, will be safer wearing one. There is no telling what kind of debris we might encounter."

"I'm getting this great visual of seeing Layla in goggles," Chuck said shaking his head. "Go on."

"The unit also doubles as a buoyancy apparatus. I will show Layla how to release a valve, which lets air escape. Allowing the air to escape will help her to surface, and then she can close it to turn it into a life preserver. If it becomes deflated, she just opens the non-return valve and blows through her mouthpiece to re-inflate the bag."

"I hope you plan on leaving that paper with me," Chuck said laughing and sitting back in his chair.

"Sorry, I get a little carried away." Joseph sat down and pulled his chair up to Chuck's desk. "I want to run something else by you and get your thoughts. I want you to secure three units so we can use the extra canister as a transport mechanism for the antiquity. Of course, there is no way of knowing how large or delicate it will be, thus our big unknown. I figure we can prepare the breathing bag so it can be opened and resealed. The idea would be to put the document in the return air canister, insert the canister into the bag, and seal the bag by sucking out the remaining air. This should create a watertight seal and provide added protection. We used a similar method on some of our covert operations. If the document is in some other configuration, we will just have to improvise on the spot. What do you think?"

"It appears you have a solid plan. Let me make some calls. Will you need some type of special diving suit?"

"No, we want to appear under the radar, so to speak. I think it best if we just wear our swim trunks. Believe me, Layla has the latest style. I got a look at her on Farouk's yacht. Given the brevity of the situation, we need Layla to draw the attention of our escorts and anyone else in the area for that matter."

"Rest assured, that type of diversionary tactic is right up her alley," Chuck said as they both imagined the scene.

Pulling a file from his desk drawer, Chuck said, "Joseph, we don't know how clear the water is around the base of the pyramid. I've been comparing old photos with some of our recent imagery taken since the end of the war. Using a technique called stereophotogrammetry, we might be able to estimate the exact location of the entrance. This technique utilizes three-dimensional coordinates, determined by the measurements from two or more images taken from different vantage points. The common points are identified on each image, and a line of sight is constructed from the camera location to the point on the object. It is the triangulation that determines the location of the point in question."

"Okay, you lost me," Joseph said raising his arms in surrender.

"Don't worry; I'll draw you a map," Chuck said as he looked up and laughed. "Since there is no telling what obstruction we might encounter, I've located a contractor who worked on the archeological dig a couple of years ago. He might be able to offer some insight."

Sitting upright, Joseph asked, "Do you think talking to an outside source is wise?"

"We need as much information as possible. I'll be careful not to arouse suspicion."

"Chuck, I am trained to work in the dark. Many of our missions were conducted in murky waters, so if you can get me close I am confident I can find the entrance. I might be able to prepare a light explosive charge if we need to clear some minor debris."

"Can you do that without collapsing the whole thing?" Chuck said with a curious look.

"I'll get you the specs. Of course, I need to keep Layla close. It will take two people to pull this job off. Once we are inside, we won't know what kind of strength will be required. I just wish she had the muscles to go along with her good looks."

"I know what you mean," Chuck said.

ゝゝゝ

Chuck employed several Europeans after the war, and Luka was one of them. They met prior to the war's end when Chuck had been asked to volunteer for one last mission. They were sent to rescue several Air Force officers who had been shot down on bombing raids across the German border. Luka escorted the officers, aiding their escape into Switzerland where they rendezvoused with Chuck's crew. If Luka had been caught, it would have meant certain execution for him and his family. Luka pleaded with the officers to take them along.

The officers thought it would be too risky and had denied his request. Chuck appealed to his Captain. His crew had seen many friends killed and knew their families would never see them again. In a small way, helping this man secure safe passage with his family gave the crew some relief. The mission ran smoothly, and everyone made it out. Luka followed Chuck to Egypt after the war where Chuck made provisions for him and his family. He would do anything Chuck asked of him.

"Luka, Chuck here."

"Chuck, it is great hearing your voice. To what do I owe the pleasure of your call?"

"I have a special favor, and I don't want you to ask any questions."

"Anything, my friend, just name it."

"I need you to secure a remote warehouse for me and set up a dummy company. Why don't you drop by tonight, and I'll fill you in on the details and provide the necessary funds."

"Consider it done."

Two days later, Luka contacted Chuck letting him know he had leased the site, which was located in Heli, a remote area around Payne Field.

Though Chuck had complete trust in Luka, he didn't feel it necessary to let him in on the whole operation. Luka knew not to question his actions.

Chuck found the contractor who had worked on the dig site, but he had not been much help. However, he was able to acquire from the Embassy aerial photos that had been taken during previous archeological expeditions. He and Mona pored over them and were successful in determining the exact location. Using the photos and special technology, they constructed a mockup of the pyramid at the remote location.

➤➤➤

"Joseph, I would like all of us to ride out to the warehouse in the morning. This will give us a chance to review the instructions in depth and fine tune our plan."

"Good, I'll pick up Layla. How about we meet you here at the Embassy, say 8 a.m.?"

"That will be great, I think you'll be impressed with the job we did."

Joseph received an urgent phone call later that afternoon from his former Colonel requesting his participation on a covert mission. Joseph wasn't under any obligation to join the mission, but as usual the Colonel was pretty convincing. He lured Joseph into believing the team couldn't accomplish their goal without him. As soon as the hook was set, the Colonel was quick to let him know there would be a helicopter waiting to ferry him out to a ship at four the next morning.

Joseph picked Layla up around six that evening and headed over to one of the local nightclubs. They enjoyed a wonderful dinner and danced up a storm. Later Joseph broke the news. "Earlier today Chuck asked if we would meet tomorrow so we could all drive out to the warehouse. However, I've been called out of town on urgent business. I tried to catch Chuck, but he had already left the office."

"How long will you be gone?"

"Hell, I don't know. The complete briefing isn't till tomorrow. I hope it won't be too long."

"I'll miss you," she said resting her head on his shoulder.

"Believe me, I'll be back as soon as possible. By the way, I need you to give this to Chuck for me," he said, pulling a piece of paper from his top pocket.

"What is it, Mr. Marine?"

Joseph laughed and handed her the paper. "These are the specifications for an explosive I need. With the phone call and all, I didn't get it to Chuck, and I sure didn't want to leave it on his desk."

"Maybe I'll take it to him, but only if you're real nice," she said reaching up and giving him a kiss.

Joseph wrapped his arms around her and held her tightly, oblivious to everyone in the restaurant. After several minutes, Joseph said, "Baby, I hate to do this, but I've got to pack and be ready to catch a flight out at four in the morning."

"That's okay I'll just go home and mope and cuddle with my teddy bear," she said pushing him back.

"Damn bear has all the fun. I promise I'll make it up to you."

"You better, soldier, or I'll let you have it. Now, on the way back to the house, will you drive me over so I can ask Darius for a ride in the morning?" Layla said as they headed for the door.

"Of course, and by the way, be sure to let Chuck know I'll contact him as soon as possible."

Layla caught Darius in his taxi, and he was more than happy to drive her the next morning.

"Oh Joseph, I so hoped we could spend the night together," she said as they pulled up to Henrietta's place.

Putting his hand up to her mouth, he said, "Maybe it's better this way. We have a lot to focus on, and getting physical could be a distraction. Besides, I don't want to mess up what we have together, how about we take it slow?"

"Have a safe trip and call me when you return," Layla said starting to choke up. She gave him a quick kiss, shut the car door, and vanished into the house.

Joseph sat there for a few minutes thinking how lucky he was. Then feeling like a million bucks, he put the car in gear and hit the pedal.

CHAPTER SEVEN

DARIUS WAS ON TIME, as usual, when he pulled up to the house and found Layla sitting on the curb crying.

"Layla, what's wrong?" he asked jumping out of the car.

"It's Henrietta; she had a heart attack this morning. The ambulance just left, but they wouldn't let me to go with her."

"What hospital did they take her to?"

"Kasr El Aini."

"Come on, get in. I'll take you."

Before Layla was settled into the seat, Darius popped the clutch and sped away. Weaving in and out of traffic and honking his horn, he navigated his way to the hospital. They rushed into the emergency area and inquired about Henrietta's whereabouts.

"I'm sorry," the nurse said, looking up through sad eyes.

"You don't understand; she is like my mother. I have to see her."

"Ma'am, she passed away upon arrival."

Layla froze and then began to shiver. Darius put his arms around her, and she buried her face in his chest. "No, no, please God don't let her be dead." Layla said.

"Sir, if you'll wait a few minutes, I'm sure I can arrange for the two of you to go back and pay your last respects. It's all I can do, maybe that would bring the two of you some peace," the nurse said in a hushed tone.

"Yes, that would be quite kind."

Once again, Layla grasped the pendant adorning her neck. Deep inside, she knew Henrietta was better off, but it was still hard coping with the suddenness of her death. Henrietta had been in failing health for some time. She had also confided in Layla that she was almost broke; her gambling had become an addiction. Layla knew this day would arrive; she just hadn't expected it now in light of all that was going on. She was hoping after they pulled off the plan with Farouk, she could take some of her earnings and pay off Henrietta's debts.

The next few days, calls poured in around the clock. Exhausted Layla said, "Darius, I can't answer another call. Unplug that damn thing..." She was interrupted by the knock at the door, "Be a dear and get that, will you?"

Darius opened the door to find a beautiful woman standing before him, "Darius, it has been too long."

"Hello, Mona. Come in. Wow, look at you, lovely as ever."

"How is our girl holding up?"

"She's taking Henrietta's death hard, but all in all, she's okay. God, it's good to see you. How is Chuck?"

"You know Chuck, always the dear."

"Come on in. Layla will be glad to see you. Lucy was just here and is helping with the arrangements."

Lucy, my, I haven't seen her in ages. How is she doing?"

"Quite the charmer, as usual. Did you know she is getting married?"

"You don't say. That's wonderful. Who is the lucky guy?'

"One of her long-term customers has been in love with her for years. The thought of not holding Lucy in his arms was driving him crazy, so he found the guts to come out and ask for her hand in marriage. Lucy had long admired him, more than any of her other clients, but never in her wildest dreams did she expect him to propose. He told her he didn't care about her past or the number of men she had slept with. All he knew was he loved her and couldn't live without her. Unlike the Lucy we know, she just melted and said yes."

"Hello Mona," Layla said walking in, curious who was at the door. Mona draped her arm over Layla's shoulder.

"Mona, Henrietta was the mother I never had. She was the one person who loved me and didn't try to abuse me. Now I feel like I let her down. We knew her health was failing. Kamuzir checked her out and suggested she go to the hospital for tests, but she was a stubborn old gal and would have nothing of it. I should have made her go. I let her down."

"Without you, Layla, she would have been lost. Don't say another word," Mona said consoling her. After a while Layla fell asleep, exhausted by the day's activities.

"Did you know about Layla's brothers?" Mona asked Darius.

"I knew she had three and a sister and was helping with their education. That's about it."

"Well, back in '48 tragedy struck the family. One brother was thirteen studying to be a hair stylist and the other was fifteen studying to be a mechanic. They'd leave home early in the morning and ride the trolley into the center of town. One day there was a collision with another trolley and five people died, among them were her two brothers. Many others were injured, one man lost his leg. It was a terrible event."

"I remember that accident; it was horrible. I was there that morning. I was driving my cab into the city to pick up a fare. I drove up right after it happened, but had no idea it was Layla's brothers. She never spoke about it." Darius said with a drained look on his face.

"When she arrived at the hospital, and they took her to a room to see her brothers. She asked the attendant where they were, and he pointed to a bed. Layla said it looked like pillows lumped under the cover. She pulled back the cover and found their bodies all tangled up together. She recognized their faces, but that was about it.

"Layla's real mother was Greek Orthodox and wanted them buried in St. George's Cemetery. Of course, she didn't have the money and in the Greek Orthodox cemetery, they have first, second, and third class burial options. Her mother was going to choose the third option, which was the cheapest.

"When Layla learned that, after three years, they exhumed the bodies, took the bones, washed them, and then put them in a small box in a special room she told Henrietta about it. Henrietta said, 'No way. Those boys deserve a proper burial.' Layla couldn't afford a proper burial, so Henrietta paid for a plot, had a mausoleum built, and ordered two carriages, one for each brother in the processional. She then ordered caskets made, and the boys were laid to rest in an honorable fashion."

"*Parole D' Honor.*[*] It is no wonder Layla cared so deeply for her." Darius said.

"Layla's deadbeat mother sued the trolley company and received about 20,000 pounds. Do you think she gave any of the money to Layla to repay Henrietta? Hell no, she squandered it on some scam business deal.

Darius frowned and said, "One would expect a mother to do what is right by her daughter. Hearing she took the money for herself should come as no surprise after all the hardship she has put Layla through."

"I know, Darius, that's why I have always respected her in spite of her life style. My mother forbade me to spend time with her, concerned people would believe I too was a prostitute, but I didn't obey her and used to sneak into the apartments she and Lucy

---

[*] Word of honor. (French)

rented from us. They were a lot of fun. I learned so much from those two," Mona said looking at him with a slight grin.

The next few days were tough, but Layla made sure Henrietta had a proper burial. She and Darius attended Lucy's wedding, where everyone had a wonderful time. The weight began to lift from Layla's shoulders as she reflected on one of Henrietta's favorite lines, "Layla, you just take those lemons life throws at you and make us some lemonade, girl."

❯ ❯ ❯

Entering the Embassy, Layla proceeded to Chuck's office. Leaning against the door's framework she said, "Hey, handsome, got some time for some hanky-panky?"

Chuck sitting at his desk looked up, laughed, and shook his head from side to side, "Get in here before someone sees you and fetches Mona. She would tear me up one side and down the other." He paused and then said, "Sorry about Henrietta. How are you holding up?"

"It's been a real bitch, if you want the truth. She was like a mother, and we had something special, her and me. Now it's gone, but I'll be okay. I'm working out of the Shepheard. God knows I need the money," she said with a sigh indicating the heaviness of her situation.

"Layla, I don't want to tell you how to run your life, but it is my hope one of these days you can retire."

"Chuck, you are a dear, and I love you. One of these days, I promise."

Pulling a paper out of her purse, she handed it to him. "Joseph asked me to give this to you several days ago; it's the description of the explosive he needs. Sorry I'm just now getting it to you. Hope it doesn't mess up our plans."

"No, not at all. Don't worry. Everything will be fine."

"Look, the other reason I stopped by, was to check on Joseph. I've been somewhat preoccupied with all that has happened. Have you spoken to him?"

"Yes, he's due back any day now. By the way, he doesn't know about Henrietta."

"I ask you, where are the real men when you need them?"

Layla and Chuck enjoyed a light moment, and then Layla said, "Okay, I guess there is no tempting you today; therefore, I will be on my way. Give my best to Mona. Tell her we are on for the bridge tournament."

"Sure thing. Take care of yourself and let us know if you need anything."

Layla turned to leave, looked back over her shoulder, and said, "I will."

Chuck reviewed the specifications. The explosive Joseph wanted was a plastic type used at the end of the WWI and the beginning of WWII. It was a green plasticized material with an almond scent made by Nobel Chemicals, Ltd. Winston Churchill had commissioned a group to keep an eye on the home front during the war. Their headquarters were at 64 Baker Street, and they were nicknamed The Baker Street Irregulars. They were considered Special Operations Executive or the SOE. They used the material for purposes of sabotage and provided it to the French resistance fighters. Thus, it was labeled in French *Explosif Plastique*.

Chuck had put a call out to all of his resources in an attempt to locate the explosive. Unfortunately, he had hit a dead end. His secretary poked her head in and said, "Sir, you have a phone call on line one."

"Did he say who it was?"

"All he said was 'Tell him the Swede is calling' and that you would know who it was."

"It's okay, he is an old war buddy," Chuck said laughing and lifting the phone from its cradle. "Luka, good to hear from you. What ya got?"

"I don't think it is best to talk over the phone. Can you meet me this afternoon over at the TWA club?"

"Sure, what time?"

"Say around 4?"

"Sounds good. I'll see you then." Chuck hung up the phone, hoping he had secured a source for the explosive. After exhausting all other resources, Chuck decided it was worth the risk asking Luka for assistance.

Chuck pulled up to the entrance and left the car idling for the attendant. He scaled the steps two at a time, eager to hear the news.

"Hey, Chuck. How is that pretty wife of yours?" Luka said as Chuck entered the club.

"Great as usual. Of course, she doesn't give me a moments rest."

"I'm sure you need a little prod now and then to stay on the straight and narrow."

"I don't mean to be short, but I haven't much time," Chuck said, getting to the point of their meeting. "What information do you have?"

"You know the military installation at Port Lyautey?"

"Yea, the old French military base."

Chuck and his B-17 crew had been ordered to land at the base on the way back from a reconnaissance mission. Their orders were to pick up some bird Colonel and transport him back to Great Ashfield Airbase in Britain. They encountered heavy weather that grounded them for several days. As custom would have it, the men at the base took Chuck's crew under their wings and showed them the local hangouts.

The base was located between Tangier and Rabat, Morocco. By 1951, it had been expanded and was a Major Naval Air Station. The United States had initiated Operation Torch securing the city of Port Lyautey and routing the German and French collaborators operating there. The base was captured with the assistance from the destroyer *Dallas*. Traveling up the Sebou River, the *Dallas* silenced all shore batteries with its guns and landed. A raider team of seventy-five men led by Captain Robert Brodie, Jr., commanding officer of the *Dallas*, disembarked and captured the field. Brodie was awarded the Navy Cross for his heroics.

The United States established the base as an Advanced Landing Ground or ALG soon thereafter. Later the base was used by the twelfth Air Force and their P-40 Warhawks. In addition, Air Transport Command used the base as a stopover enroute to Casablanca Airfield in order to transport aircraft and personnel. Not long after WWII ended, Air Tactical Command assigned several B-17s to transport key personnel from the base back to the United States.

"Yeah, but I thought everything was stripped bare and sent stateside after the war."

"It was supposed to have been, but the crews left behind took it on themselves to set aside a few items."

"And?"

"It just so happens one of the items was several cases of the explosive you've been trying to find."

"Luka, old boy, I knew you would come through. How in the world did you find out about it?"

"Chuck, you know better than to ask a question like that."

"Thanks, I owe you one."

"You don't owe me anything. Whatever you are up to, just promise you'll be careful. Things are heating up, and General Rahman is looking for an excuse to stir up more trouble."

"Don't worry I've got it under control."

CHAPTER EIGHT

J OSEPH COMPLETED HIS MISSION and had returned to his duties at the Embassy. Chuck had spent the past few weeks securing the items on his list.

"Using your suggestion about the rebreathers, I was able to make some changes to your return air canister." Chuck said picking up the pitcher and pouring a glass of water.

"Interesting. What changes?" Joseph said.

"We can assume the document is similar in size to the Rhind Papyrus, which is about 13 inches wide and 79 inches in length. If so, the canister will be perfect. I was able to reconfigure it with a removable top that's undetectable to the naked eye. Your challenge will be to keep the canister in your possession."

"With Layla as a diversion, I can pull it off," Joseph stated with confidence.

"Oh, I almost forgot, I found a source for your explosive,"

"Unbelievable. You never cease to amaze me. Where did you find it?"

"It's sitting in a Quonset hut over at the military installation at Port Lyautey. All we have to do is walk in and carry it out."

"Chuck, I'm sure it's not going to be quite that easy."

Laughing Chuck said, "I'm going to take Mona, I've reviewed the aerial photos of the base and laid out a strategy. I figure if I set up a diversion, it will give Mona time to sneak in and grab what we need."

"Do you really think Mona is up to the task?"

"Hell, she is all excited. With all the talk of secret passages and buried treasure, she feels left out. You don't know Mona very well. She is a crafty sort. If anyone confronts her, she can be rather convincing, so I'm not too concerned. It will all work out."

"Chuck, Layla knew what she was doing when she brought you in on the plan. I must say I am impressed."

"Well, don't be. We haven't accomplished anything up to this point. Everything is just bold talk. However, I have a good feeling about our mission. Besides, life has been boring here in Cairo, I am in need of some adventure. Lord knows Mona is up to it. She has been incensed by the destruction of Cairo. First her film career was sabotaged, and now Nasser has clouded the certainty of what the future holds. She is upset not knowing where we might end up. I'm thinking Maine. I have family there, and they'll fall in love with Mona."

Joseph nodded his head in agreement. "I know what you mean. I haven't given it much thought up until now. After meeting Layla, I am more inclined toward thoughts of the future. I am hoping when all this is over, she will consider putting her old life behind her."

Chuck finished the water in his glass. "Mona tells me she is somewhat taken with you too. I don't know if you are aware, but there is a strange thing about Layla and relationships. By her own admission, she has always considered herself a one-man woman. We laughed at the thought given her lifestyle; however, once you know her whole story, it is easier to embrace. She was thrown into the lifestyle by her mother. Her uncle raped her at eight, and her mother allowed a boyfriend to abuse her. She was

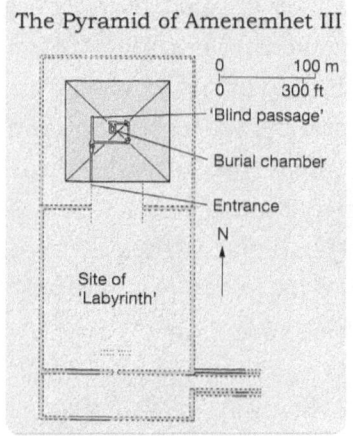

The Pyramid of Amenemhet III

| 0 | 100 m |
| 0 | 300 ft |

'Blind passage'

Burial chamber

Entrance

N

Site of
'Labyrinth'

Hawara Pyramid Interior Layout

Hawara Pyramid Entrance when dry

pulled out of school after the second grade and forced into child labor. It should come as no surprise she ended up on the street.

"Hell, she has been the sole supporter for her whole family. She buried two brothers and put another brother and sister through school. They owe her a debt of gratitude. Of course, Layla desires none of it. She considers it somewhat of a duty, if that makes any sense. Now with Henrietta's death, well let's just say, she's been through a lot."

"I had no idea she had endured such hardships."

"Oh, trust me, there is a depth to her soul that is rare in women of her caliber. She has a strong character and is very committed to those she loves. Once she falls in love, watch out. You will be hard pressed to escape her affection."

"That's just what I needed to hear. Like you, I have a good feeling about our venture."

❯❯❯

Chuck and Mona had several chalk boards set up around the mockup. Joseph and Layla arrived right on time.

With instructions in hand, Chuck pointed to the first board, "The pyramid is one of the most complex structures in all of Egypt.

It is believed Amenemhat designed most of it himself in order to ensure his body would be safe from grave robbers. He wanted to ensure his soul would survive until the time of his resurrection. Several people attempted to penetrate the pyramid, but in 1889 Flinders Petrie discovered the entrance was on the south side. This confused the Egyptologists because most pyramids had entrances located on the North side. Amenemhat III had placed the entrance in what at the time was considered a taboo location.

Enthralled by Chuck's work, Joseph asked, "Were you able to find out if the entry is obstructed?"

"No, but we should assume as much given how much time has passed and the fact it is submerged."

Picking up some of the plastic explosive from a nearby table, Joseph said, "I think I will be able to use this. We used the same material to loosen debris when we had to explore a sunken vessel."

"The entrance has steps descending to the ground below, which means you will still be swimming deeper until you reach the first chamber. If my calculations are correct, the chamber will be 20 meters from the entrance. This is where the large slab is located which makes up the ceiling. It is believed to weigh more than 20 tons."

"Excuse me, guys," Layla said.

"Yes, Layla, what is it?'

"Did I hear you correct? Was that tons?"

"Yes, why?"

"How do we know that thing hasn't already caved in?"

"We don't, but according to Petrie's notes, the ceiling showed no stress whatsoever."

"Great. That makes me feel better. It might be all over if a 20-ton piece of stone fell on my head! But, don't mind me, I'm a tough woman; I can take it." Everyone laughed as Layla rolled her eyes at Mona and said, "Men, what would we do without them and their toys?"

"Does make life more exciting though," Mona said, nodding her agreement.

"Are you two finished? I would like to continue?" Chuck said with both hands resting on his hips.

"Go ahead," Mona said and rolled her eyes.

"Okay, I will," Chuck said with a hint of frustration.

"Petrie found the ceiling slab had somehow been moved, which is incredible in itself considering the weight," Chuck pointed to one of the chalkboards. "About here, you will find an opening leading to another passage. The level in this passageway should be higher than the water line. I am hoping this point is where you will emerge."

"Chuck, do the instructions say how big the opening is?" Joseph asked.

"No, but it must have been big enough for Petrie's team to climb through, or they couldn't have navigated the structure."

"Good point." Joseph said.

"According to the instructions, the passageway branches out north and to the east. You want to take the east branch and continue about twenty meters, which will lead you to another chamber, which will be somewhat elevated, called the well chamber. It is named such because it contains two wells which lead nowhere. Amenemhat added them to confuse would be robbers. With the empty wells and blocks of solid stone along the north wall, vandals would assume they had hit a dead end. When you reach the well chamber, you are in the correct location.

"There will be a lion's eye located somewhere on the wall. The instructions are somewhat unclear at this point. I am guessing it must not be too hard to find, or more details would have been provided. Look for a drawing of a Sphinx with the head of a lion. When you push the left eye, it will depress, releasing sand behind the wall. The flow of sand will cause a shift between the floor and the wall to reveal a crevice, which will expose the entrance to a tunnel."

"If the two of you don't mind, Layla and I would like to head back to Cairo and catch the afternoon bridge game." Mona said, indicating she and Layla were bored.

Since Henrietta's death, at Mona's suggestion, she and Layla had been playing bridge more often. They both had an excellent feel for the game and had become a force to be reckoned with. The mental toughness the game required became a wonderful escape for Layla, providing much needed therapy in order for her to deal with the grieving of Henrietta's passing.

"No, we don't mind at all. Joseph and I will be by to pick you up say around six, and we can get something to eat. That is, if it's all right with you girls," Chuck said.

"Sure, but if we are winning some money we might not want to leave," Mona said looking at Layla and smiling. Layla laughed as the two of them strutted toward the exit.

"Come on, Joseph, we have work to do. Where was I?" Chuck said with a shrug of his shoulders.

"The tunnel," Joseph said, watching the ladies walk out.

Chuck continued, "Oh yes, when you reach the end of the tunnel, this is the point where it gets all mystical. It says, 'Look for a penetrating *Eye of Horus* and then back off ten paces and stare into the eye. If the eye discerns your intentions are honorable, it will begin to glow. As soon as it starts to glow, approach the eye until it separates from the stone. When it separates, stop and wait until it protrudes all the way, rotates, and locks into place. At any time the eye detects anxious movement, it will retract. If this occurs, you must flee as fast as you can. The tunnel is rigged to collapse.'"

"Oh bullshit," Joseph said as the two of them turned and looked at each other.

"That's what it says," Chuck added as they both started laughing.

"How in the hell is it going to know if our intentions are honorable?"

"Damned if I know, but I'm glad it's you and not me going in there," Chuck said grinning.

"Gee, thanks, pal. Go on, what else does it say?"

"When the eye locks in place, pull it straight out. Sand will flow from the seam between the wall and stone above. Wait for the sand to stop flowing, push the eye back in place, and drop to your knees."

"There is a blank spot at this point. It doesn't explain why you are supposed to drop down. Next, it just says to reach through the opening above the eye, locate a lever, grab, and pull it toward you. The wall will rotate outward."

"That's great. Would be nice to know all the details, don't you think?" Joseph asked.

Chuck continued reading, "The stairway is protected. Anyone descending the steps without the correct knowledge will be pierced to death."

"Oh shit, that makes me feel safer."

Chuck couldn't help but laugh at Josephs stab at humor. Pointing to one of the chalkboards Chuck said, "I took the liberty of copying this drawing from the instructions."

Looking over at the board, Joseph noticed pointed objects protruding from the walls around the steps. "Damn, Chuck, what do you make of those?"

"I've studied them and am sorry to say, I have no clue."

"I'll just have to improvise; Lord knows I've done a lot of that over the years. I guess this won't be much different. Of course, in the past I wasn't dealing with some type of mystical system."

Chuck read the next line, "Step in the middle of each platform, pausing before the next step. That's it until you reach the bottom of the stairs."

Joseph took a seat. "That's great. I'm beginning to think this is all bogus. Farouk might have made all this up, knowing how he thinks."

"Wait, let me finish before you get all cowardly on me. 'When you reach the bottom, beware of the shifting sand and remain in place until all threat has passed before proceeding. You will see antiquities all around. Look for an alabaster pot off to the side. This contains the ancient scroll. Choose the one inscribed with hieratic writing and a wax seal with the King's insignia. Upon your return, do not tarry; temptation will be your downfall.'" Chuck looked up and said, "That's the end of the instructions."

"What is hieratic writing?" Joseph asked with a quizzical look.

"Some sort of cursive writing style used by scribes when they didn't have time to use hieroglyphics. I suppose the writing is some type of ancient shorthand."

"Interesting. They were much more advanced than we give them credit for." Joseph said, running a hand through his hair and grabbing the back of his neck. He began rubbing the area around the base of his skull to ease the tension. He and Chuck spent the next two hours reviewing the instructions until Joseph was confident he had a good grasp of the situation.

Chuck looked down at his watch and said, "It's five-thirty. We had better head out. What do you think? Are you ready?"

Joseph brought his arm down and said, "Hell, Chuck, don't you know I was born ready?"

Laughing, they headed out securing the door behind them. They rode back to the Embassy in silence.

❯❯❯

Jonathan came into Chuck's office holding an open case containing plastic explosives. "Um, Chuck, you have something you want to share with your old buddy here?"

"Oh shit, where did that case come from?"

"You tell me. The courier said it was for you."

Chuck was faced with a dilemma. There wasn't time to ask the group if it were okay to bring Jonathan in on their operation.

He couldn't lie and make up some story; Jonathan was too smart for that. Knowing Jonathan's background could come in handy, Chuck had thought about asking to bring him in earlier. "Sit down, Jonathan. You have to swear to secrecy what I am about to share."

"Sure, Chuck, what's up?"

Chuck told him everything.

In shock, Jonathan sat stone faced, before saying, "You know what General Rahman and Nasser will do to you if they find out?"

Lifting his brow Chuck replied, "No, but I doubt they'll give us the key to the city. Did anyone else see the case?" Chuck asked, concern evident in his voice.

"No, I was suspicious because there were no markings on the outside. I took it outside and opened it in case it was a bomb or something."

"Good, I just ask you to keep this between us. Look you don't need to get involved, that is unless you want to."

"Chuck I haven't been this excited, at least with my clothes on, in a long time. Anything you need, I'm in."

"After we procure the document, we will be flying to Switzerland to set up an exchange with Farouk's people. This is where your help would be valuable. Until that time, there is no reason to put you in danger. The fewer of us involved at this point the better."

"Understood. I'll wait until you say go," Jonathan said, exiting Chuck's office.

Chuck picked up the phone and got Luka on the line. "Luka what in the hell were you thinking?"

Luka made a vain attempt to console Chuck. "I felt it would be too risky for you and Mona, so I called in a favor. My source broke in and stole what we needed. He sent me the case, and I delivered it to the Embassy to your attention. There weren't any markings on it, so I didn't think anyone would be suspect. I was going to call, but felt it was best to leave you in the dark just in case it was intercepted."

Chuck shook his head thinking, "What a dumb ass move that was," but he thought better of repeating it out loud. "Luka, thanks and not a word of this to anyone."

"My lips are sealed." Chuck hung up the phone thinking Luka was a good friend, but short on brains.

CHAPTER NINE

LAYLA, LUCY, AND DARIUS DECIDED TO SEE A MOVIE starring Wallace Beery opening at the Metro theatre. At the time, the Metro only showed movies produced by Metro-Goldwyn-Mayer (MGM). It was the first time they had been together since Lucy married. The movie theater was magnificent with reclining seats, plush carpeting, chandeliers, a huge screen, and a great sound system.

Before entering the theatre, they saw a mob coming down the street shouting threats and obscenities. Layla had no idea what all the uproar was about. She just knew how much the local Egyptians hated the English, French, and other foreigners. She didn't understand all the hatred. She thought to herself, "If anyone should be full of hate, it should be me."

Breaking her train of thought, Darius grabbed her arm. "Layla, you and Lucy follow me." He pushed them toward the doors leading into the theater. "These people are crazy. There is no telling what they are going to do."

Many people had been lingering outside waiting for the movie's start, but now they were rushing the doors, seeking refuge from the mob. Everyone was pushing and shoving. Layla and Darius became separated from Lucy. Breathing hard and caught in a maelstrom of emotions, they slid in behind a row of seats.

At that moment, there was a large explosion, and Darius yelled, "Get down," as he rolled over on top of Layla in an attempt to shield her from the flying debris. They heard people screaming, and after what seemed like an eternity, they looked up to see what had happened. Chandeliers were lying in heaps on the floor, and several people were stealing the crystal and ripping foam from the seats. The theatre was in shambles.

Layla's heart was pumping a hundred beats a minute as she thought, "This must be what it's like to have a heart attack." Darius took her arm and helped her up. Her head was spinning, and she felt like she might faint when Darius yelled again, "Where is Lucy?"

"I don't know. She was next to you, wasn't she?" Layla said shaking her head.

"No we got separated. No..." His voice trailed off as he looked across the aisle. The row was in shambles, and several bodies lay dead on the floor. Layla collapsed when she saw Lucy lying in a pool of blood next to a woman and her son. One of the chandeliers had dropped and crushed them. Layla tried to go to Lucy, but was restrained by Darius when he heard the mob trying to break down the front doors.

Layla knew the woman. She had trouble getting pregnant, but kept at it until ten years later she learned she was having a boy. Now here they were, dead at the hands of an angry mob. She screamed, "Why are people so cruel?" Darius was on his knees staring at the gruesome sight, one they would both remember for the rest of their lives.

The two of them crawled over the debris and made it to the rear of the theatre. Darius located the exit and slowly opened the door. To his relief the alley was clear, but further down he noticed several people passing by on the street. Layla was ready to run in an attempt to escape the horror she had just witnessed. Darius grabbed her arm and said, "Hold up, stay close to me. The street is not safe. Let's hide out in here until things cool down."

"I'm scared, Darius. Why did Lucy have to die?"

"I don't know. I am scared too, but everything will be okay if we stay calm." He consoled her by wrapping his arms around her.

They remained inside the cinema until they were sure the crowd had moved away. "Come on. I think they're gone. We need to avoid the street lights, stay in the shadows."

Metro Theatre

While hiding in the shadows of the buildings, Layla began to reflect on how she had lived her life and about how she regarded the Muslim population in Cairo. She thought, "The vast majority of Europeans know little about the inner teachings of Islam. For that matter, I don't know much about the true nature of Muslim men. I do know they are forbidden to drink alcohol, gamble, or associate with street women."

In spite of the fairness, justice, and equality specified in the Koran, many Muslim men were dedicated to harsh treatment of their women, animals, and infidels (non-believers in their faith); but, as in all religions, there were Muslim men who paid little attention to their religious duties. Instead, they lived lives that could be deemed lives of sin by the leadership of the mosques.

They thought of women as their property, hoarding them away in their homes, allowing them to come out in public only if fully covered. Maintaining honor to the Muslim man meant no daughter in his family could embarrass him under threat of death. The man's honor would be offended if the daughter had non-Muslim friends, if she dressed inappropriately, or if she refused to obey her father's demands. Many atrocities resulted, like the father who felt dishonored and shot both of his daughters in the back of his taxicab. Or the man who killed his daughter with a knife while his wife held her down and attempted to comfort her by saying, "This will be quick; you won't suffer much."

In contrast, no such rule applied to male members of the family. They were subjected only to a scolding by the father, regardless of the behavior. The men were raised to believe that all infidels were deserving of death. In fact, by killing an infidel, they were guaranteed eternal life in heaven where 72 virgins awaited their arrival. Young men were lured into the clutches of evil based on this kind of lie. Men also had the authority to divorce a wife (or multiple wives) by simply uttering three times, "I divorce you." Once stated, the divorce was final; there was nothing the wife could do.

Layla could not relate to the fact that Muslims had no feelings of remorse when killing a non-Muslim. She came to the realization that prayer and murder had intertwined to become one. It was then she realized, based on how she had lived her life, how easy a target she had become for the mob. They could justify killing her (if they needed justification) based because she was a street woman, a non-Muslim, and unveiled. Fortunately for her, the mob was more focused on killing the so-called infidels and looting. It was disturbing to see all the stores with their windows smashed.

They moved from block to block trying to put as much distance between them and the area as possible. Turning the corner, they saw another mob approaching. "Layla, quick in here," he said pushing her into a small boutique. He slammed the door and held a finger up to his lips, "Shhhh, until they pass."

Darius kept looking out the window careful to conceal his body. Whispering he said, "Layla, they're entering the British club across the street...Oh my God! They just set a man on fire and threw him off the balcony." It was then that Layla heard the ear shattering scream. Resting his back on the wall, Darius turned and looked at Layla with tears in his eyes. "Layla, what is happening?"

They slid their backs down the wall to sit on the floor. The screams continued for a while, and then everything went silent. Darius pushed himself up and turned his head in an attempt to peer out the window. It appeared the mob had left, but several bodies were lying in the street. "I pray the fall killed them," he thought to himself. "Layla, I am so ashamed."

"What do you mean?"

"I sat here while those men were killed. I didn't lift a finger to help."

"Darius, there is nothing either one of us could have done. Two against a mob would have been suicide."

"I know, but there must have been something."

"Darius, look at me. There was nothing you could do," she said, resting her hand on his arm, "but you saved my life."

Looking over at her, he realized she was right, "Layla, we need to get out of here. If we can make it to the Shepheard, we can stay there until morning."

"I'm right behind you."

Opening the door, Darius glanced from left to right making sure the street was clear. They emerged from their hiding place. "Layla, hold on to my arm and stay close."

Walking fast they headed in the direction of the Hotel, which was several blocks away. They turned onto Ibrahim Pasha Street and both gasped, "Darius no! Those idiots, how could they?"

They were horrified by the sight before them; the Shepheard was engulfed in flames. Rebel extremist were throwing Molotov cocktails and rendering the hotel to ruins for no other reason than blind hatred. It was the type of reaction Gamal Abdel Nasser and General Muhammad Rahman, leaders of the Free Officers Movement, wanted.

She and Darius fell to their knees as they observed some of the richest history in Cairo dissipate in a heap of ashes. It was a travesty, a crown jewel of Cairo engulfed in flames. Layla said out loud, "My headquarters is being destroyed. Now where will I go? What will I do? Darius, what about all the antiquities, so much beauty being destroyed, and no one seems to care?"

Shepheard's Hotel in ruins

"Layla, I can't take this anymore. I'm heading back to Italy and getting the hell out of here. My family has been hounding me to come live with them. I think it's time."

She thought how sad life had become. Lucy was dead, the Shepheard's Hotel was burning, and Darius was making plans to leave Egypt. Layla felt trapped in a storm of indignation. The day's events were almost too much for her to bear.

❯❯❯

The next day, Layla and Darius sought refuge in Darius' apartment. Intent on learning as much as possible, they tuned into the local radio station. It wasn't long before the station broadcast the first communiqué of the revolution. The speaker was a little known officer of the Free Officer movement, Anwar El Sadat. He was speaking to the Egyptian people, and he sounded like he was attempting to justify the Free Officers' actions in the take down of the monarchy, saying, "The blessed movement, our precious country had been plagued by bribery, mischief, and lack of stability at the highest government levels."

Sadat's words were pointed at Farouk and his cohorts, accusing them of malfeasance and ignorance. As such, Farouk left Rahman and Nasser no choice but to take matters into their own capable hands for the good of Egypt. He went on to assure the people that the rioters would be arrested, brought to justice, and punished. The army would be taking charge and assisting the police to ensure a peaceful transition. He laid out the punishment for anyone harboring traitors and asked for full cooperation. In so many words,

Sadat expressed desire for the public to embrace the movement's efforts with confidence.

Turning off the radio, Layla and Darius sat in silence, shocked by all they had been through.

❯❯❯

The year 1951 had passed, and the New Year had been ushered in without much fanfare. Nineteen fifty two marked seventy years of British occupation over the Suez Canal Zone. Many believed that the British attempts to rid the Egyptian authority in the Canal Zone set off the events of January 25 and 26.

On January 25, the Buluk Nizam, an auxiliary police force, occupied the Ismailia governorate and its barracks. Immediately, the British made their demand for them to clear out. The Egyptians revolted, and over fifty Egyptians were killed, another eighty were wounded, and around six hundred were taken captive.

University students heard about the incident and were reminded of the 1919 revolution, the countrywide revolt over British occupation. It had been carried out by common people under the orders of revolutionary leader Saad Zighlul and members of the Wafd Party. It ended with Britain recognizing Egypt's independence in 1922; in 1923, Egypt had a new constitution.

The students thought they were on the verge of another uprising. They took to the streets in what started as a peaceful demonstration demanding Egypt break diplomatic relations with Great Britain. Being denied by government authorities, the demonstrations became heated. The youth had a growing resentment toward the older generation and the British Western influence over the country.

Tensions escalated, and the peaceful demonstration turned into a riotous mob descending upon the wealthy districts of Cairo. In targeting the British and other foreign nationals, the mob burned much of Cairo. The violence began when some started a fire in the street. Before long, the lawless mob was burning all establishments owned by the British or other foreign nationals.

The police did little or nothing to stop the rioting. When it was over, many treasured establishments lay in ruins. Among the most well known were Badiaa Masabni's Opera Casino, the Barclays Bank, the Automobile Club, the Cicurel, Omar Effendi, the Salon Vert, and many hotels, among them the beloved Shepheard. Over seven hundred establishments were either looted or burned, and many innocent people were killed or wounded.

By sunset, the Egyptian army had restored order. Throughout the rioting, Farouk was hosting an event for 2,000 military officers at his Abdin Palace in celebration of his son's birth. He blamed the Wafdist government for failing to call in the troops. Martial law was imposed throughout the country, and a curfew was set from six in the evening until six in the morning. All schools and universities were closed and a ban placed on public gatherings. January 26 would live in infamy, known to all as Black Saturday.

In the following weeks, Farouk dismissed the Wafdist and made many cabinet appointments in an attempt to ease relations with the British, however as tension mounted, he was unable to restore confidence in his ability to rule. In trouble, he appealed to the United States for assistance and was rejected. The Cairo fires and street riots proved to be the beginning of the end of Farouk's monarchy.

➤➤➤

Not long after the events of Black Saturday, Mona witnessed a disturbing event from her balcony as she looked down toward Midan Suleman Pasha. Camelia (Lilliane Victor Cohen) was a movie star in Egypt, and like Layla was beautiful and a good friend of King Farouk. Mona had been introduced to Camelia and her mother when she started in the business.

Camellia was on her way to Paris in an attempt to further her career when she met a tragic end. The TWA flight she was on crashed and burned in the desert. All fifty five passengers were killed. The local newspapers covered the story and showed pictures of the charred bodies.

As was customary in Egypt, a procession carried the body through the streets on the way to the burial site. Because Camellia was a much loved star, many turned out for the procession. Mona was watching from her balcony when someone screamed, "*Ya Judea, ya Judea.**" People in the crowd realized the body was being taken to the Jewish cemetery. The men dropped the casket to the ground and flung open the casket. When Camelia fell out the mob started tearing at the body. Camellia's mother and family members looked on in horror.

In the midst of racial slurs and epithets, the Egyptians had accomplished nothing except to dehumanize many solely upon the basis of their religion. These dehumanizing tactics were but another warning to the Europeans and other foreign nationals that their days of living in Egypt were numbered.

---

*   She is a Jew, she is a Jew (Arabic)

CHAPTER TEN

S EVERAL MONTHS LATER, Nasser and General Rahman initiated a military *coup d'état* against Farouk on July 23, 1952, which will forever be known as the July 23rd Revolution. Farouk was in residence at his Montaza Palace in Alexandria at the time. Terrified and not knowing what his fate would be, he moved to the Ras Al-Teen Palace on the waterfront to be closer to his yacht. His captain was alerted to prepare the vessel and be ready at a moment's notice.

Nasser and General Rahman appointed a special council, and the debate about what to do with Farouk ensued among the Free Officers Movement. Some wanted Farouk's head, feeling he should be tried and executed for the crimes against the Egyptian people. Nasser and Rahman felt it best to keep the peace by exiling Farouk. Dedication to the cause to end British rule and establish a republic was the common denominator of the movement. Once the decision for exile was handed down, Farouk was given six hours to abdicate his throne and leave Egypt. They agreed to let him sail under the protection of the army on his yacht the *Al-Mahroussa*.

The Free Officers Movement was changed to the Revolutionary Command Council. The new government order was based on six primary principles: an end to occupation, an end to feudalism and monopoly, social justice, a strong army, democracy, and no more censorship. Rahman was made the President of the new republic, but he and Nasser were considered equals.

Later the same day, the military raided Abdin Palace and arrested Pulli. Farouk had been acting suspicious and secretive and had kept Pulli in the dark about all that was happening. Depressed, he had retired to his apartment complex within the palace. Among his belongings were found a key collection along with notes outlining the details of all the King's mistresses.

During this time, Farouk's people, given the short notice, were frantic. He ordered his chief steward to oversee the loading of antiquities and other items into 50-gallon drums and other containers. Servants were dispatched to Montazah Palace to gather the Queen's jewelry. The drums were delivered to the dock along with twelve heavy ammunition boxes with instructions for the Captain to load as soon as possible. When the authorities questioned the Captain about the contents, he informed them the drums were full of diesel fuel for their journey and the boxes were loaded with the Queen's personal belongings from the palace. Taking him at his word, Farouk's pilfering was complete.

Farouk arrived at the ship and the Captain informed him the loading was complete. Breathing a sigh of relief, he asked, "Has Pulli boarded?"

"No, your Majesty, the last I heard he had been arrested at Abdin."

"We're not leaving without him."

"Do you want me to make some calls?"

"No, I better handle this. Rahman is behind it, and he is eager to get rid of me. I'm sure I would have a better chance negotiating his release." Within the hour, Pulli was on board, everything was loaded, and people were lining the docks to say farewell.

Rahman had issued the following statement to Farouk:

"In view of what the country has suffered in the recent past, the complete vacuity prevailing in all corners as a result of your bad behavior, your toying with the Constitution, and your disdain for the wants of the people, no one rests assured of life, livelihood, and honor. Egypt's reputation among the peoples of the world has been debased as a result of your excesses in these areas to the extent that traitors and bribe-takers find protection beneath your shadow in addition to security, excessive wealth, and many extravagances at the expense of the hungry and impoverished people. You manifested this during and after the Palestine War in the corrupt arms scandals and your open interference in the courts to try to falsify the facts of the case, thus shaking faith in justice. Therefore, the army, representing the power of the people, has empowered me to demand that Your Majesty abdicate the throne to His Highness Crown Prince Ahmed Fuad, provided that this is accomplished at the fixed time of 12 o'clock noon today (Saturday, 26 July 1952, the 4th of Zul Qa'ada, 1371), and that you depart the country before 6 o'clock in the evening of the same day. The army places upon Your Majesty the burden of everything that may result from your failure to abdicate according to the wishes of the people."

The military honored Farouk with a twenty-one gun salute, and with tears in his eyes, he waved from the deck as the ship set sail for Italy under the protection of the Egyptian army.

The government seized all of Farouk's property and used the proceeds to pay down his debt to the people. Among the property seized were fleets of yachts, limousines, and his sprawling sybaritic estates.

CHAPTER ELEVEN

LAYLA WALKED THROUGH THE ENTRY on the way to the study. Her mind full of all that had transpired over the past several weeks, she had been in a hurry all morning. She had met early with Chuck and Mona at the Embassy. Chuck had been unable to confirm if the hunt was still on considering the military coup and Farouk's subsequent abdication. They agreed it would be best for Layla to visit the doctor.

The door to his study opened, and Kamuzir crossed the room to where Layla was standing with her back to him. He put his arms around her waist and kissed her on the neck.

"I've missed you. How are you holding up under the stress of late?"

"Doctor, they burned the Shepheard. How could they be so selfish and stupid all at the same time?"

"My dear, most of these idiots don't think past their noses. They are young and wild and give no thought to what the future might hold. Rahman and his brotherhood are nothing but a pack of wolves waiting to devour our country. Playing into their hand, King Farouk made several key mistakes, which didn't come as a surprise to those of us who knew him. Now, we must live with the consequences and try to get on with life the best we can."

Crying Layla said, "The Shepheard was my office. Now where will I operate from?"

Kamuzir's heart ached for her, and like most men he desired to fix the problem.

"I do have what I believe is some good news."

"What would qualify as good news with all that has taken place?"

"Rahman and Nasser have decided it would be important for overall relations to maintain the annual duck hunt. I still want you to be my guest. Will you do me the honor?"

"Doctor, with all the turmoil, Henrietta's death, and now Lucy's, I don't know if I would be very good company."

"Layla, you thrive in that kind of environment. As your doctor, I think it would do you a world of good. It would take your mind off of things and allow you to make some money to hold you over until you know what the future looks like." Handing her his hanky, he asked, "What do you say? Can I count on you?"

Layla took the cloth and wiped away the tears. Then with the most innocent look she could summon, she allowed a smile to crease her lips, "You know, if you were anyone else, I would have to say no, but how can I turn down my best friend. Of course, I will be your guest."

Beaming from ear to ear, he grabbed her around the waist and swung her around.

"Doctor, set me down. You are messing up my dress."

"Ummm, about that dress, it's going to be difficult to do my check up with that on."

Layla lifted it over her head. The doctor took a deep breath, then pulled her close, and kissed her. Teasing, she pulled back and said, "Not so fast, mister." She unzipped his trousers and slipped her hands down to his privates. To her pleasant surprise, the doctor was more than ready to please her.

She kissed the lobe of his ear before moving down to his neck. Kamuzir was breathing heavily, but a gentle murmur emanated deep from within his heart as she made her way down to his belly and below. When she took him into her mouth, he threw back his head, shivered, and said, "Layla, you are fantastic."

After their lovemaking, the doctor confirmed that Layla was as healthy as ever.

＞＞＞

Arriving late in the day, Layla found several workers putting the finishing touch on Doctor Kamuzir's tent. She shared what Farouk had told her. "Before King Farouk left for Rome, he suggested I visit General Rahman first, thinking it might be a good way to line my pockets. What do you think, Doctor?"

"I completely agree. In fact, he contacted me earlier this week asking if you were going to attend. He arrived earlier today so you might consider heading his way. He is going to be in great demand this week given the political climate of late. Why don't you meet me later for dinner?"

Pushing back the canvas cover, Layla took two steps, and entered the General's tent. He was sitting at a small bureau, pen in hand, completing a correspondence. The annual duck hunt was a glamorous affair, and most of the men decorated their tents with all the comforts of home. The General's tent resembled more of an office, which given his responsibilities at the time, made the most sense.

He didn't see her at first so she made her presence known by uttering a sensuous, "Umhmm."

Looking up, Rahman turned to see Layla standing in the entranceway, adorned in a full-length mink coat. His first thought, "She's gotta be hot in that coat," which led to his second, "I bet she is hot inside that coat."

"Layla, you look radiant. Sheer beauty my dear, sheer beauty," he said staring in awe.

Resting her hands on each lapel, Layla opened the coat to reveal her nakedness. Flustered, the General knocked over the inkwell on his bureau, spilling the contents over the papers on his desk.

Laughing, Layla crossed the room, picked up a towel from a nearby chair, and proceeded to clean up the ink. The mink coat remained open and exposed her bare body, "General, you look handsome, and I do believe you have lost some weight."

"Layla my darling, you are always the flatterer. How I enjoy your company. I have dropped a few pounds and can't tell you how good it feels, like I am twenty again," he said laughing.

"Um, I'm curious how it will affect our lovemaking. It has been awhile since I spent time with one so young," Layla said, bending down and placing her hands on his knees. "I'm so glad you invited me to your tent. What would you like me to do, my young tiger?"

"Grrr..." the General uttered in his best impersonation. However, being the authoritative type and wanting to feel in control, he said, "First, let us drink a glass of wine," he said, reaching for one of two glasses already filled.

Layla took a seat in the chair next to him and rested a hand on his inner thigh. With her other hand she took the glass and said, "To youth."

The General felt his penis harden and said with a slight uneasiness, "Layla, what keeps you busy these days other than your profession?" He was trying hard to give the impression he was in control of his emotions.

His reluctance to succumb to her advances made her feel uneasy. Knowing he was a curious sort, several thoughts rolled over in her mind. "Is it possible he has heard of our plan? Could Farouk be setting us up in hopes of staying in the country?" Then she reminded herself that Rahman was always hesitant, somewhat shy.

"I've been busy taking care of my mother and seeing that my brother and sister are able to carry on their education."

"How do you do it, Layla?"

"What do you mean, tiger?" She said running the palm of her hand in a circular motion on his inner thigh making sure to brush up against his new bulge.

"I mean, it is common knowledge your mother solicits suitors on your behalf. I understand taking care of your siblings, but how do you put up with that woman?"

"General, all things in life are by choice, are they not?"

Nodding in response, "Of course," he responded.

"I decided the choice was mine. I came to a revelation one Sunday when I was in such pain. Hoping God existed, I visited a church in our neighborhood. I entered and sat in the back and listened to a man dressed in black wearing a white collar. 'If you honor your Mother and Father, it will go well with you,' he said. I remember thinking at the time, 'But, God, how do I honor a mother who is beating me and sharing me with her male friends?' I heard a voice and thought someone behind me had spoken. Looking around, there was no one there. Then I heard it again and knew it was the voice of God, 'My child, rest in me. I will never leave you nor forsake you.'

"Hearing the words I felt a warm feeling flow through my mind and run down my shoulders to the rest of my body. I started crying and at that moment felt peace. I determined there was nothing more my mother, or anyone else, for that matter, could do to hurt me. I knew God would protect me. It became my decision to care for those who couldn't care for themselves, regardless of their actions. Afterwards, an unusual thing happened..." the words trailed off as she paused in reflection.

"What happened?" The General said, entranced by the unusual air of innocence flowing from her.

"My mother never hit me again and ceased being my madam. However, to show respect, I continue to support her and my siblings."

"I would have killed the bitch."

"General, let's not talk about me," She leaned over and kissed him, her lips wet with passion. He felt a spark shoot through him that ignited his manhood. He slipped an arm under the coat and pulled her naked body to his. She responded to the strength of his touch.

Picking her up he said, "What do you say we retire to my bed?" The large bed was set in an antique iron frame and covered with pillows. Layla thought about how difficult it must have been to load his tent and belongings. He laid her on the bed, and she pulled him down with her and began to undress him.

"Layla, thank you."

"Thank you? Whatever for?"

"For being so gracious and love...," his words trailed off as she caressed him. In a state of ecstasy, he didn't utter another word; he just moaned with pleasure.

The two of them rested after a long sexual encounter. The General fired up his hookah and offered Layla one of the tubes. Not fond of getting high, she declined. Instead, she waited letting the effect of the smoke have its way with him before asking, "General, I have a favor to ask of you."

"Layla, at this moment you can ask me anything, and I am sure my answer will be yes."

She continued, "I met this former navy man, a scuba diver, and he taught me how to snorkel. He was inquiring about the different sites around Cairo, and I told him I had always wanted to visit the Pyramid at Hawara. I told him the rumors about secret passages and trap doors. He suggested we go exploring, and I told him it was impossible because the entrance was flooded. Thus my favor," she hesitated rolling over on top of him allowing her nipples to brush against the hair on his chest, "will you provide a military escort and let us dive down to the entrance?"

The General, feeling himself get hard again, sighed and said, "Sure, why not. I don't see what harm that would present. When do you want to go?"

"I don't know. How about later this week when the hunt is complete?"

"Consider it done. Now where were we?"

➤➤➤

Joseph saw Layla approaching in the jeep with the soldiers. When Layla saw him, she tapped the driver on the shoulder. "Slow down. There is my friend the General told you about."

The driver obliged, and soon Layla and Joseph passed through the checkpoint and headed toward the pyramid. Upon arrival, they donned their gear in preparation to dive while the two military escorts fixated on Layla. Of course, she made sure to expose a portion of her breast as she placed the breather around her neck. She then asked one of the soldiers, "Dear, would one of you be so kind as to adjust this strap?" Almost tripping, he moved toward her, grabbed the dangling strap, and said, "*Al latul.* *"

Looking on, Joseph smiled and just shook his head.

Layla said, "Now, you two wait here and protect us. We don't want to emerge and find you missing."

One of the men responded, "The General gave us strict orders to protect you."

Joseph tied a rope around Layla's waist and secured the other end around his own. "Layla, I want you to grab my waist belt, but in case we get separated, just grab this rope and pull yourself to me."

The two of them entered the water and moved to the pyramid's edge, Joseph ran his hand along the side until he found the entrance. The pictures Chuck provided made it easy to locate the best point of entry, which was just above where they suspected the entrance to be. Running his hands around the perimeter of the entrance, he didn't find any kind of obstruction. "Good, I don't have to set a charge. Damn thing could have caused the whole pyramid to collapse and then where would we be"?

---

* Right away. (Arabic)

Keeping Layla close and his hand on the wall, they dove downward as they navigated the entrance. It was every bit of twenty meters when Joseph noticed the change in the water above; it was clear. He knew this meant they had entered some type of cavity and could surface. Tightening his grip on Layla's arm, he motioned for her to swim upward. They surfaced above the water line to find themselves inside what appeared to be a hallway of sorts.

Joseph surveyed the interior and noticed steps of stone along one side. He led Layla over to them, and there they climbed up out of the water. Layla pulled the breathing apparatus out of her mouth and the clip off her nose. Her breathing was heavy, and she sucked in as much outside air as she could. Joseph said, "Slow down. Breathe through your nose and out through your mouth." She did as he said, and soon her pulse slowed and returned to normal.

"Joseph, I don't remember ever being so scared. I couldn't see a thing, and it is hard to breathe with this thing and the clip on my nose, not to mention the terrible briny taste of the water."

"Layla, look up. This must be the slab Chuck was talking about." Above them was a solid slab of stone, which appeared to be overlapping the sidewalls of the passage. "See if you can locate the opening."

Layla pointed up. "Is that it?"

"I don't know. Let's find out." The opening looked small, but it seemed large enough for a man to crawl through. Joseph helped her back into the water, and they made their way over to the opening, "Let me go first to see what I find, and then you can follow."

Joseph grabbed the rim of the opening, lifted himself up, and crawled through. Emerging on the other side, he found himself in what appeared to be another passageway full of water.

He yelled back at Layla, "The instructions said there are supposed to be two passages one to the north and one to the east. It looks like I'll have to swim underwater to enter." Untying the rope around his waist, he continued, "I want you to wait where you are while I go explore. We only have enough air in these canisters to stay under another eighteen minutes. Once I've located the east passage and see what we're facing, I'll come back for you."

"Okay, but don't be too long. This place is spooky," Layla said, shaking off the chill.

Joseph brought two additional canisters for their exit, but he was worried they might need them to find the tunnel. Removing the unit to preserve air, he secured it with the rope. Then holding his breath, he disappeared below the water line. He had no idea how far he would have to swim to find the well chamber; the drawing had not been clear on this point. He was in need of air when he noticed a change in the water line above. Swimming as fast as he could, he surfaced inside the next chamber, gasping for air.

Taking out his flashlight, he reoriented himself, located the north wall, and looked for a drawing resembling a sphinx with the head of a lion. "How in the hell am I going to find the right one?" he asked aloud. "There must be a hundred all the same."

The builders in an attempt to thwart would be robbers had duplicated the drawings. He hit every eye in hopes of getting lucky, and after about ten minutes felt a movement. Pressing harder on the stone, he heard a grinding sound like rock moving against rock and what he assumed was sand flowing from behind the wall. If he hadn't been looking, he would have missed it. The wall shifted down and back to expose a slight fracture. Joseph wasn't sure he could make it through the opening.

He thought it best to go back and get Layla before making the next move. Retracing his moves, he slipped underwater and swam back. He crawled back through the opening and Layla gasped, "Joseph! You scared me to death! Where have you been? I thought something had gone wrong!"

"I found the entrance to the tunnel. Come on, let's move."

Joseph tied the rope back around his waist and strapped on his breathing unit. He then took Layla by the arm and lifted her up through the opening. After climbing through, he said, "Hold on to my belt. We have about thirty meters to swim before reaching the next chamber. Where is your nose clip?"

"Here in my hand."

"Put it back on and remember, breathe slowly."

He pulled her down with him, and they headed to the next chamber. Surfacing, they paddled to where Joseph had found the opening, "Joseph, it is awfully small. What happens if you can't get through?"

Joseph said, "I'll make it one way or another, even if I have to set a charge and force my way through. We didn't come this far to be denied."

Stripping off his gear and securing it with the rope, he said, "Once I make it through, hand me the gear and then take yours off and hand it to me. Keep the rope around your waist I want to make sure we stay attached. Do you understand?"

"Yes."

Joseph held his breath and drew in his stomach as far as he could and began to push through the opening. It was a tight fit, but to his surprise he made it. Layla handed him the gear and followed his lead. Soon he was shinning the light into what appeared to be a tunnel with no end. Looking up he saw a torch resting in a wooden bracket attached to the wall. There was dark gauze wrapped around the top, which upon closer inspection seemed to be soaked in an oily substance.

Pulling out a packet of matches from an airtight pouch, he said, "Layla I am going to attempt to light one of these torches, so I want you to stand back. There is no telling what might happen after all these years."

Joseph scratched the match across the rough surface until it ignited. Holding the torch as far from his body as possible, he touched the flame to the gauze. The flimsy material burst into flames and then ebbed to a soft glow emanating warmth and plenty of light.

"You ready for an adventure?" he asked after taking a deep breath.

She laughed and said, "Honey, I was born for adventure."

Returning the laugh, he checked the time on his watch and said, "Then let's be on our way."

Occasional dirt fell from the ceiling causing them to quicken their step. Joseph remained alert in case they encountered obstacles along the way. Up ahead, he saw what looked like a dead end. "Layla, we're there. Look for a drawing of an eye similar to the one you wear around your neck. The instructions say it is called the *Eye of Horus*."

"What did you say?"

"I said look for a drawing of an eye similar to the one you own."

"Joseph, the presence of an *evil eye* is not good. We could be walking into a trap? I've seen evil before, and it scares me. What if the artifacts are being guarded by the devil himself?" She said reaching for the pendant around her neck before realizing it was the first time she had taken it off.

"Layla, calm down. We don't have time for theatrics. There is no such thing as devil hoaxes. Besides, I don't believe in that crap."

"Well I do," Layla wasn't taking any chances. "If it's all the same to you, I'd rather not look. You find it, and I'll be right behind you."

"Whatever," Joseph said swinging the torch from side to side. The wall was laden with hieroglyphics. Then he saw it, an eerily penetrating eye. As he drew near to get a better look, the eye seemed to follow his movement. He couldn't help thinking, "Okay, it's just a drawing. There is nothing evil about it." However, as he reached out to touch it, a puff of wind blew across his face and snuffed out the torch.

"See, I told you, Joseph. The eye is not to be disturbed."

Joseph brought out his flashlight and scanned the tunnel. In the top corner, he noticed a crack and reaching up with his hand he said, "I feel cold air. There must be another chamber behind this wall."

To keep Layla from losing her mind, he decided not to share the part about backing off and staring at the eye. He followed the instructions and sure enough, the eye began to glow. Layla screamed. "Oh shit, Joseph. Look at that! I'm getting the hell out of here. That's proof what I say is true. The eye is cursed."

"Calm down. That was supposed to happen," He said, resting his hand on her arm.

The eye started to move, eliciting another response from Layla. "Joseph what the..."

"Don't worry; it's okay. Move back. We need to wait for it to stop and lock in place. It's the next step I'm not too sure about."

"What do you mean by that?"

"The instructions were somewhat vague," he said with a smile.

"Oh that's just great, Joseph."

Her manner caused him to laugh. "Just do as I say, and we'll be fine."

When the eye locked in place, Joseph instructed, "I'm going to push it back in and turn it. I want you to get on your knees and bow down."

"Do what?"

"Layla, just trust me, okay?"

"If you say so, but this whole thing seems suspect to me. How do we know the damn walls won't cave in on us?"

"Are you ready?" he asked reaching out toward the eye.

"No, but I guess I don't have a say in the matter."

Joseph pushed the eye and turned it. They both dropped to their knees just in time. Above the eye, a stone shot out from the wall. Joseph looked at Layla and said, "I guess whoever penned the instructions didn't think it was important to tell us about that feature."

Shaking his head, Joseph rose up and looked through the opening. It was too dark to see anything. Looking over to Layla, he said, "There's supposed to be a lever inside. We pull it, and the wall opens. I don't think I can get my hand through there. Why don't you have a go at it?"

"Joseph, I'm not about to stick my hand in that hole," she said with a look that could kill.

"Oh, all right, I'll do it."

He put his hand through the opening and felt around for the lever. Feeling something he grabbed it and pulled it out – it was a snake. Layla jumped so high she almost hit the ceiling. Joseph acted fast, snapping its head, and hurling it to the ground. Both of them heard their heartbeats echoing in the tunnel.

Shivering, Layla asked, "Did it bite you?"

"I don't think so," Joseph said looking at his hand, which was shaking. He then looked up at her and said with a grin, "Your turn."

"I'll leave before I stick my hand in that hole."

Joseph started laughing while taking out another match. He relit the torch and once again it roared to life. Both of them looked up at the crack, anticipating another breeze. When nothing happened, Joseph waved the torch in front of the hole in hopes of scaring any other vipers lurking inside. With apprehension, he reached in and located the lever. As he pulled the wall began to rotate. Once it stopped, he let off the lever in hopes it would hold.

Looking at Layla, Joseph said, "Ladies first."

"Joseph, I'm warning you."

Once through the opening, they froze, awestruck at the sight. Before them was an exceptional structure with ornate columns on either side of what appeared to be a long hall. Drawings adorned the walls between each column. Then the ground began to shake, causing Layla to scream and grab Joseph's arm. The floor shifted backward about two meters, exposing an opening to what looked like a stairway leading into a dark pit. They looked at each other in disbelief.

"Layla, it's okay. You can let go." She was holding on so tightly that she was cutting off the circulation in his arm. "Oh, I'm sorry, Joseph. This is unbelievable. Is that the secret mine?"

"This is where it gets hairy," he said, handing her the paper he had taken from his pouch, "Layla, here are the instructions. I need you to talk me through this next part." He looked over and said, "I am assuming you would rather wait here while I walk down and explore."

"You would be right," she said punching him in the stomach.

"Ouch, that hurt."

He took out the camera and took pictures in every direction while she read through the instructions. When she finished, she looked up. "Joseph, you've got to be kidding. How are you going to pull this off?"

"I don't know, but I think I'm going to need both hands for this part," he said stripping off all his gear. He secured the camera and flashlight to the front of his trunks in preparation for his journey. When he stepped down and placed both feet on the first platform, a sharp spear shot out from his left, slightly piercing the skin on the back of his left leg.

He looked back at Layla, who was frozen in place, and said, "Read the instructions. We must have missed something."

She reread, "Step in the middle of each platform, pausing before taking the next step. That's all it says."

Joseph looked down, and sure enough his left foot was a slightly off center. He felt the blood trickle down the back of his leg.

He sighed. "Great, now I understand the drawings. Sure would have been nice if they would have gone into more detail. Wish me luck. Here I go."

He jumped down about a half meter to the next platform, making sure to land with both feet in the middle. At that exact moment, three spears flew out from the sides all round him, just missing his backside, knees, and ankles.

"Woe, Layla, check this out. How am I supposed to take the next step pinned in? The Russian must have screwed up deciphering this portion of the document."

No sooner had he finished the sentence than the spears sprang back into place. All he could manage to say was, "No way." Then taking a deep breath, he said, "How did they do that?"

"Joseph, do be careful."

"Thanks for the warning."

With apprehension, he took the next step and froze. Just as before, three spears shot out and surrounded him. More spears shot out as he descended until he reached the last step. He started to jump, but something inside told him to stop.

"Read the next part," he said looking up.

"When you reach the bottom, beware of the shifting sand. Remain in place until all threat has passed before proceeding."

He made his descent to the final step, placing both feet in the middle. He froze expecting more spears; however, this time the step began moving downward. Joseph pulled out his flashlight, flipped it on, and looked around. He didn't believe what he was seeing. The walls were moving as sand flowed from top to bottom to reveal veins of gold. In front of him was an expanse with several openings leading to what appeared to be tunnels. A Pharaoh's gallery of antiquities was all around.

He yelled out, "Layla, you should see this!"

Layla lowered her upper torso into the opening, "Joseph, its dark I can't see a thing."

"Layla, what's next?"

Reading she yelled down, "Once inside, you will see antiquities all around. There will be an alabaster vessel off to the side, and it will contain the ancient scroll. Choose the scroll inscribed with hieratics and a wax seal with the King's insignia."

Looking around he located a massive alabaster pot to his right, "I see the pot. Hope there aren't any more snakes!"

Peering inside, Joseph saw what they had come for. Tied with a gold band, the scroll had elaborate drawings etched on the outer cover. Upon closer inspection, he noticed several precious stones surrounding a wax seal with an impression in the middle.

Nervous, he reached down thinking it might be booby-trapped. When he pulled it from its resting place and nothing happened, he breathed a sigh of relief before yelling, "Layla, I have the document! What's next?"

Layla called out, "Upon your return do not tarry; temptation will be your downfall."

Placing the scroll inside his shirt, he moved back toward the stairway. It was then he felt something pulling him into one of the tunnels and heard an inner voice whispering, "Come to me and I will make you rich beyond your wildest dreams. You will be more famous than the King."

He followed the voice in a trancelike state until Layla yelled again, "Do not tarry; temptation will be your downfall." She had felt a sudden need to repeat the instruction.

Her voice echoed off the walls, breaking the trance. Shaking his head from side to side, Joseph's thinking cleared. The temptation was strong, but resisting, he jumped up and landed in the middle of the first platform. He continued as fast as he could. As his weight lifted the platforms turned to sand.

By the time he reached the top, he was exhausted and started to lose his balance. Feeling he was going to fall, he sprang upward with all his might and grabbed the edge with both hands. The final platform reduced to sand dropping into the cavity below leaving his legs dangling over the expanse. Layla reached out offering her hand.

"I can't let go, or I will fall!" he yelled.

It took every ounce of his strength, but he was able to pull up and rest his waist on the rim of the opening. The veins in his arms stretched against the skin, and his muscles bulged as if ready to explode. Layla reached down, grabbed his shorts, and began to pull. He took a deep breath and pulled himself up and over the edge.

Rolling over on his back, Joseph felt his heart pounding within his chest. Layla placed her hand on his chest in an attempt to calm him. Her tender skin worked its magic, and his breathing began to slow. He pulled her toward him, and they embraced.

Joseph looked deep into her eyes and said, "Layla, we did it. We got the document. You know what else? I've fallen in love with you."

Before he could say another word, Layla brought her lips down on his. He moved his hands down and slipped them under her swimsuit. Her small bottom was tender to his touch. They made love in the labyrinth, their passion echoing through the halls.

Collapsing in each other's arms, Layla said, "I bet that was a first."

Joseph laughed. "Yeah, Amenemhat is rolling over in his tomb at this very minute."

Layla laughed too and added, "He's smiling, thinking what an afterlife!"

Enjoying the moment they lingered a while longer in a tight embrace. Feeling Joseph's strong arms around her provided a sense of peace.

"We better get back. We don't want them to come looking for us," Joseph said breaking the silence.

The guards had been the furthest thing from her mind. She responded, "Yes, as much as I hate for this moment pass."

Joseph rose up, offered her a hand, and pulled her up. They donned their suits and gear.

"Layla, that's impossible," Joseph said looking down at the opening.

"What's impossible?"

Joseph pointed, and Layla gasped, "No way, how did that happen?"

"I have no idea," he said, staring at the steps, which had reappeared.

"This place is eerie. Can we get out of here?" Layla said, clutching his arm.

Joseph pushed the lever and replaced the stone. To their surprise, the ground began to shake as the wall rotated back.

"Let's go," Joseph said after making sure everything was in place.

Upon reaching the end of the tunnel, he unscrewed the cap to his return air canister. It was a tight fit, but he was able to slip the rolled document inside. He placed the canister into the pouch in his breathing bag, inserted the small tube, and siphoned the air to create a watertight seal. Lastly he pinched the end of the tube, confident the document was secure.

Tying the line around each of their waists, he reviewed their exit plan, "Layla, when we emerge you know what to do, right?"

"I'll flirt with the soldiers to divert their attention long enough for you to secure the equipment."

"Great. If everything works as planned, we should be back in Cairo by nightfall."

Joseph checked their equipment and asked if she were ready. Layla placed the clip on her nose and nodded. They lowered themselves into the water and made their way across the expanse of the room. Reaching the far wall, Joseph broke the surface and took in fresh air. He pulled Layla by the arm up beside him.

"Are you ready to go back under?" he asked after catching his breath.

"As I will ever be," she said in a nasal tone.

Joseph held his breath, took hold of her arm, and down they went. He ran his free hand along the wall to navigate the tunnel. Reaching the end, he noticed the change in the water line above. Once again they surfaced, allowing Joseph to take a breath and regain his bearings.

With their heads above the water line, they paddled across the room until they were over the spot where the entrance should be.

"Okay, this time I'll need to move fast in order to make it out with the air in my lungs. I am going to untie the rope, but hold on to it until we reach the surface. If you have any trouble, remember how I taught you to release the air valve which will aid in your ascent."

"I remember, and Joseph..."

"Yes, baby, what is it?" Joseph said untying the rope.

"I love you too."

He leaned over and kissed her. "Let's do this."

Joseph broke the surface first, startling the two guards.

Then Layla's blonde head bobbed up out of the water. Once on land she quickly removed her breathing apparatus and shook her hair from side to side. The soldier's eyes shifted from Joseph to Layla.

"Layla, let me loosen the strap on your rebreather," Joseph said making sure the soldiers had a good view.

"Yes, please do. This bulky thing is much too heavy, and the strap is cutting my circulation."

The strap she was referring to was at the bottom of the breathing bag and ran between her legs up her bottom to the back of the unit. Joseph loosened the strap and Layla pulled it through her crotch while letting her bra strap slip to expose a portion of her breast.

The diversion gave Joseph enough time to remove the canister and place it in his bag. Then he handed his apparatus to Layla.

"Please put these in that canvas bag," she said holding out both units.

"*Aiwa ya siti,**" the soldier said nervously.

With everything secure, they climbed into the jeep and headed toward Cairo. Sitting in the back Joseph put his arm around Layla and said, "Now it's just a matter of time."

❥❥❥

"Chuck, I'm worried sick," Mona said.

"What's wrong?"

"You know good and well what's wrong. I hope nothing has happened. They were due back hours ago."

"Joseph can handle himself. I'm sure everything is fine."

"Easy for you to say. Flying in those bombers, you are used to sitting around waiting for the action. Not so with me," Mona said heading for the kitchen.

"Mona, you worry too much. If I know those two, they stopped off somewhere and went dancing." No sooner had the words rolled off Chuck's lips, before there was a knock at the door. Chuck yelled out, "I'll get it. That could be them."

The front door had a small peephole which allowed Chuck to see who was at the door. Placing his finger over the opening, Joseph yelled, "Chuck, open the damn door before I huff and puff and blow the damn thing down."

"May I help you?" Chuck said laughing as he opened the door.

"You sure the hell can. I need to pee. I'm about to burst." Joseph shot past Chuck on the way to the toilet.

After Layla entered, Chuck looked out in both directions surveying the street and surrounding area for anything suspicious.

"Chuck, you wouldn't believe what we've been through. For a while there, we thought our game was up. I'll wait for Joseph to give you the details."

---

*   Yes, madame. (Arabic)

Mona entered and ran across the room arms outstretched. "I've been worried. You don't know how good it is to see you."

Joseph emerged smiling from ear to ear. "Joseph, be careful or your mouth is going to be like that Joker in the Batman comics," Chuck said.

They all laughed at Joseph's expense. In a more serious tone, Mona spoke up. "Okay, you two, I'm going crazy here. What happened?"

"Everything went smoothly. Chuck, to my surprise, the entrance wasn't obstructed. I mean there was some minor debris, but nothing major. It was right where we thought."

"God, I bet you were happy. I was worried about you setting a charge."

"To tell the truth, I was too. Once we were inside, we followed the instructions and navigated the interior until we located the wall with the Sphinx image, or more accurately, images. The damn wall was full of them. I hit all of the eyes until I found the right one, and sure enough the floor and wall moved exposing a small opening. If you didn't look close, you wouldn't know it was there, a strange sort of phenomenon. That took us into the tunnel where we found a torch on the wall.

"You gotta be kidding," Chuck said. "That's amazing."

"Yeah, I thought so, and the top of the torch was wrapped with some sort of gauze soaked in oil."

"Would you two quit jabbering and let Joseph get on with the story," Mona said giving Chuck a hostile look.

"We followed the instructions and encountered a few problems," Joseph said looking over at Layla before finishing his sentence, "but nothing the two of us couldn't handle."

Layla just smiled and shook her head.

"Chuck, the labyrinth is not only real, but intact. It was as if someone sealed it up years ago and left. Of course, I found out about those damn spears. About took my leg off," he said pointing to the dried blood on his leg. "Guess I ought to clean that before gangrene sets in."

"Let me take a look, Joseph. Why didn't you say something earlier?" Mona disappeared into the kitchen. When she returned, she was carrying hot water and some bandages.

"Once I made it to the bottom, I couldn't believe what I was seeing: veins of gold running in a vertical path down the walls and antiquities all around. I located the document and got the hell out of there."

Excited, Layla interrupted. "On the way back, there were military transports everywhere. They had a road block set up on the outskirts of Cairo and were stopping everyone. The guys we were with weren't too happy about it and didn't plan to stop."

Joseph said, "That went over well. The guards drew their weapons and started yelling and one of our men charged his weapon. I thought we were done for."

Layla said, "Mona, I was thinking that I had almost drowned swimming inside the pyramid. I made it out alive and was about to be shot by some overzealous soldier." Layla leaned back and crossed her arms. "You know what I mean, don't you, how many times have you been threatened?"

Mona laughed and nodded. "Just another day in Egypt," she said.

"Our driver called out that they were under strict orders from General Rahman and weren't stopping for anyone. At the mention of the General's name, the guards didn't move or say another word, which our guy saw as a green light. Our other guy was yelling something into his radio. With the roar of the engine and the wind, I couldn't make out what he was saying, but it was clear that something was going down, and he didn't give a damn about us from that point on.

"I knew we needed to bail, so I told them our destination was just up ahead. They pulled over and were more than happy to let us out. We found the vehicle you left and had a hell of time getting back, but Chuck we got the damn thing; our plan worked," Joseph said as he opened the seal on the rebreather and pulled out the canister.

CHAPTER TWELVE

CHUCK ENTERED THE ROOM where Joseph and Jonathan were waiting to discuss possible options for setting up the exchange with Farouk. Several months had passed since the extraction, and the vehement atmosphere had settled from a political perspective.

"I got a call from Robert Davidson this morning, one of our C-47 pilots. He's been having trouble with one of our planes. It's scheduled for an overhaul at the airport in Geneva, Switzerland, the first of March. I think it might be a great cover for setting up a meeting with Farouk's people. We aren't required to go through customs, so there shouldn't be an issue transporting the document. What do you all think?"

"Chuck, that's perfect, I'd feel better about meeting there versus Rome." Joseph looked over at Jonathan. "What do you think?"

"Isn't there an auto show in Geneva around that time?"

"Jonathan's right. It's one of the biggest shows in the world, and you know how Farouk likes his cars. Geneva would be perfect."

Chuck nodded in agreement. "Good, it's settled. We'll get word to Farouk's people and let them know. Jonathan, will you make the necessary arrangements and coordinate with our people at the Geneva Airport?"

"You got it, boss. Not a problem."

Knowing, he was losing control of his pet project, Farouk had been anxious. Before fleeing Egypt, he sent word to Chuck saying he would be staying at the Excelsior Hotel in Rome. It hadn't come as a surprise to Chuck, knowing Farouk's taste for the most expensive accommodations. The hotel was nick-named the *Magnificent White Palace* and was located on the famous Via Veneto. It was considered a legend, hosting most of the world's celebrities, politicians, and world leaders since its beginning in 1906.

Chuck sent a simple cablegram to Farouk's attention at the Excelsior.

> *Traveling to Geneva the first part of March for routine aircraft maintenance. Will be spending a few days and plan to take in the annual auto show. Let me know if you can make it. Hope to see you soon.*
> *CH*

It had been a month since Chuck sent the cable and there had been no response until one day Jonathan walked into his office holding an envelope.

"I think this might be what we have been waiting for," Jonathan said, eager to know the contents. Chuck ripped it open and read.

> *"Your information was welcome news. I plan to attend the show in Geneva and will be arriving on the 10th of March. Will be staying at the Beau Rivage. Please forward information where to meet."*
> *AP*

The Beau-Rivage Hotel, built in 1865 by the Mayer family, was located on Quai du Mont Blanc 13, one of the most prestigious addresses in Geneva. It was quaint and luxurious with 90 rooms, each with a picturesque view of the Alps.

It was the 20th of February when Chuck sent another wire, careful not to reveal the nature of their meeting. At this late date, he knew there wouldn't be time for return correspondence.

Flying out on March 11. Will arrive sometime in Geneva around 10 in the morning. Scheduled maintenance will take several days, so I will be staying at the Bristol Hotel on Rue Du Mont Blanc. Have been missing the sweet Ile flottante et sa crème anglaise made famous at the Brasserie Restaurant de l'Hotel de Ville 19, Grand-Rue. Please join me around 6 in the evening I'll be sitting on the patio enjoying the sunset. See you soon.
CH

"Chuck, how is this going to play out?" Joseph asked.

"You and I will meet Pulli at the café and set up a time to make the exchange. Now that Farouk is out of Egypt, I hear the Saudis have been taking care of him. He has everyone convinced he is hurting for cash. My sources tell me Pulli has been traveling regularly to Switzerland on Farouk's behalf and depositing money. They also learned Pulli covered himself when setting up the accounts by requiring two signatures on all withdrawals. I think Farouk is playing the Saudis until it is safe to access the accounts."

"I didn't think Pulli was that smart." Joseph said.

"I'm sure it put a slight strain on their relationship. Hell, I don't blame him. After all, everything he owns is in Egypt, and he can kiss that goodbye."

Joseph questioned, "What about the missing gold? People at the docks said Farouk loaded several cases of ammunition. Later Rahman's people suspected they were full of gold bars from the treasury."

"For our sake, I'm hoping they are right. Rumor has it he told the Saudis he left the gold, and since they don't trust Rahman or Nasser, they believed him. They figured Rahman used it as a smoke screen so he could steal the gold for his own purposes. One thing

Farouk's Stewards

is sure, he needs the document as leverage, and he knows the only way he is going to get it is to honor his commitment to us. I'm sure the fat bastard is not hurting for cash, but unlike the Saudis I don't trust him."

"I'll second that!"

"I'll be damned if we are going to give him the original, so I'm having a fake document made," Chuck said. He intended all along to see that the document would be placed in the right hands at the appropriate time, but until such time he wasn't taking any chances.

"Good, we need to screw that bastard before he screws us."

Chuck started laughing and looked over at Joseph. "If it's just the same to you, that would be one sight I would rather not visualize."

"Don't worry, I'll shoot him first."

"You better bring a powerful gun. I hear he has put on more weight." Chuck changed the subject. "After we get our hands on the money, it will be a challenge to get out of the country. Once we are on that plane, I'm not too worried; we have diplomatic immunity. When we return to Cairo, we'll need to lay low until plenty of time has passed.

"During that time we will need to come up with a plan to determine the best way to cut a deal with whoever is in power. Once we reveal the entrance to the labyrinth and ancient mine, we should be home free. If all goes as planned, we will all ride off into the sunset never to be seen again in Egypt." Joseph and Chuck smiled at each other imagining themselves as participants in the storybook ending Chuck portrayed.

➤➤➤

Farouk's stewards, Ahmed Ali and Abdul Metaal, were standing in their usual positions listening as the King carried on a conversation with himself.

Swirling the wine in his glass, Farouk rambled, "That scum Rahman. Once I return to power, he can kiss his Egyptian ass goodbye. I am not going to hang out here in Rome when the Geneva Auto Show is on. After all, that's where Narriman took refuge. Maybe I can convince her to return. Don't get me wrong. I have no intention of crawling back to her, but I will consider a request on her part. I'm sure she will come around in time. After all, she has gotten used to the lifestyle." Looking back at Abdul, Farouk said, "Ali, secure rooms for us at the Beau-Rivage."

"Yes, your Majesty."

With Farouk's uncanny affinity for automobiles, no one would suspect his arrival at the show, thus providing the cover he desired. He had withheld knowledge of the operation from his staff with the exception of Abdul, who along with Pulli, was to handle the details. He felt the fewer who knew about their plan the better. Silently, Farouk was thinking, "With the document, surely I can convince my queen to return, and the people of Egypt will once again be endeared to me."

The people in Egypt considered Queen Narriman the "Cinderella of the Nile." She had been raised in a middle class home and was chosen by Farouk to garner public opinion in favor of the monarchy.

She often reflected at the mistake she made in breaking off her engagement to Zaki Hashem, who at the time was in the doctorate program at Harvard. Farouk had been quite the charmer and had wooed her away from Hashem. Once the engagement to Zaki was broken, she was sent to Rome to begin an intense royal preparatory program prior to becoming queen. She learned multiple languages and become an expert in Egyptian history and etiquette. Farouk had her lose weight, stipulating she could weigh no more than one hundred and ten pounds for the wedding.

She was a mere seventeen in 1951 when they married. At the time, the wedding invitation was the most coveted invitation in the world. Leaders, dignitaries, and celebrities attended, lavishing the couple with expensive gifts. Her bridal gown was adorned with diamonds, and no expense was spared. The following year Queen Narriman gave Farouk the son he desired.

Rumor had it Narriman was having an affair with Farouk's personal physician, Dr. Adham al-Nakib from Alexandria. Farouk was not moved by the rumors, thinking that she still loved him and would come running back if he were allowed to return to Egypt with honor. He was determined to win back her affection.

~~~

The setting for the auto show in 1953 was spectacular; the hall was adorned with expensive decorations. In attendance were CEO's from several major auto companies: Ferrari, Lamborghini, Fiat, and Mercedes-Benz, to name a few. The organizers planned technical presentations and a vibrant light show and constructed a test track through the streets of Geneva. Locals and visitors could be heard cheering as the cars roared past them, winding through the cobblestone streets.

Chuck and Joseph sat under the awning enjoying a beverage and watching the cars. The Brasserie Restaurant was located in a busy area of Geneva. The establishment dated back to 1764 and had a reputation for keeping everything the same. The owners of the establishment frowned at anyone who didn't conduct himself or herself in the appropriate manner and had no patience for those lacking knowledge of the dining rituals common to all upscale brasseries in Geneva. The menu was simple but sophisticated offering filets of freshwater lake perch *meunière* or the long time favorite, *longeole du val d'Arve*, Geneva-style sausages flavored with cumin. Chuck felt it was a perfect place for their initial meeting with Pulli.

Queen Narriman

Pulli was due to arrive at any moment. Neither Chuck nor Joseph had any idea how the current scenario was going to play out. One thing was for sure, they were nervous about passing off a fake. A friend of Chuck who worked for a museum in Paris had manufactured the document basing it on the Rhind Mathematical Papyrus and sent it to him in a diplomatic pouch. Like the original, they sealed it, to disguise the contents further. How Farouk intended to authenticate the document was unknown to them so the final stage of the plan hung in the balance.

King Farouk and Queen Narriman – Wedding Picture

With the Saudis providing support and his entourage still loyal, Chuck and Joseph could have their hands full. Jonathan and Joseph drafted a plan that Chuck had agreed to. There was a cable car leading up *The Salève,* known as the Genevans' Mountain, which peaked at about 4,000 feet. They agreed it would make a good place for the exchange because they could monitor who was coming and going. With the autos racing through the streets, it would be difficult to make it to the airport in a hurry, so Chuck arranged for a helicopter to ferry them. Chuck contacted Dan Harding and let him know they were planning a rendezvous with some unsavory sorts and could use a little assistance. Dan agreed without question.

Pulli showed up on time and without saying hello asked, "Where is the document?"

Chuck shrugged his shoulders, "I told you we would arrange a place to make the exchange. We don't have the document on us; however, I do have a photograph."

"Very well, let's see it."

Chuck pulled the photo out of the manila envelope and pushed it across the table.

"Where and when do you want to make the exchange?" Pulli asked as he picked it up.

Joseph leaned forward and rested his hands on the table, "Tomorrow 6 p.m., at the top of the *Le Salève* Mountain. If we suspect any foul play, the deal is off."

"Why on top of a mountain?" Pulli asked with a quizzical look.

"Gives us a better vantage to see who's with you and what you are carrying. If your intentions are what you say they are, it shouldn't be a problem. By the way, the road will be blocked so the cable car will be the only route to the top."

Jonathan had been instructed to create a diversion that would block the only road leading to the top for a couple of hours. They weren't taking any chances.

Pulli tilted his head. "You do know the mountain is in Pas-de-l'Échelle, France, so we must pass through customs to reach the cable car?"

Joseph leaned back in his chair. "Yes, we are well aware of that fact and believe neither of us would be stupid enough to sneak weapons past a customs check point. Not that you plan to carry your weapon, you know, like the one strapped on the inside of your left pant leg."

Pulli smiled. "You think you are very clever. Why not just meet at your hotel and make a quick exchange and that will be the end of it?"

Chuck looked him in the eye. "If it is all the same to you, Pulli, we prefer to handle it our way. Either you meet us on top of the mountain or kiss the document goodbye. It's up to you."

◥ ◥ ◥

The day before, Chuck and Joseph had taken the cable car to the top of the mountain and decided on the best place to meet. Jonathan positioned himself below so he could see everyone getting on and off the trolley. They tested the two-way radio making sure they could coordinate their efforts.

"Joseph, I have a strange feeling in my gut that Farouk isn't going to make the exchange easy," Chuck said as they made their way down the mountain.

Joseph placed a hand on Chuck's shoulder. "We've got a solid plan now. All we have to do is execute."

Chuck looked down at the sailboats floating on Lake Geneva and over at the Alps awash in color from the afternoon sun. "I guess you're right, I'll be glad when this is over, and we are on the way back to Cairo. Wow, this view is breathtaking."

◥ ◥ ◥

The next day, Dan flew Chuck and Joseph to the top of *Le Salève* Mountain. After they landed and made it to the drop area, Joseph called Jonathan on the radio to make sure the connection was clear. Jonathan confirmed the road was blocked and said he was in position. Now, all they had to do was wait.

Soon a taxi pulled up to the border with two men in the back, Pulli and Abdul. Clearing the checkpoint, they approached the base of the mountain where the cable car was located. Pulli emerged carrying a black briefcase and began looking around. Satisfied the surrounding area was safe, he and Abdul boarded the car for the trip up the mountain. Once the car was in motion, Jonathan continued to scan the area for anyone or anything looking suspicious. Convinced everything was proceeding as planned, he radioed Joseph and gave him the green light.

"Pulli and Abdul just boarded with four others, a couple and their two children. Pulli is carrying a black briefcase. If you don't need anything else, I'm going to head for the airport and make sure the transport is ready for takeoff."

Joseph pushed the button on the side of his radio. "Looks like we have everything under control on this end. We'll see you back at the airport, over and out."

It was an ideal time of day with the sun shooting golden sparks over the water on Lake Geneva as it melted into the horizon. The two of them looked out from their perch but kept a keen eye on the car. Chuck had the same feeling in his gut he used to get when German fighters were approaching. He shook off the feeling, thinking it was just nerves.

Pulli exited the car first and saw Chuck and Joseph standing a good distance away from the platform. Chuck motioned him over.

"Chuck, something isn't right. I feel like we are being watched. Keep your guard up," Joseph whispered.

"Do you have the document?" Pulli asked in his usual arrogance.

"What do you think? I'm standing on top of a mountain in France for nothing?"

Pulli raised an eyebrow and with a slight smile said, "May I inspect it?"

"May I inspect the briefcase?" Chuck asked in return.

Chuck had the document in a leather case strapped over his shoulder. He pulled his arm free and laid the case on a small bench. In turn, Pulli motioned for Abdul to place the briefcase on the bench next to the case.

As Chuck bent down to open the case a shot rang out, and Joseph felt a stinging bolt hit him in the chest. Chuck turned to see Joseph falling backward, blood flowing from the front of his shirt. He reached out in an attempt to catch him. Joseph hit the ground with Chuck's arms around him. It seemed like an eternity, but Chuck gathered his thoughts, looked up, and scanned the area. Another bullet rang out and

1953 Geneve Auto Show Poster

hit the ground next to him. He rolled behind the bench and saw Pulli and Abdul running toward the platform. Pulli was clutching the leather case.

The sniper had hiked up the primary trail on the front of the mountain and taken up a position with a full view of the top. His instructions had been to shoot both men after the exchange. The wind was blowing much harder than expected which had affected his calculations. The first shot hit the mark, but he wasn't sure about the second. The target rolled to the side and was no longer visible. Concerned for his own safety, the sniper shouldered his weapon and headed back down the trail.

Knowing the general direction of the shot, Chuck attempted to locate the shooter. With no success, he looked back toward the platform where Pulli and Abdul were now boarding the car. Hitting the button on the radio, he yelled, "Jonathan? Jonathan?" Frustrated by the lack of response, he decided to move toward the rendezvous point. He grabbed Joseph's leg and pulled him behind the bench. It was a struggle, but he heaved his body up and across his shoulder. Waiting several minutes, he continued scanning the area before deciding it was safe to move. He came up over the rise to see Dan standing next to the chopper.

"What happened?" Dan yelled running toward him.

Chuck shifted Joseph's body and Dan helped get him in the chopper, "That bastard had a sniper keyed in on us."

Once airborn, Chuck sat motionless staring out at the Alps for several minutes. Then turning back to look at Joseph, he said, "What we are going to do with his body? I guess we better contact the authorities and file a report?"

Chuck was in a state of shock from the whole ordeal. An ambush was the last thing he would have expected. He silently wondered about Layla. It seemed every time she allowed herself to fall in love, something happened. Now it was murder.

Chuck slammed his hand against the door. "That bastard, Pulli. If I ever get my hands on him. The years Joseph served in the war and not a scratch. I get him involved in this mess and end up getting him killed."

"Chuck, don't beat yourself up, man. Doesn't sound like there was anything you could have done. By the looks of the wound, the shooter was a professional."

Chuck sighed. "We have to get word to Jonathan. Farouk could dispatch some men to the airport and be waiting for us. Can you call the tower on your radio?"

"I'm already dialing it in."

Thinking quickly Chuck added, "Report the murder and let them know to call the authorities. I want them waiting when we land. By us making contact, they won't suspect we have been involved in any foul play. We will implicate Farouk and Pulli."

Dan grabbed the mike attached to his headset and positioned it in front of his mouth. "Geneva Tower, this is chopper Delta 22516. We are five minutes out on a northeasterly heading with an urgent mayday. Do you read?"

There was a slight crackle and the tower responded, "That's affirmative, Delta 22516. What is your issue?"

"We have a man on board who has been shot by a sniper on top of Mont Le Salve. Assistance requested."

"Roger, Delta 16. Land on #9 tarmac, and we will dispatch an ambulance."

"I also need you to get word to the pilot of our C-47 transport Alpha 4739 to let them know they could be in danger. There is no way the shooter could make it to the airport, but we suspect he has accomplices."

"Hear you loud and clear. We will contact them and alert the authorities."

"Delta 22516 over and out."

Dan looked at Chuck noticing he had turned pale, "Chuck, everything will work out. With any luck, maybe the authorities will be able to round them up before they leave town."

Chuck looked down at Joseph's blood on his shirt. "I am sure they are long gone by now. Farouk will head back to Rome, but he's in for a big surprise."

"Yeah, why is that?"

"The document he stole was a fake."

Dan looked over at Chuck, "So you were both out to screw each other? Maybe you should have arranged for the sniper."

"Hindsight is 20/20, but I guess we aren't the murdering types. What gets me is how easy it was for them. We picked the place because it was open, and there was just one way up and one way down. It never occurred to us that the openness would put us at risk. I still can't believe Joseph is gone."

Nearing the airport, Dan saw the ambulance and patrol cars. Lights were flashing obstructing his view, but he was able to land. Flipping a few switches, he cut the engine, and the rotors wound down. The ground crew helped Chuck with Joseph's body, hoisting it onto a gurney.

"I'm afraid he is already dead," Chuck said breathing heavily.

Once they had Joseph's body secure, Chuck noticed a detective motioning him over. In the officer's best attempt at English, he asked, "Could I see your identification please?"

Chuck pulled out his wallet and handed his Embassy card and passport to the officer.

"Sir, tell me what happened to your friend."

"We went up the cable car to see the sights and were standing near a small bench. That's when he was hit and stumbled backward. Another shot was fired at my feet, so I jumped behind the bench for cover. Dan here planned to meet us up top and fly us around the area. I grabbed my friend and headed toward the chopper. We contacted the tower after lifting off."

"Do you have any idea who would try to kill your friend?"

"Yes sir. As you can see by my credentials, I am with the American Embassy in Cairo. We came to Geneva for routine maintenance. When King Farouk was forced to flee Egypt, he was upset because the United States declined his request to intercede. It's my belief, he and his henchman, Antonio Pulli, hired a sniper to take us out in retaliation."

"Why would they do that?"

"Pulli was upset when they were asked to leave the country. He called me at the Embassy ranting, saying the U.S. had abandoned Farouk. I didn't say much, but rubbed a bit of salt into his wounds by saying, 'Farouk brought it on himself by raping the country's women and stealing its gold.' I don't think he took too kindly to my comment. Before hanging up on me, he told me to watch my back."

The officer stopped writing. "Interesting, Farouk and his entourage were in town for the auto show. Several reporters were frustrated because they couldn't get an interview. The tower informed me they just took off for Rome about an hour ago."

Handing Chuck's documents back, the officer said, "So let me get this straight. You think King Farouk hired an assassin to kill your friend?"

Chuck looked down at the tarmac and nodded. "Yes I do, but I think it was me they were after. Joseph was just a Marine Guard. He hadn't worked for the Embassy long. I doubt they even knew who he was. Is there any way to contact the Roman authorities and have them picked up on arrival?"

"Please give me a few minutes to finish making out my report. We will do all we can, but I wouldn't expect too much. The Italians are not very cooperative."

"Take as long as you like. We're not in any hurry."

About that time, Jonathan came running up, "Chuck, are you okay?

Chuck's face reddened with ire. "Pulli and Farouk screwed us big time. Damn! I swear those bastards are going to pay if I have anything to say about it!"

Chuck stood looking out over the runway. He hadn't felt this way since his war days. When they returned from a mission and their adrenaline had settled, the reality of the fight hit. Most of the men drowned their emotions in a double shot of scotch at debriefing. Death did strange things to the mind, and some couldn't handle it. Chuck had always been able to shake it off by tapping into an inner strength. Now he was questioning whether there was any strength left to tap.

"Chuck, we need to get the hell out of here," Jonathan's voice broke his trance.

"Yeah, I know we're waiting on the authorities to clear us. Jonathan, I thought we had all the bases covered. I don't think I will ever get the image out of my mind. Everything happened in slow motion. I've dealt with death dozens of times before. Hell, during the war, guys were killed all around me. I saw things a man is not supposed to see.

Images that can haunt you for a lifetime, but Joseph, somehow it is different. It's the first time I feel responsible."

"Chuck, you know the drill. How many men have you consoled telling them it was not their fault? Not to take it personal. This is no different. You can honor Joseph in death by what you do going forward."

Chuck looked at Jonathan, thinking how young he was to have such a depth of knowledge. Then the thought, "Damn, we are all too young to have this depth of knowledge."

"You're right. We will honor him going forward, and I have an idea how to do it."

"That's the Chuck I know. Now get us cleared and let's get the bird in the air."

﹨﹨﹨

"I have this feeling deep down in inside that not all is well, and I don't like it," Layla said shifting in her seat.

"Look, there is no use worrying about what we can't control. The guys are smart. Let's hope for the best," Mona said in an attempt to restore confidence.

"I hope you are right. With all that has taken place these past few months Egypt will never be the same. If the climate of political unrest continues, we will have no choice but to leave."

"That would be just fine with me. I'm tired of all the fighting. I don't understand these idiots. They are destroying everything I love about Egypt."

With a blank stare, Layla said, "I can't go on living this lifestyle. Something has to give. I think it's about time to consider my own future, don't you think?"

﹨﹨﹨

A contentious rivalry was heating up between Nasser and General Rahman. In secret, Nasser had held talks with the British and had signed the Anglo-Egyptian Evacuation Treaty. The treaty provided the British twenty months to prepare for a complete evacuation. The Moslem Brotherhood headed by General Rahman found out and was furious. One of their members made an assassination attempt on Nasser, but the plot was discovered. Nasser used it as an opportunity to place Rahman under house arrest and strip him of all duties. Soon Nasser was named President and held all authority.

The Suez Canal was becoming a hot zone and President Eisenhower was threatening an invasion. Word arrived at the Embassy in Cairo that an evacuation was imminent. No one knew what the future of Egypt would be, but one thing was sure, it would no longer be referred to as the Paris of the Middle East.

Meanwhile, Chuck was agonizing over the news he was on the way to deliver. He had dealt with death, and relaying this kind of news was never easy. Joseph's murder was affecting him more than any other death he could remember. The flight back had been long and given Chuck plenty of time to plot how to get even with Farouk and Pulli. The first thing he did when they landed was find a secure phone and contact Nasser's office. Wondering if he would take his call, Chuck was surprised when the President came on the line, "Yes, this is President Nasser."

"Sir my name is Chuck Gaskin. I work for the American Embassy."

Nasser said, "I know who you are. I assume you are calling about the murder of your fellow employee. Before you go on, you should know there isn't anything I can do to help. Of course, I am sorry for your loss."

"Um…, Sir that's not the sole reason for my call. I have two important documents I think you would have an interest in obtaining."

"What documents would you have that would be of interest to me?" Nasser said in an arrogant tone.

"One has instructions how to find an ancient mine hidden in the labyrinth near Hawara Pyramid, and the other is an ancient papyrus we found inside the mine," Chuck said hoping his words had the desired effect.

"Interesting, and how did you happen to find these documents?" Nasser responded after a brief silence.

"King Farouk and his companion Pulli."

At this point, Chuck heard Nasser clear his throat before saying, "You have my attention. Go on."

"A now deceased archeologist approached Farouk about a find at one of their dig sites. It was a coded document which Farouk hoped would confirm a legend he had been told as a child. His great, great grandfather Pasha Muhammad Ali believed there was a hidden gold mine at Hawara.

"The legend was that Amenemhat III from the twelfth dynasty found the mine while building the pyramid and labyrinth. He also found an ancient papyrus rumored to contain the mystical powers of the ancient pyramids. In his later years, paranoid the document would be stolen, he hid it inside the mine for retrieval in the afterlife.

"Farouk was obsessed believing the information would somehow help him return to Egypt and restore his family to the throne."

Agitated Nasser said, "That son of a bitch is never returning to the throne in Egypt if I have anything to say about it, and right now I'm in charge."

"I share the same sentiment. After purchasing the document, he sent it to a scientist in Russia who was working on a super computer. He was successful in breaking the code and sent back a document containing instructions on how to find the mine. However, upon receipt Farouk had a problem; you had relegated him to his palace. After all the years searching, he found evidence supporting the legend, but he couldn't act on it."

Nasser spoke up, "So how did you get involved?"

"Before Farouk headed for Rome, he contacted a friend of mine saying he would pay a lot of money if he would help him extract the papyrus. My friend asked for my help, so we met with Farouk.

"It was our intention to turn the instructions over to the Egyptian authorities. However, with all the turmoil we weren't convinced who best to contact. Since he was willing to pay two hundred thousand pounds, we decided to go forward with the plan."

"So tell me more about this plan."

"We had a young lady trick General Rahman into allowing two of our team to access the pyramid after the duck hunt last year," Chuck hesitated and let this information sink in.

"That idiot couldn't secure his zipper. It's a known fact women have a hypnotic effect on him. Go on," Nasser said letting out a sigh.

"Armed with the instructions from the deciphered document, my team penetrated the pyramid at Hawara and made their way into the labyrinth where they found the ancient papyrus."

"You're telling me that the labyrinth exists?"

"That's correct, sir. The mine is full of antiquities; however, we removed just the papyrus, knowing what would happen if your authorities caught us, not to mention our own government. Afterward, I set up the meeting with Farouk's people in Geneva to make the exchange. That's when they double crossed us and shot my partner."

After pausing a few moments to let Chuck's words sink in, Nasser finally said, "So, let me get this straight. You steal one of our antiquities and attempt to sell it to Farouk for a tidy sum and you expect me to welcome you with open arms?"

Chuck responded with confidence, "Not quite, but close. We took a fake papyrus to the exchange. Like I said, our intention always was to hand over the instructions to the proper authorities. Our intention didn't change when we came into possession of the papyrus, but considering you and the General have been in a power struggle, we made the decision to wait and see who would be the victor, thus my call today."

Nasser said, "So how do I view this papyrus and determine its authenticity?"

"That leads to the main reason for my call. We could very well turn over the papyrus and be on our way, but then you wouldn't have an opportunity to implicate Farouk and Pulli in the murder of my associate."

"Go on."

"My sources say Farouk was incensed when he found out Pulli botched the exchange and brought him a worthless papyrus. It is my contention he would still like to get his hands on the original."

"So what do you propose?"

"I'm proposing a sting operation. We no longer have an interest in the money, but we want them held accountable for our man's death.

"I would like to set up a second meeting in Rome and plant a wire in order to get a confession. With the confession, they could be picked up, returned to Egypt, and tried for the murder. It would endear you to the United States, we would be vindicated, and you would be the one to announce to the world one of the greatest finds in Egypt's recent history."

"Interesting, continue."

"My team will assist me in setting up the meeting. I will have the original document in my possession. We will need to work out a signal so that once I have an adequate confession your people can be ready to move in and make the arrest."

Nasser responded, "I don't think the Italian authorities will be too accommodating. What do you think their reaction will be?"

"Given their response thus far, I don't believe they will offer any resistance. I know the Swiss will be delighted to close the case. You and your people will have a valid reason for the extradition so there's no need to worry about public sentiment. More important you will have the original document and Farouk's money."

Nasser pondered the proposal. "Let me give it some thought. Where can you be reached?"

"I might have jumped the gun in my assumption that you would have an interest. Please forgive me if I have over stepped my boundaries, but I'm preparing to leave within the hour and will be unavailable."

A long silence ensued, and Chuck began to think the connection had been lost when Nasser spoke, "Mr. Gaskin, I believe we can do business. I'll put you in touch with my people in Rome. I will give them instructions to cooperate in setting up the sting. If what you say is true, and you are able to accomplish the abduction, I would like to meet you."

"I'll be back at the Consulate afterward. I would enjoy that meeting."

"When should I tell my people in Rome to expect you?"

"With all the turmoil of late, I can't say for sure. It would be better if I contacted your Embassy when I arrive.

"Agreed, ask for Rajad. He will be the one to assist you and make sure everything is in place on our end. Mr. Gaskin, one more thing..."

"Sir?"

"Don't try to fool me; I am not Farouk!"

"Of course not. I'll look forward to our meeting when this is all over."

⟩⟩⟩

Chuck knew telling Layla was not going to be easy. He and Mona had been so excited that she and Joseph had hit it off. Joseph had been willing to accept her no questions asked. Now he didn't know how she might respond. He feared it might push her deeper into the lifestyle she longed to escape.

Mona and Layla had finished with their bridge game and were sitting down having a drink when Chuck walked in. "Mona, look Chuck's here!" Layla said, pointing toward the entrance.

Mona jumped up, ran over to him, and threw her arms around him. At once she sensed something was wrong. The waiter approached and asked, "Mr. Gaskin, would you like something to drink?"

Chuck glanced up at the waiter. "Yes, please bring me a double scotch straight up, any brand will do."

Layla turned toward Mona and gave her a questioning look. He wasn't a heavy drinker and seldom ordered a double of anything. Chuck pulled out a chair, sat down, and said, "I have some bad news."

Layla had a sinking feeling as his words lingered in her ears. With a hint of anxiety she said, "Chuck where is he...where is Joseph?"

The waiter interrupted setting the glass on the table and asked, "May I get you anything else?'

Mona said with anxiety in her voice, "No, we are fine. Chuck what is going on?"

Chuck picked up his drink and swirled the liquid. Looking over at Layla, he took a deep breath and said, "Joseph has been murdered."

Layla dropped her glass which shattered as she froze in a state of shock.

"What happened?" Mona said grabbing Chuck's arm as the room began to spin.

Chuck told them everything, and all the while Layla sat stone-faced not saying a word. The moisture was evident around the edges of her eyes. Mona put her arms around her, and Layla laid her head on her shoulder. She looked up at Chuck through her own tears.

He shrugged his shoulders, shook his head, and whispered to Mona, "There was nothing any of us could do."

Chuck took a big swig of his drink allowing the scotch to burn away the frustration he was feeling.

Layla straightened and said, "What are we going to do now?"

Chuck set his drink down and said, "Look, it's too soon for us to discuss the future. Why don't we take a couple of days to let the dust settle, and we can talk more?"

"Chuck, look at me," Layla said in a stern voice.

Chuck turned and looked her in the eyes, "Yes."

"Do I look like a woman who needs to wait a few days mourning like some housewife? No offense, Mona."

"None taken."

"No, far from it," Chuck said.

"Then let's talk about it right now and figure out what we can do to get back at those two."

Chuck pulled his seat closer to the girls and said, "The way I see it, we can sit back and let the authorities handle it, or we can take matters in our own hands."

Looking confused Layla said, "Do we know who did this?"

Chuck continued, "It would be impossible for us to determine who the shooter was. However, we know Farouk and Pulli were behind it. I've got a plan."

"Why does that not surprise me?" Mona said.

"Look, the Italian authorities have been alerted, but because Joseph's murder happened in Switzerland, they won't do much. We have to believe Farouk was upset when he found out the document was a fake. I intend to contact him and find out just how bad he wants the original. I'm guessing he will jump at the chance to set up a second meeting. However, this time things will be different."

Layla said, "What do you mean different? I thought we had a good plan the first time. What makes you think a second meeting would be any different?"

"If we can somehow expose Pulli and Farouk, there might be a chance to implicate them, so I contacted Nasser."

Layla almost fell out of her chair. "You called Nasser? What on earth for?" She shot Mona a look, and then they both turned back to Chuck awaiting his response.

"He knew about the murder and was quick to tell me there wasn't anything he could do."

Mona said, "So he must have known Joseph worked for the American Embassy."

"Yes, he did."

Chuck related his conversation with Nasser, and the ladies hung on every word.

Mona asked, "So is Nasser in support of the sting?"

"He agreed and is putting me in touch with his people in Rome to work out the details. After speaking with Nasser, I contacted an old acquaintance and asked him to get a feel for Farouk's routine in Rome.

Layla's thoughts drifted back in time. She remembered how jovial Farouk was around other people, always the comedian and the center of attention. She doubted he had changed much since his arrival in Rome.

"He should be easy to track considering he relishes the limelight," Layla said looking up.

Chuck responded, "I'm counting on it and have an idea how we can approach him without bringing attention or leaving a trail back to us. Assuming I am right, and Farouk still wants the document, he will agree to a meeting. Layla, it might take us a while, but we'll get them one way or another. If it's the last thing I do on this Earth, I pledge to you, they will pay for Joseph's death."

"I believe you, Chuck," Layla said allowing a faint smile to cross her lips.

Chuck took another sip of his drink, "We'll have a courier deliver a series of anonymous notes once we know his routine. The last message will instruct him where to meet for the exchange. We'll have him squirming."

Layla chimed in, "Won't Farouk try to catch the courier and attempt to find out where we are so he can come after us?"

"The courier won't know us or our whereabouts. I'm going to plant a wire at the meeting place. Nasser's people will be stationed nearby, and once I get the confession, they will close in and make the arrest. Farouk can't afford to do something stupid in public. The press would eat him alive."

"Chuck, you never cease to amaze me. I should have known you were up to something," Layla said, somewhat relieved.

Chuck leaned forward in his seat and lifted his glass, "Here's to Joseph."

CHAPTER THIRTEEN

THE KNOCK ON THE CABIN DOOR came again, only this time louder. Spence had risen from their berth to grab a towel that he was now wrapping around his waist.

Opening the door, he asked. "Yes, what can I do for you?"

"Sir, I was told to deliver this envelope to Miss Layla Donan," said the young ensign standing at attention.

"Thank you. I will give it to her."

"No sir. I was instructed to hand deliver it to Miss Donan."

"Sailor, I think it will be just fine if you give me the damn thing. She is unable to come to the door at this time."

"Sorry, sir. Orders from Ambassador Raymond Hare were specific on that point."

"Oh, very well, just a minute." Spence slammed the door in frustration and turned to face Layla standing behind him dressed. Taken back Spence said, "Ambassador Hare? What business do you have with him?"

"Spence, you're a dear, but I had better not keep the sailor waiting." Layla moved past Spence, opened the door, and stepped out on the deck.

The sailor, still standing at attention, was quick to eye her up and down as she moved closer and said, "Hello."

Blushing he said, "Ma'am I have an important correspondence from Ambassador Raymond Hare. My orders were to hand deliver this to you."

Thank you," Layla said taking the note from his hand.

As the sailor rotated on his heels and walked away, Layla wondered why she would be getting a message from the Ambassador. She turned to see Spence standing in the doorway.

"Are you going to just stand there or open the damn thing?"

Spence, I told you this is personal. Now be a dear and go back inside I will return soon to finish what we started."

Spence shrugged his shoulders and said, "You had better; otherwise, I might go crazy."

Layla turned and walked down the narrow deck toward Mona's room. She assumed it was from Chuck, but why it was addressed to her was anybody's guess. She would find out soon enough. With all they had been through, it was best for them to stick together. They were hoping their sources were correct, and Farouk was still in Rome; their plan depended on him being there. She knocked on Mona's door.

Opening the door, Mona said, "Layla, hey, come on in. Are you okay?"

"Yes, but a sailor brought me this envelope saying it was from Ambassador Hare. I thought it best to come down, and we could open it together."

Layla tore open the envelope and unfolded the letter. As she began to read she fell back onto the bunk.

"What is it? What does it say?" Mona said.

Layla looked up, tears forming in her eyes and read from the letter.

Miss Donan,

It is with great regret I wish to inform you of the death of our friend Chuck Gaskin. I am sending this via courier thinking it best if you break the news to his wife, Mona Gaskin. Local Egyptians stormed a restaurant night before last and threw Molotov cocktails setting the building on fire. Chuck and his associate from the Embassy, Jonathan Bartlet, helped everyone escape. When Chuck didn't emerge Jonathan and the others feared the worse. It is assumed he must have been trapped inside. Let Mrs. Gaskin know we are still investigating the incident. I will leave word at the Port Authorities office in Rome to help her contact our Embassy. They can help with final affairs. Please offer my condolences.

Sincerely,
Ambassador Raymond Hare

Shocked by the news, they both froze. Then Mona began sobbing. "Layla, what am I going to do? I can't believe it. Chuck can't be dead. No, no, no..." Layla wrapped her arms around Mona and didn't say a word.

Her mascara running down both cheeks, Mona looked up at Layla and repeated, "I can't believe it. Chuck can't be dead."

"Oh Mona, I am so sorry. I don't know what to say. Maybe once we get to Rome, we will know more."

The rest of the trip would be a blur to Mona. Layla asked if she could share her berth. She didn't think she could go back to Spence, not after what she had just read. She was not in a loving mood. They read and reread the letter, not believing what it said. Neither of them knew what to do. It was like being in a dream, but there was no waking from this dream.

Layla broke the silence. "After all we have been through, it is not fair that Chuck should die. Mona, it is my fault. It is that cursed eye; my whole life it has plagued me. I have worn this stupid amulet around my neck thinking it would protect me. First Joseph is murdered, and now Chuck is feared dead. I am beginning to think rather than protect me it has been the very thing cursing me. This damned thing has become a weight."

≻≻≻

After reaching Piraeus, Greece, the evacuees' journey had taken on a more pleasant atmosphere. The scenic beauty of the Greek Islands made the trip seem more like a pleasure cruise. Chuck received a final message from command confirming the success of the evacuation. It was from Exodus 3.8,

> *So I have come down to deliver them out of the hand of the Egyptians, and to bring them up from that land to a good and large land, to a land flowing with milk and honey, to the place of the Canaanites and the Hittites and the Amorites and the Perizzites and the Hivites and the Jebusites*

At this point Chuck and Jonathan were tired of being holed up at the Cecil. They heard it rumored there was a restaurant safe for Americans and other foreign nationals. They decided to take a chance and go out for dinner. Grabbing a booth near the rear of the restaurant, they relaxed and discussed their options. The news from Ambassador Raymond Hare that they were expected to remain at the Embassy until further notice came as a complete surprise. They had been excited about meeting the girls in Rome and executing the plan. Now they were perplexed about what to do.

Everything seemed so upside down. Even Chuck's calm demeanor was being threatened. "Jonathan, these Egyptians are crazy. Here we are stuck in the middle of this crap. I don't know about you, but I've just about had it. Home is looking good about now. I just hope they don't plan on keeping us here too long."

"I know, Chuck. Sometimes I wonder why I didn't just head home when I had the chan...."

Jonathan's words trailed off as the front glass shattered, and the floor burst into flames. People screamed as the fire began to spread. Their training kicking in, Jonathon and Chuck shot out of their chairs.

Chuck yelled, "You help the people in here! I'll get the people in the back!

Jonathan headed for the front of the restaurant yelling for everyone to get out. About that time, two more bottles came barreling through and exploded. There were about twenty people rushing for the door. Flames caught a woman's dress on fire. Jonathan grabbed a tablecloth, threw it around her, knocked her to the ground, and rolled her until the flame was extinguished. Helping her up, he pushed her toward the front door. About that time, the cooks and other attendants were right on his heels. Everyone ran into the street; they could hear the sirens as they approached.

People were screaming, and the scene was chaotic as Jonathan looked for Chuck. Then the building exploded and became a raging inferno. Chuck was nowhere to be found.

Believing Chuck had made it out, Jonathan continued his frantic search through the crowd. Running over to several people wearing aprons, he yelled, "Did you see an American?

One of them spoke first. "Some guy rushed into the kitchen yelling fire, grabbed the mop hose, and started spraying us down. He said we needed to head toward the front as soon as possible, so we ran through the flames. That's the last I saw of him."

Jonathan turned his head from side to side in a vain attempt to locate Chuck. He yelled again, "Did anyone else see what happened to him?"

Another person said, "I don't know what happened, but he saved our lives." They stood looking at the building thinking the same thing. "If he got stuck in there, he is dead for sure."

Jonathan sat down on the curb, put his face into his hands, and let the tears that had been bottled up for years flow. His thoughts pierced his soul as he reflected back to that night in Geneva when Joseph was murdered. "It wasn't supposed to work out this way. They were supposed to deliver the document and collect their payment. Now Mona and Layla are on the evacuation ship heading to Rome, and Chuck is dead."

CHAPTER FOURTEEN

FAROUK WAS NOT HAPPY FINDING OUT the document was a fake and was on the verge of a breakdown. "Pulli, I dare those bastards cheat us out of what is rightfully ours. How could they?"

"Your Majesty, I don't think they are giving it much thought. After all, we murdered their friend. I am sure they are wondering the same thing about us."

"Shut your mouth, Pulli. I am sick of your bullshit. You have been a pathetic bastard your whole life. If you had any brains at all you would have inspected the document before any shots were fired. Now, instead of killing them both, one of them is still alive, and my sources say the local authorities are appealing to the Saudis. They are perpetuating the rumor that somehow we were behind the murder of the American. With tension already strained, the Saudis might hand us over to Nasser just to keep the peace.

"Since the war began, everyone's running for cover, and no one wants to upset the Americans. All I wanted was the document. Was that too much to ask from anyone? That document was our ticket back to Egypt, and now we can forget returning. Not to mention that bitch ex-wife of mine is now sleeping with my doctor."

Pulli thought better than to utter another word. He motioned for Abdul to come over where he was sitting. With his finger, Pulli gestured for Abdul to come close and whispered, "Get a sedative and bring it along with a glass of water. We must calm him down before he has a heart attack."

"Yes sir."

Abdul returned with a tray and walked over and offered it to the King, "Your Majesty, I took the liberty of bringing you a little something to calm your nerves."

Farouk looked up and said, "Abdul, blessings my friend. Finally, someone who cares about me. Thank you, I believe I will."

Farouk downed the sedative and chased it with water. Pulli was relieved, knowing the drug would take affect soon and spare him from further verbal abuse. He would check with his source and find out if the Swiss account had been cleared. Farouk would be much happier knowing the money they had stowed away was accessible.

CHAPTER FIFTEEN

Spence had waited patiently for over an hour, but he couldn't take it anymore. He knocked on Mona's door in hopes Layla was inside. Layla opened the door, stepped out onto the deck, grabbed him around the waist, and said, "Hold me, Spence."

"Layla, what is going on?" Not knowing what else to do Spence complied and wrapped his arms around her.

Layla looked up at him her eyes blood shot, the tears still streaming down her cheeks, and said, "Chuck is dead."

Spence's eyes widened. "What, how, when…?"

"There was a fire at a restaurant in Alexandria, and Chuck was trapped inside. He was assisting others when the fire broke out, but he never came out. The building burned to the ground. That's all we know for now. The note from Ambassador Hare said for us to contact the authorities in Rome for assistance. We hope to know more at that time."

Spence held her tightly and said, "Look, Layla, I'll put everything on hold. Anything you two need, I am at your service. We will find out what happened."

"Thank you, Spence. That would be great. I don't think either Mona or I have it in us at this point to make any decisions."

When the ship pulled into port, the scene was hectic. Women were chasing after their children, and no one seemed to know what to do or where to go. The Italians attempted to keep order, but the lack of communication made it difficult. The US Embassy employees seemed just as clueless.

Spence grabbed one of the crewmembers and asked for help. They offloaded all of Mona's and Layla's luggage and his duffle. He then went to the Port Authority office and inquired if there had been any messages left for a Mona Gaskin. Sure enough there were two envelopes with her name on them. The gals were standing next to the luggage embracing when Spence approached. The emotions of the moment mixed with the commotion of all the kids running around made the situation harder to bear.

"Mona, these two envelopes were left with your name on them."

Mona recognized Chuck's writing on one of the envelopes and tore it open. She let out a scream that pierced Spence's ears and caused Layla to jump back a foot.

"Mona, what is it?"

Mona grabbed Layla and swung her around and jumped up; then she gave Spence a kiss. "Chuck isn't dead! He is here and waiting to meet us!"

"What...how in the world...that's great," Layla said, a little more than confused.

"It doesn't say what happened, and I don't care. All I know is he is alive, and that's good enough for me. Spence, be a dear and get us a taxi."

"Sure thing," Spence said running from the pier.

Mona read the note out loud,

"Mona

I'm in Rome. Meet me at Hotel Nazionale, located at Piazza Monte Citorio, 131, as soon as you arrive. I will fill you in on everything when you get here.
Love Chuck

Chuck thought it best if he booked a suite at the Nazionale, which was a good, but lesser known hotel. Situated near the Piazza Montecitorio Square and the Italian Parliament, it provided a perfect venue for their purposes since everything central was within walking distance.

"Unbelievable, whew...I don't know how much of this I can take. What's in the other envelope?" Layla said.

Mona tore it open and read it in silence then said, "It gives instructions on whom to contact at the Embassy about Chuck's death." She crumpled it and threw it in a nearby trashcan.

"Layla, how do you feel about Spence?"

"Are you asking if I trust him?"

"Yes. Don't you think we need to be careful about sharing our plans with him until we know more about him?"

Layla shot her a sly look and said, "I looked through his duffle and his wallet while he was sleeping."

"Oh, you are the sly one, aren't you?"

They both let out a laugh and hugged, needing the comic relief the moment afforded.

"Well, what did you find?"

"All his credentials were there and seemed in order. However, there was a letter in his duffle, which leaves me suspect. He is to be awarded a medal called the Navy Cross when he returns stateside."

"Why is that confusing?"

"He must be lying about something. He is wearing a Marine uniform, so how does he win a Navy award?"

Mona let out a big laugh.

"Why are you laughing?"

"Chuck told me about the different awards. The Navy Cross is given to people in the Marines or Navy. It is one of the highest awards for valor in combat, second only to the Medal of Honor. He must have done something heroic, that's for sure."

"Be careful not to say anything, or he will know I went through his things."

"Your taken with him, aren't you, Layla? How soon we forget the past."

"Come on, Mona. I'm not that coldhearted. Joseph meant the world to me, but a girl has to move on. I can't help it if Spence just happened to come around at the perfect time. After all, you have to admit, he's a good catch. Maybe my luck is changing after all."

"He is charming, but let's be careful until we find Chuck," Mona said, with caution in her voice. Pointing to the pendant around Layla's neck, she added, "Why don't you let that represent your past and put to rest your old life style?"

A slight smile creased Layla's lips as she ripped the *evil eye* from her neck. "I don't need this damn thing anymore," she said flinging it as hard as she could. It landed in the white foam of the surf and soon vanished below the water line. A weight immediately lifted from Layla's shoulders.

"What are you looking at, ladies?" Spence said looking down at the water.

Winking at Mona, Layla said, "Oh nothing, just burying the past. Did you find us a ride?"

"What do you think?" He pointed to a taxi waiting nearby.

Riding through the narrow streets of Rome on their way to meet Chuck, the girls felt an electrifying presence. They spoke to each other in French, a language Spence had not mastered. He remained quiet for most of the ride with an intuitive sense there was something they weren't telling him. He couldn't help thinking that it would be nice to meet Chuck and spend sometime around another man for a change.

The driver pulled up to the curb in front of the Hotel, and before the car came to a stop, Mona jumped out and dashed inside. Approaching the front desk, she asked in her best Italian, "*Mi scusi sir, che è Chuck Gaskin in camera?**"

The clerk said, "Mrs. Gaskin I presume?"

"Yes, this is she."

"Mr. Gaskin asked if you would join him at Checchino dal 1887, it is a short distance away on Via Monte Testaccio, 30. He said to let you know he would be waiting on the patio. You should enjoy the setting. It's a quaint restaurant still run by the family who started it back in 1887. I might add it's the best place in town if you want true Roman cuisine."

Mona didn't say another word, but turned on her heels and ran back to the car. "Spence, would you be a dear and check you and Layla into the hotel? Chuck wants us to meet him at a restaurant nearby, and we have some private business to discuss. I promise we won't be long."

Looking over to Layla, Spence frowned, but before he could say anything, Layla said, "Spence, please don't take offense. A lot has happened of late. Be a dear and check us in."

She reached up and gave him a kiss, and the two women got back in the taxi. Spence stood on the curb watching as they pulled away.

The taxi came to halt in front of a weathered building adorned with a faded awning. Entering the restaurant, they were directed toward the patio where Chuck was waiting. As soon as he saw them, he rose and opened his arms, "Hey gals."

Mona strolled over and slapped him across the face as hard as she could.

---

*   Excuse me sir, which room is Chuck Gaskin in? (Italian)

"What in the hell was that for?" Chuck said rubbing his cheek.

Tears forming, she said, "Chuck Gaskin, how could you let me believe you were dead?"

"What do you mean? How did you know about that?"

"Ambassador Hare sent word to the ship informing me you had been killed in a fire in Alexandria. I was sick to my stomach."

He held his arms out and said, "Come here, baby."

"Don't you baby me; you damn near gave me a heart attack! What if I would have killed myself or something?"

"Okay, okay. Calm down and I'll explain. I figured I would make it to Rome before the news reached you, and everything would work out. How was I to know the Ambassador would send word to the ship?"

"Well, you should have." Then looking over at Layla, Mona said, "Calm down. Calm down, he says. I'm told my husband has been killed in a fire, and I'm on my way to Rome without a clue what the future holds, and he tells me to calm down. Why, if I wasn't so glad to see you, I would kill you a second time."

They all started laughing. Chuck grabbed her, wrapped her in his strong arms, and kissed her with passion. He then whispered in her ear, "I'm glad you missed me, baby."

Mona just melted in his arms and said, "Don't ever do that again, Chuck."

"I promise, never again."

Chuck motioned for them to sit down. "Let me tell you what happened.

"After we finished the evacuation, Ambassador Hare contacted me and stressed the need for us to remain in Egypt to assist with Embassy business. It came as a total surprise. Jonathan and I were not real happy with the decision.

"The next day we heard it rumored there was a safe restaurant for foreign nationals." Chuck proceeded to tell them what happened in the restaurant the night of the fire. "When I hit the street every-one was in a state of panic, so I ducked into a nearby alley. My chest was pounding, and I couldn't catch my breath. I sat down in hopes of regaining my strength. That's when it came to me. It was a per-fect opportunity for me to escape Egypt and try to make it to Rome. I avoided the crowd and made it back to the Cecil where I contacted Commander Brown. I knew he was still in Alexandria, and he was someone I could trust."

Mona interrupted, "You told him about our plan?"

"No, not exactly. I shared the details surrounding Joseph's death and how we believed Farouk had orchestrated it in retalia-tion for the United States not coming to his aid. I told him about our desire to investigate and that I couldn't go to the authorities with the information until we had more evidence. I told him I was supposed to meet you in Rome, but Hare's last minute deci-sion to keep us in Egypt threw a wrench into our plan.

"He arranged for a chopper to ferry me out to a ship in the sixth fleet heading for Rome. The Captain was a good friend and owed him a favor. They must have been a considerable distance in front of your ship, and that's how I arrived before you.

"Oh, I didn't tell you this. Brown suggested we let the Embassy in Alexandria go on believing I was killed in the fire. He said when the time came for me to return, he would speak with the Ambassador. He figured if I could implicate Farouk and Pulli in the murder, the Ambassador would be more than understand-ing."

Mona said, "What about Jonathan? Does he know you are alive?"

Chuck squinted and with a slight tilt of his head said, "I hated to leave Jonathan, but felt the less he knew the better. I fig-ured the news would reach Farouk at some point, and it might aid us in our little plan. Besides, Jonathan is capable of handling everything in my absence. When I get ready to return, I plan to contact him and get him to run interference for me. He'll understand."

Then with a broad smile Chuck said, "So here I am, ready to get down to business."

Mona cleared her throat and said, "We have another minor problem."

Chuck rolled his eyes and threw his head back. "What now?"

"Layla met a Marine on the ship and has become smitten, so to speak. Don't worry; he doesn't know about our plan."

The deep breath Chuck took could have been perceived as frustration, but actually, it was more a sigh of relief. He said, "Layla, I'm glad you found someone to take your mind off of Joseph. Tell me about him."

Layla looked over at Mona and then back at Chuck. "When we boarded the ship in Alexandria, there were women and children everywhere. You arranged for Mona's berth, but must have forgotten about me."

Chuck roared in defense, "The hell I did. There were supposed to be two berths located side by side."

Layla went on. "It doesn't matter now. This nice Marine asked to help with my luggage, so I figured what the heck. One thing led to another, and before you know it I was sharing his berth. He earned a Navy Cross!"

"Well, that's impressive. I mean no one in the Marine Corps receives that high of an honor without earning it. Where is he now?"

"He is checking us in at the hotel and looking forward to meeting you."

"Okay, let's play it by ear. If he proves trustworthy, in time we can fill him. Right now, we don't have to tell him anything. In fact, we need to maintain a low profile. He'll be a good cover for you.

We'll let the hotel assume the four of us are on vacation. The last thing we want is attention. The fewer people who see us, the better, thus the reason I picked that particular hotel. It's not one of the more popular ones, but it is close to everything.

> > >

Farouk was depressed over all that was happening to his world. His Queen was marrying his former doctor, he been exiled from his homeland, and people were spreading rumors about his affairs. Then word had arrived from Cairo, that Chuck Gaskin had been killed in a fire. The document he had been searching for all these years had been within his grasp. Now the house of cards had tumbled, and his life was a mess.

He decided the best thing was to take in the opening of La Tosca at the Opera House and afterward make love to ease his sorrows. As was his custom, seated next to him was a cute young blonde. Feeling a tap on his shoulder, he turned to see the curtain move but no one there. Looking down, he noticed an envelope on the floor. He picked it up, opened it, and read,

"The opportunity to acquire the document is still in play"

Farouk looked out over the rail at the audience, hoping to catch a glimpse of someone looking toward his loge. He scanned the audience, looking for anything which might provide a clue to who had delivered the note. Triggering the desired effect, Farouk turned to his young companion and said, "I have some urgent business to attend to. We need to return to the hotel."

Farouk and his companion made their way to the front doors where he summoned his chauffeur to bring around the car. Back at the hotel, Pulli was reading the note that had just been slipped under the door of the suite,

"You killed my friend and I gave you a forged document."

Farouk barged into the room and in his deep baritone voice yelled, "Pulli, where are you?"

"I'm in the toilet. I'll be out in a minute." Pulli emerged holding the note.

"What's that in your hand?"

"Someone slipped a note under the door. Either he is alive or someone else is screwing with me."

"What do you mean? Who's alive?"

"Chuck Gaskin."

They traded notes, and after reading Farouk's note, Pulli looked up at him and asked, "So what do you think?"

"No way to tell from these. If it were me, I'd want revenge for my friend's death, but given the fact all the American scum have been evacuated, whoever it is must be interested in the money."

ﹾ ﹾ ﹾ

The next day was like any other, but there was sense of excitement in the air. Mona and Chuck were sitting on the patio drinking their coffee. There was a nice breeze, and the birds chirping gave evidence the day was in full swing.

Chuck took a sip of his coffee and said, "The final note is set to be delivered early this morning. Farouk should be squirming right about now."

ﹾ ﹾ ﹾ

Farouk and Pulli sat on the terrace overlooking the square as Abdul served the usual breakfast. Farouk's weight had ballooned to well over three hundred pounds. Pulli sat across from the former king as he gorged himself wondering how anyone could eat that much and not throw up. He was disgusted at the sight.

"We need to find out who is delivering the notes and interrogate them. If we can find out where he is staying, we can steal the document and rid ourselves of his petty game."

Abdul walked up to the table and held out an envelope. "Sir, I found this on the floor near the door."

Wiping his mouth with his cloth napkin, Farouk took the envelope and looked over at Pulli. He took the note out and read,

Piccola Trattoria

'Let's finish what we started. Meet tomorrow at noon on the patio of Piccola Trattoria with the agreed amount, and you will have your document. No bullshit this time, or it will be you bleeding on the ground!'

"Pulli, how do we stand with the bank?"

"Everything is in order."

"Set up a meeting so we can withdraw the money. You and Abdul will be meeting whoever is sending these notes. I want to play along on the outside chance they have the document. There might still be a chance to recapture my throne."

"How do we know it's not some kind of trap?"

"What would be their incentive? They can't pass a stolen antiquity of that magnitude without exposing themselves."

"Good point. Why don't I take Abdul with me, and if the opportunity presents itself, I'll silence whoever shows up. The last thing we need is the Italian authorities stirred up over an ancient Egyptian antiquity. I'll make sure it's clean."

Farouk leaned forward and grabbed Pulli by the collar. "Don't mess this up, do you hear me? I want that document. If they walk away with the money so be it. Its small change compared to what that document is worth."

He leaned back and yelled at Abdul to bring him a cigar, "Let's have a smoke and celebrate. The Gods are favoring me; I can feel it."

❯❯❯

The next day Chuck, Mona, and Layla rose early and met at the hotel restaurant. They were excited to find out how the day's events were going to unfold.

Spence awoke to find Layla's side of the bed empty. He was perplexed by how she slipped out without him knowing. He dressed and headed downstairs in hopes of catching her. On the way, he knocked on Chuck and Mona's door, but there was no answer. He felt that feeling he had known during the war when he intuitively knew the enemy was near. It was a feeling which had helped him save many men's lives.

Descending the stairs and walking toward the patio, he saw the three of them sitting at a table enjoying their morning coffee. Relieved he said, "Good morning everyone. Layla, you sure woke up early." He bent over and gave her a kiss on the cheek.

Layla said, "Have a seat Spence. Isn't this a wonderful day? Mona and I were just talking about some of the shops we want to explore. Chuck has Embassy business to attend to. Do you mind if us girls do a little shopping and have lunch together?"

"No not at all. In fact, I have some personal business of my own to attend to."

Spence's curiosity had been aroused ever since it was discovered Chuck was alive and waiting in Rome. He had been wondering if this woman he was falling in love with was somehow using him. The previous day, he left Layla to get dressed and headed downstairs for a cup of coffee. Chuck and Mona were sitting on the patio as he approached. He overheard Chuck talking about their plans. He hadn't been able to make out the whole conversation because of the morning traffic. Chuck said something about a document exchange with Farouk and how he was needed back at the Embassy in Cairo. That's when Layla walked up and ended his eavesdropping.

Now here they were, all with separate plans for the day, none of which included him. Chuck signed the room number on the bill, and everyone rose from the table. "How about we all meet back here later this afternoon, and we'll have dinner?"

"Sounds good to me," Spence said.

Layla reached up, kissed Spence's cheek, and whispered in his ear, "Later I'll treat you to dessert in our room." Then, arm in arm, she and Mona darted for the street. Chuck excused himself as well. Spence waited a few minutes and then took off in Chuck's direction.

❳ ❳ ❳

Farouk and Pulli met with the bank President and withdrew the desired funds, which Pulli placed in a black briefcase. Farouk wished him luck and headed back to the hotel to await the outcome. Pulli was concerned about not knowing whom they would be meeting. One thing he knew for sure, whoever it was would be intent on avenging the American's death.

After Farouk was out of range, Pulli turned to Abdul, "I know you have been faithful all these years, but Farouk is losing his grip. I have no intention giving an American infidel two hundred thousand pounds for some ancient piece of paper. I propose we split the money. It would serve us both well in retirement."

"Are you proposing we skip the meeting?"

"No, we'll make the meeting, but I'll have a surprise for them," Pulli lifted his pant leg revealing the gun with the attached silencer taped to his ankle, "You be ready to grab both cases when I make my move."

"Sounds like a repeat of our previous meeting. Do you think we can pull it off?"

"Not for sure, but be ready, for I'll act fast. They won't know what hit them."

The two of them headed toward the restaurant, Abdul with a tight grip on the briefcase.

Meanwhile Chuck arrived early to make sure everything was secure. Nasser's men had searched all nearby buildings to make sure they didn't have a repeat of what had happened in Geneva. His men were disguised and in place. The agreed signal was Chuck's cigar. He would pretend to be lighting it in celebration of the exchange. At that moment, they were to converge and make the arrest. There was a van waiting to whisk Farouk and Pulli off to the airport where a plane was fueled ready for takeoff. If everything went as planned, the Egyptians would have the antiquity, a case full of cash, and Farouk and Pulli back in Egypt by the end of the day. Chuck would breathe easier knowing there was a certain virtue in the sacrificial atonement for Joseph's death.

Chuck watched as Pulli and Abdul neared the restaurant, Abdul with the briefcase at his side. Chuck hit the switch on the recorder which he had taped under the table. Standing Chuck held out his hand. "Hello, Pulli, we meet again."

Pulli looked like he had seen a ghost. "You! We thought you were dead, caught in a fire."

"Would have been convenient for you considering Farouk wasn't happy you botched the job in Geneva."

"I want you to know we had nothing to do with your friend's death."

"Pulli, the past is past. All I care about is making this exchange and heading back to America. But there is something you need to know. There is a sniper with a rifle pointed at your forehead right this minute."

Pulli and Abdul nervously scanned the surrounding area. Gaskin had presented them with an option they had not considered.

"Doesn't feel too good now, does it?" Chuck said harshly.

"What do you want, Gaskin?"

"You and Farouk had Joseph killed with a bullet meant for me. Maybe it's time you paid for his murder."

"Look, Farouk is half mad. He was paranoid when he found out you wanted to meet on top of some mountain. He wanted you dead and ordered me to make sure you never made it to the bottom."

Chuck's eyes narrowed, but he kept his cool, "Enough, let's just finish what we originally set out to do. I don't want to ever see your disgusting face again?"

Abdul was fidgety his head darting from side to side, looking to see if he could locate the shooter.

"Abdul, look at me," Chuck ordered. "I'm assuming the case by your side contains the money."

"Two hundred thousand pounds," Abdul said looking into Chuck's eyes.

Chuck didn't see Pulli pull the gun, but then he didn't see Spence either. Out of nowhere Spence emerged and in one fluid motion grabbed the gun, slid his free arm around Pulli's neck, and tightened his grip. Pointing the gun at Abdul, he said, "If I were you, I would sit very still about now."

Chuck lit the cigar, and all hell broke loose. The van pulled up next to their table, and Spence was grabbed from behind by two men. Two others grabbed Pulli, Abdul, and both cases. People around the restaurant scattered in a state of shock.

"The American is with me. It's okay. Let him go," Chuck yelled.

Chuck stripped the tape from under the table and handed Rajad the recorder, "Here is your confession. Now that you have what you came for, let's don't draw any more attention than is necessary."

The men let go of Spence, and Rajad extended a hand. "Egypt is in your debt, Mr. Gaskin. Nasser asked me to have you call when you return to Cairo."

"Say nothing of it; it was my pleasure to rid the street of that scum," Chuck said taking a puff off the cigar and extending a hand.

Chuck looked over and momentarily locked eyes with Pulli before the men shoved the scrawny Egyptian through the side door of the van. Chuck blew smoke into Pulli's face and smiled. The engine roared as Nasser's men raced from the curb.

Hearing sirens off in the distance, Chuck looked at Spence and commanded, "We need to get the hell out of here before the local police arrive."

They raced away from the restaurant, careful to run the opposite direction from where they were staying. Doubling back, they made their way to the hotel.

When the key turned in the knob, Mona grabbed the lamp on the table, ready to smash any unwanted visitor. Chuck entered, smiling from ear to ear, but her surprise was seeing Spence walk in behind him.

Noting their apprehension, Chuck said, "Don't worry. If it wasn't for your Marine here you might have received another note stating I had been murdered. Farouk pulled a no show, and Pulli planned to shoot me and steal the case. Spence came out of nowhere and foiled his plan. Nasser's men stepped in and grabbed Pulli and Abdul. At least, someone will stand trial for Joseph's murder."

Mona smiled and said, "I anticipated a successful mission, so I took the liberty of buying a bottle of the restaurant's best champagne. What do you say we drink a toast?"

Layla approached Spence and slipped her hands around his waist. "I'm sorry. I hope you understand my reluctance to confide in you. Will you forgive me?" Spence grabbed her, swooped her off her feet, and kissed her. Chuck smiled at Mona and lifted his glass.

CHAPTER SIXTEEN

NASSER WAS ELATED AT THE NEWS. The team he had sent to Rome was in transit. He was disappointed Farouk was not among their cargo, but he reveled in the thought that Farouk had lost his two closest confidants. He would not rest until Farouk was either brought to trial or dead. It didn't matter which; they both held equal appeal.

Chuck arrived at the airport in Cairo, and Commander Brown was there to pick him up. The two of them drove to the Embassy to meet with Ambassador Hare. He was incensed by the fact he had not been pulled into the loop, but the Commander, true to his word, covered for Chuck by saying he had orchestrated the events after the fire.

Jonathan was both shocked and angry to see Chuck. Only after hearing Chuck's reasoning for leaving him in the dark did he calm down. "Hell, Chuck, I would have done the same thing. All I know is that it's good to see you. Good to have you back."

"You might not be so excited when I tell you Nasser wants to meet and that you are going with me."

"I have no desire to meet him, and what does he want with you?"

"When I contacted him about the sting operation, he said if we pulled it off he wanted to meet me on my return. I don't want to go alone. You gotta come with me."

"Oh, that's great. You leave my lily white ass in the dark, thinking you were dead, and now you want me to go with you to face the firing squad."

Chuck started laughing; it felt good after all he had been through.

"He isn't going to line anyone up in front of a firing squad. He has Pulli, the document, and Farouk's money. What does he have to gain by implicating me? Besides, why would he invite me to the palace? He could just send the police after me."

Chuck confirmed the meeting with Nasser at the Abdin palace, and it was agreed Jonathan could accompany him. Chuck felt more at ease knowing Jonathan would be joining him.

Upon arriving at the Palace, they were taken to Nasser's office. Smiling, Nasser rose and extended his hand. "Chuck Gaskin?"

"Yes sir."

"We meet at last."

Turning toward Jonathan, Chuck said, "This is Jonathan Bartlet from our Embassy."

"Nice to meet you. Please the two of you take a seat," Nasser said returning to his own seat. "You must tell me about Rome."

Chuck related the events surrounding their plan, how they lured Pulli to the meeting place and were able to secure the confession. He finished by saying, "I regret not being able to deliver Farouk."

"We are pleased at the outcome. Farouk will get his one day, but now I am sure he is feeling lonely after losing his closest, no his only, allies." Nasser motioned to a member of his staff.

Soon after the steward approached, carrying a case which Chuck recognized as the case Pulli had with him at the restaurant. He glanced at Jonathan and then back at the case.

Taking the case and extending it to Chuck, Nasser said, "It is with great pleasure on behalf of the Egyptian people to offer you a reward for putting you and your team in danger and preserving a treasured Egyptian antiquity."

"I don't know what else to say, but thank you. It comes as a complete surprise. May I ask why?" Chuck said clearing his throat.

"The money doesn't let Farouk off the hook with me, so I consider it appropriate to use it as payment for bringing an American Embassy employee's murderer to justice. Shall we make an appearance and let the world know?"

"If it's all the same to you, Sir, we would rather not assume any of the credit. The payment is reward enough. Why don't you and your men take the credit? I am sure it will help to mend relations with our country. I'd call that a win-win for all involved, wouldn't you?"

Nasser smiled. "I like you, Mr. Gaskin. I will honor your desire."

Jonathan and Chuck stood, shook Nasser's hand, and exited the palace. On the way out Chuck smiled as he whispered to Jonathan, "I'll be damned. Who would have thought it after all we have been through?"

EPILOGUE

LAYLA AND SPENCE WERE OFF on another adventure of sorts. Layla had become an accomplished bridge player and was playing the professional circuit. With three kids in tow, she still didn't miss a tournament.

Chuck and Mona had settled in Spain. Life was somewhat boring, but they were comfortable and surrounded by many good friends.

"Chuck, please come in here. We are getting ready to play poker," Mona called from the other room.

Chuck was entranced by the article he was reading from Time magazine dated Friday, March 26...

Midnight on March 18, 1965 Farouk was dining at the Ile De France restaurant in Rome. Twenty-eight year old blonde, Anna Maria Gatti, was sitting next to him. He ordered his usual fare of lobster, oysters, roast lamb, cake, and fruits. He finished eating around 1:30 in the morning and lit up a Cuban Havana cigar. Then it happened, he dropped dead, face first into his food.

Farouk was just forty-five years old. His death was ruled a heart attack, but curiously, the former Cairo Ex-governor, General Ibrahim Baghdadi, had taken a job at the restaurant as a waiter. Baghdadi, nicknamed the "Assassin," was also a member of Egyptian Intelligence.

Though not proven, Chuck assumed Nasser had the last laugh. Farouk's death was the virtual end of the Mohammad Ali Dynasty. Chuck set down the article and called to his wife, "Mona, tell them to deal me in."

THE END

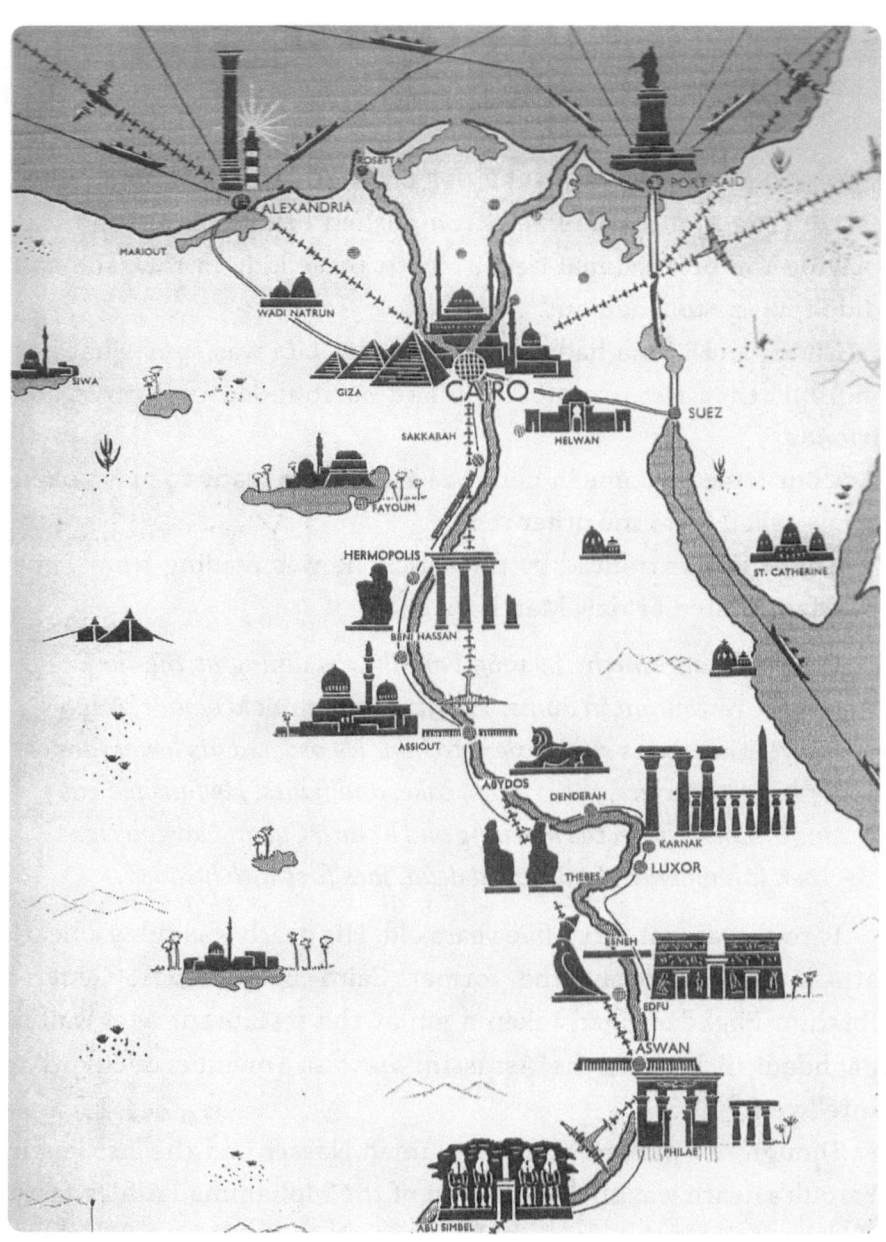

Ancient map of Egypt

APPENDIX

Ammenemhat III

Amenemhat III (also spelled Amenemhat and known as Amenemmes III), king of ancient Egypt (reigned 1818–1770 BCE) of the 12ᵗʰ dynasty, brought Middle Kingdom Egypt (c. 1938–1630 BCE) to a peak of economic prosperity by completing a system to regulate the inflow of water into Lake Moeris in the Al-Fayyūm depression southwest of Cairo. The resulting stabilization of the water level also drained some of the marshes that had surrounded

*Amenemhat III
Berlin Museum*

the old lake. As part of this great work, the labyrinth described by the Greek historian Herodotus was probably built nearby, just south of one of Amenemhat's pyramids at Hawara, in Al-Fayyūm. It was probably a multifunctional building—palace, temple, town, and administrative centre. To celebrate the reclamation of 153,600 acres (62,200 hectares) of land for agricultural use, Amenemhat erected two colossi of himself nearby, also described by Herodotus. A second pyramid, located at Dahshūr, was built for his interment.

Amenemhat also worked the turquoise mines at Sinai with unprecedented intensity. Permanent quarters were erected for the miners, with wells nearby and fortifications to repel Bedouin raiders. A temple to the goddess Hathor was also built. Likewise, quarries throughout Egypt and Nubia to the south, were the site of much activity to support the king's building enterprises. Except for minor punitive raids, his reign was peaceful.

Source: Encyclopædia Britannica

Rhind Mathematical Papyrus

"It is not a theoretical treatise, but a list of practical problems encountered in administrative and building works. The text contains 84 problems concerned with numerical operations, practical problem-solving, and geometrical shapes.

"The Rhind Mathematical Papyrus is also important as a historical document, since the copyist noted that he was writing in year 33 of the reign of Apophis, the penultimate king of the Hyksos Fifteenth Dynasty (about 1650-1550 BC) and was copied after an original of the Twelfth Dynasty (about 1985-1795 BC.)"

"The Rhind Mathematical Papyrus dates to the Second Intermediate Period of Egypt and is the best example of Egyptian mathematics. It was copied by the scribe Ahmes (ie., Ahmose; Ahmes is an older transcription favoured by historians of mathematics), from a now-lost text from the reign of king Amenemhat III (12th dynasty). Written in the hieratic script, this Egyptian manuscript is 33 cm tall is made up of multiple parts making which in total make it over 5m long, and began to be transliterated and mathematically translated in the late 19th century.

In 2008, the mathematical translation aspect is incomplete in several respects. The document is dated to Year 33 of the Hyksos king Apophis and also contains a separate later Year 11 on its verso likely from his successor, Khamudi."

Source: http://en.wikipedia.org/wiki/Rhind_Mathematical_Papyrus
Image Source: British Museum

HERODOTUS'S ANCIENT HISTORICAL ACCOUNT OF THE EGYPTIAN LABYRINTH

Herodotus, known as the "Father of History," was a well-respected Greek historian who lived in the fifth century BC (c.484-425 BC). He was the first historian to systematically encapsulate his findings, testing their authenticity and deliver them in a cohesive narrative.

Herodotus considered the labyrinth to be a complex maze-like structure which surpassed even the pyramids. The following is his eyewitness account describing the labyrinth at the base of the Hawara pyramid in the Faiyum Oasis.

Herodotus

"Moreover, they decided to preserve the memory of their names by a common memorial, and so they made a labyrinth a little way beyond lake Moeris and near the place called the City of Crocodiles. I have seen it myself, and indeed words cannot describe it; if one were to collect the walls and evidence of other efforts of the Greeks, the sum would not amount to the labor and cost of this labyrinth. And yet the temple at Ephesus and the one on Samos are noteworthy. Though the pyramids beggar description and each one of them is a match for many great monuments built by Greeks, this maze surpasses even the pyramids. It has twelve roofed courts with doors facing each other: six face north and six south, in two continuous lines, all within one outer wall. There are also double sets of chambers, three thousand altogether, fifteen hundred above and the same number underground. We ourselves viewed those that are above ground, and speak of what we have seen, but we learned through conversation about the underground chambers; the Egyptian caretakers would by no means show them, as they were, they said, the burial vaults of the kings who first built this labyrinth, and of the sacred crocodiles. Thus we can only speak from hearsay of the lower chambers; the upper we saw for ourselves, and they are creations greater than human. The exits of the chambers and the mazy passages hither and thither through the courts were an unending marvel to us as we passed from court to apartment and from apartment to colonnade, from colonnades again to more chambers and then into yet more courts. Over all this is a roof, made of stone like the walls, and the walls are covered with cut figures, and every court is set around with pillars of white stone very precisely fitted together. Near the corner where the labyrinth ends stands a pyramid two hundred and forty feet high, on which great figures are cut. A passage to this has been made underground."

Source: Herodotus, with an English translation by A. D. Godley. Cambridge. Harvard University Press. 1920. Book 2, Chapter 148.

PETRIE'S EXPEDITION TO HAWARA

Throughout the 1800's, several expeditions intent on exploring the mysteries of the pyramid were conducted. One of the most prominent expeditions began in January 24, 1888, and was led by William Matthew Flinders Petrie. His team penetrated the pyramid and explored its inner chambers where they discovered incredible passages, trap doors, and the King's sepulcher (burial chamber.) Petrie documented their findings in his book *Kahun, Gurob, and Hawara*, published in 1890.

After a year of tunneling into the structure, Petrie's team found a hole forged by ancient treasure seekers. Entering through the hole and carefully navigating the interior, Petrie was able to locate the entrance passage. He also found a cartouche on a bit of alabaster vase with the name Amenemhat III.

The entrance was a sloping passage leading to a small antechamber. Proceeding from this room led to a chamber under the first trap door. Petrie wrote, "The trap-door system used three times in this pyramid was arranged by roofing a chamber with a sliding block of stone, the side of which thus covered the end of the high-level passage, the floor which was on a level with the roof of the chamber. Of these trap-doors only the first had been drawn, the others were carelessly left in their recesses and presented no obstacle to the plunderers who had broken their way past the first."

Using the size of the doors, Petrie estimated them to weigh 22 tons. One might ask how these doors could be manipulated, and Petrie goes on to explain, "All the trap-doors have a groove along the sides to allow of a rope being passed around them whereby to drag them along in their recesses." Historians can only assume that the workers in great supply during the pharaonic times used rope, sledges, and rollers to manipulate these massive structures.

"Hawara is situated 90 km south of modern Cairo at the entrance to the depression of the Faiyum oasis. The Egyptian name Hw.t-wr.t, "great temple", refers to the labyrinth. The location is marked with the pyramid of Amenemhat III, the last great king of the 12th dynasty (about 1855-1808 Before Common Era). The pyramid he built at Hawara is believed to post-date the so-called "Black Pyramid" built by the same ruler at Dahshur. It is this pyramid that is believed to have been Amenemhat's final resting place. In common with the Middle Kingdom pyramids constructed after Amenemhat II, it was built of mud brick around a core of limestone passages and burial chambers and faced with limestone. Most of the facing stone was later pillaged for use in other buildings (a fate common to almost all of Egypt's pyramids), and today the pyramid is little more than an eroded, vaguely pyramidal mountain of mud brick. The entrance to the pyramid is flooded to a depth of 4-5 meters by groundwater.

"In 2008 the Mataha expedition researched the lost labyrinth of Egypt at Hawara. A legendary building lost for 2 millenia under the ancient sands of Egypt. Bringing the highest level of technology to unlock the secrets of the past. The sand of Hawara was scanned by the Belgian Egyptian expedition team. Although ground penetrating techniques are used by archaeologists for years, the Mataha-expedition (Mataha = labyrinth in Arabic) was the first to apply this technology at Hawara, to solve the enigma born in the Renaissance for once.

"The results of the Hawara geophysic-survey are officially released for the first time in August 2008, by the National Research Institute of Astronomy and Geophysics (NRIAG, Cairo) at the Workshop in Cairo, to the persons directly related with the Hawara preservate masterplan of the Supreme Council of Antiquities. The Mataha

Expedition results were secondly published in the scientific journal of the NRIAG in fall 2008. Thirdly, all Mataha-expedition research information was exchanged on the Public Lecture at Ghent University (October 2008) in the presence of the Belgian press.

"The Mataha expedition geophysic research confirms the presence of archaeological features at the labyrinth area south of the Hawara pyramid of Amenemhat III. These features covering an underground area of several hectares, have the prominent signature of vertical walls on the geophysical results. The vertical walls with an average thickness of several meters, are connected to shape nearly closed rooms, which are interpreted to be huge in number. Consequently, the geophysic survey initiated with the permission of Dr. Zahi Hawass the president of the Supreme Council of Antiquities, and conducted by the National Research Institute of Astronomy and Geophysics (Helwan, Cairo) with the support of Ghent University, can now officially verify the occurrence of big parts of the Labyrinth as described by the classic authors at the study area."

Source: http://www.labyrinthofegypt.com
Mataha Expedition Hawara 2008

PHOTOGRAPHIC CREDITS